"MORE POWE[R]" GOLD SHOUTED.

"Keep her steady, Wong!"

At the helm, the young ensign struggled to comply, but the turbulence around the tiny starship had grown more violent. Another blast of superheated, superdense gas erupted beneath the ship, which listed sharply to starboard. The roar of the storm outside the vessel had become overpowering, and the bridge lights flickered erratically.

Gomez looked up from the damage reports that were flooding in from engineering and glanced at the main viewscreen. The small, vulnerable-looking Work Bug was fighting its way through the fiery maelstrom, back to the *da Vinci*, but the constantly shifting currents tumbled the tiny craft end over end, spinning it in all directions, trapping it halfway between the two starships. *Come on*, Gomez thought as she watched the Work Bug struggle forward. *Another half-kilometer—you can make it.*

A massive, spinning pillar of liquid-metal hydrogen—fresh from the planet's core—formed between two enormous cloud layers and grabbed the Work Bug, pulling it in quickly shrinking circles toward what Gomez realized would be almost certain destruction. She thought of Kieran, trapped inside the small craft, and felt a chill wash through her as she watched Bug One accelerate toward its doom.

STAR TREK®
S.C.E.

Book Six
WILDFIRE

KEITH R.A. DeCANDIDO, DAVID MACK,
AND J. STEVEN YORK & CHRISTINA F. YORK

Based upon *Star Trek*® and
Star Trek: The Next Generation®
created by Gene Roddenberry,
and *Star Trek: Deep Space Nine*®
created by Rick Berman & Michael Piller

POCKET BOOKS
New York   London   Toronto   Sydney

POCKET BOOKS, a division of Simon & Schuster, Inc.
1230 Avenue of the Americas, New York, NY 10020

This book is a work of fiction. Names, characters, places and incidents are products of the authors' imaginations or are used fictitiously. Any resemblance to actual events or locales or persons, living or dead, is entirely coincidental.

 STAR TREK is a Registered Trademark of Paramount Pictures.

This book is published by Pocket Books, a division of Simon & Schuster, Inc., under exclusive license from Paramount Pictures.

ISBN: 0-7434-9661-2

First Pocket Books paperback edition November 2004

10 9 8 7 6 5 4 3 2 1

POCKET and colophon are registered trademarks of Simon & Schuster, Inc.

Type design and layout by Zucca Design
Cover art designed by Keith Birdsong

Manufactured in the United States of America

Enigma Ship, *War Stories*, and *Wildfire* were each previously published in eBook format. *War Stories* and *Wildfire* were published in two parts.

For information regarding special discounts for bulk purchases, please contact Simon & Schuster Special Sales at 1-800-456-6798 or business@simonandschuster.com.

CONTENTS

ENIGMA SHIP

J. Steven York
& Christina F. York

1

"U.S.S. Lincoln *to* Vulpecula, *the* Arch-Merchant *has dropped out of warp again. Let's circle back on impulse and see what's broken this time.*"

Second Mate Wayne "Pappy" Omthon muttered a curse and shut down the *Vulpecula's* warp drive. The freighter shuddered and the lights on the cramped bridge flickered as it shifted to impulse.

Pappy turned the command chair to face the sensor console and get a fix on the *Arch-Merchant*, wincing at the chair's squeak. He'd get it oiled as soon as he had time.

The image on the screen was fuzzy, so Pappy slapped it with the flat of his pistachio-green hand, a practiced maneuver that instantly, if temporarily, cleared up the image. He'd earned the nickname "Pappy" by being far younger than the captain and most of the crew serving under him, a point he was still defensive about. But he prided himself on knowing the ship's quirks as well as any old-timer.

The *Arch-Merchant* was venting plasma coolant. Pappy sighed, ignoring the sensor display, which had gone all fuzzy again. "That ship," he announced, without a trace of irony, "is a piece of junk." He slapped the sensor display again, then put in a call to Captain Rivers in her cabin to advise her of the situation.

Rivers was, as he'd expected, mildly drunk. The captain instructed him to use his own judgment, and not to call her again unless there was a core breach. Pappy grunted as the intercom screen went blank, then set a reverse course. It was business as usual.

Both the *Vulpecula* and the *Arch-Merchant* were privately owned freighters operating on the edge of former Cardassian space. The fall of the Cardassian Union and the aftermath of the Dominion War had thrown the region into chaos, creating lucrative new trade opportunities, and new dangers as pirates and raiders moved in.

Federation starships were spread thin and overworked, so freighters often formed small, impromptu convoys for mutual protection and safety. Pappy didn't fear the danger much, but he was just as happy when they were transporting some cargo important enough to Federation interests to warrant a starship to escort their convoy.

On this run, the two ships carried power station components, Cardassian war salvage from abandoned bases now needed to rebuild Cardassia Prime. If Pappy found it ironic that the Federation was paying to ship Cardassian war materials to restore Cardassia, he never would have said so. It was exactly the sort of situation a tramp freighter captain lived for. It was Pappy's ambition to buy the *Vulpecula* from Captain Rivers one of these days. His share of profits from this run would be one more step in that direction.

If they ever got to Cardassia.

"*Vulpecula* to *Lincoln.* How long are we going to be delayed this time?"

One of the secondary viewscreens cleared, and the angular features of a human Starfleet officer appeared. *"This is Captain Newport. Shouldn't you be addressing that question to the* Arch-Merchant?"

Pappy grinned, he hoped not too much. "Since it's my guess your engineers will be doing the repair work, I thought you'd know best."

Newport chuckled. *"My chief engineer is putting together a repair party right now. We should know more after they beam over. Tell me, why is it—*" He hesitated. "*How to put this politely?*"

"I won't make you ask the question, Captain. The *Arch-Merchant* is a corporate ship. She looks clean and sharp for the stockholders, but she's lucky to make it out of orbit without shedding a nacelle. We're a tramp, and independent. Our ship looks like the rattletrap she is, but we keep the important systems in top shape, appearances be damned. Most of the time, we're all we've got out here."

Newport nodded. "*Well, thanks for being the less troublesome part of this mission.*" He glanced to one side. "*Looks like the* Arch-Merchant *managed to plug the plasma leak on their own. Uncommonly resourceful of them. Now if we can just—*"

The screen went blank. No static, no interference, no sign of a problem on the Federation ship. It just went blank. Startled, Pappy glanced up at the main viewer. He could see the *Arch-Merchant*'s plasma cloud, a tiny smudge against the darkness, glowing in reflecting starlight, but the *Lincoln* was gone.

He slammed the intercom panel. "Condition red, all crew to emergency stations. Possible hostiles incoming!" Then, after a moment's hesitation, "Captain to the bridge."

He knew the result of that last command: the captain would at least attempt to sober up first. If he was lucky, he might see her on the bridge in an hour or so.

He hailed the *Arch-Merchant*. "Did you see what happened to the *Lincoln?*"

The reply was audio only and crackled with static. The voice was high, tinged with incipient panic. "*No,* Vulpecula, *our sensors are down too. Are we under attack? We can't see anything. We're dead in space! Don't leave us!*"

"I'm not leaving anybody, but I'm busy here. Save your questions and send out a distress call for me, will you?" Pappy closed the channel and turned his attention to the sensor screens. No hostiles, no radiation or debris, no cosmic storms, nothing that would account for the *Lincoln*'s disappearance.

He reviewed his own sensor logs, replaying the event. The *Lincoln* vanished, without violence or explosion. He slowed down the replay, then slowed it again. He squinted. The *Lincoln* didn't just vanish. It was as though it had run into an invisible rift in space and been swallowed. A wormhole? He shook his head. He should have picked *something* up on sensors.

He heard the bridge doors slide open. The *Vulpecula* was highly automated, and the tiny bridge had only two stations. The second was staffed only during shift changeovers or critical operations such as docking. Or during emergencies, so he wasn't surprised to hear someone slide into the seat behind him. He was surprised to catch a strong odor of Saurian brandy.

Turning his head, he caught the captain's eye.

"Carry on, Pappy. I took a handful of stims, but she's still your ship for now." She tapped the controls to activate her station. "Just tell me what you need."

That explained the smell. The stims were burning the alcohol out of her system. Pappy tapped at the command console, transferring information to the secondary station.

"The point at which the *Lincoln* disappeared is on your sensor display. Run a detailed scan on the area in front of it. Look for anything unusual." Pappy ordered all stop, and kept his distance. If something had pulled the *Lincoln* in, it wouldn't do to be pulled in as well.

The secondary consoles chirped and beeped as the captain entered commands. Finally she looked up at him, her dark eyes red and tired, but sobering by the minute. "There's something out there, a discontinuity, like somebody blew an invisible bubble and the *Lincoln* just ran into it."

Pappy frowned, his sharp eyebrows drawing together into a vee. "How big a bubble?"

The captain consulted her displays, rubbed her eyes, then checked them again. "I'm reading a sphere a hundred kilometers across. We just missed running into it ourselves." She sighed. "This is trouble."

"Our convoy partner is disabled, we're facing off with an invisible threat the size of a moon, one that just took out an *Intrepid*-class starship without firing a shot. Yeah, that would be one definition of 'trouble.'" He tapped the thruster controls.

It was the captain's turn to frown. "What are you doing?"

"Getting in closer," he replied. "Somebody may need rescuing."

The *U.S.S. da Vinci* was a small ship. Even with a limited crew of about forty, its interior was crowded and cluttered by Starfleet standards, a situation not improved by the preponderance of engineers in its crew. In general, they were pragmatic about their use of ship's spaces. It wasn't unusual to see someone overhauling environmental suits on a briefing room table, storing salvaged alien propulsion components in a corner of the transporter room, or playing Andorian Juggle-ball in the shuttlebay.

Lt. Commander Kieran Duffy could even remember a time when all the corridors of deck six had been briefly converted into a miniature golf course, complete with holographic windmill. The exception to all this madness, by unspoken consent, was the mess hall. Not that it was reserved solely for eating, not at all, but it was reserved for quiet conversation, reading, social gatherings, and the occasional spontaneous musical interlude. No plasma torches, no alien artifacts, and no extreme sports allowed.

That was why Duffy liked it there, why it was the place

he retreated when he needed to work or think, when his quarters became too cramped or lonely. The lights were kept low, the dark maroon chairs were inviting, and the clusters of small tables fostered quiet conversation. It was the *da Vinci*'s living room, the place he came to bask in the feeling of family, and be reminded why he *really* liked having one of the few private cabins on the ship.

He'd picked a choice seat for himself near one of the scattered windows, where he could watch the stars, and ordered a quinine water from the replicator. Leaning back in the lightly padded chair, he put his feet on the table and sat back with an oversized design padd propped up in his lap.

He'd just gotten comfortable, opened his work space, and managed to move exactly one line in the display when he sensed someone standing behind him, and a very familiar scent of herbal shampoo. Commander Sonya Gomez leaned into his field of view, looking at the padd.

"What're you doing?"

He pulled the padd protectively to his stomach. "Nothing. Just doodling."

Gomez glanced at the table, and Duffy hastily put his feet on the floor. "That was a starship. You're doodling a starship?"

"So?"

"Pretty elaborate doodle. How long you been doodling?"

He sighed and lowered the padd back to working position. "Six months."

"That's some doodle." She leaned closer, her body nearly touching his shoulder, and this time he didn't try to hide his work. "I didn't know you were interested in ship design."

"Isn't every engineer, on some level?"

"So you're designing a ship?"

"An S.C.E. ship."

"We've got one of those already."

The doors opened, and Gomez drew back a fraction. Fabian Stevens and P8 Blue came in. Stevens headed for the replicators, while Pattie scuttled across the floor on all legs, popping to an upright stance only when reaching Duffy's table. "Greetings. I see you are designing a ship, Commander."

"So I've heard," said Gomez. "An S.C.E. ship, I'm told."

"We've already got one of those," said Stevens, who approached the table with two cups in hand. He gave one to Pattie. "Here's your 'swamp tea,' whatever that is. I don't really want to know."

"Thank you," said Pattie.

"That's what I told him," Gomez said.

Duffy sighed. "The *da Vinci* is a great ship, but she isn't designed for the kind of missions we go on. No ship is, really. Tugs are slow, short-range, and don't have the shops or crew capacity we need. A general purpose design like this *Saber*-class is small and maneuverable, sure, but it's too fragile for heavy work, and it also doesn't have the cargo, shop, or laboratory space we could really use."

Gomez's interest was piqued. "So you're designing a ship with our needs in mind?"

Duffy shrugged. "It's just an exercise, a dream ship, really. Gives me an excuse to broaden my knowledge of ship's systems."

"It resembles a *Norway*-class," observed Pattie, shoving a second small table next to Duffy's.

"I used that as a starting point, but see, the engines are uprated, and the whole front of the saucer section opens up like—no offense, Pattie—like insect mandibles, to form a miniature drydock. We can pull things partially inside the ship for inspection or repair."

Pattie tapped a foreleg at a part of the diagram. "What are those?"

"Heavy tractor beam emitters, for towing."

"You should add six smaller ones," said Pattie, "for precision manipulation of objects in space."

Duffy nodded. "Good idea."

"And more Jefferies tubes," said Pattie. "I like Jefferies tubes."

By now, several other crewmembers had entered the mess hall, including the chief of security, Lt. Commander Domenica Corsi, and the chief medical officer, Dr. Elizabeth Lense, and all of them seemed to be gravitating to the table. Stevens shoved another table over, and sat next to Corsi.

"Idea," said Stevens. "An industrial replicator, so we don't have to replicate small parts and put 'em together into something big. And maybe a second hololab."

Gomez sighed, and Duffy imagined he could feel the warmth of her breath on the back of his neck. "A second holodeck would be nice. Then it can double for recreational purposes."

"Holodecks are nothing but trouble," said Corsi. "We'd be better off without any. More quantum torpedoes would be good, though. I'm very in favor of more torpedoes."

Lense reached across the table and tapped Duffy on the wrist. "Put in a Risa deck."

Duffy looked up at her. "What's a Risa deck?"

She shrugged. "Risa in deck form. Sounds good to me." She saw the look in Duffy's eyes. "What do you expect? I'm a doctor, not an engineer."

He looked back at his padd. "You're not taking this seriously." He scowled at her, but couldn't hold it for long. "Besides, I like my Risa in chewable, cherry-flavored lozenge form, anyway."

A faint vibration in the hull stilled the conversation, and all eyes went to the windows, where beyond the nacelle the stars shifted into streaks of light. "We've gone to warp," said Duffy.

Gomez seemed to be assessing the vibration in the deck. "About nine-point-six-five. We're in a hurry."

"The inertial dampers need tuning," said Pattie.

Stevens nodded, touching a bulkhead with his fingertips. "Somebody should check those plasma injectors too."

Corsi rolled her eyes. "How did I get stuck on a ship full of engineers?"

"Dumb luck?" Stevens said with a smile.

Captain Gold's voice came from the intercom. "*S.C.E. staff to the observation lounge.*"

"Right on schedule," said Lense, taking one last sip of *raktajino* before heading toward the doors.

"Showtime, people," said Gomez, leading the rest of them out.

Duffy sighed and cleared the padd's display. "One plasma conduit," he muttered, before following the others into the corridor. "I got to move one lousy plasma conduit."

2

Captain David Gold sat alone at the table in the *U.S.S. da Vinci's* observation lounge. Carefully spaced around the long black table stood a full complement of vacant chairs, all Starfleet standard issue, save for Blue's at the other end of the table. At his elbow was a rapidly cooling bowl of matzoh ball soup, and the grim visage of Captain Montgomery Scott filled the main viewscreen in the wall to his right.

He glanced briefly into the soup, decided the color of

the broth was too pale, the sheen of fat on top somehow wrong. He set it on the table to finish its thermodynamic journey to room temperature. No matter how many times he had the crew tweak the replicators, they could never produce even a faint shadow of his wife's wonderful homemade soup.

Captain Scott seemed to notice the bowl for the first time. *"Sorry about your lunch, David. This is one of those instances where seconds could mean the difference between life and death."*

Under better circumstances, Gold might have grinned. Captain Scott was a man out of time, an officer from the golden days of two-fisted space exploration. He didn't shy from the dramatic, or even the melodramatic. It was something Gold liked in Scott, even as he found it sorely lacking in himself. "My people are on their way, and we're already en route at maximum warp. It sounds like we should hit the ground running, so to speak."

"Aye, that's the way I see it. Everything we've got on the situation has been transferred to your computers under the heading 'Enigma,' but I wanted to brief you all personally."

The door opened and the S.C.E. crew began to file in, led by Gomez and Corsi.

Gold nodded to acknowledge their arrival. "Warm up your padds, there's work to be done."

"Always is," replied Gomez, pulling out her personal access data display.

Corsi's reaction was different. She stopped and studied the captain, her eyes narrowed. He could see her mind working furiously.

Corsi wasn't an engineer, far from it. Beyond field-stripping a hand phaser in the dark, or setting a demolitions charge, she steered clear of technical subjects. If the current mission concerned her, she knew there was a threat involved, either to the ship, or the crew. Playing watchdog to a ship full of egghead engineers, often oblivious to their own safety, was her job. She took it very seriously.

Lense, Soloman, Blue, Abramowitz, and Stevens quickly followed and took their seats, Blue scuttling across the room and crawling onto her special chair at the far end of the table. Gold noticed Duffy bringing up the rear, a distracted frown on his face.

"Computer, display file Enigma on the main viewer." A screen on the wall lit with the files entry screen, Scott's image shifting to an inset in the upper-right-hand corner.

Gomez frowned as she looked over the file's contents. "This is a search-and-rescue operation? I'd think there were better-equipped ships in the sector for that."

Scott sighed. *"Well now, that's the rub. The* U.S.S. Chinook *is already on station, but they're having no luck getting inside the bloody thing, or even figuring out what in blazes it is. Command has a vital relief mission for them across the sector, and they're going to have to get under way in just a few hours."*

"More vital than a missing starship?" Gold asked.

"According to Starfleet Command, this is classified as a salvage operation where the Lincoln *is concerned. We know the* Lincoln *struck what they're calling a navigation hazard at sublight speed. The object is about a hundred kilometers in diameter, and the* Lincoln *didn't come out the other side. That means it was likely decelerated from two hundred and fifty thousand KPH to the navigation hazard's speed, about ten thousand KPH."*

Gold felt his jaw clench involuntarily as he thought about it.

Shaking his head, Stevens said, "Even with inertial dampers, that should have torn the *Lincoln* to shreds, and turned its crew into paste. Not something I'd wish on my worst enemy."

"That's what Starfleet assumes, Mr. Stevens. There's

also the matter of a freighter crewman who disappeared inside the object under less violent circumstances. Starfleet hasn't given up on him, but the Chinook's *mission is of planetary importance. They expect you go in, rescue that merchantman if possible, recover any wreckage, and deal with this blasted navigation hazard, but that's nae the way I think. The crew of the* Lincoln *is as certain paste as I'm seventy-five years dead on a derelict ship. Until I see evidence of the wreckage and the bodies, we'll be working on the assumption that those people are alive and in need of our immediate help."*

This time Gold did grin, just a little. Scott had come back from the dead more than once, after all. "If I'm ever in trouble, Scotty, I should have someone like you looking for me. Fine, search and rescue, then. By the book. If there's any way possible, we'll be bringing them back alive."

Scotty's lined face brightened a bit. *"Aye, I knew I could count on you lot. It's stumped the science types on the* Chinook, *so I'm hoping an engineering approach will do better. Just don't forget the main thing is to crack that egg open and get any survivors out. Captain Gold, I'll stop my meddling and let you get on with your work. Good luck to ye, and keep me posted."*

The screen blanked, replaced by an annoyingly incomplete scan of the enigma object.

Gold turned back to the crew. "We'll be pulling alongside the object in about eight hours, but we should know what we're doing when we get there. Comments?"

Blue made a little bell-like noise, her equivalent to clearing her throat. "Captain Scott's egg metaphor, while gruesome, appears quite accurate. It seems impossible to understand this object from surface observations. To understand it better, we'll need to find a way to penetrate to its interior."

Gomez nodded. "That's what we'll need to focus on, then."

"Remember," Gold said, "our immediate goal here isn't complete or immediate understanding of the Enigma, it's results. We'll try anything, and we'll try everything."

"It would help," Stevens said, "if we could see inside the thing."

"Good point, Fabian," Gomez said with another nod. "Take the lead on that. Find us a window inside that thing, visual, sensors, probing with a long metal rod—anything that'll give us some useful information."

"One more thing," said Stevens. "This freighter crewman, Wayne Omthon, who's lost inside? I'm pretty sure I've met him. My parents run a shuttle service in the Rigel colonies, and he's hauled express cargo through there while I was visiting. Apparently Rigel is a regular stop for his ship."

"It's a small galaxy," said Corsi.

"But I wouldn't want to paint it," said Duffy.

Gold talked over their banter with the ease of long practice. "Can you tell us anything useful about him?"

Stevens scratched his chin for a moment, considering. "Mom once said he was part-human, part-green Orion. Not sure why that was noteworthy."

Corsi grinned, as though someone had just told her a secret joke.

Stevens studied her face for a moment, puzzled, then moved on. "He has a good reputation as an engineer. Apparently he's come up with some innovations to improve the engine efficiency on Profit-class Ferengi-built freighters, which have been widely adopted."

Gold mulled this for a moment. "You think that's significant?"

"Reports are he's smart and resourceful. He may have found, or at least stumbled upon, a way to open a chink in the Enigma's hide. Maybe if we can figure out how he did it, we won't have to reinvent the wheel."

"It's worth keeping in mind," Gomez said. "Thanks,

Fabian." She turned her attention to Blue. "Pattie, assuming we can find a way inside the Enigma, we'll need contingency plans for sending a team inside, and what they'll do once they get there. I want you working on that." Her gaze shifted briefly to Soloman, who sat silently, listening intently, and yet contributing little. "Soloman will work with you. Soloman, you're checked out to operate an EVA pod, right?"

It was difficult to read the little Bynar's expression, but Gold thought he was surprised. "Commander? Er— I have access to all operational manuals and training materials though the ship's computers, as well as an accumulated six hundred and thirty-two thousand hours of flight logs—however, in terms of practical experience—"

"Blue," Gold interrupted, "see to it that Soloman is checked out on the simulator and ready to fly by the time we arrive. They're so automated, I could train a Denebian mud-monkey to fly an EVA pod. I imagine the finest computer expert in Starfleet should have no trouble."

Soloman blinked. "May I inquire—?"

"I doubt we'll just be able to beam into this thing," Gomez said. "We'll need our team out there in suits, and I'll want someone standing by just outside, to observe and provide assistance if necessary. In an EVA pod, you'll be able to get up close and personal with it, and comfortably stay on station much longer than someone in a space suit."

Soloman shifted uncomfortably in his seat. It was an uncharacteristically human gesture. "Commander, I do not know if—"

"You can do this, Soloman. You *will* do it."

"Yes, Commander."

"That covers the major assignments. The rest of you provide any support or resources you can. Teams should coordinate and share information. I'll expect progress reports at least an hour before we drop out of warp."

Gomez looked at Gold, who gave an approving nod. "Good," he said, and glanced around the room. "Anything else?"

"Animal, vegetable, or mineral?" Carol Abramowitz, the team's cultural specialist, asked.

Gold looked at her. "Excuse me?"

Abramowitz shrugged. "Sorry, Captain. Just thinking out loud. That seems to be the fundamental question, the one the *Chinook* couldn't answer. Is the Enigma animal, vegetable, or mineral? Knowing which one would give us a better idea what approach to take in breaking it open. But without breaking it open, there's no way to answer the question."

Following the meeting, Captain David Gold returned to the bridge of the *da Vinci,* more as a matter of his own comfort than of any necessity. As the doors parted, he basked in the atmosphere of the place: the subdued lighting that reflected his own preferences, the chatter of com traffic, the cool, efficient voice of the computer issuing from several consoles simultaneously, and the focused energy of his bridge crew as they went about their job.

As usual, the tactical officer, Lieutenant McAllan, bellowed, "Captain on the bridge." Gold had given up trying to break the by-the-book lieutenant of the habit.

He stepped up to the command chair, slid his fingertips across the cool metal of its arm, and settled into the cushions.

It was a comfortable chair, perhaps the most comfortable one he'd ever sat in, yielding where it needed to, and yet supporting his back firmly. When he sat in it, his body naturally fell into the correct posture, both comfortable and alert.

He wished he had a chair that felt this good in his

cabin. If they ever had to abandon ship, he'd get the crew off first, then hope there was a spare escape pod for the chair.

"Status report, Wong."

Wong swiveled in his chair to face the Captain. It was an annoying habit common to Academy graduates these days. *Keep your eyes on the road,* thought Gold, but he said nothing. *I'm just being an old curmudgeon. The ship can fly itself for a minute.*

"On course at warp nine point five, captain. All systems nominal. ETA, sixteen hours, thirty-six minutes."

"Steady as she goes."

Wong nodded, and turned back to his console.

About time. He smiled at himself. *You are turning into a curmudgeon, David Gold. Keep this up, and you're going to start to frightening your great-grandchildren as much as your junior officers. Appreciate what you've got here.* She was a good little ship, and this was a good chair. Not the most glamorous command in Starfleet, and there were probably those who would look at it with some scorn, but it suited David Gold, and he knew it.

S.C.E. ships didn't go looking for battles, nor did they seek out strange new worlds. Often enough, those things found them, but that was almost never the plan. Captain Gold believed he spent as much time shepherding his brilliant and sometimes eccentric crew as he did charting courses across the galaxy. This ship and her crew faced battles of a completely different kind, and together they made discoveries no less profound, no less important. Moreover, everywhere they went, they left things better, things built, repaired, restored, improved. They made a difference.

It was something he wouldn't trade for anything.

The turbolift doors slid open and Corsi stepped onto the bridge. Gold knew from the look on her face that something was bothering her, yet she hesitated to approach him.

"Back so soon, Corsi? Come. We'll talk."

Gold stood, a bit reluctantly, and gestured to the door of the ready room. Corsi followed as he crossed the short distance, and stepped inside.

"I was wondering, Captain, why I didn't receive a specific assignment regarding Enigma."

Gold stood near the doorway. He faced Corsi, her concern clear in her expression. "You're my chief of security, Corsi. You know your job."

"Exactly, sir. We're moving into a threat situation. I should be part of the planning."

"You know your input is always welcome, Corsi."

"I meant a *specific* part of the planning."

"This mission has potential hazards, yes, but this Enigma object isn't something I'd classify as a threat. It's made no overt hostile moves, demonstrated no weapons capability, nor even the ability to move at warp."

Corsi frowned. Her face was tight, drawn. She worried too much, relaxed too little. Gold wondered if it was his job as captain to try and change that.

"Captain, a volcano isn't hostile either, and yet it can be plenty dangerous."

Gold nodded. "Corsi, I understand how you feel, but this is still an engineering problem, and perhaps I put you in the middle of engineering problems too often. There are times that's necessary and appropriate, but I don't see that this is one of them." He watched her frown deepen. "When you're put in the middle of an engineering problem, Corsi, I sometimes wonder if it compromises the engineering, and if it compromises the security concerns as well. Let the individual teams handle the engineering matters."

"Even when I know they'll be putting themselves in danger?"

"I said you know your job, Corsi. Be watchful, keep them safe, but give them the space to work. You're a professional, but so are they. Trust them as you trust yourself."

"Bridge to captain." It was Lieutenant Ina, at ops. *"We have an incoming transmission from the* Chinook."

He could still read doubt in Corsi's face, though she'd never question his orders. He smiled reassuringly. "Let's try something different this time. It could be good. You never know."

As Gold stepped back onto the bridge, his smile faded, and he slipped back into business mode. "On screen, Ina."

It had been a number of years since their last encounter, but he recognized Christa Otis, captain of the *Chinook*. He tried to remember the circumstances. Some casual gathering of senior officers on Starbase 96? He was twenty years Christa's senior, which still made her a seasoned officer by most standards. Still, he felt a certain fatherly affection for her. He briefly considered making small talk, but something in her expression told him this wasn't the time. Worry lines wrinkled her forehead, and her skin seemed pallid.

"David. I didn't know they were sending you, but I'm glad. Right now it means a lot to me that I'm turning this situation over to someone I trust."

"What's wrong, Chris?"

Her jaw clinched, and she looked away from the screen. *"I've got orders to get under way to Salem II, David, maximum warp. Unless we can stop the blight there immediately, three hundred million people are going to starve, come harvest time. There's no choice at all."*

"Chris—"

"I'm leaving without two of my people, David. They were setting navigation buoys around the thing when they, and the buoys, just vanished." Gold could see the effort it took for her to control her anger, in the tight line of her jaw, and her ramrod-straight posture. *"It got*

*bigger, just swallowed them up, and there's not a blasted
thing I can do about it."*

Gold glanced over at Corsi, who, despite her best
efforts at restraint, was giving him the "I told you so"
face.

3

"How," asked Carol Abramowitz, grunting as she
slammed a handball off the far wall of the court, "did I
get this assignment?"

Dr. Lense dashed to intercept the ball, smashed it
with rocketlike power. It bounced off the wall and was
past Abramowitz before she could react. Lense recovered the ball and bounced it against the floor so that it
snapped back into her hand. "As I recall, 'this assignment' was your idea. 'Is it animal, vegetable, or mineral,
that is the question.'"

Abramowitz sighed and wiped the sweat off her
upper lip. "I know that, but I'm a cultural specialist.
None of those really fall into my area."

"I'm a doctor, and the captain asked me to assist.
That makes even less sense, if you want to think about it
that way. I'd say he wants a couple of intelligent people
not locked into some fixed technical or scientific view-
point. This doesn't fit into any neat categories. Maybe
trying to make it fit is what threw the *Chinook* off."

Abramowitz sighed again, lifting her short black hair
off her neck. "What's the score?"

"I'm winning," said Lense.

"I don't doubt it, but what's the score?"

"I play to win. I'm winning."

"But the score?"

"I'm not keeping score, I'm just winning."

"You're not keeping score?"

"Don't need to. If you want to, you keep score."

"I don't know how. I've never played handball. I swat this ball against the wall until I miss, that's all I know. Why are we playing handball?"

"You want my help? I think better while breaking a sweat."

"That makes one of us." She plopped down in the corner, her back against the glass observation wall.

Lense put her hands on her hips and frowned. "You're no fun at all." She waited to see if Abramowitz would react, which she didn't. "I've got the rec room for thirty more minutes. The computer can shift things around and we can play something else. Racquetball, roto-goal, Bolian squash—there's a ping-pong table that pops out of the floor."

"I don't play any of those, or Aztec basketball either."

"What? Oh, never mind. What do you play?"

"Golf."

"Golf?" She looked around the room.

"The walls don't move that far, trust me."

It was Dr. Lense's turn to sigh. She shuffled over and sat down facing Abramowitz. "Animal," she said.

"What?"

"Animal, that's my answer. The Enigma is some kind of space-dwelling organism, like the space amoeba."

Abramowitz looked up and brushed a strand of damp hair out of her eyes. "You're making that up."

Lense shook her head. "It's the subject of many a trick question at Starfleet Medical. In 2268 the *Enterprise*, A or B or X or something—I don't remember which one— encountered an eighteen-thousand-kilometer-long space-dwelling amoeba that consumed an entire star system before they could stop it."

Abramowitz shook her head. "I didn't know that."

"Anyway, Enigma hasn't shown signs of intelligence, and it doesn't have warp drive. It does have camouflage, and it does ingest things, possibly as food. Ergo, animal."

"Mineral," Abramowitz said suddenly. "Or mechanical anyway. It's some kind of probe, or maybe a cloaked ship on autopilot, the crew long dead. They could have lost warp drive in deep space, and couldn't fix it. The crew died of old age, or they just ran out of food and air, but the ship is still going its merry way, running on autopilot."

"So why does it keep swallowing things up?"

Abramowitz took a deep breath, considering the problem. "If it's a probe, it could be taking samples, or collecting specimens. Maybe it's trying to recruit a replacement crew."

"I like my solution better."

"If your 'solution' is correct, then roughly one hundred and fifty people are being digested by an amoeba as we speak. If my theory is correct, then they may be safe and waiting for rescue. I like mine better. A *lot* better."

Lense reacted as though she'd been slapped. She slammed the ball against the floor so hard that the crack hurt Abramowitz's ears. "You think I don't? But we have to face the possibility. Get back to me when you're willing to." She got up and stormed out of the rec room.

Abramowitz just sat, trying to figure out what had just happened.

Duffy pushed a solitary black bean around his plate with a fork. He had been doing so for somewhere between two minutes and an eternity now, and it was driving Gomez, who sat across the mess-hall table from him, crazy.

"Kieran, would you please eat that, or put it out of its misery."

He put down his fork and looked up at her. "Sorry, thinking."

"Thinking is good. Sharing is better. I could use some ideas here."

"What we need is a can opener."

"A what?"

"Can opener. A device to open cans. Didn't they teach Waldport's *Principles of Parallel Technologies* when you were in the Academy?"

"They taught his theories. The book wasn't required reading."

"Then you know most technological civilizations develop parallel technologies, and Waldport's first example is the can opener. Almost every civilization known develops a system of preserving food in metal cans. The surprising thing is that the device to open these cans, a can opener, often isn't developed until later, sometimes hundreds of years later. You should read the book. It's one of the foundations of the Prime Directive, the idea that every civilization develops warp drive."

"And every civilization develops can openers."

"Almost."

"Almost?"

"That's Waldport's argument against his own principle. Vulcans never invented the can opener."

"Vulcans?" Sometimes following Kieran's conversational leaps was enough to make her dizzy. As though this assignment didn't already have her going in circles.

"Never developed cans. They preserved food by drying, salting, or a kind of bacterially induced homeostasis. No cans. No can openers."

A pattern was beginning to emerge. "So, you're saying that the Enigma may be a ship of some kind, representing an advanced civilization that somehow managed not to develop the warp drive, like the Vulcans and their nonexistent can openers."

"I'm saying that the Enigma is a big can, and we need a can opener to get inside."

Gomez looked down at her half-eaten curry rice, and after a moment's consideration, pushed it away before she started playing with her food too. "I'd say we know two, maybe three, different ways to crack Enigma already."

Duffy leaned forward on his elbows and raised an eyebrow slightly. "How so?"

"Well, first there's the brute force method. Crash into it at a significant fraction of the speed of light. It worked for the *Lincoln.*"

"Okay, I'm scratching that one off my list right now."

"Don't. We won't want to get in that way ourselves, but maybe there's some way we can use it, to send in a ruggedized penetrator probe, or spear some kind of pipe into the surface for access, like a giant hypodermic needle."

"There's a joke there somewhere. Maybe two or three. But go on, what's the next method?"

She frowned. "Well, that's the problem. We know, but we don't know. This freighter pilot managed to get himself in somehow. So did the two from the *Chinook,* and they managed to carry a dozen marker buoys with them."

"Well, this Omthon guy was apparently actively trying to get in. It's hard to tell, really; the sensor logs from the freighter were of such poor resolution. But we have recordings of the *Chinook* incident in crystal resolution in every wavelength known to the Federation, and we know they were only fixing a buoy near Enigma, not trying to get in, and were just swallowed up."

"Ah, but that swallowing, that's the only proactive thing that Enigma has done since we've encountered it. I think they, or the buoys, did something to trigger it. If we can figure out what that is, it's like having the key to the door."

"The trouble with that is, assuming that any of them are still alive in there—and I am—none of them have come back out. Me, I want to go in, but the coming out part, this is also part of the plan."

Gomez considered this for a moment. "We need a can opener," she finally said.

"I think I heard somebody suggest that idea."

She gave him a look that had stopped strong men in their tracks, but he just shrugged and grinned at her.

"But we need one that also works from the inside," she continued. "That means we can't just duplicate one of the methods for entering Enigma, we have to understand how it works before we find ourselves trapped." She stood up abruptly. "Come on, time to look at those sensor logs again."

Duffy groaned, loudly. "We've been through them a dozen times," he protested, but he was already climbing out of his chair to follow her.

"Then that obviously wasn't enough," she shot back over her shoulder, as she led the way out of the mess hall.

Soloman stared intently out the viewplate, watching floating debris drift by only inches from his face. "This is entirely illogical, P8."

"Concentrate on flying the pod," P8 Blue's voice came from a hidden speaker. *"Besides, you're a Bynar, not a Vulcan. Stop sounding like one."*

"Computers are inherently logical, and Bynars are a computer-based society."

"Yes, but you're a passionate people too, even though you don't often express it so other humanoids can understand. You delight, you fear, you love. I've seen it. Look out!"

A proximity klaxon sounded, and Soloman was

alarmed to see an ejected warp core tumbling toward him like a giant baton. He fumbled with the unfamiliar joystick, feeling the pod twist end over end, but the warp core grew ever larger in his view. In a panic, he hit the main impulse thruster, feeling the rumble as it fired just a meter or so under his feet.

The warp core slid out of view beneath the window, but smaller pieces of debris bounced noisily off the hull around him. He flinched as a jagged piece of metal bounced off the window just over his head, but the transparent aluminum held. In a moment, he was clear of the debris field, looking down on the shattered saucer section of the *Galaxy*-class ship. "Very well, then, I *fear* this assignment."

P8 made a dry, crackling sound. Soloman suspected the sound corresponded to a human sigh, though he wasn't certain. Bynars had no exact equivalent to either noise.

"Only a grub is mastered by their own fear. Well, grubs and green males, but that's another matter. In any case, while you failed to handle that situation the way I would have, it all worked out with only minimal damage registering on the pod."

Soloman muttered a string of binary code that did not have a direct translation, but could best be rendered in the human tongue as, "Dammit." "I failed to recover the data core. We will be unable to determine why this ship broke up."

"The wreckage isn't going anywhere, Soloman. Safety is always the first concern."

"Now, but what if the lives of my teammates depend on me?"

"Then I have every confidence you will do what is necessary. Besides, in a real emergency it isn't likely you'll need the joystick."

There was a clunk and a whir, and the EVA pod's hatch swung open. Soloman blinked against the glare of the *da Vinci*'s shuttlebay, and looked down at P8 Blue, standing on her hind legs just outside.

"Enough simulations for now. We need to work on the mission planning for Enigma."

Soloman nodded gratefully, and climbed down the steps to the shuttlebay's deck. The *da Vinci*'s two shuttles were parked just a few meters away, leaving little room for anything else in the small bay. He took one last look up into the pod's cupola, and watched the simulated starfields projected onto the windows flicker and vanish.

Soloman took a step, and nearly stumbled. Bynars were not a strong people, and the session had been taxing. His hands ached from manually operating the controls.

P8 watched him flexing his fingers, and made a comforting sound. "Sorry to push you so hard, but time is short. The simulation programs we have on hand are very advanced, worst-case scenarios that would challenge even an experienced pilot. And I know that operating the controls manually, rather than through direct computer interface, put you at a disadvantage, but that was something you had to learn. Under the circumstances, you did well."

They stepped through the pressure doors into an interior corridor, and headed toward the workroom where they had set up shop for their part of the mission.

"Thank you." Soloman still felt uncertain.

"How did it feel?"

"Feel? Do you mean in the tactile, or the emotional sense?"

"In the less tangible sense. Operating a spacecraft, even one this small and limited, is a profound experience, from both a sensory and emotional standpoint. Sometimes the best way to evaluate it is on a nontechnical level. How does the pod feel to you?"

Soloman hesitated. There had been fear, excitement,

and exhilaration, but something else nagged at him, some aspect that colored all the rest. "It felt—lonely."

P8 dropped down to scuttle on all eight legs. "That's not what I would have expected."

"Nor I. I thought that since—losing my bond-mate, I thought I had become somewhat immune, or at least numbed, to the feeling of being alone. Yet I have spent most of my time on this ship, surrounded by my crew-mates, interfacing with its computers. I've not been truly as alone as I imagined. In the pod, immersed in the simulation, hearing only your voice, without even the pod's pathetically limited computer for company, I was more alone than I think I have ever been, and I know that in a real mission, it would be even more extreme."

P8 stopped, then scuttled around in a semicircle to look up at Soloman. "I am sorry. I didn't see what a personal challenge this could be for you, and I'm sure Commander Gomez didn't either. I will talk with her. I'm sure we can get someone else to go out in the pod."

"No," said Soloman, surprised at his own resolve, "that will not be necessary. I look forward to the mission not with dread, but with anticipation. Flying the mission, operating the manual controls, that feeling of being alone. I felt—empowered."

P8 stood on her hind legs, antennae waving excitedly. "Good for you, my friend! It is amazing what this Enigma can teach us about ourselves. I have heard it said that when one looks into the abyss, they see only themselves." She turned and walked through the door of their workroom.

Feeling just a little dizzy, not from fatigue, but from amazement, Soloman followed.

4

To Captain Gold, the *da Vinci*'s shuttlebay seemed like a giant's closet: crowded, and badly in need of being cleaned out. There were two shuttlecraft wedged into the compact space, plus a Work Bee and several EVA pods. Along every wall and in various alcoves, all manner of large equipment was stowed: phaser drills, portable tractor beam emitters, cargo-sized pattern enhancers, magnetic grapples, spools of carbon nanotube cable, color-coded drums of lubricants and plasma coolant, and other tools of the S.C.E. trade.

On most Federation starships, the shuttlebay was a neat and spacious hangar, kept clear of all but a few shuttles and perhaps a visiting ship or two.

Well, Gold smiled to himself as he threaded his way through the clutter, *most shuttlebays don't have to work for a living.*

He stood before the closed bay doors, and glanced over his shoulder at the observation windows. As he expected, the station was not staffed, and he was alone. Good. "Computer, active force field, open shuttlebay doors."

"Command authorization required."

"Authorization Gold, ten-forty-five."

With a whir, the doors parted. There were many unusual aspects of the *Saber*-class design: the warp nacelles connected to the outside edges of the saucer, the deep-keeled engineering section trailing aft with the warp-core in the rear, and the shuttlebay doors that opened forward, just under the main bridge.

The doors stood open, and Gold watched the warp-streaked stars passing by, the vastness of space sepa-

rated from him by no more than a few inches and a
force field.

One more thing about this command that he
wouldn't trade for anything. The sailing captains of old
could stand on the bow of their ship, lean over the rail,
and look out at the vast and wondrous sea. So too could
Captain David Gold. He could almost imagine the stellar winds on his face.

"That's dangerous, you know." The voice belonged to
Corsi. He heard her sharp footsteps as she walked up
behind him. Even in the cluttered shuttlebay, there was
a military precision to her step.

"The universe, or just where I'm watching it from?"

"Both. If you weren't the captain, I'd be busting your
chops about safety protocols."

"Then it's good to be the captain."

"Would the captain be prepared to accept a lecture
on safety protocols?"

"No."

"A reminder?"

"Noted and ignored."

They stood silently for a while, Gold looking at the
stars, Corsi contemplating the force-field control panel.

Gold sighed. "You're taking all the fun out of this,
you realize?"

"It's my job."

"Well, you're good at taking the fun out of things.
You clearly aren't here for the view."

"I had the computer track you down. I wanted to discuss ship's discipline."

"Somebody else's chops you want to bust?"

"Not that kind, Captain. Maybe discipline isn't the
word. Mood, maybe even morale, though that isn't my
area of expertise."

"Obviously." When Corsi ignored the sarcasm in his
tone, Gold said over his shoulder, "Go ahead."

"People are acting strangely, even for engineers.

They're acting almost"—she hesitated, as though searching for the proper word—"almost giddy. I'm even seeing it in my security people. I don't understand it. This is a very serious mission."

Gold nodded. "Close shuttlebay doors."

He turned away from the closing doors and faced Corsi. "It's understandable, Corsi. You've never been on this kind of mission before, have you?"

"What kind of mission would that be, sir?"

"We're investigating the disappearance of a Federation starship with all hands. Despite Captain Scott's boundless optimism, we all know, on some level, there's a chance we won't be finding survivors."

"We've investigated ship disasters before, much worse than this." Her tone was puzzled, and a frown creased her smooth brow. "The *Beast*, *Friend*, the *Senuta* ship, those Breen and Jem'Hadar ships during the . . ."

"Those were alien ships. This is a Federation starship, full of Starfleet personnel, people like us."

"So was the *Defiant*," Corsi said almost defensively.

"Yes, but we knew the *Defiant* crew was already dead before we even started that mission. I'm not saying that these people value the lives of aliens or non-Starfleet crews any less. But we all come out here knowing there are dangers, knowing that the universe could reach right out and smite one or all of us. Knowing we may find a ship with all hands lost is a stark reminder of our own fragility, our own mortality."

"You're saying they're scared?"

"Not at all, not in any pejorative sense, anyway." Gold clasped his hands behind his back and paced across the small open space behind the closed doors, his head down and his voice low.

"I've been in the fleet a long time, Corsi. I've lost too many crewmates and friends, seen wars and disasters, and generally spent too damn much time in the close proximity of death. That's not unusual in these days. Not after the Dominion War and the Borg. It's an unhappy accident of history that most everyone on board this ship, directly or indirectly, has had a taste of what we could be facing."

He stopped his pacing and glanced at Corsi, then looked back at his feet. "What I'm saying is that sometimes the only way to look the reaper in the eye, feel his cold breath on your cheek, and not to run screaming, is to laugh in his face. Trust me, this is only what *anticipation* of a possible disaster has done to them. If we find ourselves trying to sort body parts out of wreckage, you'll hear gallows humor that will curl your toes."

"You don't have a problem with that?"

He looked up then, and chuckled sadly. "You'll probably find me in the thick of it, Corsi. It's human nature. It's healthy. It's not your way of coping apparently, but for your sake, I hope you have some way of releasing the tension. You must be feeling it too, and I need my chief of security functioning at one hundred percent."

She nodded. "Yes, sir. Thank you for clearing that up for me." She turned and headed for the inner door.

"And, Corsi?"

"Yes, sir?"

"You're thinking like a senior officer. I like to see that. You could be first-officer material one of these days, maybe even the big seat."

"That wasn't what I was thinking about, sir."

"Sometimes you choose the seat, Corsi. Sometimes the seat chooses you."

Corsi stepped into the corridor and stopped, considering the captain's words. She was feeling the pressure, the apprehension of what they might find when they dropped out of warp in a few hours. She tapped her combadge. "Corsi to Stevens."

"Stevens here."

"Are you busy just now?"

"I'm in my quarters. I was hoping for a few hours' sleep before we roll up our sleeves and start working on Enigma." There was a pause. *"Why?"*

5

"Kieran."

The voice came out of darkness. It was a pleasant voice, a voice he liked. It was the message he didn't like.

"You're sleeping, Kieran."

It was Sonya's voice.

"Resting my eyes."

"Well, you snore when you're resting your eyes. You should have Elizabeth look into that."

"I'm going to rest them a little longer."

"Can't. Captain Scott is returning our call."

Duffy opened his eyes. He lifted his chin from his fist, which had been propping it up during his "rest," and looked around the hololab.

Sonya grinned at him, looking rested and alert. He knew she hadn't slept any more than he had. Where did that woman get her energy?

"Look alive, Lieutenant Commander, the boss is on the line."

He glanced over at the wall-mounted viewscreen just in time to see the Starfleet logo vanish and be replaced by the image of Captain Scott. *"Commander Gomez. Sorry I took so long to return your call. Meetings."* He grimaced, as though the one word explained everything. *"What can I do for you?"*

"Sorry to bother you, Captain, but our investigation into Enigma has turned up something that requires your expertise."

Scotty brightened. *"Well, why didn't ye say so, lass? What have ye found?"*

Duffy felt awake enough to dive in. "Captain, we've been reviewing the sensor logs from the *Chinook* and the freighter. The *Chinook* data hasn't been terribly useful, but the freighter logs are a different matter. The quality is so bad we've had to filter and massage it a dozen different ways to get the resolution we needed, but we think we have something."

"I'm transmitting a segment of the enhanced and restored visual record," Gomez said.

Scott's image on the screen was replaced by the visual playback. A space-suited figure floated in what seemed to be empty space. The suit was orange, an armored shell topped by a transparent bubble, with a bulky backpack studded with thruster nozzles, and a large toolpack attached to the belt. The man inside the helmet was humanoid and looked about thirty, perhaps younger, in human terms. But he was not human. His bright green skin made that clear.

Only when one looked closely was it apparent that *something* was just in front of the man, a discontinuity, like the edge of a soap bubble the size of a moon. He reached for the discontinuity and his hand stopped against the nearly invisible surface, like a mime touching the walls of a make-believe box. Then he reached into the pouch and pulled out an odd-looking tool.

"Computer, freeze playback," Gomez said. "Do you recognize the tool, Captain Scott?"

"Well, it's no human manufacture, but I'd say it's a magnetic probe o' some kind."

"Right," said Duffy, "we think that's exactly what it is. Probably Andorian, from the looks of it."

"Now, watch," said Gomez, resuming the playback.

The suited man pressed the tip of the probe against the discontinuity, and twisted a control. The probe began to disappear inside, which was surprising, since, in this case, inside only looked like more empty space. But as it pierced the surface, it began to disappear. The man withdrew the tool, and adjusted the controls some more. The tip of the probe began to glow. He pressed it against Enigma again.

Suddenly, something flared, and a circular opening perhaps two meters across appeared around the tip of the probe. The man leaned forward, looking inside. Little of the interior could be seen, but there was light coming from inside. The man crawled through the opening and disappeared from view, leaving the floating probe in the middle of the opening.

After a slight delay, he reappeared, grabbed the probe and pulled it inside. The opening narrowed as he did, and he could be seen switching the probe off, at which point the opening vanished completely.

Captain Scott reappeared on the screen, nodding. *"So y'think a magnetic probe can be used to get inside Enigma?"*

"We hope so," said Duffy. "But we want to understand how it works before we try it ourselves, and that's why we wanted to talk to you about the magnetic probe."

Scott looked puzzled. *"What's to tell? Do you not know all about magnetic probes?"*

A sheepish look crossed Gomez's face. "Sir, nobody in Starfleet has needed a magnetic probe in fifty years. We assume the freighter has some systems old enough or primitive enough to make one useful, but we're just not sure."

"Well then, lass, I'm nae sure if I should be flattered or insulted, but I can tell you all you need to know. In my day, we used them to work on the magnetic and force field antimatter containment. I once used one to save

the Enterprise *when we lost control of the antimatter flow."*

Gomez nodded. "The Kalandan Outpost incident. I've read about it in the texts." She shuddered slightly. "The idea of manually shutting down a runaway antimatter drive using a hand tool seems—forgive me, sir—"

Scotty grinned. *"Insane? Lass, I would have said the same thing, but it's amazing what a motivated engineer will do to save his ship—as you should know, or have ye forgotten the* Sentinel *so soon?"*

Duffy had to hide a grin of his own at Gomez's abashed look. She had, after all, pulled several stunts during the Dominion War during her time serving as chief engineer of the *U.S.S. Sentinel.* "In any case," he said, "that's why we called you. This thing was designed for working on magnetic containment, yet somehow it opened an iris in a holographic force field."

Scotty looked surprised. *"A hologram, you say?"*

"We don't know what's inside Enigma yet, but we're pretty sure the outside is a holographic projection over-laying a regenerative shield system. We've never seen anything like it."

"We knew Enigma wasn't truly cloaked," said Gomez. "Cloaking devices generally bend or transfer electromagnetic radiation around or through a ship. Enigma isn't *that* well hidden, if you know where to look and look closely enough in the right way. I don't think it's meant to sneak up on people—more like cam-ouflage, a system designed to allow it to go unnoticed in the vastness of space. When we see 'through' Enigma, we're actually seeing a holographic representation of what the stars on the other side look like, not the stars themselves. And the really curious thing is that, while Enigma isn't truly invisible, it's equally difficult to see in most every wavelength and form of energy known. We've tried everything from gravitons to tachyons. There could be thousands of Enigmas wandering through

our space, and pretty much the only way we'd ever discover them is by accident."

"Like, say, by running into one," added Duffy.

"So what we need, sir, is the missing link between the
magnetic probe and shields. That we don't find in the
books."

Scotty considered the problem, idly stroking his
mustache with a fingertip as he did. *"Tell me, did you
ever hear of the Nelscott flip?"*

Gomez blinked. "Sir?"

*"When I was on the asteroid freight run at Deneva, the
lads there pulled a wee trick on me. They used a magnetic
probe to invert the phase of the gravity generator under
my cabin."*

Duffy chuckled.

"Aye," said Scott, *"it plastered me to the ceiling until
they switched it back again. Some engineer named
Nelscott stumbled on the trick, and they pulled it on every
new officer aboard."*

"That makes sense," said Duffy. "You can't have
shields without gravitron generation, and if you flip the
phase, the local fields would repel each other, creating
our doorway. We've got the 'can opener' we were looking for, and now we have a pretty good idea how it
works."

Gomez nodded. "Thank you, Captain. We couldn't
have figured it out without you."

*"Any time, lass. Anything else I can do, let me know.
Also, since this concerns holograms, there's a lad you
might want to look up. Top man in the field, or so they tell
me."*

"Broccoli!" Duffy said suddenly.

"I beg your pardon?"

"You mean Reg Barclay, right?"

"Aye, that's the one. He's at Project Voyager *on Jupiter
Station."*

Gomez smiled. "We served with him on the *Enter-*

prise, Captain. He's actually quite a skilled diagnostic engineer—holography's just what he, ah, established his reputation with. We'll definitely get in touch with him, though."

"Meanwhile," said Scotty with a dramatic sigh, *"I'm due in another blasted meeting. Admirals."* His image flickered out, to be replaced by the Starfleet logo.

Duffy shook his head. "Haven't talked to old Broccoli in years. Been meaning to get in touch with him ever since he tracked *Voyager* down in the Delta Quadrant."

"If I remember correctly," Gomez said with a smile, "Captain Picard gave a cease-and-desist order on that nickname."

Laughing, Duffy said, "Like that was gonna stop me. C'mon, let's put a call in to Jupiter Station. Fabe should talk to him too. He may have some ideas how to see inside that holographic shell." He sighed. "Which would help us on our biggest unknown on a list of many. Our can opener should get us in, and in theory, out as well. So if our freighter pilot had the same can opener too, why did he go in and never come out?"

Abramowitz sat at her cabin's small workstation, reviewing reports from the other Enigma teams. It seemed as though everyone was making progress but she. The latest development was from Stevens, who, thanks to his consultation with holographic expert Reginald Barclay, thought he had a way of scanning Enigma for life signs. The technique didn't promise a great deal of accuracy or detail, but it might tell them something about what they were dealing with.

She pushed her chair back, and stared at Stevens's report glumly. *Just good enough to prove me wrong.*

A movement in the corner of her eye made her look up at her cabin's open door. She liked working with the door open, a habit she'd developed as a student. Dr. Lense stood in the corridor just outside. Abramowitz could see her lips moving. Lense was clearly unaware Abramowitz couldn't hear her.

Abramowitz waved her inside. Lense looked puzzled, stepped through the door, and immediately jammed her index fingers into her ears.

"Sorry," said Abramowitz, raising her voice to be heard over the music. "Computer, mute audio!" She hadn't even been conscious of the music until it was gone. "There's an audio damping field across the door. Ensign Conlon rigged it up. Probably something to do with her cabin being across the hall."

Lense glanced at the door. "Imagine that." She shook her head as though clearing her ears. "Was that *drad* music?"

"Nausicaan tusk opera. It doesn't sound a thing like *drad* music."

"Sorry, I'm not a connoisseur of pain. It's all pretty much 'ouch' to me." She took a deep breath and shifted nervously from one foot to another. "Look, this isn't starting out well. I just wanted to—and don't get used to this, because I don't plan to make it a habit—but I wanted to apologize, both for walking out on you earlier and for being less than helpful on this assignment."

Abramowitz shrugged. "You've got other work. I assumed you were getting sickbay ready for possible casualties."

Lense shook her head. "Not that much to do, really, until we know more. I've got Wetzel, Copper, and Emmett," the last being the ship's Emergency Medical Hologram, "replicating and stockpiling extra medical supplies, but they're more than capable of handling it."

She glanced at the nestlike pod where Abramowitz's roommate, P8 Blue, slept. The cabin was small, like all the others on *da Vinci,* and the alien pod made it feel even more cramped. Without waiting for an invitation, Lense sat down on the bunk. "Fact is, I saw things during the Dominion War that nobody should ever see. I thought I had gotten over it, and in a way, I have. I'm ready to handle the obvious nightmares lurking out there: the wreckage, the casualties, the bodies beyond help, the scattered remains that don't even resemble bodies anymore. All that I'm ready for. I can take it. What I can't take is the nervous laughter of people about to brush shoulders with death."

Abramowitz turned to face her. It never occurred to her that the doctor would feel that way—especially after how she handled herself on Sherman's Planet. "I didn't mean—"

Lense waved her off. "You didn't do anything. It's me. Maybe one day you'll understand, but for your sake, I hope you never do."

They were quiet for a while. Then Lense raised her chin and looked up at Abramowitz. "I've been thinking about our question, and I think you're right. This thing is artificial. A probe, a ship, a robot, something like that. If it were an animal, it would clearly have to be a sophisticated one. Even a space amoeba has a 'flight or flight' reflex. This thing doesn't. It's not chasing food, and it's not running away. It's not defending itself. It's just hiding, just going about its business, hoping not to be seen, not to be engaged." She grimaced. "I can relate to that."

"Mineral, then," said Abramowitz, avoiding the personal comment. "A ship, or something like it. But a ship would be 'animal' too, it would have a crew."

Lense shook her head. "Not a conscious one. 'Fight or flight' again. Maybe it's just a probe, but it seems far too big and sophisticated. Too simple-minded even for a robot. Maybe the crew is dead. Maybe they abandoned ship. Maybe this is a sleeper ship, and the crew is in suspended animation." She considered her last statement. "Yeah, that sounds about right to me. These 'enigmans,' whoever they are, whatever they want, they left home a very, very long time ago."

6

Captain Gold reached the bridge just as the *da Vinci* came out of warp. He slid into the big chair. "Put the Enigma on screen."

The beta shift conn officer glanced back at him. The ensign at the post was new, a Betazoid, having just transferred in from the *U.S.S. Hood.* "It already is on screen, Captain. There just isn't much to see."

Gold wondered if she'd simply anticipated the order, or if she was reading his mind. *Stop that.* He watched her face for a reaction. No, he didn't think so. It took a lot of restraint for a Betazoid to function well as a Starfleet officer. The concept of private thoughts didn't come naturally to them.

"Ensign—Deo, is it?"

She nodded.

"Deo, overlay a tactical grid on the object, based on our sensor scans. I'd like to at least know *where* to look."

She tapped her console. A grid of yellow lines appeared, outlining the shape of the object.

He'd been expecting—well, he wasn't sure what he'd been expecting. A sphere possibly, or some other geometric shape. Instead Enigma was lumpy and irregular, like a cluster of grapes, or perhaps a bag full of soccer balls. Moreover, even that shape didn't appear to be static. As he watched, the spherical lumps moved slowly across the surface, even sinking inside to be replaced by others rising to the surface. "Are we getting any sensor readings from inside the object at all?"

"No, sir," said Deo. "We can detect a bit of displacement at the boundaries that allows us to tell where that boundary is, but when we look deeper, all we see is—uh, whatever's on the other side."

Gold nodded. Stevens's modifications to the deflector dish couldn't be performed while they were at warp. It would be several hours before they knew if his plan to probe Enigma would work.

Deo was still looking at him. Something seemed to be bothering her. "Sir, there is something else. Enigma has a . . . telepathic component."

"The *Chinook* didn't report anything like that."

"Perhaps they didn't have any telepaths on board, sir."

"Can you read it, communicate?"

"No, sir. I get a sense that it is reading us in some way, and not much more. I can't even tell you if it's alive, or if we're being read by one consciousness or many. The telepathic probe is passive, inert, and very subtle."

"If you sense anything more, let me know immediately."

From behind him, the beta-shift tactical officer, Ensign Anthony Shabalala, said, "Captain, there's a ship approaching, and we're being hailed. It's the freighter *Vulpecula*."

"Give me visual."

The woman who appeared on screen was human, in her fifties, and looked like she hadn't slept in a long time. Her eyes were red-rimmed with fatigue, and her close-cropped gray hair stood out at odd angles.

"*Captain Gold, I've been expecting you. My name is Dee Rivers, captain of the* Vulpecula. *After my first officer disappeared, and those people from the* Chinook *disappeared, I didn't know what to expect from that thing, so I pulled the ship back a few million kilometers to wait.*"

"Thank you for staying on station until we arrived."

She sighed deeply, and dug at her scalp with nervous fingertips. "*Captain, that's my first officer in there. Pappy's a damned fool to have tried rescuing those people, but I'd like him back anyway, if you can manage."*

"We'll do what we can, Captain Rivers." *Pappy?* he wondered, but didn't ask aloud.

"We're a for-profit ship, Captain. I've loitered here longer than I can afford, and certainly longer than was safe. I've lost my convoy partner, my Federation escort, and there are a lot of raiders between here and Cardassia. I can't wait here to see how this turns out, but we'll stop back by after we drop off our cargo."

Gold nodded in a manner he hoped was reassuring. "I understand. If necessary, we can arrange transport to return your Number One."

"He's my retirement plan, Captain."

"Excuse me?"

"He's saving to buy this ship from me, and I'm counting on that to set me up for my declining years, a nice little hut on a beach somewhere. I really need him back."

"I see." Gold felt his tone turn chilly.

Rivers had turned away from the screen, as though she was about to disconnect, but turned back to look at him. Her shoulders sagged, and something in her seemed to melt, revealing a profound sadness. *"He's a fool, but a good fool, Captain. Bring him back to us. Please."*

Before Gold could respond to the pain in her voice, Rivers's image blinked out.

Duffy pulled the gauntlet over his hand and flexed his fingers experimentally in front of his face. "I love this part."

Gomez glanced at the panel on her left wrist, punched in the commands to start a space-suit self test, and looked up at Duffy. Like her, he now wore a complete environmental suit, minus the helmet. "Putting on gloves?"

"Putting on a space suit. Makes me feel like an

ancient knight preparing for the joust." He squirmed his shoulders and arms, testing the fit of the suit.

She pointed at the rack in the locker room wall behind him. "Excuse me, Sir Talks-a-Lot, but you're standing between the fair maiden and her lovely helmet."

He stepped aside as she plucked two helmets from the rack, handing one to him, and putting the other over her head, twisting it until the molecular seals engaged. She tapped the wrist panel again. *"You hear me, Kieran?"*

"Loud and clear, milady."

She tapped again. *"Gomez to Soloman. Communications check."*

"I—" Soloman seemed distracted, but not, as she had feared, distressed. *"I hear you well, Commander. My module is checked out and ready to fly—I believe."*

Just then, P8 Blue scuttled through the outer door into the locker room. She stood up on her hind legs, and made an annoyed clicking noise. "Aren't you ready yet? It must be very bothersome being so sensitive to vacuum."

Pattie's exoskeleton allowed her to endure vacuum with no special gear. All she needed was a special communicator with a pickup inside her breathing cavity, some safety gear, and she was ready to go.

Gomez grinned. *"Not according to Lt. Commander Duffy. He likes the outfit."*

That annoyed sound again. "Clothing, also something I find difficult to fathom." She strapped on a simple equipment harness. "I find this confining enough."

The locker room had two outer doors. The right-hand one led directly to service airlock two, the other to the shuttlebay. Duffy followed Gomez through the left door.

One of the Augmented Personnel Modules had been rolled up to the doors on its service stand. The module's hatch was closed, and Duffy could see Soloman through the cupola windows in the top, his bald head reflecting the blue interior lighting. The module was spindle-shaped and about three meters tall, with a control cupola at the top. The wide midsection was ringed with specialized work arms, the narrow base surrounded by maneuvering thrusters, and tipped with the orange glow of a tiny impulse drive. The module was more spacecraft than space suit.

Pattie tapped a wall panel, activating the force fields across the main doors. A warning klaxon sounded as the outer doors slid open, revealing the stars beyond.

Duffy stared, trying to decide which of those stars was real, and which was the holographic surface of Enigma. He couldn't be sure, but he trusted the module's instruments would get them where they needed to be. He could see Soloman working inside the control cupola, then a series of grab-bars and footholds folded out from the module's smooth sides.

Pattie's voice sounded over everyone's comm. *"Everyone attach your safety lines."* She climbed onto the side of the module.

Duffy let Gomez go first, then climbed up himself. The force clamps made the footrests feel slightly sticky as he moved his feet. He snapped his safety line into an attachment socket. "I'm secure."

"I'm go," Gomez said.

"Secure and ready," said Pattie.

"Away team to da Vinci," said Soloman. *"We are ready to disembark."*

B.J. O'Leary, the engineer on duty at the control gallery, replied, *"Ready."*

As they waited, Duffy could hear only his own heart and breathing, the whir of the suit's fans, and his comrades' voices in his helmet speakers.

"Disengaging artificial gravity," said O'Leary.

Duffy felt his stomach jump, and fought the instinct

that said he was falling. He looked down to see the tractor beams lift the module from its cradle and sail it smoothly out of the shuttlebay.

"I still don't see why we didn't just beam out," P8 said over the link. *"It really makes much more sense."*

Duffy managed to catch Gomez's eye, and winked, though he doubted she could actually see him. "I suppose we could have," he answered. "But where's the fun in that?"

"Lt. Commander Duffy." Soloman's voice was tight, a little strained. *"I really do not see that a discussion of 'fun' is appropriate at this time."*

Duffy knew when he had pushed far enough. Pattie was right. They could have beamed out, instead of riding the module through the force field. But the sensation of his suit pressurizing as it passed from the atmosphere of the shuttlebay to the vacuum of space was a rare experience, and not one he would pass up easily.

With Enigma almost impossible to see with the naked eye, Duffy's gaze was drawn back to the *da Vinci*. The shuttlebay opened the front of the saucer section like a misplaced grin, the two shuttles just inside reminding him of teeth. The *da Vinci*, which seemed so small from inside, was huge from out here. The saucer swept out on either side of them, and he could see the warp nacelles and the engineering hull trailing away from them in the distance.

They climbed above the plane of the saucer section, and he looked down at the bridge, suppressing the urge to wave.

"You're doing very well, Soloman," said Pattie.

"This is much easier than the simulation," replied Soloman, his voice calmer now that the tractor beams had released them and he had control of the module. *"Nothing is exploding. Nothing is trying to crush us. None of my systems are undergoing cascade failures. My direct computer interface is working."*

"Better to be overprepared," said Pattie, *"than under-prepared."*

Duffy and Gomez shared a chuckle, and he glanced over at her, her face just visible inside the bubble of her helmet. She grinned bright enough, he was sure, for them to see it back at the ship. *She's loving this too.*

"Stevens to away team."

"Gomez here."

"Commander, the deflector modifications are done, and we're ready to take a picture of Enigma."

Duffy saw Gomez's eyes widen. *"I thought you wouldn't be ready for another two hours, or I would have delayed the mission. Should we head back to the shuttlebay?"*

Stevens chuckled. *"Somebody named Scott once told me to always pad my repair estimates. Anyway, no need for you to return to ship, the neutrino flux is harmless, and the direct EM burst from the torpedo will be very localized. In fact, this times out pretty well. Just pull back a couple kilometers and enjoy the show."*

"Soloman," ordered Gomez, *"get us out of the line of fire."*

"Yes, Commander. Firing main thruster."

Duffy felt a slight push down onto the footrests, and the module began to accelerate away from the *da Vinci*. The ship grew slightly smaller for several minutes, until they rolled over, and the module braked to a stop.

"Gomez to Stevens, we're standing by at a safe distance."

"Stand by, we're almost ready to launch."

"Explain to me again," said Pattie, *"what this 'X-ray' is?"*

"Sure," said Duffy. *"It's an internal imaging technique we used to use on Earth. Radiation was directed through a solid object onto some kind of sensitive receptor or film that could create a shadow image. It was used to test metals for cracks, even image people for medical purposes."*

"Bombarding living beings with radiation just to examine their insides? My people never developed such a thing."

Duffy chuckled. "Not likely you would. All your bones are on the outside, where you can just look at them. Anyway, Doc Lense mentioned this to me, and that gave me the idea on how to take a peek inside. See, the problem is that Enigma's broad-spectrum holograms fool all our sensors. They seem to know when they're being scanned and increase their resolution. The closer we look, the more realistic their holograms. Our sensors are *too* good. We hope if we take a big, crude, fast, shadow picture of Enigma, it will overwhelm their ability to cloak themselves. Instead of radiation, though, we'll use a torpedo modified to produce an intense burst of neutrinos, and we've modified our deflector dish to be the image pickup."

Duffy looked up as he spoke and saw the port over the *da Vinci*'s forward torpedo launch slide open. "They're getting ready to fire."

"Stand by," Stevens's voice came through his speakers. *"Fire torpedo on my mark."* A pause. *"Mark."*

A bright object—the torpedo all but hidden behind its own thruster flare—shot from the tube, running in a straight line only long enough to clear the ship, then curving around the bulk of Enigma. They couldn't see the hidden ship, but the curve of the torpedo's course, for the first time, gave them a sense of its size. Duffy found himself whistling.

Intellectually, he had known it was big, but that was much different than having a *feel* for the thing. It reminded him of the time he'd first walked the wooden deck of the restored Brooklyn Bridge in New York, back on Earth, and imagined building those stone towers using nothing but steam and muscle. Then, as now, Duffy had suddenly felt very small.

He was surprised that he could tell when the torpedo

crossed Enigma's "horizon" and continued around its back side. At that point, something about the torpedo looked *different* in a way he couldn't define. Perhaps the speed and brightness of the torpedo were already overwhelming Enigma's holograms in some subtle way that the eye, an amazingly sophisticated instrument in its own right, could detect.

Then came the explosion.

There was no sound, of course, and his helmet visor automatically compensated for the glare. But the flash was brief, and his visor almost instantly reverted to a normal view. In that moment, he could swear he saw the stars behind Enigma shimmer slightly, as though the hologram had momentarily become unstable. Then it was gone, and Enigma was hidden in its cloak of secrecy. Almost.

"Away team," said Stevens, *"we've got good data on the dish over here. We're analyzing it right now. Getting some gross readings. There's a lot of Starfleet-issue duranium alloy in there, consistent with the mass of the* Lincoln.*"*

Duffy felt a tightness in his chest. Of course the duranium was in there, but in what form? The seconds ticked by.

"Away team, we're—she's intact! The Lincoln's *still in one piece!"* In the background audio, Duffy could hear cheers. He surprised himself by letting out a whoop and pumping his fist at the stars. He surprised himself even more when he leaned over and gave Gomez an awkward hug. More surprising yet, she hugged back, laughing all the while.

"What," said Pattie, a puzzled tone in her voice, *"was all that about?"*

"Elation," said Soloman. *"A release of accumulated emotional tension. A human thing, perhaps, but I felt some of it myself. Our comrades are quite possibly alive."*

P8's pickup transmitted an odd, tinkling sound. *"Our orders were always to proceed on that assumption."*

"Sorry, Pattie," said Duffy. "Humans can't just be ordered to be optimistic. There's hope, and there's justified hope, and most of the crew just crossed from the former to the latter."

"Gold to away team."

Duffy was surprised to hear the captain's voice. He quickly let go of Gomez's waist and tried to put himself back into professional mode.

"You heard the man," the captain continued. *"If there was ever a doubt, this is now definitely a rescue mission. Get us inside."*

"Aye, sir," responded Gomez. *"Soloman, take us in."*

7

Dr. Lense leaned over Stevens's shoulder and stared at the console. "How much do you trust this data?"

Stevens shrugged. "I'm guessing maybe seventy percent accuracy. All our information is inferred, and Enigma was trying to mask our pulse."

On a viewscreen to Stevens's right, a tall, nervous-looking officer with a high forehead looked on. Lense understood that his name was Barclay, and he was some kind of expert on holotechnology.

Barclay shook his head in wonder. *"A neutrino hologram. I—I wouldn't even have thought it was possible."*

Stevens looked up at the screen and smiled wryly. "They haven't seen anything like this in the Delta Quadrant, Lieutenant?"

"Voyager has encountered some amazing things. But nothing like this."

"So you're saying Enigma represents a more advanced technology than ours?" Stevens said.

Barclay seemed hesitant to commit. *"In some ways, but there's no sign of warp drive. You're familiar with* Principles of Parallel Technologies?"

Stevens nodded. "It's already come up several times since this mission started. You think this is the exception that proves the rule?"

Barclay's eyebrows lifted. *"Technically, the exception can never prove the rule, but it's possible this is an exception of some sort. Waldport thought the urge to explore and to seek simulated experiences, through storytelling, or more advanced technologies like holodecks, were interrelated. Perhaps that might lead the occasional civilization down a different—different technological path."*

Lense squinted at the readouts. "I'm not an engineer, but how different are they? I mean, the ship hypothesis is mine, but shouldn't there be more *metal* in there?"

Stevens shrugged. "Given the resolution of this method, we pretty much had to know what we were looking for, so there could be lots of nonduranium alloys inside there that aren't showing. But we do show plenty of carbon-organic signatures, and only a small number of them correspond to the *Lincoln* crew. If we assume those are living creatures, and not corpses or somebody's food supply, then it still looks like a ship."

"There's—there's something else that's bothering me," said Barclay. *"You said that Enigma showed some sign of—telepathic capabilities?"*

Lense nodded. "According to our Betazoid crewmember, yes. Why does that bother you?"

"If we assume the crew have some telepathic abilities she's picking up, then probably not. But if it comes from the holographic systems, possibly. Starfleet Intelligence, years ago, did some studies of a telepathic hologram feedback system. A system like that is capable of showing a

viewer exactly what they expect to see, and that feedback can be quite—powerful."

"Holodiction," said Lense.

The very word made Barclay squirm in a way Lense found intriguing. She'd have to ask Gomez or Duffy, who served with him in the past, about his background sometime.

"No, not holodiction—though it could lead to that, I suppose. What we're talking about is an absolute suspension of disbelief, about hyperreality. The mind providing the source of the illusion is hypnotized—seduced by the illusion, until they find it almost impossible not *to accept as reality."*

P8 Blue looked up from her tricorder, antenna waving excitedly. Her voice sounded over Duffy's com-link. *"I think I have an idea how the* Lincoln *survived the impact."*

Duffy, who floated at the end of his safety line several meters away, grunted in response. His attention was focused on the magnetic probe they'd only recently replicated, based on seventy-year-old Starfleet blueprints. Of course, they'd added some modifications: a long-duration power supply, extra field strength, and a whole suite of telemetry sensors that would provide data to the highly modified tricorders that they also carried. Still, some small part of his mind was listening to Pattie. "Do tell," he finally said.

"The interstellar medium is rather thin out here, but Enigma *is still sweeping a wide swath though interstellar gas and dust. I've observed several microparticle dust impacts while you've been working.* Enigma *doesn't sweep them away with a deflector, like a Federation starship, and there's been no energy release consistent with an impact. I believe* Enigma *uses some combination of force fields and gravity control to gently brake objects it encounters. Meanwhile, it should leave a 'hole' in the*

interstellar medium which would be possible to follow, but it does not. That means that it's leaving a trail of dust and gas behind as it moves."

"Like," said Gomez, *"soldiers covering their tracks to avoid detection."*

"Exactly," said Pattie. *"But the composition has been subtly altered. Enigma is using the objects and gas it collects as raw materials, and ejecting waste products."*

Duffy frowned. "You think the *Lincoln* will be cut up for raw materials?"

"Possibly," said Pattie, *"but perhaps not. In any case, there is a mechanism that could have 'collected' the* Lincoln *without substantially damaging it."*

Gomez leaned back. *"Did you copy that,* da Vinci?"

"We did," said Corsi's voice. *"We're monitoring you very carefully."*

"Thanks, Mom," said Duffy. "We promise not to leave the yard."

Duffy thought he heard a slight growl, but it was hard to tell. Corsi's voice returned, crisp and professional. *"Are you sure you don't want a security team out there with you?"*

"No," said Gomez, before Duffy could reply. *"Nothing Enigma has done so far seems to constitute aggression. Having a bunch of goons with phasers waiting around might be seen as provocative. It would only put us in danger."*

"My people are not 'goons,' any more than yours are 'grease monkeys.'"

Gomez chuckled. Foley, one of Corsi's security people, had let the "grease monkey" quip slip a week earlier, and Gomez was milking it for all it was worth.

"What," asked Corsi, *"is taking so long?"*

"We're being methodical," answered Gomez.

"That's 'safe' in security speak," said Duffy. "Besides, I'm almost"—there was a click, and the end of the magnetic probe began to glow a soft blue—"ready."

"Be careful," said Gomez, *"that you don't depolarize your own suit seals."*

"Careful, careful," Duffy replied in a sing-song tone. He pushed the probe closer to Enigma's nearly invisible surface. There was no question this time. The stars imaged near the probe began to shimmer and swirl like runny watercolors.

"Check your safety lines," warned Pattie. *"If we pierce the field, atmosphere could vent from inside."*

Duffy tugged at the line, and braced himself as he turned up the probe's gain and pushed it against the force field. Suddenly the image melted back, shimmering waves moving outwards from a hole that seemed, literally, to appear out of empty space. "It's working!"

As the opening reached half a meter or so, Duffy reduced the gain and allowed it to stabilize. There was light inside, and he got an impression of a large space.

Gomez checked her tricorder. *"I'm getting a reading from inside. There's a breathable nitrogen-oxygen atmosphere, with enough residual force field to keep it inside. It's like the fields in the shuttlebay. Radiation flux is above background but nothing we'd need to worry about in the short term, even without our suits."*

Duffy leaned closer to the opening. He could see large machinery inside, dun- and gold-colored metals, pinstripes of silver and black, and glowing blue panels that pulsed with energy. "Will the force fields keep us from getting inside?"

"It shouldn't be a problem. Try pushing your hand through."

"Wait," said Corsi.

Duffy grimaced. They had a ship to rescue.

He plunged his hand through the field before any superior officer had time to reformulate that thought into the form of an order. There was a slight, springy, resistance, like punching through a thin sheet of rubber. He stopped only when he was up to the shoulder in

Enigma. He wiggled his fingers experimentally. "Still attached," he announced.

"Guys," Stevens's voice cut into the circuit, *"Corsi is turning all red. For your own safety, I recommend not returning to the ship right away."*

"We will," Corsi's voice was slow and controlled, *"have a talk about this later."*

"Gomez." It was Captain Gold's voice this time. *"What do you see?"*

"It looks like some kind of mechanical space, Captain. Possibly a power generator or an engine room, though the technology is unlike anything I've seen before. No sign of crew. Everything appears automated."

"Captain," said Duffy, "we have to go inside. We can't tell much about Enigma from out here. It's also possible that once inside, we might be able to get a message to the *Lincoln,* either with our combadges or through an internal communications system we can tap into."

"Captain," Corsi's voice rose in warning.

"Stand by, away team."

The bridge circuit was muted. Duffy exchanged glances with Gomez. He wondered what the proverbial fly on the wall would be hearing right now.

"Commander." It was Corsi. *"I'll be monitoring the situation from here. I have a team suited and ready for immediate beam-out in case there's trouble."*

"It'll be fine," said Duffy. "There's a duplicate magnetic probe on one of Soloman's manipulator arms. The module has enough power to hold the breach open indefinitely, which our portable model can't do. Soloman can monitor us from outside and provide a communications relay."

"Very well," said Gold, *"permission to enter the Enigma ship is granted."*

They withdrew the portable probe, and replaced it with the one on Soloman's pod. With the increased power available from the pod's mini-fusion reactor,

Duffy felt comfortable upping the gain to give them a two-meter opening. Gomez insisted on going first, but there was no shortage of volunteers. They were all eager to examine Enigma's mysterious workings.

There was an operational gravity field inside Enigma, roughly half a standard gravity, and it was oriented so that the opening dropped them onto an angled wall. A towline from the module was fed through the opening first, to allow them to climb down to a level deck about eight meters below. Duffy watched, feeling a slight bit of disorientation, as Gomez lowered herself down.

She waved. *"Comm check. Do you read me out there?"*

"Signal gain is down seventy percent," reported Soloman, *"but I still read you fine, and I'm relaying a clear signal back to the ship."*

P8 Blue was next in. She bypassed the line, her eight legs allowing her to scurry directly down the wall in the reduced gravity.

"Wish me luck," said Duffy, as he waved at Soloman in his cupola and climbed through the opening.

"Despite considerable effort on my part, I still do not understand the indeterminate nature of luck. I wish you success, not failure."

Duffy chuckled. "Close enough." He felt the gravity field grab him as he passed through the force fields, and climbed hand over hand down the line. He dropped lightly to the deck—it was a little like his first walk on Mars—and joined the others in looking around.

The space was dimly lit, and their hand-lights helped them pierce the shadows. A large cylinder, covered with glowing blue panels along its length, stretched from one end of the space to the other, a distance of perhaps fifty meters. Duffy was drawn to this device, while P8 scrambled inside a large copper-colored piece of machinery at one end of the room. Gomez focused on some illuminated wall panels that might be controls or readouts.

With the oxygen-nitrogen atmosphere confirmed, both Duffy and Gomez took off their helmets to conserve their suits' respective air supplies.

Duffy walked along the length of the device, feeling the pulse of power from inside as his glove slid along its mechanical supports. He knew instinctively it had to be some kind of engine. He stopped occasionally to take a tricorder reading, then moved along. He'd traveled the full length of the device before coming to a conclusion. "I think this is a space drive, a caterpillar."

Pattie's head popped out of an opening in the top of the device she was examining. "Excuse me? That last part can't possibly have translated properly."

Duffy laughed. "I wasn't talking about one of your family members, Pattie. It's a kind of theoretical reactionless drive. Inside this cylinder, a bit of space is being pinched, kinked. The drive then uses that kink to pull itself forward. Once the kink has been pulled through the length of the engine, it's released, a new one forms at the other end, and the process repeats itself.

"It's like an inchworm crawling along—again, no offense—or one of us climbing that line hand-over-hand. It's a perfect stealth drive, no exhaust products, no radiation, no thermal emissions, just a few stray gravity waves that these people apparently have the technology to mask. Thing is, this kind of drive should require a lot of power."

"Two things," Pattie said. "One, you really don't need to apologize every time you make a metaphor to an Earth-based insectoid or vermicular life-form."

"Sorry." Duffy grinned.

"Secondly, I believe that this device I am studying is the source of that power. I believe it may be a zero-point energy collector."

Duffy whistled softly. "Literally energy from nothing. The Federation's never been able to make that one work, though we've had the theory for centuries. Couple this drive to that collector, and you've got about as close to a perpetual motion machine as you'll ever see."

"I'm not having much luck making sense of these panels," said Gomez. "For all I know, I'm trying to decipher a decorative wall hanging. But there's definitely control activity behind it. If I can find a way to tie in a hard connection for Soloman, maybe he can access their control circuits from outside." A puzzled look crossed her face as she studied her tricorder. "Is anyone else getting unusual readings?"

Duffy stopped what he was doing. "What kind of readings?"

"These tricorders are modified to be especially sensitive to photonic force fields. Kieran, can I borrow the magnetic probe?"

Puzzled, he unhooked the tool from his belt and handed it to her.

"My readings are inconclusive," she explained. "This is the only way to be sure."

She activated the probe to a low gain and pushed it *through* the lighted panel.

Duffy looked around the room, as though seeing it for the first time. "This is all a hologram."

Gomez nodded. "A much more sophisticated one than we've ever seen, but yes."

"Look at this," said Pattie, gesturing at a series of flashing green panels along the wall. "These lit up when you pushed the probe through the panel. You may have disrupted something."

The flashing lights reminded Duffy of something. As he thought of it, he became aware of something else, a tone at the high end of his hearing range, pulsing in time to the lights. "This is an alarm of some kind," he said.

Just then, a bulkhead at the end of the room irised open, and a floating ball of light passed through.

Corsi's voice sounded tinnier even than usual over

the com-link. *"Away team, get out of there. We can't get a transporter lock with you inside. Move closer to the opening."*

The ball of light stopped in front of Duffy and changed shape, dimming as it did, and taking the form of something froglike, upright, and only vaguely humanoid. The frog-thing considered him with wet, yellow eyes. "This is a class one service area," it said. "You can't be here." It reached out to Duffy with a webbed, many-fingered hand. "Good-bye," it said.

Duffy faded out of existence.

8

Captain Gold paced the length of the observation lounge. "I want options."

Stevens leaned back in his chair, fingertips pressed together. "I can send out more 'pinger' torpedoes. The pulse should be detected by the modified tricorders the away team has."

Gold stopped and looked at him. "What does that do for us?"

"Well, they already know we're here, and we're looking for them. It should allow them to get a fix on the pulse. If they're lost inside and trying to find their way out, it might help."

Gold nodded. "Sounds good. How long?"

"I've got a second torpedo in the tube, two more on the fabrication bench. I think a shot an hour indefinitely."

"Do it. Pulse every hour, on the hour, ship's time. A

logical schedule will make it easier for them to find the pulses if they need multiple fixes along the way."

Corsi looked at Gold, her expression dark. "I should have had a team in there with them."

Gold glared back. "I'm looking for options, not 'I told you so.' If your people were in there, we'd be looking for them too."

"Options, then," said Corsi, her posture ramrod-straight. "Stevens replicates a half-dozen more of these magnetic probes and shows my people how to use them. Then I lead a team of my people inside that thing, and we start poking holes in holograms until we find our missing people and bring them out."

Lense cleared her throat. "Enigma has an interior volume of just under half a million cubic kilometers. You could be looking a long time."

"Then," said Corsi, "if we can't find them, we'll find someone or something that knows where they are." She scowled at no one in particular.

Gold knew her anger was directed more at herself than anyone else, but that conversation would have to wait. He shook his head. "I think that's out of the question unless we have some idea where to look."

"The easiest way to do that," Abramowitz cut in smoothly, "would be to ask them. Have we learned anything else that might let us communicate with them?"

"Actually," said Stevens, "some of their tricorder readings from inside Enigma were relayed back to us. Data transmission was slowed by the intervening force fields so we didn't get everything, but I'd say in those few minutes we learned more about Enigma than the *Chinook* did during its entire study." He licked his lips. "I think we can punch a comm signal in that they could translate through their modified tricorders."

"We need more than a signal." Corsi was like a belligerent dog with a bone. "We need intelligence. Can you improve the images you have of the interior? Maybe find our people, or at least the *Lincoln?*"

"We've been reviewing the data from the first imaging pulse, but I don't know there's much I can do to improve on it. We have a mass of duranium we believe to be the *Lincoln.* We have various other scattered duranium traces, none of which add up to a hundred-kilometer ship, or anything remotely like it. We have organic concentrations that we believe to be lifeforms."

Gold stopped his pacing, and stared hard at Stevens. "How many, Stevens?"

"Somewhere in the neighborhood of thirty million." Stevens looked grim.

Corsi's mouth fell open. "Thirty million people in the crew, and nobody is answering our hails?"

Stevens shrugged. "They could be unconscious, or dead, for all we can tell. We could be reading farm animals, or the occupants of a zoo. They could be some other kind of biological concentrations entirely—trees or bioreactors full of bacteria. We just don't have the resolution to tell. However—" He seemed reluctant to continue.

Gold crossed his arms over his chest. "Spit it out, Stevens."

"During the first burst, we observed some minor disruption of the holographic matrix. Given that, and our success with the modified magnetic probe, it's just possible I could come up with a special torpedo to disrupt at least their outer holograms. It might be only be temporary, twenty minutes or so while the fields regenerate, but it would give us a look at what we're dealing with. It might let us get a direct comm signal in, or beam our people out."

"How long?"

Stevens punched at the screen of his padd. "We'll need to run some more analysis on the data. More scans next time we pulse Enigma. Design and fabricate the weapon. Maybe thirty hours."

"Make it twenty," said Gold.

Duffy looked down at the surf sloshing around the boots of his space suit. "I am definitely overdressed for this beach."

He, Gomez, and P8 Blue were standing on a sandy coastline under a sunny pink sky. Pattie—smaller, lower, and generally more vulnerable to the waves—scuttled up the sandy slope away from the water. Thirty meters beyond, a cliff made of dark volcanic rock reared up into the sky.

Gomez looked at him. "Any idea how we got here?"

"Felt like a transporter to me."

"Where," asked Pattie, "do you think we are?"

"Still inside Enigma, I'd say." Duffy took out the magnetic probe and looked around for something to test it on. He could have simply tried it on the sand, but the environmental suit made it difficult to bend that far.

Ten meters to his right, a black outcropping of rock the size of a shuttlecraft rose up out of the sand. He trudged over, activated the probe, and shoved it against the outcropping.

To his surprise, the probe didn't penetrate, but neither was the surface entirely solid. Instead, it gave slightly, like wet leather.

There was a rumble, almost subsonic, so deep and loud Duffy felt it in his rib cage as much as he heard it. "Ouch," said the universal translator, in the very generic voice it reserved for the most extremely alien of languages.

A few meters to his left, a flipper the size of a man lifted out of the sand, traversed a five-meter arc, and dug into the sand. With a grunt, the "outcropping" laboriously pulled itself a few meters farther up the beach.

Duffy staggered back, then turned and ran from the

behemoth. He managed ten meters or so in the clumsy environmental suit before looking back.

The thing wasn't chasing him. It labored to move on land, and he could have kept ahead of it at a slow stroll. "Did that turtle just talk?"

"Do not mock me, small visitor," said the behemoth. "No turtle am I. Rogendera Godo-*click*, I am, far-traveler, brave adventurer, home from the stars after many seasons' travels. Home to lay her eggs in familiar sand, and tell her children tales of distant worlds. Home to stay am I."

Gomez stepped closer. "You're a space traveler?"

"I was, as you must be. Strange is your form and speech. Never your like have I seen before, not in all the travels, mine."

"We're space travelers," said Duffy, "but we're a little lost." He considered a moment. Whatever this thing was, it was real, and it didn't seem to know it was on a ship. "In your travels, did you at some time collide with some unseen object?"

"This happened on the four-hundred-and-sixth day of the twentieth season of our voyage through the black ocean. We were trapped for a time, but we escaped and after many adventures on the black ocean, returned here, to these fine sands."

"Kieran," said Gomez, "maybe we shouldn't talk about this with the 'locals' till we know more."

"Yeah, I think you're right."

"Friends," said Pattie, "we are not alone."

They turned to see a bright ball of light emerge from the cliff face. As it approached, it dimmed and changed form, into something more humanoid this time.

The being was shorter than Duffy, with caramel-colored skin, its head owl-like and topped with short brown feathers. The eyes were yellow, which surprised Duffy not at all. "This isn't your story," said the owl. "You must not interfere."

Duffy turned to the behemoth. "Nice meeting you, but I think we'll be go—"

"—ing." Duffy staggered as the gravity changed.

Clouds of dust blew past him, kicked up by elephant-sized beasts that marched single file through the marketplace, cargo carried in slings tied between the tail of one animal and a blunt horn on the nose of the next.

One of the beasts contemplated him with a blue eye the size of his fist, a gaze suggesting intelligence, if not sentience. Then it snorted and moved on.

The plaza was crowded with thousands of people representing dozens of races, none familiar to Duffy. Open-air stalls sold goods of all kinds: food, artwork, and items of unfamiliar, yet obviously advanced, technology.

The first impression had been of a primitive market, but Duffy realized this might be an illusion. The primitive aspects might be recreational, or perhaps ceremonial.

Certainly, everyone seemed to be having a good time. He had the impression of a vast party, or a fair.

He, Gomez, and Pattie stood close together, earning no more than the occasional curious glance in the sea of races. This was obviously a place used to unfamiliar visitors.

"I believe," said Pattie, "we have been sent somewhere where we can do the least harm."

Duffy nodded. "That light entity was real, and he was clearly upset we were interfering with the alien's 'story.'"

Gomez looked around. "I wonder how much of *this* is real? Not much, I'd wager."

"I agree," said Duffy. "This was created for someone else's benefit, and it could be only a few of the thousands of beings here. Maybe only one of them."

Gomez pointed toward a largely empty seating area.

In the middle was a large platform with an elaborate machine on it, constructed of brass and glass pipes. It might have been a sculpture, or a musical instrument on a stage, it was hard to tell.

"Since we aren't likely to find anyone real to talk to, I suggest we sit down and assess our situation."

There were benches and perchlike rails, in a variety of sizes. Duffy found one that looked right and sat down, Gomez taking the seat next to him.

Duffy reflected on their situation, and nodded his head in amazement. "The *Lincoln* can't be the first ship to get trapped inside Enigma. There must have been dozens, hundreds maybe, and nobody escapes because they think they already have. They continue their voyages, go home, even die of old age, never realizing that they're living in a holo-simulation."

"Agreed," said Pattie. "This obviously has been going on for a long time. None of these species are familiar to us."

"Based on its course," said Duffy, "Enigma just crossed the Ronde void, a region almost devoid of stars. The area beyond it is unexplored by the Federation. All we know about it is from scattered reports purchased from the Ferengi. I bet that's where these species came from." He watched as a turbaned vendor draped a jeweled chain around the neck of a skeptical customer. "But we've got no way of knowing if all of them are really present, or if they're simply re-created from someone's memory."

Gomez watched another of the "elephant trains" pass by, this one carrying egg-shaped gondolas full of passengers.

"What I don't understand is how anyone could *not* know they're in a simulation, after they've seen the kinds of things we did."

P8 reared up on her back four legs, her antenna waving. "We did not enter Enigma on a colliding ship. Our experience may not be typical."

Duffy shrugged. "She's right. Maybe there's an automatic response to a ship collision, and they just end up in simulated space until a more complete simulation can be created."

Gomez nodded. "Of course. They wouldn't need a simulation until the colliding ship was supposed to reach a planet."

Duffy frowned. "I have one other concern. If we do find our way out, how do we *know* we've found our way out? We could end up like the rest of these prisoners, passengers, whatever you want to call them. We could be back on the *da Vinci*, happy as *targ*s in blood, when we're really still in a simulation."

"The difference between all of them, and us," Gomez said, holding up the magnetic probe, "is that we have the key to reality." She activated it, and pushed it through the metal bench.

Pattie made one of her contemplative noises. "The light entity—do you think it is part of Enigma's crew, or some aspect of the ship's automated systems, or its holoprogramming?"

"Maybe part of the program," said Gomez. "It seems pretty single-minded."

"I am not so sure," said Pattie. "If all these other beings can survive here, there's no obvious reason the crew shouldn't be alive as well."

Duffy looked up at a nearby vendor's tent. "Maybe we should just ask. Here it comes."

They turned and watched as the ball of light approached. It changed form; this time it was fully humanoid—Bolian, to be exact—and it wore a Starfleet uniform. "You don't belong here," it said, "but now I know where you do belong."

"We're from the Federation Starship *da Vinci*," said Gomez, standing and showing her open hands. "We mean no harm to this ship. Are you part of its crew? We need to speak with the crew."

The pseudo-Bolian looked puzzled. "I am a keeper of order. I keep the stories on their paths. You don't belong here. You take me from my own story, and I wish to return to it."

"Please," said Gomez, "are you real?"

She reached for the magnetic probe again, activated it, and extended it toward the Bolian.

He shimmered, and for a moment Duffy could see what was underneath—a floating machine a little bigger than his torso. On top of it, a small creature looked out at him with intelligent yellow eyes.

Then the Bolian was restored, an annoyed expression on his face. He pushed the probe away, seemingly no longer affected by it. "That device interferes with the story. It disrupts the experience. You should not use it." He frowned. "You don't belong here."

Gomez's eyes went wide. "Kieran, helmets, *now!*"

Duffy affixed his helmet to his head, just as the Bolian image reached out a hand, and his stomach lurched—

9

They were floating, floating among stars. Duffy was relieved to see that his helmet's seals were intact. A quick glance over to Gomez showed that hers was also.

Gomez, meanwhile, looked at their Nasat companion. *"Pattie, are you all right?"*

"I'm fine. Like you, Commander, I anticipated this and closed my breathing passages before our transport."

Duffy looked around. "Is this really space? The stars *look* right."

"That doesn't mean anything," said Gomez, *"but there's nothing to test with the probe. If it's real space, though, where's the* da Vinci*?"*

Duffy activated his suit's communicator. "Away team to *da Vinci*, do you read? Can you get a transporter lock on us?"

"Stand by," said an unfamiliar voice, *"we're homing in on your signal."*

Duffy saw something moving at the edge of his vision, and turned to face it—a bright, moving dot that quickly grew larger in the distance.

"It's a Federation ship," said Pattie, *"but it's not the* da Vinci*."*

As Duffy watched, the dot resolved itself into the sleek shape of an *Intrepid*-class starship. He could just read the markings u.s.s. lincoln across its bow when the transporter effect enveloped him.

Fabian Stevens put down his molecular welder and looked up over the torpedo casing on his workbench.

Across the hololab, Soloman sat bolt upright in a chair, looking straight ahead, unmoving. Only the furious flashing of the lights on his belt-mounted data buffer hinted at how hard he was working.

"Thank you," said Stevens, "for your help on programming, Soloman. This is well beyond my humble computer skills."

Soloman turned his head slightly toward Stevens. "Thank you for asking me. The construction of a narrow-bandwidth, data-redundant, self-installing message worm to operate in the limited environment of a tricorder is a stimulating challenge. It is good to have function, to participate in the rescue of my crewmates. I feel"—he paused, as a rapid burst passed through the data buffer—"responsible for their disappearance."

Stevens shook his head. "Now, that's just silly, Soloman. There was nothing you could have done. If you hadn't been standing by, we might not even have been able to warn them."

Soloman blinked rapidly. It reminded Stevens of the lights on the data buffer.

"Lt. Commander Corsi had me beamed from the module immediately after their disappearance. If I had been on station, I would have been in a position to be of more assistance, to observe the situation directly and provide data necessary to their rescue."

"Beaming you back was Corsi's call, and Captain Gold's, Soloman." Stevens retrieved a relay from the parts replicator. "The module is still out there, operated from the bridge. It's keeping the breach open, just in case, and relaying sensor readings. I'm not sure what else you could be doing out there."

"If they should return, they will need me to pilot them back to the ship."

Stevens bent over the torpedo casing, and fitted the relay into place. "They can be beamed back, or the module can be flown home by remote control."

Stevens glanced up as the lights on Soloman's data buffer abruptly went dark, and he turned to face Stevens. "They will need someone to be waiting there for them when they return."

Stevens considered this for a moment. He couldn't argue. Part of him wanted to be out there too.

Soloman broke the silence. "We Bynars, we are aware that we are . . . unusual among humanoid species; that some species look upon us with disfavor."

Stevens blinked in surprise, the relay momentarily forgotten. "What do you mean?"

"We are small. We are physically weak. We are linked closely to computers in a way that some humanoids find disturbing, or even repulsive. Even our aversion to ambiguity is disturbing to some. Yet we have always reached out to other species. We are a curious people. But some say we are not brave."

"Soloman, I don't think anyone on this ship questions your courage—"

"I wonder. What if Lt. Commander Corsi beamed me back in anticipation that this was my wish?"

"Trust me, Soloman, she would have done the same for any of us." Stevens chuckled dryly. "She's protective of us crazy engineering types. I think that's why the captain pulled her back a little this mission, to remind her we need room to work."

"Yet I have noted that she will place herself, and her security people, in danger."

Stevens nodded. "When the situation calls for it, yeah. But that's what they're trained for, and she trains them hard." He waved a hand in the direction of the corridor. "Haven't you seen them working out down at the court? When Lense isn't playing handball, anyhow. When we pull into a starbase, while the rest of us are taking shore leave, Corsi is rotating her people down so they can run combat simulations on a real holodeck."

"I do not like uncertainty," said Soloman. "I do not seek danger. Yet I would prefer to be out in the module, waiting for my crewmates. Do you know what the Klingons say of my people?"

"No."

"They say 'a Bynar never stands alone.' I gather they mean great disrespect in this. Yet when my friends disappeared, I was as alone in that module as I have ever been in my life, even more alone than when 111 died. Yet I did not wish to return to the ship. I wished to fulfill my duties, to be of service to my shipmates. I would be there still, if I could."

Stevens grinned. "You've come a long way, Soloman. You can watch my back anytime."

Soloman blinked, then turned away. The data buffer began to flash again. "I will take that as a compliment,

Fabian, but I do not consider your back to be especially interesting."

Stevens laughed and picked up his tools. "Let's get this done. We have a message to send."

It's good to be out of the space suit, thought Gomez, adjusting her fresh uniform, even if it made her a little nervous.

She half expected the "Keeper of Order" to appear through the wall of their assigned quarters at any moment and transport them somewhere else, but logically, that wasn't going to happen.

Whatever force controlled their fate on Enigma, had decided they belonged on a Federation vessel. This was likely their final destination.

Large windows lined the curved wall. To all appearances, the *Lincoln* was under way at warp speed.

A set of doors opened, and Duffy emerged from an adjoining bedroom.

They'd been assigned to a large guest suite, and even with three of them, it was luxurious by the standards of the *da Vinci*. Even Captain Gold's quarters weren't this big.

"Interesting that we got VIP quarters," she said. "But I'd feel a lot better about it if there weren't a pair of armed security officers standing outside."

The cushions on the couch under the windows stirred, and Pattie emerged from where she'd tunneled in to rest. "I feel much refreshed," she said.

"Good," said Gomez, "I wish I'd had time for a nap myself. We need a clear head here."

Duffy looked puzzled. "We were looking for the *Lincoln*, and we've found it. If our situation isn't perfect, it's much improved. Moreover, this ship is real. We've tested it."

She nodded her head toward the windows. "But is that real? We assume not, but we can't be sure."

"If it is a simulation," said Pattie, "then whose simulation is it? We know Enigma's holographic systems have a telepathic capability they use to create their simulations. In this case, would it base the simulation on the thoughts of the entire crew, or perhaps just one individual?"

"Judging by those guards outside," said Gomez, "we don't know what we're dealing with here. Clearly somebody, probably Captain Newport, is suspicious of us. If the simulation is based on his thoughts— Well, remember what Reg warned us about. He may not *want* to know this is a simulation."

The door slid open, and an Andorian security officer leaned in. "The captain will see you now."

The three of them followed her to the elevator, and three decks up to the captain's ready-room off the ship's bridge.

Captain Newport sat behind his desk, the top empty except for a three-dimensional chessboard in the center. A green-skinned man dressed in civilian clothing sat in a chair to his right. They appeared to be in the middle of a game. From what Gomez could tell, the green-skinned man was winning.

Both men stood as they entered the room. The green-skinned man seemed to study them with special interest.

The captain put out his hand to Gomez. "I'm Captain Newport; welcome to the *Lincoln*."

"I'm Commander Sonya Gomez, first officer of the *U.S.S. da Vinci*, and this is my second officer, Lt. Commander Kieran Duffy, and one of our engineers, P8 Blue."

He gestured at a trio of chairs arrayed around his desk. "Please sit down."

Gomez and Duffy took their seats. P8 climbed into the chair, but it wasn't designed for her, and she perched awkwardly on the arm.

Gomez turned her attention back to the green man. She became aware of a curious smell, a little like sage and cinnamon. It wasn't at all unpleasant. "You must be Wayne Omthon, first officer of the *Vulpecula*."

He smiled nervously. "Ex–first officer, actually. My former captain and I had a falling out. That's why I'm still on the *Lincoln*. They've made me their guest until we meet up with a ship headed back to Orion."

Gomez tried to hide her puzzlement. "I'm sorry to hear that."

Newport's eyes narrowed. "If you don't mind my asking, how do you know his name, and how did you come to be floating in mid-space, six light-years from the nearest star, and conveniently right along our course?"

Gomez glanced at the others, uncertain what to say next. Well, try the truth. "Well sir, we were sent to rescue you after a collision you had with an object we call Enigma."

Newport still looked serious, but he laughed. "If you'd hoped to rescue anyone, you might have brought a ship."

She studied the room casually, trying to get some sense of the officer she was dealing with. A collection of antique gunpowder-and-bullet firearms filled a glass case behind his chair. A small shelf of old-style paper books was displayed in a glass case with an elaborate lock, on the wall to his left. She could only just see the title of one of them, *The Spy Who Loved Me*. It appeared Newport had an interest in espionage.

"We did, sir, an S.C.E. vessel. In fact, we sort of expected them to pick us up, not you."

"You said you're from the *da Vinci*. We show that vessel in transit to Deep Space 7, nowhere near the so-called Enigma object."

"Yes, sir," said Gomez, "that was our course before we were called in to investigate your ship's disappearance, but we diverted in response to the *Chinook*'s call. You never left the Enigma, sir. This is all an illusion."

Newport's face started to redden. "You're not the first to try and sell me that bill of goods. This is no illusion. This is a Federation starship." The captain stood so abruptly his chair nearly fell over. "I want to know what's going on here, what's affecting the minds of my crew. Even Mr. Omthon was confused when we first brought him aboard, though his mind has since cleared. Just what are you? Telepaths? Changelings? Section 31?"

Gomez noticed Mr. Omthon looking at her with an odd expression; not threatening, but pained, almost apologetic. Something in his eyes told her confronting Newport wasn't the way to go.

She also wondered about Newport's grip on reality. Telepaths were a semi-reasonable paranoia, but all the shape-shifting Changelings that ruled the Dominion had gone back to the Gamma Quadrant after the war, and Gomez didn't even know what a "Section 31" *was*.

"Sir, I'm telling you what I believe to be true. I will admit that, since leaving our ship, we've been feeling some, uh, confusion. Disorientation. Perhaps your doctor should take a look at us."

Newport's expression immediately softened, and he looked hesitant. It was almost painful to watch a Starfleet officer in this condition. Clearly this was his personal simulation, and he was deeply locked into what Reg had called "hyperreality."

Newport took a deep breath, slowly released it, then sat heavily back in his chair. "Understand, Commander Gomez, I'd like to believe you. Our scans tell us you are what you claim you are, though we know scans can be fooled. All of your identification data match the Federation database, and we do show you assigned to the *da*

Vinci. But you must understand, we escaped this 'Enigma' days ago, with the help of Mr. Omthon here and the aid of the *Chinook.* We're now three and a half light-years away from your Enigma, and your story doesn't make a bit of sense."

Gomez looked over her shoulder at the guard who now held their tricorders and the magnetic probe. They were being led down a corridor, and this time the security officers had their phasers drawn.

They were being led to the brig, not the VIP quarters.

Newport had been conflicted about giving the order, but he seemed to be sinking into a paranoid fantasy, finding spies behind every bulkhead.

She wondered what it was like to have almost god-like power over events and your surroundings, and to have no idea it was happening. To have no idea any of it might, or might not, be real.

For Newport, the universe was exactly what his unconscious mind expected it to be. It was no wonder he was intoxicated by the experience.

Enigma was a trap from which so many had never escaped, and Gomez could understand, with frightening clarity, exactly why.

The tricorders, both clipped to the guard's belt, began to chirp a warning tone. The guard stopped and stared at them suspiciously, then pulled one out and flipped it open. "What's this?"

"I have no idea," said Gomez. "I didn't leave mine running." She looked at Duffy, who shook his head.

The guard stared at the screen, licking his lips nervously, then turned the tricorder around so that they could see it. Gomez read the text there.

"WILL ATTEMPT TO SHUT DOWN ALL ENIGMA HOLOGRAMS AND FORCE FIELDS, 2100 HOURS SHIP'S TIME. BELIEVE WE WILL SUCCEED. WILL

ATTEMPT TO LOCATE AND RESCUE THEN. THIS IS OUR ONLY TRANSMISSION TILL 2100. MAZEL TOV.—GOLD."

The guard looked worried. "What does this mean?"

"For us," said Duffy, "it's great news. For the countless other beings I suspect are on this ship, it means an ugly death in the vacuum of space."

Gomez nodded grimly.

Pattie looked up at them. "Then we have all reached the same conclusion."

"Enigma is not a ship," said Gomez.

"A ship, perhaps," said P8, "but not as we know it."

"More of a self-sustaining holographic construct," said Duffy, "pretending to be a ship. If the *da Vinci* actually has found a way to shut it down, everyone on board not protected from space by a ship, suit, or," he nodded toward Pattie, "their own physiology, will be killed. We could be talking about millions of sentient beings."

The guards all looked concerned and confused, but nobody was insisting they continue toward the brig. The crewman holding the tricorder shook his head in confusion. "What are you all talking about?"

"What I've been trying to tell you all along," said Wayne Omthon, stepping out from an alcove where he'd evidently been hiding. "None of this is real. It's some kind of illusion, and we're all trapped inside."

Duffy nodded. "You weren't dumped directly into this simulation either, were you? You saw enough of the rest of Enigma to suspect this wasn't real."

"And to suspect that the *S.S. Vulpecula* that came to pick me up wasn't real either. This ship, this crew, are the only things I know for sure are real, so I picked a fight with my captain, or her simulation, to contrive a way to stay here. Fortunately, Newport and I have become chess buddies."

He grinned, and somehow Gomez felt compelled to grin back, despite the dire situation they were facing.

"Being good enough at chess to be a convincing loser has its value," he continued. "He hasn't been in a huge hurry to get me off the ship, and I've managed to build a level of trust."

The security guard reached a decision. He glanced at his fellows to confirm they were in agreement, then handed Gomez her tricorder. "We've got to get out of sight. In here," he said, leading them into a service area, and pulling the cover off a Jefferies tube.

They all climbed inside, crawling through the low tube. "I'm Lieutenant Roth," said the guard with the tricorders. "These," he gestured at the other security officers, "are Chen and Vaches."

"Okay, my turn to ask what the heck is going on," said Duffy.

They reached a service junction where there was room for them all to stop and talk in secret.

"I never though I'd be saying this," said Roth, as he handed Duffy and Pattie back their gear, "but this is mutiny. We've all known the captain was acting strangely, and Mr. Omthon has been trying to tell us we're trapped in some kind of simulation that's somehow affecting the captain's mind."

"It's not his fault," said Gomez. "The simulation is being created from telepathic scans of his subconscious, and it's much more realistic than any holodeck. It's almost like he's intoxicated, or hypnotized. He isn't responsible for his actions."

Roth sighed. "None of us could dismiss it, but we weren't reluctant to embrace it, either. Then Mr. Omthon here showed up, and the pieces started fitting together."

"The first officer is with us," said Omthon, "but he's under too much scrutiny to act directly. I think we've got maybe a third of the security force, several of the senior staff, and I've managed to convince most of engineering, but this could get ugly."

The youngest of the security officers wiped his mouth with an unsteady hand. "That message. It sounds like we could just sit tight. In a few hours we'd know. For sure. The captain would see too."

"We do that," said Duffy, "and millions could die, starting with—" He blinked. "The away team from the *Chinook*, where are they?"

Roth looked surprised. "They beamed back to the *Chinook*. Last I knew they were headed into Starbase 12 for resupply."

"I'm afraid the *Chinook* is on its way to Salem II," said Gomez, "without those two crew members. The ship they beamed aboard is a holographic simulation, one that's going to blink out of existence at 2100 hours and leave them floating in space. It's barely possible that the *Lincoln* or the *da Vinci* can find them and transport them aboard before they die, but there will be too many to save."

"Other ships," explained Pattie, "have become trapped here. This may have been happening for centuries."

"Mutiny," said Roth, seemingly just trying out the word, but every time he said it, he made a face as though he'd tasted something sour.

"Wait," said Gomez, grinning, then laughing. "Maybe we don't need to mutiny. You saw what happened when we challenged Captain Newport's vision of reality? What if, instead, we give him exactly what he wants?"

Duffy looked skeptical. "We've got just a few hours to pull a con on the captain, and find a way to get a message to *da Vinci*."

"We can do it, and try to pick up the *Chinook* away team while we're at it." Gomez felt a surge of adrenaline. It was a risk, a huge one. But it was their only chance.

Duffy shrugged. "You're insane, but I'm game. What choice have we got?"

"None," replied Gomez.

"One problem," said Pattie, "can we get to Starbase 12 before 2100 hours?"

Omthon shook his head. "This is a fast ship, but not even at maximum warp."

"If this were real distance, in real space," said Gomez. "It isn't, so we're just going to have to change the laws of physics." She looked at Duffy. "You ever hear of something called 'Section 31'?"

"Never."

"Me either, which is funny, considering we're about to join."

10

Gold stood in the shuttlebay, hands clenched behind his back, gazing out into the unmoving stars. Here, in the darkness of deep space, he could clearly see the colors, a red giant here, a yellow dwarf there, a glowing stellar nursery looking like luminous cotton candy.

It was beautiful.

It was false.

He knew he was looking at Enigma, that it filled a sweep of sky that encompassed his entire view, but his eyes told him otherwise. He could just make out the flashing formation lights on the Augmented Personnel Module, still standing vigil at the gates to Enigma, but otherwise, the sky seemed empty.

He held up his hand near the force field, feeling the tingle of energy, and perhaps only imagining he could feel the bite of bitter cold.

He heard a footstep behind him. Some senses, at least, were still trustworthy.

"Come to lecture me, Corsi?"

The security chief stepped up beside him, and looked out into the star-flecked darkness. "Not at all, Captain. I was hoping you wouldn't mind some company."

He said nothing, and neither did she. Finally, after several minutes, she broke the silence. "It's hard, isn't it? Knowing what orders to give, what decisions to make?"

"It's very hard. Especially when people's lives are on the line, and people's lives are *always* on the line. There's never enough time, never enough information, never enough certainty."

He shrugged toward the flashing lights of the module. "He's back out there. Soloman. He asked to go back out and wait, and I gave permission."

He paused to see if Corsi had anything to say. She remained silent.

"Sometimes," he continued, "you just have to trust people, that they'll do the right thing, that they'll make things work. When you have a good crew, that's the best thing you can do. Just don't get in their way."

Corsi chuckled slightly. It was a startling sound, coming from her. "You think I need to learn not to do that, don't you, sir?"

"You should let them run, Corsi. The trick is, you shouldn't let them run too far."

"Is that what happened this time, sir?"

He smiled sadly. "That's the hardest part about making decisions, Corsi. Sometimes, you make the wrong ones. But you can never be certain until it's all over."

"And now?"

"Now, we see what happens."

*   *   *

Captain Vince Newport, exhausted and vaguely troubled, stepped through the doors into his quarters. It was dark inside.

"Lights," he said, and took two more steps before realizing nothing had happened. "Lights," he said again, more forcefully this time.

"Lights," said another voice, "reduced intensity."

The lights brightened slowly to a soft glow, revealing a woman sitting on the couch under the windows. Newport recognized Commander Gomez, casually holding a phaser on him. She smiled at his look of surprise.

"I believe," he said stiffly, "I sent you to the brig."

"We didn't like it there, Captain, and we simply don't stay where we don't want to stay." She shrugged. "We're very resourceful people. It's a job qualification for our line of work."

"You *are* Section 31. I knew it."

Gomez's smile faded. "You don't know anything, Captain, and if you do know anything, you should forget it." Her voice was harsh. "Who we are is on a need-to-know basis, and frankly, you just don't need to know." She looked down at the phaser. "I'm sorry about this, Captain, I just wanted to make sure we had time to talk uninterrupted. Do I have your word, as a Starfleet officer, that you'll hear me out?"

"My word," said Newport. "You have it."

Gomez lowered the phaser, placing it on the cushion next to her, still within easy reach. "Be assured, Captain, our interests in the current situation are the same. We work for the security of the Federation, and that security is threatened."

Newport nodded as she continued.

"As you suspected, your ship has been under a subtle kind of attack, and it all centers on the Enigma object."

He chuckled. "You're not going to tell me we're still trapped inside again, are you?"

"No, of course not. We were testing you. Your resolve. How easy it is to deceive you. You passed, Captain, which is very, very good, because we need you right now. The landing party you returned to the *Chinook* were not the same personnel that left that ship. They were alien imposters, and it is vital we get them into custody and onto this ship before they have a chance to act."

Newport's eagerness quivered in his voice. "The *Chinook* is at Starbase 12. We could be there in just over a day."

She laughed. "That will be too late, Captain. But I did say we were resourceful. Perhaps you're wondering where my comrades are? They're covertly making certain modifications to your deflector dish and warp drive. These modifications would be much easier with your cooperation."

"What kind of modifications?" He licked his lips, and Gomez suppressed a triumphant grin. She had been right.

"The handheld device we arrived with, you saw it?"

"You said it was a magnetic probe."

"Yet it doesn't look like any magnetic probe in your database, does it?" She rose in a single swift motion, retrieving her phaser and holding it lightly at her side. She wouldn't need it, but it was part of her masquerade. "It looks just enough like one to obscure its real purpose. It's a warp slipstream overdrive module, secret technology obtained from salvage of an experimental Jem'Hadar strike ship. With it, the *Lincoln* can reach Starbase 12 in less than three hours. Once there, it will be up to you to arrange for the transfer of the false personnel to your ship. I'm confident you can handle the assignment."

Newport squared his shoulders, pleased with her endorsement.

"They shouldn't give us any trouble," she said. "They can't without exposing themselves."

"You need *my* help."

"The Federation needs your help, Captain, and your pledge of secrecy. Can we count on you?"

A smile crept across Newport's face. "You bet you can. I'll talk to my chief engineer, arrange full cooperation."

"Thank you, Captain Newport." Gomez started for the door, anxious to make her escape.

"What should I do next?" Newport asked.

She turned back, her expression serious. "Make your call to the chief engineer, then go to the bridge and set course for Starbase 12. Have your conn officer engage at warp six-point-seven. By then, the first modifications to your warp drive should be complete, and that will get us there in plenty of time." She grinned. "Then you can find out just how fast your ship can go. I think it will exceed all your expectations."

Gomez looked out an open sensor port through the deflector dish. Beyond the glowing blue of the grid, the sky shimmered in waves of rainbow colors, and multi-colored stars streaked past at a furious pace.

Duffy was standing next to her as they were making modifications to the deflector. "Well," he said, "I'll say this for Captain Newport, he's got a vivid imagination. I always wondered what slipstream overdrive travel would be like. Whatever a slipstream overdrive is."

Gomez and Omthon wrestled a field booster coil into its mounting, as Pattie crawled underneath to secure it in place. Gomez stopped to wipe the sweat off her brow. "I was improvising. I thought I did pretty well, under the circumstances. I even remembered to tell him we wouldn't need to use the deflector while in slipstream, which makes our work down here a lot easier." She turned to Omthon. "Thanks for your help. I'm not anxious to involve the *Lincoln*'s engineers in our changes here, but getting a message out to the *da Vinci* is going to be a close thing."

He smiled. "Nobody wants out of this place more than I do."

The smile made her blush for some reason, and there was that smell again. "Has anyone ever told you your skin is the color of pistachio ice cream?"

He laughed.

"Or that you smell nice?" That slipped out somehow, and it surprised even her. She glanced over and saw Duffy giving her the eye.

The smile faded, and he seemed embarrassed. "My grandmother was green Orion. It's the pheromones. They're more prominent with the females, but males have them too. I've spent most of my life trying to figure out if it's a blessing or a curse."

Gomez felt herself blush even more. *Idiot, idiot!* "Pheromones," she said, trying to sound professional. Duffy was still looking at her. *Well, a little jealousy isn't necessarily a bad thing.*

Mercifully, Pattie changed the subject. "We're cutting it close. It will be small satisfaction knowing we saved the *Chinook* team if millions of sentients die."

Gomez shook her head. "I'm open to suggestions, but those Cochrane solenoids we installed have to be brought up to working temperature slowly, or the cores will crack. Simulated laws of physics we can monkey with, but this is real equipment, and real physical laws. We aren't even sure this is going to work."

"I wish," said Duffy, "we knew how *da Vinci* did it. I suspect they used one of Fabe's modified torpedoes to transmit Soloman-designed software to our tricorders, but we don't know. We'll just have to hope our method works."

Roth emerged into the sensor room, climbing down a ladder from a Jefferies tube.

"Well," he said, "the captain has it all set. The *Chinook* personnel are being kept busy at the local Starfleet adjunct's office until we arrive and can beam them over." He blinked. "Hey, couldn't they be here already? This is a simulation, they could be a few hundred yards away."

"Or tens of kilometers," replied Gomez, "and even if they are close, we'd never be able to find them and get a transporter lock through all the force fields and holograms."

"You know," said Duffy, "if this works, we'll be punching a narrow-bandwidth EM hole through Enigma to the outside to get our signal through. You could do the same thing to create a sensor window. Aim it like a searchlight, and you could scan anywhere in Enigma."

Gomez grunted. "I wish we had an extra day to work on that idea. I wish you'd come up with it before we started our modifications. In fact, I wish you'd come up with it before we got stuck in Enigma in the first place."

"Sorry," Duffy said with one of those irritatingly endearing grins of his.

"Well, it's too late now. As Captain Scott once said to me, 'Sometimes, lass, you're just stuck with plan A.'"

Stevens settled the torpedo onto the launch cradle and disconnected the anti-gravs. He checked the torpedo room's status display, satisfied himself everything was in order, and tapped his combadge.

"Stevens to bridge. I'm ready to fire down here."

Gold replied, *"We'll need a few minutes to have Soloman pull back to a safe distance. You're early, Stevens."*

He chuckled. "Somebody named Scott once told me to always pad my repair estimates."

"I'll just bet he did. Stand by."

*   *   *

Though the *Lincoln* hadn't yet reached Starbase 12, Duffy and Omthon headed to the transporter room. Depending on how things went, they might need to bring the *Chinook* people rapidly into their conspiracy.

Pattie stayed behind in the sensor room to initiate their communications pulse just as soon as the solenoids were ready.

"There'll be a security team at the transporter room of course," said Duffy, looking to make sure there was nobody else within earshot, "but Lieutenant Roth is leading it, and he's handpicked the team."

Omthon didn't seem to be listening. "She's a beautiful woman."

Duffy managed not to trip over his own feet. He kept looking straight ahead. "Who?"

"Sonya Gomez."

"I hadn't noticed," Duffy said glumly.

"It's a good thing Sonya has been dealing with Captain Newport, Mr. Duffy. You are a very poor liar."

Duffy considered for a moment. "That smell thing, it doesn't come in a bottle, does it?"

Commander Gomez loitered off to one side of the *Lincoln*'s bridge, pretending to examine the vacant engineering station. A few of the bridge crew gave her the occasional curious glance, but largely, she went unnoticed.

She glanced back at Captain Newport, who sat in the big chair like Zeus on his throne. He rubbed his chin, and stared intently at the main viewer. They'd be dropping out of warp in a few minutes.

She wondered how Pattie was doing. It was impossible to know precisely how much thermal shock the solenoid cores could take, or exactly when they would be ready. *At least we'll save the* Chinook *people.*

But then she had an ugly thought. They were only

assuming the simulation would bring back the real *Chinook* away team in response to Newport's perceptions.

But what if they were somewhere else, lost in their own simulation? What if, instead of the real away team, Enigma gave them back only holographic duplicates? Then they might not be able to save anybody at all.

Stevens stepped out of the turbolift and onto the *da Vinci*'s bridge.

Gold looked at him curiously.

"Nothing more I could do down there, Captain. I figured this would be the place to watch the show. In fact"—he glanced at the tactical station—"I was wondering if I could push the button?"

Gold nodded. "Be my guest."

McAllan moved out of the way to allow Stevens access.

"Just one thing, Stevens."

"Sir?"

"Don't miss."

Duffy and Omthon stopped just outside the transporter room, and Duffy groaned. "Not now!"

The ball of light hovered just outside the door, then shaped itself back into the form of the Bolian officer.

"Listen to me," said Duffy, "your ship is in danger. You have to listen to me."

The Bolian looked annoyed. "You disrupt the simulation. You must be isolated."

"Captain," said *Lincoln*'s conn officer, "we're being hailed. A ship is matching course with us."

"On screen."

Gomez looked up and gasped. She'd seen the ship before, but only as a drawing on a padd. It was Duffy's S.C.E. ship.

"They're the *U.S.S. Roebling*," reported the ops officer. "Sir, they're asking us to beam over a Commander Gomez, a Lt. Commander Duffy, and Crewperson P8 Blue."

Gomez blinked. *Roebling.*

She remembered the name from her engineering history class. A nineteenth-century engineering family back on Earth. If memory served, they designed and built the Brooklyn Bridge. Duffy had mentioned visiting the Brooklyn Bridge to her once.

Enigma had to be plucking things from Duffy's mind, only they didn't realize this ship was real only to him.

"Captain," said Gomez firmly, "that is not a Federation ship; it's an alien imposter."

"Captain," said the ops officer, "all their Federation identity codes verify."

"Check your database. You'll find no *U.S.S. Roebling* listed, nor will you find any ship matching that configuration. Look at it! It's a poor copy of a *Norway*-class vessel," she added with a mental apology to Duffy.

Newport looked at her. He nodded. "What should we do?"

"I recommend evasive action. Fire on it if you have to, but don't let it delay us getting to Starbase 12."

As abruptly as he'd appeared, the false Bolian was gone. Duffy was surprised he hadn't been transported elsewhere, but he somehow didn't think it was over.

As they entered the transporter room, the deck shuddered slightly. Duffy immediately knew what had happened.

"That was a torpedo launch! What in blazes is going on up there?"

Roth was at the transporter console. Duffy slid in beside him. "We're still not in transporter range." He glanced at the sensor display, then did a double take. "There's another ship registering out there."

Omthon leaned closer to see. "Do you recognize it?"

"Oh yeah," said Duffy, feeling another torpedo fire, "I recognize it. And I think Commander Gomez does too."

"Torpedo away," said Stevens. He watched the torpedo streak toward Enigma, heading straight for its heart. But the torpedo wasn't designed to penetrate it, or even touch it.

It would explode just short of Enigma's surface, and a carefully tuned magnetic plasma burst would shred Enigma's holograms like confetti.

Duffy watched the screen anxiously. "The *Roebling* is trying to get multiple transporter locks on us, probably to beam the three of us troublemakers off the ship, but they can't do it while our shields are up."

"We're almost to Starbase 12," said Roth, his fingers flexing nervously over the console.

Omthon looked at Duffy. "They'll have to drop shields to beam the *Chinook* people on board. We've got a problem."

"What," said Duffy sarcastically, "another one?"

P8 watched the sliding temperature scale on the wall console, her front leg hovering over the control. Just a little more. A little more. *Now.*

Soloman watched the torpedo sail past his module, and he did not hesitate to follow as it approached Enigma. Bynars did not have the excessive sensitivity to glare that humans had, so he had instructed the viewport not to polarize, as he would still be able to see everything.

Then it happened.

The torpedo exploded into an expanding ball of yellow plasma that struck Enigma. The force fields shimmered with arcs of energy, and the holograms began to flicker. At last, Enigma would be revealed.

"Good luck, my friends," said Soloman, surprised at his words, especially given that there was nobody there to hear.

Stevens watched the tactical console in disbelief. "Captain, there's a message coming from inside Enigma. It's from Commander Gomez. It says—" His gut suddenly knotted, and misery crept into his voice. "It says, 'Life or death, do not disrupt Enigma. Do not fire on Enigma.'"

"Something's happening," said Omthon, looking at the exterior view on a wall-mounted viewscreen. As he watched, the floating top that was Starbase 12 flickered, as did the *Roebling* flying close formation with them, the blue planet in the background, and the very sky itself.

"We're too late," said Roth, his face turning pale.

Duffy pushed him aside, scanning frantically for the combadges he knew would be there. For a moment, there were thousands, and then there were only three. "I've got a lock! Energizing!"

Three stunned Starfleet crewmen materialized on the transporter pad, but Duffy knew it wasn't enough.

"Great Emerald gods," said Omthon, staring at the screen, dumbstruck. "There must be millions of them, and they don't have a chance."

11

Soloman's eyes widened. Something was wrong.

As the holograms faded, there should have been a ship, a hull, but there was only space, and that space was not empty.

There was a vast cloud: unidentifiable pieces of machinery, most no bigger than his module. A few ships, most of them looking abandoned and derelict, some eroded as though by long corrosion.

But mostly there were bodies, beings, people flailing about, horrified as they found themselves dumped, unprotected, into space.

Soloman reacted instinctively. He saw a being near him, six-legged, pink-skinned, huge blue eyes that shined with both terror and intelligence.

He activated the thrusters, simultaneously extending a manipulator arm from the pod to grab the floating body. Two meters short, the pod stopped and rebounded.

He'd hit something. A force field.

Soloman accessed the module's sensors and scanned the cloud. He read air, and several other exotic breathing mixtures, encased in millions of individual force-field bubbles.

Then he looked up again. He'd missed something the first time, because it blended in with the stars. In fact, it looked like a cluster of stars, but there were far too many of them.

It took him a while to realize there was one star for each bubble.

Captain Newport stared openmouthed at the view-screen, his face ashen. He turned to look at Gomez and blinked, like a man waking from a dream. "I've done something terribly wrong, haven't I?"

She glanced over at him, still transfixed by the screen. It seemed as if everything that could go wrong had, and yet it was somehow working.

The *Chinook* crew were safe; the *Lincoln* was, in more ways than one, free of Enigma; and Enigma's countless unwilling passengers were still alive, though for the life of her, she couldn't figure out how.

"In the end, Captain, you did the absolute best thing you could do, even if you didn't know you were doing it." She glanced at him, trying to look reassuring. "This isn't your fault."

"Captain," said the ops officer. "We're being hailed by the *da Vinci*, sir. I'm reading her thirty kilometers off our port bow, though I can't tell you how she got there, or what happened to Starbase 12. It's like we jumped thirty light-years in an instant."

"We didn't go anywhere, Lieutenant." Newport looked over at Gomez. "Right, Commander?"

Before Gomez could answer, her combadge chirped. *"Sonnie, it's Kieran. Meet us down at the transporter room. And, ah, bring Captain Newport, if he's in the mood to come. There's someone here you really should see."*

Gold ran to the hangar deck. He had to see this with his own eyes.

As the outer doors opened, he saw Enigma, spread out before him, re-forming itself. One by one, the bubbles of air transformed into opaque, golden holographic bubbles, no longer hidden from view.

At first they were scattered, but then they began to cluster together, blending, rebuilding, and reinventing what it had been before.

As the full shape of Enigma began to re-form, Gold saw a dark speck, moving rapidly against the golden mass, a speck that rapidly grew larger and resolved into the sleek form of an *Intrepid*-class starship.

The *U.S.S. Lincoln* was back.

His combadge chirped. It was Corsi.

"Captain, the Lincoln *is returning hails. Our missing people are on board, safe and sound, and they have the missing freighter crew member and the* Chinook *personnel as well."*

Despite himself, he broke into a broad smile, and barely kept from laughing. He was glad Corsi wasn't there to see. At times like this, he wasn't the most dignified officer in the fleet.

But it seemed she didn't need to see. *"Enjoy the moment, Captain. Corsi out."*

She understood. She was coming along, this Corsi. Like him, she knew it was all over but the shouting. Like him, she knew that apparently, this time at least, he'd done the right thing. And she knew what that meant.

She's going to make somebody a fine first officer some day, maybe even have a ship of her own.

"Captain Core-Breach," he said out loud. "It has a nice ring to it."

Gomez and Newport arrived at the transporter room just as Roth emerged with the *Chinook* party, looking confused, but unharmed. Roth made hesitant eye contact with Newport.

"Sorry, Captain," was all he said.

Newport pushed his lips together and nodded sadly. "You did all right, Roth." He patted him on the shoulder. "We'll talk later."

They stepped into the transporter room to see Duffy and Omthon standing with the holographic Bolian. Newport seemed puzzled.

"Captain," said Duffy, gesturing at the Bolian, "meet a *real* alien imposter."

The Bolian bowed his head in greeting. "We call ourselves the Quanta. We owe you thanks for waking us from our long sleep. We owe you apology for the trouble we have inadvertently caused yourselves and others we have encountered. It is time you knew our story."

"You never developed warp drive," said Duffy.

"We did not know that was unusual until we met you. We encountered other beings with this technology, but by then we were not—lucid. Only in our stories and dreams could we do such things, but we did not give up on our dreams of the stars. One day, some of us determined that we would go, no matter how long it took. But by that time our stories were quite developed. They were what we were, and we brought them with us."

"Your holoprograms," said Gomez. "You built your entire ship out of holotechnology, self-powered, self-sustaining."

"It worked well. We visited many worlds, until we reached the void where stars were far apart. Somewhere, on the edge of that gulf, we fell into our dreams and did not come out. From time to time, we encountered other beings such as yourselves, but by then, our stories had grown stale and repetitive, and we welcomed the new stories these beings brought with them."

"You were like me," said Newport, "denying reality, incorporating anything that challenged it into your fantasies."

"Until," said the Bolian, "like you, Captain, we were forced to confront reality in a way we could not deny."

"What I don't understand," said Duffy, "is how you and all your 'passengers' survived without your holotechnology, or even how you're maintaining this form. At minimum. Your systems are only now rebooting."

"Your ship disrupted our independent holographic projectors, the telepathic systems that maintained our ship's systems and ran our gross simulations. But we have developed our holotechnology over a long time. We are more intimately associated with it than you imagine. Each of us has individual holographic capabilities as well. These forms I have adopted, have aided in communication, but it is time that you saw us as we really are."

Abruptly the Bolian faded. It brightened into the familiar ball of light, then that too dimmed, revealing what was hidden within.

The device was as they had glimpsed in the alien marketplace. About the size of a human torso, perhaps a little larger, it floated a meter above the deck, apparently supported by antigravs or force beams. The curved surface was intricately inlaid with tiny, jeweled hexagons, which Gomez guessed corresponded to the holodiodes on their holodecks, though vastly more sophisticated.

But their eyes were drawn irresistibly to the transparent dome on top, and the tiny being housed inside.

It was covered with brown fur, and looked at them with large yellow eyes. The top of it was domed, and Gomez supposed that was the brain case. Under this was a tiny, flattened body, and four useless, atrophied limbs.

Various tubes and wires connected the body to the machine, providing life support. Gomez doubted the entity could live more than a few minutes without it.

Gomez would have loved to study the technology the "holobody" represented, but there was a shimmer, and as though shy, the creature was again shrouded in a glowing ball of light.

12

Duffy sat in the dining hall, studying his padd and the flat diagrams of a nonexistent ship that covered it. He thought about the holographic *U.S.S. Roebling* and sighed.

He wished he'd gotten the chance to beam on board, see what it was like. Then he remembered Captain Newport, and decided he was just as happy to have missed it. Maybe next time they were docked at starbase, he'd reserve a holodeck for a little while. That would be good enough.

Gomez walked over, carrying her lunch on a tray, and sat down across the table. Corsi and Stevens were right behind her. "Mind if we join you?" asked Gomez.

Duffy nodded at the other empty seats at the table. They all sat down. Corsi leaned toward Gomez conspiratorially.

"So," she said, nodding toward the corner table, where "Pappy" Omthon sat talking with Ensign Conlon and Robins from security, neither of whom seemed to be able to stop giggling, "how long is he staying?"

"For a week or so, till we can rendezvous with his freighter."

Corsi grinned. "As far as I'm concerned, he can stay as long as he wants." She almost giggled herself.

Corsi?

Corsi turned to Gomez. "Have you—*smelled* him?"

Duffy frowned at her. "He gets that a lot, you know."

"It's happening," Stevens said suddenly. Everyone—the four of them at the table, Omthon and his two new friends, and Drew and Hawkins from security, who were sharing lunch across the mess hall—all rose from their seats and made for the windows. Enigma was breaking up, its vast cluster of grapes turning into clumps of two or three or four.

Duffy pressed his nose against the cool transparent aluminum. They were going home, the lost people of Enigma. The Quanta had warp drive now. *Holographic warp engines that work. That's something I'd like to study.*

Ironically, they'd had the knowledge of warp capability for hundreds of years, since the first warp-capable ship became trapped in Enigma's web and its crew was read by their telepathic computers. But by then it had seemed to the Quanta as only one more fantasy among many.

Only now were they lucid enough to put the knowledge to practical use. Now they would take their lost people home, those that wished to go. Others had built lives on Enigma. They would stay, and join the Quanta on their explorations of the universe.

"There." Conlon pointed. There was a streak, a flash, then a cluster went to warp.

Then another, and another.

Then hundreds, thousands. And then they were gone.

"There's something you don't see every day," Drew said.

Hawkins smiled. "On this ship, that's saying something."

"A beautiful end," said Omthon, "to a long nightmare."

Duffy gazed out at the stars, the sky, suddenly empty. "Mazel tov," he said.

P8 Blue watched gratefully as Abramowitz left their shared quarters to begin her watch. She scrambled down from her bed and pulled open her locker. She hesitated, then reached inside.

It had to be done.

She removed the magnetic probe with her front legs, checked it carefully, then turned it on. She shoved the probe against the front of the locker. Metal struck metal with a clunk.

P8 made a rattling sound that, for a human, would have been equivalent to a satisfied sigh.

It never hurts to check.

WAR STORIES

Keith R.A. DeCandido

ANDROSSI VESSEL OVERSEEN BY BIRON
STARDATE 53675.1

Sub-Overseer Howwi's voice awoke Overseer Biron out of a sound sleep. *"Attention, Overseer. Your presence is required on the flight deck. The client has arrived one hour, fifteen minutes early for the engagement."*

Biron was instantly awake, his annoyance at the interruption leavened by the information contained in that interruption. He checked the time-keeping device in his quarters, which informed him that it was one hour and ten minutes prior to the scheduled time of the engagement with the client. This meant that Howwi had been awakened and informed of the early arrival first, then it was left to the sub-overseer to inform Biron.

He climbed out of his hammock and dressed. Biron made a note to investigate who spoke to the sub-overseer rather than Biron himself. Proper protocol dictated that the overseer be informed immediately of such a change in scheduling. One of the lower officers—or worse, one of the workers—had decided to inform the sub-overseer instead rather than risk the ire of the overseer by waking him up. A foolish notion, that. If it was an officer, that person would be severely disciplined. (If it was a worker, the solution was much simpler: death and replacement. Workers were, after all, easy enough to come by.)

Once he had dressed and put in the five nose rings that symbolized his position as overseer, he exited his cabin and proceeded to the flight deck. He entered to see

Sub-Overseer Howwi and the four workers presently on duty stand up in his presence. They remained standing until Biron had taken his seat at the front left of the deck.

"Open a communications frequency to the client," Biron said as the five others retook their seats.

The face of a Yridian appeared on the viewscreen. A like image did not appear on the Yridian's screen—Androssi protocol dictated that they never transmit visual communications to any but other Androssi, and even then, such a practice was frowned upon. It was a security risk, after all.

"May I assume I'm speaking to Overseer Biron?" the Yridian asked.

"You assume correctly."

"Excellent." The Yridian bared his teeth in what Biron assumed to be an expression of pleasure. *"I'm sorry I got here early, but my previous engagement was, ah, cut short."*

"Your itinerary is of no interest to me. I wish to conduct a business transaction. I have been informed by reliable sources that you have information regarding Starfleet."

"Some, yes. I can give you ship and personnel movements from up to one month ago. Given sufficient incentive, I can cut that down to a week or two."

"Ship and personnel movements are also of no interest to me. What I require are log entries."

Again, the Yridian bared his teeth, but Biron noted a subtle difference in his facial structure this time. *"That will cost more."*

"I expected as much. Provide me with a price."

Biron noted two things. The first was that the Yridian's protracted pause was ostensibly to consider what price he would name, but Biron knew that he was simply delaying in a futile attempt to pretend that he had the upper hand in this negotiation. Biron knew that the

Yridian already had a price in mind, but wished to make the acquisition of these logs seem more difficult than it truly was. Biron had expected this behavior and did not concern himself with it.

The second thing he noted was that Howwi looked uncomfortable. Biron had only just ended Howwi's period of punishment—he had continued to perform his duties as sub-overseer, but at half-pay—for his succumbing to Starfleet treachery on the abandoned Cardassian space station Empok Nor, so he was unlikely to raise an objection to anything Biron did at this juncture.

And Biron could understand why Howwi was befuddled by the nature of this particular client interaction.

The Yridian finally spoke. *"I take it you've scanned my ship, Overseer?"*

Biron looked over at Howwi, who nodded. "Yes, we have."

"Then you know what a mess it is. You're supposed to be the best tinkerers in the galaxy. If you can upgrade my clapped-out ship—give me a full overhaul—then I can get you whatever logs you want. Just official ones, though, not personal." Again, the bared teeth. *"Even I have my limits."*

"Your terms are acceptable." Biron entered data into the console in front of him in preparation for transmitting it to the Yridian ship. "I am transmitting the specific personnel whose log entries I wish to peruse. I wish to obtain entries dating back at least two years."

The Yridian nodded. *"Fine."* His fingers played over his own console. *"I'm sending you the parts of the ship I want upgraded."* He looked down. *"Getting the data now."* He frowned. *"I'll need two weeks at least to gather this all up."*

Next to Biron, Howwi was perusing the Yridian's list. The sub-overseer muted the transmission, then spoke.

"We will require that time period to obtain the materials to perform the required upgrades."

Biron nodded, and Howwi deactivated the mute function. "That is also acceptable. We will part ways and reconvene at these coordinates in two weeks' time."

"Excellent! It's a pleasure doing business with you, Overseer Biron. See you in two weeks."

With that, the Yridian ended the transmission.

Turning to Howwi, Biron said, "Begin procedures for acquiring everything on the Yridian's list. Use ship's stores for as much of it as possible—even if it is already earmarked to be used on a future endeavor."

Howwi hesitated. "Sir, I—"

"Your objection is both anticipated and noted, Sub-Overseer." Under other circumstances, Biron would discipline Howwi for even considering questioning his orders.

But these were very peculiar orders.

"You have my assurance that all your concerns will be addressed before this endeavor is completed."

Seeming relieved, Howwi said, "Of course, sir. Thank you, sir."

The sub-overseer's unvoiced complaint was a valid one. After all, as a ship in the Androssi fleet, their mission was to provide material requested by the ship's Elite sponsor. Their sponsor had made no such requests recently, and certainly had done nothing that would lead Biron to contact this Yridian for Starfleet log entries. Should their sponsor request an audit—as was his right at any time—he would not be pleased by the expenditures that would be used for an unauthorized endeavor. It could have a serious impact on Biron's ability to provide for his sponsor and, by extension, his crew.

But Biron needed this information.

It was unworthy of him, it was true, but he did not care. Not after the second humiliation.

The first time Biron encountered the Starfleet starship *U.S.S. da Vinci* on the planet designated Maeglin, their crew managed to outmaneuver him. It was the first time Biron had ever failed in a mission for his Elite sponsor. That first time, however, Biron could very easily attribute to random chance. After all, mathematically speaking, Biron's ability to always fulfill the requests of his Elite sponsor was bound to end eventually. Even the best overseer sometimes fails. The Elite accept this, as long as such occurrences were rare and not damaging. Indeed, Biron's own sponsor was understanding about the failure of the Maeglin mission.

But then Biron was thwarted again, this time at the abandoned Cardassian mining station Empok Nor—and it was again due to the interference of the crew of the *U.S.S. da Vinci*. True, that mission had become untenable in any case; the client who was to provide the holo-emitters required by the sponsor was overly demanding and eccentric, and was proving very difficult to work with.

However, Biron did not take kindly to failure. The best response to such was to eliminate its cause. So he set out to do what he could to eliminate the threat posed by the crew of the *U.S.S. da Vinci*. The personnel he had requested logs for included several members of that ship's complement, including most of its officers and all the personnel assigned to the ship's Starfleet Corps of Engineers.

Armed with this knowledge, Biron would find a way to end their threat to his continued ability to provide for his sponsor.

The two weeks passed. All the material needed to perform the necessary upgrades to the Yridian's ship were obtained and stored in Dimension 7 until they needed to retrieve them in order to perform the upgrades.

Biron's ship arrived at the rendezvous coordinates at

the designated time, to find that the Yridian was once again early. The overseer found that he preferred clients who were early to those who were tardy, as far too many of his clients had been. Timely clients were easier to deal with.

"Open a communications frequency to the Yridian," Biron said.

The Yridian's face reappeared on the screen. *"I have obtained as many of the logs as I was able, dating back to the war against the Dominion. This includes not only logs from the* da Vinci, *but also the* U.S.S. Lexington, *the* U.S.S. Sentinel, *and Starbase 92."*

Rarely was Biron surprised by something, but this Yridian had accomplished it. "That is far more thorough than I was expecting."

"I was simply accommodating your request, Overseer. Several personnel on your list were serving in those other places during the time frame you gave me." Baring his teeth again, he added, *"It is my hope that my adherence to the full letter of our agreement will be reciprocated."*

"It will be. Please transmit the data, and we can begin to perform the upgrades."

"Sorry, but no. First of all, I'm not foolish enough to transmit data this sensitive on an open channel. It's all contained in a storage unit, which I will hand to you. Second of all, that handoff will not take place until all the upgrades are finished." Biron was about to object, but the Yridian, apparently anticipating this, continued speaking. *"If you wish to inspect the storage unit to verify that it does contain the asked-for data, you may—but the unit stays with me until the upgrades are done."*

Biron seethed for a moment. He did not wish to wait to peruse the logs. But he could contrive no reason why the Yridian should accede to his desire to do so without Biron fulfilling his portion of the agreement.

"Very well. We will engage our matter transfer device and materialize upon your ship in order to inspect the unit and effect the upgrades to your vessel within ten minutes."

The upgrades took two days. When they were completed, the Yridian's ship had had its sensor efficiency increased by twenty-five-point-nine percent, its cruising speed increased to an FTL of 4.0 from its previous maximum of 2.14.

The Yridian, of course, felt the need to inspect all the changes, from the new antimatter containment unit to the burnished chrome used as molding on the helm console. Biron had seen the latter as an absurd extravagance, but this *was* a decadent alien species, and could not be held to the standards of the Androssi.

After his inspection, the Yridian stood before Biron—presently standing on the cramped flight deck of the Yridian vessel—and bared his teeth wider than he had at any time in their short acquaintance. "Overseer, I thank you from the top of my head. This outstrips even what I had heard about your people's prowess with engines. I daresay you'd give Starfleet a run for their money."

The praise of aliens was of no consequence. "May I take the storage unit containing the log entries now?"

"Of course." The Yridian went to a small panel under his environmental control console and tapped a sequence of alphanumeric characters onto a touch pad, taking pains to block the exact sequence from the view of Biron or either of the workers still present. He then opened the door, revealing the storage unit. "Enjoy the reading. There are some gripping accounts of the war there, as it happens."

Biron simply nodded to the workers, who removed the unit from the Yridian's hands. Then Biron activated his subspace communications device. "Sub-Overseer Howwi. Activate the matter transferral beam and transport myself, the workers, and the storage unit back to the ship."

"Acknowledged."

"It was a pleasure doing business with you, sir," the Yridian said, just before the matter transferral beam conveyed Biron to his vessel.

Seven minutes after the Yridian ship engaged its warp drive, Biron turned to Howwi. "Engage the dimensional blockers on all the equipment we installed upon the Yridian ship."

Howwi was inappropriately enthusiastic when he said, "Yes, *sir.*" However, Biron was willing to forgive it. The sub-overseer added, "Dimensional blockers now read active. All equipment registers in Dimension 7."

Biron nodded and rose from his chair. The others on the flight deck did the same. "I will be in my quarters," he said and departed.

The Androssi had retrieved all of their equipment, including the new acquisitions, which would be potentially useful in future endeavors, and therefore would not be deemed untoward in an audit. Said equipment included an antimatter containment unit, but did not include the antimatter itself. The Yridian and his ship would by now have been eliminated by the catastrophic collision of the Yridian's antimatter with the matter of the ship itself, no longer separated as they were by a containment unit. Thus, there was no danger of reprisal from the Yridian.

Now Biron had the information he needed. The only net loss was that of one irrelevant alien life and time: the time spent obtaining material and upgrading the Yridian ship, and the time that Biron would now spend reading over the log entries of the hated crew of the *U.S.S. da Vinci.*

The log entries were not up-to-date, but the Yridian had said that there would be a gap between what he could acquire and the present day. The most recent entries related to a medical crisis on Sherman's Planet that the *U.S.S. da Vinci*'s chief medical officer, Dr. Elizabeth Lense, was able to solve with the aid of Fabian Stevens, a member of the ship's Starfleet Corps of Engineers team. Biron found the method Dr. Lense used to be of interest, and added it to his ship's database.

Once again, Biron found himself baffled by Starfleet's continued insistence on aiding others for no obvious benefit. In this particular instance, the crew of the *U.S.S. da Vinci*—with the exception of five of its complement—were also in danger from the pandemic that infected the population of Sherman's Planet. Even so, Biron doubted that the ship's crew's reaction would have been any different if none of them were in danger.

He decided to read through the logs of the chief medical officer. Hers, he noticed, were only on the *U.S.S. da Vinci* since shortly after the cessation of hostilities between the Dominion and the alliance among United Federation of Planets, the Klingon Empire, and the Romulan Star Empire. Prior to that, as the client had indicated, she served on a different vessel, the *U.S.S. Lexington*.

Sitting in his quarters, Overseer Biron began to peruse the log entries of Dr. Elizabeth Lense. . . .

U.S.S. LEXINGTON STARDATE 51246.9

The first thing Elizabeth Lense did when she entered her quarters on the *Lexington* was check her personnel file.

She hadn't been on board the *Lexington* in almost a month. Her quarters were just as she'd left them—not that she cared. All that mattered was whether or not Commander Selden kept his promise.

After keeping me in his damn dungeon imagining vast conspiracies to create genetically enhanced doctors in Starfleet . . .

But no, there was nothing about the Starfleet investigation into whether or not Lt. Commander Elizabeth Lense, chief medical officer of the *U.S.S. Lexington*, top of her class at Starfleet Medical, had violated the Federation law forbidding postnatal genetic enhancement.

Of course, she hadn't. The whole idea was patently ridiculous. And if the Federation wasn't presently embroiled in a war with an enemy ruled by shapechangers who had spent the last several years fomenting paranoia throughout the quadrant, it no doubt would have been investigated quietly and with a minimum of fuss.

Instead, the revelation that the salutatorian of her class, Julian Bashir, had been illegally genetically enhanced by his parents when he was six led some to think that Lense, having, in essence, beaten him, might also be so enhanced.

So they locked her in a room on Starbase 314 and went over her life with a fine-toothed comb. End result: she was an absolutely brilliant and completely human physician, who had been kept off active duty, and probably costing lives with her absence, because some admiral somewhere thought it was a good idea.

Part of Lense wanted to resign right there.

Instead, she returned to the *Lexington*. There was, after all, a war on.

The door chime rang. "Come in."

Heather Anderson walked in. Lense had been hoping that Captain Eberling himself would come by. *The son of a bitch owes me that much, at least. I always thought Starfleet captains defended their officers when they're falsely accused.*

Instead, he'd sent the first officer to do his dirty work. Lense had never liked Anderson much. She wasn't sure why, there was just something about the older woman that rubbed her wrong.

"Good to see you again, Elizabeth."

"Commander, I only just reported on board—"

"Uh, it's 'Captain' now, Elizabeth—but 'Heather' is just fine. They're sending us right back to the front lines, so we're probably going to all be in close quarters for some time."

Lense frowned, only just now noticing the fourth pip on Anderson's collar. "What happened to Captain Eberling?"

Anderson's lips seemed to twist oddly. "Didn't they tell you?"

"They kept me in a room for a month, Comma— Sorry, *Captain*. The war could've ended while I was in there, and I wouldn't have known."

"I'm afraid that Captain Eberling died at Tyra."

Blinking, Lense said, "I'm sorry?"

"Captain Eberling is dead."

Anderson went on for several seconds. Somewhere, in the back of her head, Lense registered the captain's words explaining that over a hundred ships were at Tyra, and only fourteen, including the *Lexington*, made it out in one piece. However, Eberling was fatally wounded on the bridge.

"Damn . . ." Lense muttered.

"There was nothing you could've done," Anderson said.

"Hm?" Lense was confused by the statement.

"The captain was dead before he ever got to sickbay. Your being here wouldn't have made a difference."

Lense wanted to say any number of things. She wanted to ask about the other people she might have been able to save if she had been where she belonged. She wanted to say that she would never get the chance to get the apology from Eberling that she felt she deserved. She wanted to say that she wondered what it meant that her first thought upon learning of the death of a man she had once respected was self-righteous anger. She wanted to ask how the hell Anderson knew what difference her being there really would have made. She wanted to say that she had no desire to serve under Captain "Heather is just fine" Anderson, regardless of rank.

She said none of those things. Instead, she just said, "Thank you, Captain."

Anderson smiled. Or, rather, her lips upturned. Smiles tended to brighten faces and show some kind of humor or joy. But the rest of Anderson's face remained as pursed and humorless as always. "It's 'Heather.' And don't mention it. There's a senior staff meeting at 1100 in the observation lounge. I'll give everyone the mission specs there." Her lips turned downward into a frown that was as unconvincing as the smile. "It won't be another Tyra, I promise you that. In fact, this may give us a chance to get some of our own back."

With that, Anderson left Lense alone to figure out how she felt.

The mission the *Lexington* went on wasn't another Tyra.

It was worse.

Dominion forces were threatening the border near the Setlik system. The site of a major battle during a previous war between the Federation and Cardassia, it was once again a flash point in this war in which those two nations were only supporting players. The *Lexington* was one of six *Nebula*-class vessels assigned to the sector, along with the *Honshu, Sutherland, T'Kumbra, Monitor,* and *Aldebaran.* In addition, they had support from ten *Norway*-class ships. Intelligence reports indicated a distinct possibility of an attempt to take Setlik by a small garrison of Cardassian ships, led by one

Jem'Hadar strike ship, and this force would be more than enough to deal with it.

Typically, Intelligence was both absolutely right and completely wrong. The Dominion/Cardassian forces *did* try to take Setlik—but with two very large garrisons of Cardassian ships and six Jem'Hadar strike ships.

The *Narvik*, *Oslo*, *Lillehammer*, and *Bodø* were destroyed before the *Lexington* had a chance to even go to red alert.

Lense had been on the bridge at the time. She was discussing the possibility of setting up one of the shuttlebays to handle triage in case things got bad. Said discussion was taking place with the new first officer, Commander Fiona Galloway, since "Heather" was busy with other concerns. This suited Lense just fine.

Then the tactical officer—some Bolian ensign who didn't look old enough to have a ridge—announced the arrival of over a dozen warp signatures, and then four of their support ships were gone in plumes of flame, and a Jem'Hadar ship was firing on the *Lexington*.

Galloway bellowed, "Damage report!"

Man-Fai Wan, the second officer, said from the ops station, "Multiple hits to decks nine, ten, eleven, and twelve."

Lense tensed. Sickbay was on deck nine.

Wan continued: "Hull breach on deck twelve. Plasma fires erupting on all four decks."

So much for "getting our own back," Heather, Lense thought angrily, and said, "I've got to get to sickbay."

Nobody spared her a glance as she headed to the turbolift.

"Target that Jem'Hadar ship and fire all phasers." That was Anderson's voice.

"Load torpedo bays."

"Sensors indicate that the *T'Kumbra*, the *Tromsø*, and the *Trondheim* are trying to cut a wedge in the Cardassian ships."

"The *Honshu*, *Bergen*, *Sutherland*, and *Stavanger* are chasing the ships going after Setlik IV."

"Course 189 mark 2, then hit them with—"

Whatever it was Anderson wanted to hit them with was lost to the turbolift doors closing. "Sickbay," Lense said. *Plasma fires. I'll need to get the burn units up and running.* She tapped her combadge. "Lense to Kumagai."

Silence greeted her request.

Damn newbies. The *Lexington*'s medical staff had almost doubled—from eleven to nineteen—in the month she was away. Lense's staff now included two more doctors, twice as many nurses, and an additional medtech. Kumagai was one of those two doctors—an ensign, fresh out of Starfleet Medical, with a specialty in treating burn wounds (hence his assignment to a ship on the front lines).

"Lense to Kumagai," she repeated.

Again, silence.

She tried her assistant, who had filled in as CMO while she was away. "Lense to Cox. Julianna, you there?"

More silence.

"Lense to Cavanaugh. Lense to Griscom."

She sighed. With all those people, *one* of them should have replied.

"Lense to sickbay, *someone* report!"

The turbolift doors opened onto deck nine. Uniformed personnel ran back and forth, some carrying what looked to Lense's untrained eye like equipment to be used in repairs. People shouted at each other, both across the hall and over intercoms and combadges.

As she walked closer to sickbay, she started to notice the burning smell. It had the distinct metallic odor of a plasma fire, but it was more of a lingering smell than an active one. *Good*, she thought, *that means the fire-suppression systems are working.* The computer could starve a fire with force fields, and it usually had a quick enough response time that damage was often minimal.

The moment the doors to sickbay started to part, she spoke. "Why the hell isn't any—?"

Whatever she planned to say next caught in her throat.

Sickbay was full of bodies.

The smoky metallic smell from the plasma fire lingered, but it was mixed with the equally metallic odor of blood.

This wouldn't be unusual in the midst of a large-scale battle, but for the fact that it was all medical personnel. The biobeds were empty, but members of her staff were sprawled about. Julianna lay on the floor, third-degree plasma burns all up and down the right side of her body. Next to her was Nurse Rodgers, like burns on her left side. They were both dead.

There was a giant hole where one of the bulkheads used to be, a force field over that hole, through which she could see dozens of badly burned pieces of whatever normally was inside starship bulkheads.

The fire-suppresion systems did *work*, she thought through the shock, *just not fast enough.*

She forced herself to look around. *Triage. See who needs immediate attention.* Half the equipment in sickbay was also burned. She heard moans, and one person screaming. Nobody seemed to be in any shape to help out.

"I need a doctor here!"

That voice came from the doors, which had just parted to reveal a lieutenant she didn't recognize carrying in an ensign she also didn't recognize. This was due in part to the blood obscuring both their faces.

Somewhere in the back of her head, she cursed Cox for not giving the crew adequate first-aid training—the lieutenant was carrying the ensign like he was bringing his bride across the threshold instead of in a proper "firefighter's carry"—then remembered that Cox was lying dead at her feet.

"Computer, activate EMH."

A short, male human figure appeared in the center of the room. "Please state the nature of the medical emergency," the figure said in a haughty tone.

"There's a war on," Lense said dryly. "Examine the people on the floor. Do triage, and treat the most gravely injured first. There's no support staff handy, so you'll have to find everything yourself."

The EMH looked around. "I'm a doctor, not an archaeologist."

"Move!"

"Of course." The EMH knelt down to start examining those on the floor.

Lense pointed to the lieutenant. "You—set her down there, then you sit here."

"I'm fine, Doctor, it's all her blood on me. I need to get back to engineering."

She waved him off. "Fine, go."

Sickbay's supposed to be the best protected part of the damn ship, she thought as she ran a scanner over the ensign. *The Jem'Hadar managed to penetrate it with one shot. That's ridiculous. They're supposed to build ships that are able to defend against our foes.*

As the biobed readings came through—broken arm, a combination of electrical and plasma burns on both legs, several cuts and contusions, and a concussion— Lense thought, *Of course, we didn't know about the Dominion when they built the* Lexington. She'd heard stories about how the Jem'Hadar could walk through force fields and had technology far beyond anything the Federation had ever seen.

If we can't protect sickbay, how the hell are we going to protect the rest of the ship?

She managed to stabilize the ensign and apply a dermal regenerator and a sedative. As long as she lay still and remained sedated, her body would eventually heal.

"I've completed the triage," the EMH said. "One requires immediate surgery. Two will require surgery within the next three hours. Three are stable and sedated. The remaining eight are deceased."

Lense closed her eyes. She had sent four medtechs to various parts of the ship to facilitate the transportation of wounded. She had been on the bridge.

The EMH had just listed the remainder of the *Lexington* medical staff.

"Get started on the surgeries."

"Excuse me?" the EMH said archly.

"We're about to get inundated with wounded, and we're a sickbay of two. One of us needs to be able to diagnose in an instant and make judgment calls as to what treatment to perform; the other needs to perform those treatments. I think we know how that division of labor should go, yes?"

"A logical course of action, I suppose." The EMH sounded almost grudging.

Who the hell programmed this monstrosity, anyhow? "So why are you standing around? Get to work on that patient who needs immediate surgery!"

"There's no need to yell, Doctor," the EMH said as he went over to prepare for surgery. "Of course, without a nurse, this will be most difficult."

"My heart bleeds for you," Lense muttered.

"Doctor?"

Lense turned to see that her metaphorical words applied to someone else in reality—a patient was being brought in on an antigrav gurney, blood pouring from a chest wound. With a start, she recognized the patient as Jenson, one of the three medtechs she'd sent out—and she had no idea who it was navigating the gurney.

"What happened?" she asked as she ran the scanner over the wound. Eyes widening as the tricorder told her that there was a massive arterial tear, she said, "Never mind." Jenson had seconds at the most.

She took a quick look around, but the only instruments nearby were fried by the plasma fire. The spares were across the room in a drawer—they may as well have been in the Gamma Quadrant, for all the good they did her right now.

The hell with it. She shoved her decidedly nonsterile hand into Jenson's chest cavity and tried to close the arterial tear with her fingers. If she could just hold it shut, the blood would keep pumping.

It was a ridiculous gesture. It had no chance of actually working. She could barely get a grip on the artery with the blood pouring out of Jenson's body. But she had to try.

She looked up at the person who'd brought Jenson in, and saw that he had one pip on his uniform. "Ensign, get over to the set of drawers on the far wall. In the second from the top is a tray. Bring the whole thing over here, *now!*"

"Yessir," the ensign said, sounding almost relieved to be given an order.

It took the rest of Garth Jenson's life for the ensign to make it back with the tray. By then, he had lost too much blood—no amount of infusion would do the trick, especially given how much more he'd lose in the time it would take to repair the artery.

Lense closed her eyes, counted to five, then opened them.

The smell got worse.

Again, she asked, "What happened?"

"It all happened so fast. We were just standing there down on deck twelve, talking about—something." The ensign almost giggled. "I don't even remember, but we were having one of those stupid arguments that's about nothing at all, but neither side will ever back down for anything, no matter what the other one says?"

Lense bit her tongue. She had plenty of arguments like that on Starbase 314 recently.

"And then all of a sudden, the red alert went off, and we all started to go to battle stations, and Jenson—I don't know why I remember this part particularly—but Jenson said to Halprin, Wilhoite, and Soriano, 'We'd better get a move on.' And then—"

"Wait a minute," Lense said, stunned at this revelation. Those were the other three medtechs. Now that she had a moment to think about it, none of them should have been on deck twelve. Jenson was supposed to be down in engineering, with Wilhoite on deck twenty, Halprin on deck eight, and Soriano on deck two. "They were all together?"

"Yes, sir. Along with me and . . . and Ensign Hasegawa. We were all going to report to our duty stations, when . . . when the bulkhead ripped off."

Lense recalled Wan's damage report. *Hull breach on deck twelve.*

The ensign shook his head. "Soriano, Wilhoite, and Halprin were blown out into space, sir, along with Hasegawa. A piece of shrapnel tore through Jenson's chest before the force field kicked in. I don't know how I managed to make it through without a scratch." The ensign smiled, but like Captain Anderson's, it didn't reach the rest of his face. "I guess I'm lucky, huh?" he asked, not sounding like he felt in the least bit lucky.

"Go to your duty station, Ensign. I get the feeling they're going to need you, wherever that is."

Mithra to sickbay—we've got wounded down here. Where the hell are your people?

Lieutenant Commander Rachel Mithra was the chief engineer. "They're all dead or incapacitated, Commander." *Think, think, think.* "Are transporters still operational?"

What difference does that make? Shields are up.

"Think inside the box, Commander—we can beam intraship with shields up, yes?"

What? Oh, yeah, of course we can. Sorry, Doctor, it's a little—"

"Save it. Feed the coordinates of your wounded to the transporter room and beam them directly in here."

For the next hour, the *Lexington* sickbay was unusually quiet. The EMH performed its surgical procedures with a minimum of fuss, a maximum of competence, and a healthy dose of smugness, but with no support staff, neither it nor Lense had anyone to talk to but each other, and Lense deliberately kept that interaction to a minimum. The only constant noise was that of the transporter as it beamed in the latest casualties, punctuated by the occasional scream of pain.

The smell of blood got worse. Lense would have thought she'd get used to it.

It took a brief lull to realize that there were no other casualties being beamed in. She was about to contact the bridge for an update, when Commander Galloway came stumbling in, carrying another crew member—in, Lense noted, a proper carry. She quickly took stock of the wounds on Galloway's head and torso.

"I'm fine, but Fornnel here needs help."

Galloway gently laid the officer down on a biobed. With a start, Lense realized it was the same Bolian whose youth she'd been lamenting back on the bridge. Blue blood coated his entire right arm.

"We need to talk," Galloway said seriously after setting him down.

Lense called the EMH over and had it work on Fornnel, then regarded Galloway with an expectant look.

"Transporters are down. That was a *very* clever idea of yours, but the Jem'Hadar have made it impossible. The bridge has been compromised—Captain's setting up in the auxiliary bridge with Wan."

As Galloway spoke, she was clutching the right side

of her belly with her right hand. The blood that covered that hand was red, so it definitely didn't belong to Fornnel.

"Tell me the rest while I examine you."

"I'll be fine," she said, backing out of sickbay. "I saw about ten other wounded people on the way here—without the transporters, we'll never get them here. They're worse off than me. Be right back."

Before Lense could say anything else, she left.

Lense was just starting to debate the efficacy of going after her, when she heard a wheezing noise. Antonacci, one of the engineers, was going into shock. "Dammit!"

More hours passed. She stabilized Antonacci, and she and the EMH dealt with the casualties as Galloway and others brought them in. Some even made it in under their own steam.

Too many of them died.

Somehow, Galloway kept coming in with more wounded, even though the red stain on her uniform jacket kept getting bigger each time. At least five people survived who wouldn't have without Galloway playing medtech.

If I'd had the entire staff, if half my equipment hadn't been fried, if I'd been here the past month and not let discipline and training slip with my absence . . .

It would still be a nightmare. People would still be dying, there'd just be more of us watching.

The smell of blood never left her nostrils, and she was sure that it never would.

Another hour, and the not-especially-reassuring voice of Heather Anderson sounded over the intercom. *"Attention all hands, this is the captain. We have destroyed the Dominion forces that tried to take Setlik. With the arrival of replacements from the Third Fleet, we're standing down from red alert. Once warp drive is repaired, we will be setting course for Starbase 375 for repairs."*

When the captain signed off, the EMH approached. Lense wondered where Galloway was—she hadn't seen the first officer in quite some time.

"All the patients are stable, Doctor. And—oh, dear."

"What is it?" Lense followed the EMH's glance—it was peering at the floor.

She saw a figure sitting there, next to the corpse of Dr. Cox, staring lifelessly ahead, seated as if she'd plunked herself down there for a quick rest.

Fiona Galloway.

"Dammit, why didn't she let me help her?"

With surprising gentleness, the EMH said, "Because she thought it was more important to help others."

Lense let out a very long breath. *Maybe I* should *have resigned,* she thought—not due to outrage at the way Starfleet treated her, but so she wouldn't have had to face this nightmare ever again.

Anything to never smell the blood.

"Yeah." She shook her head. "C'mon, let's check on our living patients."

ANDROSSI VESSEL OVERSEEN BY BIRON
STARDATE 53678.4

Overseer Biron read through the logs from the *U.S.S. Lexington* with a mixture of admiration and confusion.

The former came from Elizabeth Lense's ingenuity in accomplishing her appointed task with no staff and limited equipment.

The latter came from that appointed task. In particular, the actions of Fiona Galloway filled him with utter confusion. Why would the Starfleet equivalent of a sub-overseer waste time and energy, and sacrifice her own life, just to preserve the lives of inferiors? It was an appalling misuse of resources. What did a mere engineer matter? Such people were easily replaceable. Someone who can perform the task of second-in-command of a ship—especially one as large as the *U.S.S. Lexington*—was a person for whom the preservation of life should have been a far greater priority.

Biron was unable to determine why Dr. Lense had been temporarily reassigned to the Federation starbase designated number 314 for a month's time. He did, however, know that she specifically requested a transfer to the Starfleet Corps of Engineers after the war's end.

Furthermore, he noted that she was the only doctor assigned to the *U.S.S. da Vinci*, aside from an upgraded version of the Emergency Medical Hologram that assisted her during the combat in the Setlik star system. The *U.S.S. da Vinci* was, after all, a much smaller ship than the *U.S.S. Lexington*, and did not require as extensive a medical staff.

He mentally stored these pieces of information along with the others he'd gleaned from his reading. Dr. Lense was a critical asset to the functioning of the vessel, given the obscene importance Starfleet placed on the lives of irrelevant life-forms. That was something Biron knew he could exploit.

Biron noted that several log entries were from the Federation starbase designated number 92. He soon realized that Bartholomew Faulwell, the language and cryptographic specialist assigned to the *U.S.S. da Vinci*'s Starfleet Corps of Engineers team, had been assigned there during the time period of the war. Confusingly, Faulwell appeared to be of Starfleet's worker class, even though he obviously had the skills of an officer. *I will never understand this Federation*, he thought.

Faulwell had not been directly involved in either of Biron's previous encounters with the *U.S.S. da Vinci* at either the Cardassian station Empok Nor or at the planet Maeglin. Therefore, Biron was unfamiliar with him. Apparently, he was stationed at this particular starbase during the war, and assigned to interpret and translate Dominion communication codes into something that could be read by the Federation.

That is a valuable skill, Biron thought, and began reading.

STARBASE 92
STARDATE 52601.6

Bartholomew Faulwell had been sitting outside Commander DuVall's office for two hours. He had kept himself occupied by reading one of the books he had loaded onto his padd—it was what he intended to use to read himself to sleep that night, of course, but he could always get his hands on another one. And it was a good read—a historical novel about twenty-first-century space travel by a very talented woman named Almira Van Der Weir. Bart had also read many straight histories about so-called boomers in the days before the Federation's founding, and Van Der Weir was one of the few fiction writers who captured the essence that Bart had found in the histories. Portraying the frontier spirit was easy enough—pretty much every halfway decent novel set in that time period managed that—but few were able to leaven it with the very real hardships they endured. *Then again, in our replicator age, hardship's a tough one to handle—though I suspect the last couple of years have cured us of* that *little bit of compla-cency.*

Of course, Bart would rather have been doing something productive with his time. Since the start of the war with the Dominion, Bart had been applying his skills as a cryptographer to cracking Dominion and Cardassian codes. With the entry of the Breen into the war, he assumed that his sudden reassignment to Starbase 92 had to do with their codes.

So he'd hopped the first runabout he could get on and reported to the station commander immediately upon his arrival at the large top-shaped station that orbited Calufrax IV.

And then he waited.

Finally, the doors parted and a very short, balding, round human came out. He didn't so much walk as waddle.

"You must be Faulwell. Come in." Then he turned and went back into his office, obviously expecting Bart to follow him.

No apologies, no pleasantries, just ordering him in. *This is gonna be fun,* Bart thought with a sigh as he got up, turned the display of his padd off, and followed the commander into his domain.

Said domain was fairly utilitarian. Usually Starfleet officers tended toward a minimum of décor—enough to show that there was a person occupying the space, but not enough to scream out their personality through interior decorating. It was the enlisted folk like Bart himself who tended to make their working spaces over into their own image.

DuVall, however, took the former to an extreme. There was nothing here that didn't belong: the standard-issue desk with equally standard-issue viewscreen/computer on it, the two guest chairs, the computer display on the wall, and damn little else. No pictures, no personal effects, no wall hangings, nothing.

"Have a seat," DuVall said, even as he fell more than sat into his own chair.

"My orders," Bart said, "were to report here right away, but not why."

"Of course not," DuVall said after snorting derisively. "I won't kid you, Mr. Faulwell. There's a war on."

Bart bit back a sarcastic response. It didn't do to antagonize one's commanding officer within five minutes of meeting him.

DuVall continued. "You probably don't know this—and once you leave this room, I expect you to continue not to know this—but the war's going pretty badly for our side."

In fact, this was common knowledge, but again, Bart refrained from comment.

"With the Breen's damned energy-dampener keeping us and the Romulans out of the battle, we have to rely on the Klingons to hold the border. Now, between you, me, and the viewport, there's nobody I want next to me in a fight more than a pissed-off Klingon, but I want 'em backing me up, not going out in front. No discipline, if you know what I mean. And the numbers just don't add up."

He leaned forward, hitting Bart with what might have been a penetrating glare on a face that wasn't so—there was no other word for it—chubby. "That's where you come in, Mr. Faulwell. Now, more than ever, we have to rely on knowing where the Dominion is going to attack. Unfortunately, they've upgraded their code, and we can't figure it out. Your job is to crack it."

Bart nodded. "Of course, sir."

"Don't give me that, 'of course, sir,' crapola, mister. Look, I know your type."

"Type?"

"Yeah, you noncommissioned academic types. I read your file. You enlisted seventeen years ago to go on one of those long-term exploratory missions. Probably figured you'd meet lots of nice little alien life-forms that you could make friends with."

In fact, the seven-year mission of the *U.S.S. Pisces* was meant to do exactly that, and they made several first contacts, at least one of which was on its way to Federation membership. Bart had joined Starfleet specifically for that mission, serving as the ship's linguist, but he found he enjoyed the challenges Starfleet had to offer, and reenlisted when his term was up.

"Well, this is the other side of the coin, Mr. Faulwell. This is the real deal. The Federation's counting on you to come through, are we clear?"

Unable to resist, Bart said, "So clear I can see right through you, sir."

"Excellent," DuVall said with conviction. "That's what I want to hear. You'll be heading up a team of crypto specialists. I understand you've worked with some of them before. Your liaison to me will be Lt. Commander Anthony Mark. In fact, he should be here." He stabbed angrily at a control on his desk. "DuVall to Mark."

"Mark here."

"Why the hell aren't you in my office, mister?"

A pause. Then, slowly: *"I've received no orders to report to your office, sir."*

"Well, you do now. Get your posterior over here, Commander, and I mean *now*. Our crypto spook is here."

Spook? Bart thought, but didn't pursue it. He just hoped Mark would arrive soon.

When he did, about a minute later, Bart tried to keep his jaw from falling open.

Since he was a teenager, Bart had always had a physical ideal in his head for the perfect mate. In the forty years since, he had yet to find anyone even close to that ideal—which, he supposed, accounted for his appalling lack of success with any kind of long-term relationship in those years.

The person who walked into Commander DuVall's office fit most of the criteria of the ideal he had created in his head at the age of fifteen: tall, but not too tall; curly blond hair, but not too curly; hazel eyes; long fingers. The only thing missing was a beard, but looking at Lt. Commander Mark's face, Bart saw that a beard wouldn't work right on that face. (As opposed to Bart's own. He had no appreciable chin, which his slightly scraggly brown beard nicely covered up.)

If he likes swimming and Van Der Weir's historicals, I'm going to start believing in fate. . . .

"About time," DuVall said, though Bart couldn't imagine, on a station this size, that Mark could possibly have arrived any sooner. "This is Faulwell—he's the new head of the crypto project."

"So you indicated, sir," Mark said in a deep voice. "I'll escort him to his quarters and call a meeting of the staff for 1900 hours."

"Can't be at 1900. I have a meeting with Admiral Koike at 1900, and he'll want a progress report. Make it 1700."

"Sir, it's 1705 now."

DuVall blinked. "It is?"

"Yes, sir."

"Dammit, where the hell did the day go?"

"And, sir," Mark added, "Novac and Throckmorton won't be back from Starbase 375 with the updated files until 1830."

Bart frowned, wondering why files had to be brought by hand. Then he realized that it was probably for security reasons. Subspace communication wasn't always safe. *If it was,* Bart mused with a small smile, *I'd be out of a job.*

He also, as DuVall had indicated, knew at least one of those names, assuming it was Roxana Novac to whom Mark referred. Until the war, she had been on the staff of the Tamarian liaison's office, trying to further contact with the Children of Tamar, a race who spoke purely in historical metaphor. She had done some excellent work in determining how the Tamarians developed their singularly peculiar form of communication, and Bart was grateful to have her on the team.

DuVall pounded the desk with his fist and stood up. "Dammit, what the hell kind of chicken outfit are we running here?"

"Sir, you can tell the admiral that everything's under control, that our team is together, and that they will work hard to crack the code as soon as possible."

"We need it sooner than that, mister, if we're going to win this thing." He sat back down. "All right, have the damn meeting without me, if you think it'll do any good. But I expect a full report and transcript, and I want progress reports from both of you twice a day, understood?"

Bart stood up, taking the phrasing as a dismissal. "You'll have those reports, Commander, I promise."

"I'd better. Dismissed."

"If you'll come this way, Mr. Faulwell," Mark said, indicating the door to DuVall's office with his hand.

As soon as the door shut behind him, Bart said, "Let me guess, you deliberately set the meeting for 1900 because you knew he had that meeting?"

Mark sputtered a laugh. "Was I that obvious?"

"No, but *he* was."

"Yeah, well. He's not as bad as he seems." Mark chuckled. "In fact, he *couldn't* be as bad as he seems. But he's a very good administrator, and he's run this place phenomenally well for the last ten years. It's just—"

"What?" Bart prompted.

"He's got Starfleet in the blood. Mother was Starfleet, grandfather was Starfleet, all four great-grandparents were Starfleet—all the way back to '61." Mark didn't need to explain which year ending in "61" he meant— everyone knew that was shorthand for 2161, the year the Federation was founded. "But they all had pretty impressive careers—ship captains, war heroes, historic first contacts, that sort of thing. All he's done is distinguish himself as a bureaucrat. And then a war hits, and he finds himself on entirely the wrong end of it."

Bart nodded as they entered a turbolift. Starbase 92 was about as far from the front as possible, which was why so much important crypto work was being done here, away from the fighting.

"Habitat level." The turbolift started to move horizontally. "So he makes up for it by doing the tough-guy military act. We all make sure he feels properly appreciated as the last line of defense against the Dominion, and everyone's happy. Things actually run pretty smoothly here."

The lift started to move downward. "So who all is on the team? I assume Novac is Roxana Novac?"

Mark nodded. "Terence Throckmorton is her partner—they've been working together since the war started." He grinned, a bright smile that seemed to light up the turbolift. "I also think that she's going to ask him to marry her, if he doesn't beat her to it."

Bart returned the grin. *Always good to know some of the gossip going in—*

"The others are T'Lura of Vulcan—"

"Good." Bart had never met the woman, but her work on translating the notoriously difficult Breen language had been invaluable.

"—Ganris Phrebington—"

A Gnalish, his knowledge of sibilants in particular might be useful in this sort of work. Bart had met Phrebington a few times, and found him off-putting, and not nearly as talented as he himself thought he was.

"—and Janíce Kerasus."

Blinking, Bart said, "Kerasus? She's still alive?"

Again, Mark grinned. "If you're *very* nice to me, I won't tell her you said that. Yeah, she's still alive. A hundred and sixty-five, and still going—well, not strong, exactly. She spends more time in the infirmary than any other single place, but her mind's still as sharp as ever, even if her body's breaking down on her."

The lift came to a stop and the doors parted. "So what's the problem with this new code?"

"Hell if I know," Mark said with a shrug. "I'm just the liaison officer. All I know about language is that my universal translator mostly works."

"Fair enough."

"Here we are, Mr. Faulwell."

"Please, it's Bart. Hell, if you want to be formal, it's 'Dr. Faulwell,' but that just makes me feel like a stuffy old academic." He grinned. "Of course, I *am* a stuffy old academic, but that doesn't mean I want everyone to think I am."

"Bart it is, then. And I'm Lieutenant Commander Mark. Or 'sir.'" He held the straight face for about a second. "Or 'hey you.' I answer to all three."

"'Hey you' it is. Where is this meeting at 1900?"

"The wardroom. The computer can direct you."

"Great. Thanks, Commander Hey You."

Mark shook his head. "You're welcome, Bart."

Three weeks later, Bart Faulwell and his team were no closer to a solution than they were when they started.

The meeting on Bart's first day hadn't taken too terribly long. Everyone introduced or reintroduced themselves to their newest boss. Novac and Throckmorton were truly a pair, finishing each other's sentences and talking over each other. T'Lura said very little, but her few comments were incisive. This was in direct contrast to Phrebington, who had several dozen ideas, only some of them worthwhile. And then there was Janíce Kerasus, a frail old human woman who looked like she would keel over at any second.

Bart was sitting in his quarters, going over the latest

samples Starfleet Intelligence had provided, these from the few Klingon ships that had survived the attack on Avinall VII. They'd been working for days on end with no progress. Bart hadn't realized that running this team would mostly consist of playing den mother to a bunch of opinionated specialists. Bart had always enjoyed the research for its own sake and for the intellectual rewards you generally got at the end. This group, though, was more interested in justifying their own pre-existing theories. Phrebington mostly expounded on his own ideas about everything, whether or not they related to reality; Kerasus spent most of her time poking holes in Phrebington's theories (not a difficult task, as Bart had encountered Swiss cheese with fewer holes than the Gnalish's ideas about cryptography, but Kerasus applied herself to that particular task with special glee), and Novac and Throckmorton were in their own world and had to be repeatedly reminded that there were four other people involved. T'Lura was the only one who had been easy to work with, as she shared with Bart the love of research for its own sake—though, naturally, she didn't express it as overtly as Bart did.

"Mark to Faulwell."

Only when he almost fell out of his chair, startled, did Bart even realize that he had fallen asleep at his desk. Bart had always preferred to work at his own pace and simply catch naps where he could, but Commander DuVall insisted on a more rigid schedule, and the rest of the team was already locked into it, so Bart was stuck with it as well. It was playing merry hell with his admittedly eccentric circadian rhythm.

"Faulwell here. What can I do for you, Hey You?"

"Bart, no offense, but that joke stopped being funny the first eight hundred times."

The next words came out of Bart's mouth unplanned. "Tell you what—meet me for dinner tonight and I'll stop."

"All right, then, it's a date."

Bart blinked. Then he blinked again. *My God, he said
yes.* He was already in shock at himself for asking in the
first place—which he chalked up to exhaustion lowering his resistance—but Mark actually said yes.

"Bart, you there?"

"Uh, yeah. What say we meet at that Trill restaurant
at, ah"—he checked the chronometer on his desk
—"1930?"

"Will do."

"Great."

"That's not why I called."

"No, you called to remind me that DuVall wants my
evening report in ten minutes and I better get it to him
before he gives me the evil eye."

*"His eye isn't evil, it's just misguided. Even so, I'd
rather it wasn't guided at you."*

"Not to worry, Commander Hey You, he'll have it on
time. I even made sure I spelled all the words right this
time."

"You said you'd stop that if I met you for dinner."
Mark's voice sounded mock-petulant.

"You haven't actually *met* me for dinner yet. I know
you officer types, always making promises to us enlisted
folk. I want proof."

Mark laughed. *"Fine. I'll see you at 1930."*

"The problem," Bart said between mouthfuls of the
yellow-leaf salad the Trills called *grakizh*, "is that there
isn't anything to work from. Anytime you've got a code,
there's some kind of base for it. Something to build off
of. Every Dominion code up until now has had similar
algorithms at the root. Or at least similar enough that
we could extrapolate *something*. Sometimes we've been
lucky enough to stumble into things, and sometimes
they've been careless. But this latest one—it just doesn't
match anything—no mathematical or linguistic pattern

we've seen before, from the Dominion, from the Breen, from the Cardassians. It's a big mess."

"Sounds it," Mark said, leaning back in his chair, having long since finished his meal by dint of not being able to get a word in edgewise.

"I'm sorry," Bart said sheepishly. "I've been talking shop all night."

Mark grinned. "That's all right—I would've just spent the whole meal bitching and moaning about Commander DuVall. This is a nice reminder that other people have problems too."

"Yeah." Bart took a bite of his *grakizh*.

"Maybe the Dominion's come up with an unbreakable code."

"No such thing—remember, if there's no way to decode it, there's no way the other side gets the message. Of course, it could just be something straightforward and simple and we're overthinking it." Bart chuckled. "Overthinking is definitely an occupational hazard with this bunch."

"Well, I hope for my sake you come up with something soon. DuVall got a very terse communiqué from Admiral Ross today and—well, let's just say that the abused tend to kick downward."

Bart gave Mark a sympathetic look. "I'm sorry, Commander, but—"

Mark laughed.

"What?"

"'Commander'?"

"Well, I can't call you 'hey you' anymore. I promised."

Mark nodded. "Fair enough. Anthony will do, I think."

"Fine, Anthony." Bart speared the last of his *grakizh* with his fork. "Actually, one of the more famous 'unbreakable code' stories was from Earth—the Second World War. One side's code kept being broken by the other side, so instead of an actual code, they transmitted everything in an obscure language by a people they'd conquered over a century earlier. That 'code' was never broken during the hostili—" Bart cut himself off. "My stars and garters, I think that's it."

"What's it?"

"We're complete and total idiots." He got up. "I've got to go. I may have stumbled onto the right track."

Mark grinned. "Then we both have to go." He tapped his combadge. "Cryptography team, please report to the wardroom immediately."

"So you're saying—what *are* you saying?" Phrebington said. The lizardlike Gnalish was standing in one corner of the wardroom, pointedly positioning himself as far from Kerasus as possible. The elderly human, for her part, sat placidly at the head of the wardroom table, with Throckmorton and Novac sitting to her left, T'Lura on her right. Anthony stood leaning against a rear bulkhead, with Bart sitting at the other head of the table.

Bart leaned forward. "I'm saying that we need to try investigating a language from the Dominion that's as obscure to us as the Navajo language was to the Axis powers in World War Two on Earth."

"Ah, yes, because, after all, we've had such tremendous cultural exchanges with them," Phrebington said with a snort.

"Mr. Phrebington's sarcasm notwithstanding," T'Lura said, "he is right. Our cultural information on the Dominion is limited."

"We know about their language, though," Kerasus said in a voice that was at once paper-thin and rich with authority. Bart had spent the last several weeks wondering if he'd be able to pull that off when he was that old.

"What do we possibly know about their language?" Phrebington asked sharply.

Her tone now withering, Kerasus said, "Quite a bit, if

you actually have paid attention to the recorded conversations and discussions involving the Founders, the Vorta, and other Dominion members. Untranslated, of course."

"What good would that do?" Novac asked, sounding confused.

Throckmorton added, "It's not like they'd use a language we're familiar with for their code."

"If they had, we'd have found it weeks ago," Phrebington said, "and I'd be back on Gnala where it's safe."

Bart smiled a small smile. "If you give Janíce a chance, I'm sure she'll elaborate."

Kerasus smiled right back. "Thank you, Bartholomew." Bart generally hated being called by his full first name, but he couldn't bring himself to be annoyed when Kerasus did it. "My point is that it can't be anything relating to the Founders or the Vorta in any case, because their actual language is too simplistic. The Founders didn't even have a concept of vocal speech until they encountered solids. They communicate with each other through that Great Link of theirs, and only use a very basic spoken language—it's the one they programmed into the Vorta and the Jem'Hadar as well. It makes them very easy to translate, which can be useful in diplomatic circumstances, though it makes for wretched poetry."

Bart laughed. So did Novac and Throckmorton and Anthony. Phrebington didn't. (Neither did T'Lura, but that was to be expected.)

"In any event," Kerasus said, "that would explain why they haven't used a purely linguistic base for their codes prior to this. The people running this war have only the simplest of linguistics to go on. It makes sense that only now, when we've done such a fine job of breaking through their codes, that they're trying more esoteric methods." The old woman's breathing became more labored as she finished. "If we're going to try this solution, we—we need to look to another—another member of the Dominion."

"Hadn't we already established that?" Phrebington asked snidely.

Anthony, meanwhile, walked over to where Kerasus was sitting. "Are you all right?"

She nodded quickly. "Yes, I'm fine. Just a bit—a bit too much there."

"As I suspected," Phrebington said, "talking too much will get the best of her."

Bart sighed. "The problem is, we don't have any kind of cultural database on the Dominion member worlds. We can try to compare it to the ones we do have some records on from trips that ships made to the Gamma Quadrant, but I can't imagine they'd have used anyone that was visited by an allied ship in the past."

"That doesn't mean we shouldn't investigate those languages," Novac said.

"Just to rule it out," Throckmorton added.

Nodding, Bart said, "You two handle that, then. I think Deep Space 9 has complete records of all the Gamma Quadrant worlds that have been visited since the wormhole was discovered."

"It's a waste of time." Phrebington started to walk toward the door. "This is an utter waste of time."

Anthony moved to block the door. "You haven't been dismissed yet, Mr. Phrebington."

"Commander, it's late, I'm tired, and I'm not in the mood for tiresome—"

"I'm not terribly interested in what you're 'in the mood for,' Mr. Phrebington." Anthony spoke in a moderate tone, the picture of calm. "We've all got a job to do here, and it's an important one. Lives depend on what this team accomplishes here. And by putting that uniform on, you have already committed to doing whatever is necessary to keep those lost lives to a minimum. So what you're in the mood for really doesn't enter into it.

Now, you're not leaving until Mr. Faulwell or I dismiss you. Is that clear, Mr. Phrebington?"

In direct contrast to the barking tones with which DuVall had asked that last question three weeks earlier, Anthony was downright conversational, giving the words no more weight than if he were asking Phrebington for a cup of coffee. Yet it was much more effective, as the Gnalish turned tail (literally) and went back to where he'd been standing against the bulkhead.

"There is a possibility we have not considered," T'Lura said.

"What's that?" Bart asked, grateful to the Vulcan woman for changing the subject—or, rather, getting back to the original subject.

"It is true that the Federation has had comparatively limited contact with the Dominion, and that Romulan and Klingon contact has been even less. However, there are other nations in the Alpha Quadrant."

Novac chuckled. "It's not like the Cardassians or the Breen are going to share their cultural databases with us."

T'Lura steepled her hands together, elbows resting on the wardroom table. "I was referring to the Ferengi."

That got everyone's attention. Bart noted that Anthony had a particularly wide-eyed look, as if he were disappointed in himself for not thinking of it first.

Phrebington, of course, sounded more disappointed in T'Lura. "The Ferengi? If you were anyone else, I'd say you were joking."

"Insults are not necessary, Mr. Phrebington," T'Lura said primly. "First contact with the Dominion was, in fact, made by the Ferengi Alliance, and they have made numerous trade agreements with a variety of Dominion races. It is quite possible that there are those in the Alliance who have the information we need."

"That's the most ridiculous thing I've ever heard,"

Phrebington said. "Is this what we've come to? Relying on the Ferengi?"

Grinning, Bart said, "Oh, the Ferengi can be damn reliable. You just have to know how to acquire the information."

Throckmorton frowned. "I don't think Commander DuVall would be able to requisition gold-pressed latinum for this."

"That won't be necessary," Anthony said. Bart couldn't help but notice the mischievous smile on his face. "I think I can find what we need. I'll need a couple of days to track down the DaiMon I'm thinking of."

Novac shrugged. "We'll need that long to go through what we have on the Dominion in any case."

"At least," Throckmorton said.

"All right, let's pursue this," Bart said. "Meantime, the rest of us keep doing what we've been doing. Just because this is a possibility doesn't mean it's the only one. We may get lucky. Dismissed."

Phrebington muttered, "Lucky—*that* would be a first."

"War's full of firsts, Mr. Phrebington," Anthony said with a grin. "I'd say we're due for one."

The next week was chock full of activity.

Novac and Throckmorton went over the known data about Dominion linguistics, paltry as it was, and concluded, unsurprisingly, that there was no connection between it and the new code.

Bart, T'Lura, and Phrebington continued to search for more ways to crack the code, with the same lack of success they'd been having since Bart's arrival.

Kerasus, unfortunately, spent the week in the infirmary, her inability to catch her breath during the meeting turning out to be a symptom of some lung trouble. The starbase doctor assured everyone that it was routine for someone of her advanced age, and she'd be released in a few days, "if not sooner." The last was added in an exasperated tone that suggested to Bart that the older woman didn't appreciate being bedridden when there was work to be done.

As for Bart and Anthony, they had dinner at the Trill restaurant the following night to "finish off" the previous dinner. Then they met again the next night. Soon, it became a nightly ritual. After five days, Bart accompanied Anthony back to the latter's quarters after the restaurant closed, since they weren't finished with their spirited discussion (Bart was having far too much fun, and they were being far too civil, for it to be categorized as an argument) about literature. Anthony didn't like anything written since around 2350 or so, preferring the neo-Gothic books of the earlier part of the century. At the end of the night, Anthony promised to read Van Der Weir, though Bart suspected it was mostly just to shut Bart up about how excellent her work was.

The morning that the Ferengi DaiMon finally arrived, Bart had spent the night in Anthony's quarters, his happiness with his private life now in inverse proportion to his frustration with the lack of results in the crypto project.

DuVall, Anthony, and Bart met with the Ferengi, a short, rotund man named Bikk. The DaiMon sat his portly form at the foot of the wardroom table, opposite DuVall.

"So," the commander said, "Mr. Mark tells me that you're something of an expert on the Dominion."

"Something like that," Bikk said with a toothy smile that made Bart want to run to his quarters and make sure all his possessions were still there. "I spent a year living in the Gamma Quadrant, supervising Ferengi interests on behalf of Grand Nagus Zek."

Anthony nodded in appreciation. "That must've required a hefty bribe."

"Several dozen, actually, but those have been recouped a thousandfold. The Tulaberry wine business is quite profitable on that side of the wormhole. Not only that, but the person I had to give the most kickbacks to was later stripped of his standing by the Ferengi Commerce Authority, so now I keep even more profits. It's quite a tidy arrangement."

"Especially since you've been selling information about the Dominion to allied powers," Mark said. "Not to mention arranging the talks between Gul Dukat and the Vorta that led to Cardassia joining the Dominion."

Bart swallowed. He hadn't known this. Based on the sputter that came from the head of the table, neither did DuVall.

"You mean to tell me that you're responsible—"

"Now, now, Commander," Bikk said, not at all flustered by this revelation. "Don't give me your superior, self-righteous Federation posturing. Outrage that a Ferengi will sell out to the highest bidder is a waste of your time and mine. If you didn't think I could be bought, I wouldn't be here."

"I ought to haul you up on charges right now, Dai-Mon."

"In which court, Commander?" Bikk stood up. "I see no reason to listen to this. Mr. Mark, I was under the impression that a serious business offer was being made."

"It is," Anthony said with a glare at his CO. "We're looking for a complete linguistic database of all the Dominion member races."

Bikk threw his bulbous head back and laughed before sitting back down. "And what makes you think I have such a thing?"

"Because you're you, Bikk. Because you lived in the Gamma Quadrant for a year making huge profits—yet your personal bank balance when you left was almost exactly the same as when you arrived. To me, that means that you spent your profits. And again, because you're you, you probably spent that money on amassing information that you could sell on this side of the wormhole."

Face darkening, voice deepening, Bikk asked slowly, "How did you learn what my personal bank balance was?"

Anthony just grinned in response. Bart had to hold back a grin of his own. Starfleet Intelligence had impressive resources when they put their minds to it, and a Ferengi who lived in the Gamma Quadrant for a year was definitely going to be a very large reading on SI's sensors.

"Never you mind how we got it," DuVall said quickly. "The point is, we know what you've been up to, Dai-Mon."

Realizing that he wasn't going to get a straight answer, Bikk leaned back in his chair. "Assuming I *have* such esoteric information, what would you be prepared to offer me in exchange for it?"

Anthony leaned forward. "You're familiar with the Breen energy-draining weapon, yes?"

"Of course. And only the Klingons can defend against it, which is, by the way, a sad commentary on the state of this little war you're fighting. You'd have been better off entering a trade agreement like we did."

"We're not profiteers, mister," DuVall said.

Bikk shrugged. "Your loss, our gain."

"Your gain, anyhow." Anthony smiled. "We're developing a countermeasure against the Breen weapon. You can have access to all our research—"

"As if I'd need it. *We're* not at war, Mr. Mark."

"—and to the method for countering the weapon once we have it." Anthony continued as if the Ferengi hadn't spoken.

DuVall stood up and fixed a furious gaze on his adjutant. "Are you out of your mind?"

Without looking at DuVall, Anthony said, "Starfleet Command has already signed off on this, sir."

"Dammit, we shouldn't be giving these big-eared cretins access to our military secrets."

Bikk smiled that unctuous smile again. "Your commander has a point. Besides—"

"Don't kid yourself into thinking that the Dominion will stop with the allies. If we lose this war, Ferengi independence won't be long for this galaxy. And you never know when you might need a defense against a Breen ship."

A pudgy hand ran thoughtfully over the edge of Bikk's right ear. "Perhaps." He stood up. "I will consult my copious files and see what I can provide."

As soon as the Ferengi left, Anthony let out a long breath. "That went better than expected."

"Yup."

Bart turned to look at Commander DuVall and was shocked to see that the station commander was *smiling*. It was a sight Bart hadn't seen in his month on the starbase and found it more than a little disconcerting.

"Good work, Mr. Mark," DuVall continued. "I think we've baited this particular fish lock, stock, and barrel."

Wincing at the mixed metaphor, Bart said, "You mean to say—"

"Yes, it was an act, Mr. Faulwell. You don't *really* think Mr. Mark here would go over my head like that, do you?"

"The thought had crossed my mind," Bart said dryly.

Anthony chuckled. "Bikk likes the idea of being the cause of some kind of rift between Starfleet officers. Especially if I'm one of them. He and I have—well, a history. That's how I know he's got what we need. He's an information pusher, and this is exactly the sort of thing he'd have access to."

"I just hope it pans out. We're still taking a stab in the dark with this whole idea. It could wind up being nothing." Bart let out a long breath. "I'd hate for us to give away important military stuff for nothing."

DuVall shrugged. "It's not like we wouldn't have shared the data with the Ferengi if they asked."

"But they wouldn't ask," Anthony added. "They'd assume they'd have to pay for it. So we might as well oblige them."

"Well, good work," Bart said with a grin.

"Glad we have your approval, Mr. Faulwell," DuVall said snidely. "Now if you'll excuse me, I have actual work to do. There's a war on, you know."

"I've heard that," Bart said with a straight face.

DuVall ignored the crack and left the wardroom, leaving Anthony and Bart alone.

"So, what say we celebrate tonight?" Anthony said. "Maybe do dinner in my quarters instead of at the restaurant?"

Bart grinned. "Works for me."

DaiMon Bikk returned the following day with a complete linguistic database of Gamma Quadrant aliens known to the Dominion—and known to nonaffiliated people such as the Dosai and the Wadi—and Anthony provided him with all the data from Starfleet Headquarters on their progress in combatting the Breen weapon, with the promise of more to come. The morning's dispatches had told of a Jem'Hadar ship outfitted with the energy-dampening weapon that had been captured by rebel Cardassians and brought to Deep Space 9. Studying the weapon itself would no doubt provide the breakthrough needed. Bikk seemed very pleased with this news, though he was not as thrilled with this transaction as Bart might have expected.

"He's just cranky because we were able to learn his personal bank balance," Anthony said in bed that night when Bart broached the subject. "That's the functional equivalent of peeking into his bedroom. But he'll get over it."

A day later, Bart sat in the starbase lounge drinking a cup of coffee, rereading an old Van Der Weir, and lamenting the starbase's inability to do a proper French roast, when his combadge sounded with the papery voice of Janíce Kerasus, newly released from the infirmary. *"Bartholomew, you need to come to the lab right now."*

Tapping his combadge, Bart said, "What is it, Janíce?"

"Paydirt."

Grinning, Bart left his coffee unfinished and went straight for the lab, where the rest of the team was waiting.

"We've found our Navajo," Kerasus said as soon as the doors closed behind Bart. "It even follows the same pattern."

Bart frowned. "What do you mean?"

"There's a small tribe of aboriginal types on the Karemma homeworld. They live on a small island in the middle of one of their oceans. They don't care about technology, or—" Kerasus interrupted herself with a coughing fit.

Novac took over as Kerasus reached into her tunic to retrieve her medication. "They have a ridiculously complex language. The UT can't make heads or tails of it, but it's a perfect match for the new codes. All we've got to do is build a translation matrix."

"All we've got to do?" Phrebington said irritably. "The universal translator insists that it's random noise. I'm not completely convinced that it *isn't* random noise and that Ferengi cheated us."

"Even the UT isn't perfect," Throckmorton said. "Hell, it sometimes still has problems with the Klingon language."

Phrebington made a disparaging noise. "That's not

evidence of anything. The Klingon language really *is* random noise—"

"Let's get to it, people," Bart said quickly before another argument erupted.

He and Anthony exchanged a quick glance. Finally, it looked like they were on the right track.

ANDROSSI VESSEL OVERSEEN BY BIRON STARDATE 53678.5

According to the remainder of the logs the Yridian provided, Faulwell's team was able to build a translation matrix for the language and decode the Dominion transmissions. It required manually adding a subroutine to all universal translator devices, which struck Biron as inefficient. Androssi computers were equipped with dimensional enhancers to allow such upgrades to be performed instantaneously on all equipment. *Yet another way in which the Federation is demonstrably inferior to us.*

It made Biron's defeats all the more galling.

Biron studied several other missions of the *U.S.S. da Vinci* itself, from their assorted construction missions (an irrigation system on a desert world designated Elvan; a subspace accelerator on the crystalline world designated Sarindar), salvage missions (a one-hundred-year-old Starfleet starship, the *U.S.S. Defiant* from an interphasic rift in the fabric of space; an alien vessel that the *U.S.S. da Vinci* crew members gave the inappropriate name "the *Beast*," but which was in fact a ship belonging to a species known as the Hlangry, which Biron himself had also encountered two-point-nine cycles earlier), and rescue missions (prisoners from the malfunctioning prison designated the Kursican Orbital Platform; the mining colony of Beta Argola from an attack by the species known as the Munqu).

He noted several references to Commander Sonya Gomez's exploits during the Dominion War on the *U.S.S. Sentinel* and decided that it was time to read about some of those missions as well. . . .

U.S.S. SENTINEL
STARDATE 52646.1

Lt. Commander Sonya Gomez had been wandering the halls of Deep Space 9 since the *Sentinel* docked at the station a few hours ago.

I can't believe I'm lost. I never get lost.

It was a point of pride with her as much as anything. She had always had a dead-on sense of direction. Within three months at the Academy, the fourth-year cadets were asking *her* for shortcuts around campus. On the *Enterprise,* the *Oberth,* Altair IV, and the *Sentinel,* she knew her way around almost instantly, and never needed to consult the computer for directions.

Yet this Cardassian-built space station was vexing her.

As she turned a corner from one identical dark corridor into another identical dark corridor, she took refuge in a familiar face heading toward her.

"Chief!"

Miles Edward O'Brien looked up from the padd he was studying to see Gomez. "Sonya! Er, sorry, Commander."

Gomez grinned. "Sonya's just fine, Chief. How've you been?"

"About like you'd expect," the taller man said with a wry smile.

"Are Keiko and Molly doing all right?"

"Just fine, all things considered. Keiko's not thrilled with being this close to the front, but with the way things are going, no place is all that safe."

Remembering the images of the Breen attack on San Francisco that she saw in the *Sentinel*'s observation lounge, Gomez was forced to agree. "I know what you mean."

"Oh, and Molly has a brother—Kirayoshi."

That put the smile back on Gomez's face. She had always thought the chief and Keiko Ishikawa made a good couple, and she was glad to see that her instincts had proven correct. *If only those instincts had been as accurate with Kieran,* she thought, then put it out of her head. She and Kieran Duffy had broken up when she transferred off the *Enterprise* to the *Oberth* almost eight years ago. They had promised to keep in touch, but didn't. At times she missed him horribly, at times she forgot all about him. She idly wondered if O'Brien had heard from him—after all, the chief had remained on the *Enterprise* for another year and a half after she left before he took over as chief of operations at DS9.

Instead, she kept the topic comfortable. "I hope his birth went more smoothly than Molly's."

"You could say that. Worf didn't have to deliver this one, at least."

Gomez laughed. Worf's impromptu midwifing of Keiko had happened less than a week before Gomez left for the *Oberth*, and had gotten her a lot of storytelling mileage on that one-year assignment. She had forgotten that the Klingon, too, was now assigned to DS9. *It's like it's old home week. . . .*

O'Brien continued. "But, ah, it was actually Colonel

Kira who carried the baby to term. It's a *very* long story," he said quickly, obviously not wanting to get into it.

Taking the hint, she said, "I wish I had time to hear it, but I need to get to the meeting in the wardroom."

"I won't keep you, then," O'Brien said.

"Actually, I need you to tell me how to get there. I've gotten completely turned around."

Chuckling, O'Brien said, "Cardassian architecture." He quickly gave a series of clear directions that included a turbolift ride two levels up.

"I really did get lost, didn't I?"

"A bit, yeah," O'Brien said with a smile. "Don't worry—I won't tell. Your reputation's safe with me."

"Thanks. And give my love to the family—oh, and in case I don't see him, say hi to Worf for me."

"Will do. Take care, Sonya!"

Following O'Brien's directions brought Gomez to the wardroom in under three minutes, and only five minutes after the meeting's official start time—which meant, of course, that not everyone was there and it hadn't begun yet. Gomez's CO, Captain Anna Maria Amalfitano, was already present, along with the *Sentinel*'s first officer Lt. Commander Kuljit Patel. Gomez took some satisfaction out of the fact that she couldn't see their tactical officer, so she wasn't the last one to arrive.

Of course, given the crowd in the wardroom, she might have missed Grimnar, their Bolian tactical officer, but a two-meter-tall blue-skinned humanoid tended to stand out, even in a room full of Klingons, Romulans, and Starfleet officers. The senior staffs of the *Musashi* and the *Fredrickson* made up the remainder of the Starfleet personnel, and she assumed that the Klingons and Romulans were involved in whatever their mission was.

Grimnar finally came in about two seconds before the arrival of Admiral Ross, Captain Sisko, General—

no, Chancellor Martok, and a Romulan admiral she didn't recognize. As soon as they did, many took seats, with most of the rest standing along the walls, as there were far more people than available seats. Gomez found herself wedged between a surly-looking-even-by-their-standards Klingon and a bored-looking Starfleet officer with full lieutenant's pips.

Sisko began without preamble, speaking in an intense, deep voice. "The mission we have for you all is twofold. The *Sentinel*, the *Musashi*, and the *Fredrickson* will be dispatched to the Dominion outpost in Sector 25013."

Amalfitano blinked. "That's a bit deep into enemy territory, isn't it?"

Martok chuckled. "Not as deep as others shall go."

"A fleet of twelve warbirds, aided by some Klingon vessels," the Romulan said, sounding almost pained at having to even acknowledge the Klingon contribution, "will be moving under cloak to the Orias system. That system is under constant antiproton scan by the outpost you will be attacking."

Nodding, Amalfitano said, "So you need us to take down the outpost, or at least distract them long enough for the cloaked ships to sneak in and wipe out the shipyards on Orias III?"

"Exactly," Sisko said. "With the Breen energy-dampening weapon neutralized, and the Cardassian resistance sabotaging their ships, we need to strike at a decisive target and start to get our momentum back. We think this attack on Orias will aid in that."

"The timing will be critical," the Romulan added. "We won't be able to communicate with each other, obviously, so you must arrive at the outpost at the designated time so we can begin our run."

One of the other Starfleet captains asked, "What kind of defenses can we expect?"

Ross spoke up then. "Intelligence reports indicate

that there are only two Jem'Hadar strike ships guarding it."

The third Starfleet captain made an irritated noise. "Not to put too fine a point on it, Admiral, Captain, but aren't three ships a bit—well, inadequate? We'll be lucky to get that far into Dominion territory as it is."

There were some rumblings from the Klingons at that, but Ross simply said, "Unfortunately, you're all we can spare. We're putting together a massive offensive against the Dominion. This is one of many strikes we're attempting simultaneously to keep their forces spread thin. We have to press the attack now."

"However," Sisko said, "you will have a relatively easy time getting there. Thanks to the Cardassian resistance, we've been able to obtain a course that will get you to the outpost without encountering any patrols. It's a less direct route, so you'll have to go at warp seven most of the way to get there at the pre-arranged time."

Patel said, "This is assuming that the patrols stick to their assigned routes. We can't very well count on that."

"We're past the point where we can play things safe, Commander," Sisko said just as the Klingon next to Gomez made a disparaging comment under his breath about Patel's lineage.

Before her first officer could say anything else, Amalfitano spoke. "We'll be fine, Captain, don't worry. We'll clear a path for the rest of you," she added, looking around the room.

Then her gaze fell upon Gomez. *This is my moment, I guess*, she thought. The chief engineer hadn't really needed to be at this briefing, but she had come up with an idea that the captain wanted brought up in front of Sisko and the other higher-ups. "Captain, Admiral, if I may?"

"Yes, Commander Gomez, what is it?" Sisko asked.

Both Martok and the Romulan bristled, but Sisko

and Ross each gave her expectant looks, as if they were genuinely interested in what she might have to say. Gomez took that as an encouraging sign. "We might be able to do better than just having a specific course. We can alter our ships to make us look like Cardassian freighters."

"We've tried that in the past," Sisko said. "But at this point, the Jem'Hadar and the Cardassians know to look for it."

"With respect, sir, those had been changes to the shield harmonics. What I'm suggesting is altering the warp fields of the ships. We've tested it on the *Sentinel*, and it should fool even Dominion sensors at warp speeds."

One of the Romulans sneered. "And when you come out of warp and are revealed to be a Federation ship?"

"We keep the warp field in place. As long as they don't do an intensive scan, they shouldn't be able to tell the difference between it and a hull configuration. In fact, we can also change the shield harmonics to match. They're less likely to look for that bit of misdirection if the ship's warp field reads as an allied ship."

Ross seemed intrigued by the idea. "Can you maintain warp seven with this reconfiguration?"

Gomez blinked. She hadn't thought of that—but then, she hadn't known they'd be forced to maintain warp seven until two minutes ago. "I'm afraid not. We could only do warp four—any higher and the modified warp field will tear the hull apart."

"Then it won't be practical for this mission. Still, it's a good idea. Send the specifications on that to the station—and," he added with glances at Martok and the Romulan admiral, "we'll share it with everyone here, see if we can make it work across the board." He turned back to Gomez. "Good work, Commander."

Gomez nodded, but was still disappointed. She was sure that the trick would work—but not at warp seven.

She had been hoping for a practical test, and this mission would have been ideal for it.

The good news was that the route provided by the Cardassian resistance had done the trick, and the three Starfleet vessels arrived at the outpost unmolested. The other good news was that Intelligence was right, and there were only two Jem'Hadar strike ships guarding the outpost.

The rest of the news was rather bad.

For one thing, the outpost itself turned out to be armed with energy weapons of a type Gomez didn't recognize. They plowed through the *Fredrickson's* shields with little effort, leaving the *Excelsior*-class ship a sitting duck for the Jem'Hadar. It was destroyed within two minutes of their arrival in the sector.

"Steinberg, give me a reading on that damn weapon!" Gomez bellowed at her assistant chief.

In a voice as calm as hers was frantic, the black-haired lieutenant said, "I'm almost finished with my analysis, Commander."

"Finish faster." She gazed at the viewscreen that showed what the bridge had on their main viewer. The *Musashi* had gotten some shots into the outpost before one of the Jem'Hadar ships cut them off. Now each ship had the Jem'Hadar on their tail, with the outpost itself taking potshots as well.

The *Sentinel's* shields were now down to twenty percent.

Patel's voice sounded over the comm systems. *"Divert power to shields."*

In addition to getting their new assignment, the *Sentinel* had gotten crew replacements at DS9. One of them, a kid who didn't look old enough to be let out of his house alone, said, "I can't get the power to divert to the shields!" Gomez could hear the panic in the young man's voice.

"Take it from wherever you need it, Ensign, just keep the shields up."

"No, it's not that—the control circuits are fused."

Gomez rolled her eyes. "If you can't reprogram, reroute."

The ensign nodded quickly. "Right, of course. Sorry, Commander."

"Just keep your head cool." *Was I ever that young and stupid?* Gomez thought.

"Commander," Steinberg said, "if we bring the shield frequency down to the lower regions, we should be able to defend against the outpost's weapon."

"Lower?"

"Yes, sir."

It was a counterintuitive move—which, no doubt, was the Dominion's thinking.

The baby ensign said, "Shields back up to eighty percent."

"Nice work," Gomez said. "Steinberg, bring the frequency down."

"Aye," the lieutenant said.

She tapped her combadge. "Bridge, we're lowering shield frequency—that should allow us to defend against the outpost. Recommend transmitting data to the *Musashi* immediately."

"*Acknowledged,*" Patel said. "*Good job, Gomez.*"

The Jem'Hadar ship then fired on them again, pounding at the shields.

"At this frequency," Steinberg said, "we've got to keep them at sixty percent, or the Jem'Hadar will rip us to pieces."

Gomez went through the mental picture of the *Sentinel* in her head. The *Akira*-class ship had a compact, retro design, reminiscent of the old pre-Federation Earth starships. There wasn't a lot of wasted space. Still . . .

"Bridge, we need to evac decks eight, nine, and ten

right away." Those were crew quarters, holodecks, and recreational facilities—none of them necessary right now, and only minimal staff was there at present.

Amalfitano and Patel, bless their hearts, didn't even question the request. *"Attention all hands,"* Amalfitano said. *"This is the captain. Evacuate decks eight, nine, and ten immediately."*

"Steinberg, the second everyone's out of those decks, cut off all power, and divert as much of it as you can to the shields." Silently, Gomez cursed whichever idiot designer thought it was a good idea to make holodeck systems incompatible with other ship systems. *We really could use that power right now.* But at least the other power that was used for those decks would be put to good use.

Chatter from the bridge came over the intercom.

"Continuous fire on the Jem'Hadar."

"Their aft shields are failing."

"Concentrate fire there, Grimnar."

"Aye, sir."

"Tenmei, bring us to 253 mark 9, try to drive a wedge between them."

"Direct hit—our shields are down to sixty-five percent."

Steinberg looked at Gomez. "Sir, we can't keep this up—if we stick with the lower frequency, we're more vulnerable to the Jem'Hadar."

"We're not exactly overburdened with options," Gomez said.

"Shields are down."

Gomez turned. "What the hell happened?"

Steinberg checked a console. "Lucky shot—they got through to one of our emitters."

"The Jem'Hadar don't rely on luck," Gomez said. "And neither do we—reroute, get the shields back up to full. Are those three decks evacuated yet?"

"Not yet."

"We can't wait, divert the power."

"Aye, sir."

Even on as small a ship as the *Sentinel*, there was considerable waste in the life support system. Even with it taken off-line, there would be enough air just sitting in the corridors to last a couple of hours, and at red alert, they'd probably all have wristlamps in any case. *And if they don't, that's just too damn bad,* she thought, a bit unkindly. *They should've evac'd by now.*

The young ensign—whose name, she finally remembered, was Natale—said, "Shields back up to full. Sir, this juryrig won't last, request permission to rewire junction 92A5."

Gomez frowned, then smiled. "Good idea." That junction was a backup for holodeck systems, and could easily accommodate a shield rerouting, at least for a couple of hours. It would take a few minutes, but the present setup would hold in the meanwhile.

"Thank you, sir." Ensign Natale moved off, grinning with an enthusiasm that Gomez remembered seeing in the mirror back when she was the dumb young ensign and Geordi La Forge was the chief engineer doling out praise only when earned.

She often missed those days on the *Enterprise*. She had so many good friends there—Lian T'su, Reg Barclay, Gar Costa, Wes Crusher, Ella Clancy, Denny Russell. Even La Forge was more a friend than he ever really was a CO.

And, of course, Kieran. Lovable, goofy, wonderful Kieran.

One of the other engineers cried out from near the warp core, startling her out of her all-too-brief reverie. "Commander, containment system's fluctuating—we've got to take the warp drive off-line."

Dammit, dammit, dammit. "Do it." She tapped her combadge. "Bridge, we've lost warp drive."

"Not much of an issue right now," Patel said. *"At least you got shields reenergized."*

Gomez pursed her lips. "Yeah, but our hat's running out of rabbits."

As if on cue, one of the Jem'Hadar strike ships exploded.

"Maybe yours is." Gomez could visualize Patel's toothy grin.

"Sir, the Musashi *has lost shields. The other Jem'Hadar ship is moving in."*

"Tenmei, cut them off, draw their fire."

"Aye, sir."

The maneuver apparently worked, as the *Sentinel* started taking dozens more hits, from both the outpost and the Jem'Hadar. "We can't keep this up," Steinberg said, the first sign of tenseness creeping into an exterior that was normally a Vulcanlike calm; the noncoms had nicknamed him "T'Steinberg."

"Easy, Steinberg, we'll be fine." Gomez tried to sound reassuring, but she was too busy trying to figure out what the *Musashi* was doing. *It looked like . . .*

No!

The *Musashi* was on a suicide run—headed straight for the outpost.

The Jem'Hadar realized it too, obviously, as it and the outpost both changed their firing pattern to concentrate on the *Musashi.*

Amalfitano's voice cried out, *"Tenmei, get between them and the* Musashi. *We have to give them time!"*

Two seconds that seemed like hours passed, and the *Musashi* rammed into the Dominion outpost, annihilating it.

Sonya Gomez learned the most valuable lesson of her life shortly after she reported to the *Enterprise,* and the Borg carved a section out of the ship's hull, costing the ship eighteen crew members. When she found she couldn't get her mind around the loss of eighteen people, La Forge had said the words that she spoke now, over a decade later, to her staff:

"We'll have time to grieve later. Steinberg, get the shields back to their regular frequency. Ensign, how's our juryrig?"

"Almost done," Natale called out from under a console.

"Be done, I want this ship with full defenses."

"*Grimnar*," Amalfitano was saying even as Gomez spoke, "*give the Jem'Hadar everything we've got.*"

Two seconds that actually seemed like two seconds later, the Jem'Hadar ship exploded in a satisfying conflagration, a plume of fire that was quickly consumed by the vacuum of space.

Which left the *Sentinel* alone amid a cloud of debris that used to be four starships and an outpost, behind enemy lines, without warp power.

"*Engineering*," Patel said, "*how soon can you get the warp drive up and running?*"

Gomez and Steinberg walked over to inspect the warp core. "Give us a minute."

Amalfitano said, "*Make it a quick minute, Commander—the Jem'Hadar called for backup, and I really don't want to be here when they arrive.*"

Grimnar's voice cut in. "*Long-range sensors are picking up a Breen ship.*"

"*Then we're dead.*" That, to Gomez, sounded like Ensign Simas, a notorious doomsayer whom Gomez had rotated out of the engine room due to the effect he had on morale. She wondered how the hell he contrived to get bridge duty.

She also wondered if there was some way she could change the readings that were now displayed in front of her and Steinberg.

Patel said, "*Grimnar, how soon before the Breen get here?*"

"*At present speed, one hour, ten minutes.*"

"I was afraid of that," Gomez said. "Captain, we won't be able to get the warp drive up and running in less than two hours."

What if we do a cold restart?

Gomez couldn't help but smile. "That estimate was *with* a cold restart, Captain."

"They'll know we're an enemy vessel a lot sooner than that," Grimnar said. *"The debris will mask us for a little while, but the closer they get, the more likely they are to see us for what we are, in which case they may increase speed."*

"No they won't," Gomez said without even realizing at first why she said it. Then she spent half a second thinking it through. "Steinberg, get to work on the warp core. Natale, you're with me—we need to bring the warp field on-line and reconfigure it."

Natale frowned. "What's the point of bringing the warp field on-line if we can't go to warp? Isn't that a huge waste of energy—especially if we don't have the matter/antimatter system on-line?"

The ensign's question was reasonable. Without the power provided by the constant annihilation of matter and antimatter in the core, the ship was running on emergency power. *But then,* Gomez thought, *if this doesn't constitute an emergency, I don't know what does.*

Before she could explain things to Natale, Amalfitano asked, *"Are you thinking what I think you're thinking, Commander?"*

"Yes, Captain—we're going to reconfigure the warp field so those Breen think we're a Cardassian freighter."

Patel chuckled. *"I guess your idea gets a practical run-through after all, Sonya."*

"So it would seem, sir, yes."

"Get someone up here to install the holofilter on the comm systems," Amalfitano said. *"We're gonna need to talk our way through this too, and I think I'll be more convincing as a gul than a captain."*

"Yes, sir."

Gomez sent two of her people up to the bridge, then sat down with Natale and called up her specs for the warp field reconfiguration. Natale whistled. "Impressive work, Commander, if you don't mind my saying so."

"I do mind, Ensign," she said, all seriousness—then broke into a grin. "Say that again after it works."

"Yes, sir," Natale said, returning the grin.

Good, Gomez thought, *he's set the grief aside. He's not thinking about all the people who've died today—he's focused on what he has to do to keep himself from being added to the list. That's the only way we're gonna get through this.*

Amazingly enough, the Breen bought it.

Gomez had been far too busy—first getting the warp field realigned, then helping Steinberg and the others get the containment unit up and running so that they could use the warp drive—to know what was happening on the bridge. All she knew was that the Breen ship went away after what she imagined was a tense fifteen minutes.

One hour and forty-seven minutes after they started, Gomez tapped her combadge and said, "Bridge, warp drive is on-line."

"Two hours, huh?" Patel said.

"We were motivated to speed it up," Gomez said with a relieved smile at Steinberg, who returned it.

"Good work down there," Amalfitano said. *"But keep that realigned warp field. We're not on a timetable now, and I'm just as happy to stay at warp four if people will think we're Cardassian."*

"No problem, Captain."

She gave Steinberg a glance, and he nodded. "On it."

Taking a look around at her staff, she took pride in what they had accomplished. In what *she* had accomplished. The idea of realigning the warp field had come to her in a night of tinkering—one of those inspirations that suddenly slams you behind the eyes. She stayed up all night working out the logistics, then brought it to Patel, who in turn brought it to Amalfitano, who told her to bring it to the meeting on DS9.

An inspiration that quite probably saved all their lives.

It wasn't until they crossed safely back into Federation space—after being passed by several Jem'Hadar ships that didn't challenge them—that Gomez allowed herself to feel for the hundreds of people lost on the *Musashi* and the *Fredrickson*. The grief was only slightly alleviated by the news that the strike on Orias III was successful. It was a major victory for the Alpha Quadrant.

ANDROSSI VESSEL OVERSEEN BY BIRON STARDATE 53678.9

Biron was starting to form a clearer picture of what it was that had enabled the crew of the *U.S.S. da Vinci* to outwit and defeat him on two occasions. It was something he never would have deduced based on the empirical evidence he had acquired in his face-to-face encounters.

The crew of the *U.S.S. da Vinci* improvised.

Biron always approached every mission with a carefully laid-out plan. True, there were always variables, but rarely did they impinge upon the plan to a degree that was mathematically significant.

On the other hand, the *U.S.S. da Vinci* crew seemed to be able to adapt to variables with great ease. Where the variables—mostly introduced by the very presence of the *U.S.S. da Vinci*—on the planet Maeglin and at the space station Empok Nor had proven to be too much for Biron to overcome, his opponents seemed to thrive on it.

Perhaps it was because they were so actively involved in military engagements. While Biron did occasionally have to defend his ship and engage in battle situations, they were comparatively rare. Androssi military engagements were handled by the Elite's standing army, supplemented as necessary by members of the worker class conscripted into service.

He would need to factor this ability into his plans.

That and the Starfleet people's inexplicable predilection for forming personal attachments. That was a definite weakness that Biron needed to exploit.

He made a note of these items, and then continued his research. One particular mission of the *U.S.S. da Vinci* conducted during the war against the Dominion piqued his interest. . . .

U.S.S. DA VINCI
STARDATE 51993.8

Fabian Stevens materialized in a remarkably tiny transporter room.

At least this one can be called a "room," he thought. During his last Starfleet tour, the young engineer had served on the *U.S.S. Defiant,* a warship that had a transporter room so small, they referred to it as the "transporter bay." This ship—the *Saber*-class *U.S.S. da Vinci*—was only slightly larger than the *Defiant,* which gave it at least the capacity to have a proper transporter *room*.

He looked over to see that the Nasat engineer—she called herself P8 Blue, but told Fabian that "Pattie" was an acceptable form of address—and the golf ball had both materialized next to him.

It wasn't really a golf ball, of course—unless the golf game was being played by creatures fifteen times the size of humans—but the spheroid's resemblance to an outsized version of the ball from the Earth game was uncanny. Its surface was a glossy white substance of some kind, and covered with slight circular indentations. It had no visible seams; the small indentations enabled it to sit still on a flat surface without rolling.

"Welcome to the *da Vinci*," said a steady voice from the mahogany-skinned Vulcan who stood on one side of the transporter console. "I am Salek, first officer of the *da Vinci* and commanding officer of the S.C.E. team aboard ship. You must be Stevens and Blue."

The Nasat—who looked like a giant blue pillbug, albeit with eight legs—made an odd tinkling noise, then said, "Correct."

"Reporting for duty, as ordered, sir," Fabian added.

The tall, sandy-haired human who stood on the other side of the console from Salek grinned. "And that must be our new toy."

"Yes, sir, it is," Fabian said.

"I'm Kieran Duffy—second officer of the ship, second-in-command of the S.C.E. team. You're looking for second-best, you come to me."

Fabian smiled. "I'll keep that in mind, sir." He'd been worried when he found out that the S.C.E.'s CO on this ship was a Vulcan that things would be stiffer and more formal than he was used to. If this Duffy character was any indication, though . . .

Turning to the transporter operator, Salek said, "Chief Feliciano, transfer the device to the lab."

"Yes, sir," said the black-haired human.

Salek turned back to Fabian and Pattie. "Your personal effects—including your larvae," he added with a look directly at Pattie, "have been sent to your cabins. The majority of the complement of the *da Vinci* share quarters. You will be sharing accommodations with our cultural specialist, Dr. Abramowitz, and Stevens will do likewise with our linguist, Dr. Okha."

"Sounds chummy," Fabian said.

One of Salek's eyebrows climbed up his forehead. "In a word, yes. Duffy will escort you to your quarters. It is now 1432 hours. The entire S.C.E. team will meet in the lab at 1500 hours to discuss our mission."

Pattie made another tinkly sound. "We'll be there, sir."

"Good. Come with me," he said to the Nasat, and led her out of the room.

Fabian regarded the second officer. "A linguist and a cultural specialist? I thought you S.C.E. types built bridges and orbital platforms and stuff."

Duffy smiled. "Only if we have to. Didn't you read up on us before taking this glorious assignment?" he asked as they departed the transporter room and turned left.

"Honestly, no. Until two days ago, I thought I was being assigned to Utopia Planitia. Then I find out that there's an opening on the S.C.E. team on the *da Vinci*—I didn't even know there were S.C.E. teams on ships."

"Yup. Have been for as long as there's been a Starfleet. Right now, we've got four *Saber*-class ships that all have the same kinda setup. The *Musgrave*, the *T'Pora*, and the *Khwarizmi* are the other three. We gad about the galaxy, righting wrongs, saving damsels in distress, and reaping glory worthy of our exalted status."

Fabian blinked. "Really?"

"No, not really. Actually, we gad about the galaxy fixing things, saving machines in distress, and getting no glory whatsoever, but what the hey—it's a living. And sometimes what we have to fix is written in another language or it belongs to someone else, so people like Chan and Carol come in handy." They walked up to a door. "Here you go."

Shaking his head, Fabian said, "Bunking up with someone else—it'll be like old home week."

"How so?" Duffy asked with a slight frown.

"I used to serve on the *Defiant* under Chief O'Brien. We—"

A huge grin bisected Duffy's face. "You know the chief?"

Laughing, Fabian said, "Know him? He ran me ragged for two years. Actually, he was great to work for."

"I bet he was. He and I were both on the *Enterprise* together. Hey, look, the quarters are pretty boring, as quarters go, and we've both got half an hour—let me buy you a drink, and we can compare Miles O'Brien stories."

"Sounds good to me, Commander."

Twenty minutes later, Fabian was halfway through a cup of coffee—he hadn't really gotten a good night's sleep since leaving Mars for Starbase 375, thence to meet up with the golf ball and Pattie and then report to the da Vinci—and Duffy was on his second quinine water with a twist of lime. Fabian was hearing all about the chief's wedding.

"We had a pool going as to how badly Data would screw up the dancing, but he was sure-footed as all get-out. You would believe an android can cha-cha?"

"Where'd he learn?" Fabian asked.

"Rumor had it that Dr. Crusher taught him, but I never bought that. Crusher never seemed to me to be the dancing type." He gulped down the remainder of his water, then asked, "So what's your story, Stevens? What brought you back into Starfleet after two years under the chief's thumb?"

"Well, my tour ended right after we lost a good friend of mine—Enrique Muniz. Good guy, great engineer, awful poker player."

Duffy smiled. "Everything you want in a shipmate."

"Something like that. He died on a mission to salvage a Jem'Hadar ship." Fabian shook his head. "It's funny, I always knew the risks, but it never seemed real until Muniz died. So I decided I'd had enough. I didn't re-up, went home to the Rigel colonies, and helped my parents out with their shuttle service while I tried to figure out what to do with my life."

"And you figured you'd come back to Starfleet?"

Fabian nodded. "The war kind of figured it out for me. I was bored to death on Rigel, and I realized I missed Starfleet. And then, when the war kicked into high gear, I—well, corny as it sounds, I figured it was my duty to sign back up. Besides, I figured there'd be a need for engineers."

Duffy grinned. "You got that right." He looked up. "Computer, time?"

The time is 1457 hours.

"We'd better get going," Duffy said, getting up. "Don't want to be late for your first meeting."

"That would be bad, yes," Fabian said, also rising.

"We'll pick this up later. If nothing else, I want to know exactly how it is that the chief had a second kid by way of a Bajoran major."

"Okay, but only if you tell me how Commander Worf, of all people, midwifed Molly."

Another grin. "Deal."

"The device was found in the wreck of a Jem'Hadar ship that was taken from Chin'toka three weeks, four days ago," Salek said as he stood next to the golf ball.

The *da Vinci*'s main lab was a good-sized room—for a ship this small, anyhow—currently occupied by Salek, Duffy, Pattie, and Fabian, as well as two short, dark-haired humans, one male and one female, and a Bynar pairing. The latter wore civilian garb; Fabian had had no idea that there were any Bynars working with Starfleet, though he was grateful. No better computer experts existed in the galaxy.

First Duffy had performed the introductions. The humans were Chan Okha, ship's linguist, and Carol Abramowitz, the cultural specialist. The Bynars had the designations of 110 and 111, though Fabian knew it was going to take him weeks to remember which was which. They didn't look alike, of course, but they were sufficiently similar—and seemed to cluster together and move as a unit—making it difficult to know where one short, bald-headed, slim-limbed alien began and the other ended.

"The ship itself provided no useful intelligence that Starfleet did not already possess, but this device was found on the vessel's main bridge. P8 Blue was part of the team that salvaged the device." Salek then nodded at the Nasat.

Standing on her hind legs, Pattie stepped forward. "Thus far, there isn't much to tell. The device doesn't have any obvious function, and scans have detected material unknown to Starfleet databases. However, the scan we did was cursory at best."

Duffy smiled. "So our job is to curse a bit less?"

Making another one of those tinkly sounds, Pattie said, "Something like that, yes."

Fabian noticed that Salek made no reaction to Duffy whatsoever. He would have expected some kind of noise of disapproval from the stolid Vulcan, but Salek remained all business. *That'll teach me to stereotype people*, he thought ruefully.

One of the Bynars started to speak: "We might be able—"

Then the other Bynar continued. "—to integrate with—"

"—the computer systems of the device—"

"—and learn its function."

Okay, Fabian thought, *that's going to take a lot of getting used to.* He knew that Bynar pairs were heavily integrated, but he'd never actually met any before, and so was unaware that they finished each other's sentences like that.

"That would be a logical step to take," Salek said. "However, precautions should be taken."

Abramowitz said, "So Okha and I are here, why exactly? Cheerleading?"

Salek regarded the woman. "I assume, Dr. Abramowitz, that you are sufficiently versed in the cultures of the Dominion member races that the Federation and its allies have come into contact with that you might be able to provide some insight into the device."

Okha grinned. "And I can cheerlead in fifteen different languages. Thirty, if you count the dead ones."

"Really?" Duffy said. "How *do* you say 'sis-boom-bah' in Old High Andorii?"

While the banter went on, Fabian noticed something: the surface of the golf ball looked familiar somehow. He hadn't realized it before, but Salek's comment about Dominion member races started the gears turning in his mind.

Before he could pursue this, he noticed a subtle change in the vibration of the bulkheads.

Duffy looked up. "We just went to warp."

"Warp eight, from the feel of it," Pattie said.

Fabian frowned. "Feels more like warp seven to me."

Salek raised an eyebrow again. "We are, in fact, traveling at warp seven-point-three."

Pattie made another tinkly noise—Fabian noted that each one had sounded different, and he wondered if he'd ever figure out how they related to her emotional state.

"*Saber*s are like the *Defiant*," Fabian said to the Nasat. "Overpowered and undersized, so it's easy to overestimate how fast they're going."

"Two quatloos to the new guy," Duffy said with a grin.

A voice sounded over the speakers. "*S.C.E. team, report to the observation lounge.*"

"That's us, folks," Duffy said. "Let's go."

Within a few minutes, they all reassembled in the observation lounge, another small room, but this one with a big window that looked out on the distorted starfield that indicated that the *da Vinci* was at warp. Three others were present in addition to the group that had been gathered in the lab. One was a medium-height human with snow-white hair, bushy eyebrows, and grandfatherly blue eyes. The four pips and red trim on his uniform indicated that he was Captain David Gold. From what Fabian understood, the captain had no background in engineering, so he was unclear as to what the older man was doing supervising a group of engineers.

Then he thought about the engineers he'd known in his time, and realized that it was probably better this way. . . .

The other two were a human woman with blond hair tied back severely in a bun and a Bolian man with no hair whatsoever. The former wore gold, the latter blue, which made it tough to tell where his collar ended and his neck began. The thickness of the ridge that bisected his face and the looseness of his skin indicated that he was quite old.

Everyone sat except for Pattie, who explained quickly that chairs on starships "weren't built with me in mind," and Gold began the meeting.

"First of all," he said in a pleasant but authoritative voice, "I'd like to welcome our two new crewmembers aboard. Fabian Stevens, P8 Blue, welcome to the *da Vinci*. I'm Captain David Gold, and they tell me I run the place. I assume you know most of the team. This," he indicated the human, "is Lt. Commander Corsi, our chief of security, and our chief medical officer," he now indicated the Bolian, "Dr. Tydoan."

The Bolian nodded his head and said, "A pleasure. You'll both need to report for physicals within the next three days."

"Assuming they have time to," Gold added quickly. "I know we've got that widget from Starbase 375 to look at, and that still needs to get done. But we've got another priority ahead of it." The captain touched a control on the desk, and the viewscreen behind him lit up with a schematic from what looked to Fabian like a standard Federation communications relay station. Such stations were positioned throughout Federation space, boosting comm signals a thousandfold and allowing near-instantaneous communication across most of the Federation. During the war, those relays were of even greater value. Fabian also noticed that the one showing on the screen had taken some rather severe damage.

"This is a comm relay in the Phicus system. Some Cardassian ships carved a chunk out of it yesterday, and we need to fix it, pronto."

Corsi leaned forward. "Sir, the Phicus system is hardly what I'd call secure. We've been holding on to it by our fingernails."

"Calm down, Corsi," Gold said, "we're gonna have support. The *Appalachia* and the *Sloane* will meet us at the relay."

Fabian recognized both ships as *Steamrunner*-class vessels. *Not bad for support*, he thought, *but a hair skimpy*.

Apparently, the security chief felt the same way. "Sir, that's insane. The Cardassians have been dancing on the edge of that system for weeks. We can't go in there with only two ships for backup. Starfleet has to—"

Gold held up a hand. "Way ahead of you, Corsi. I already asked Starfleet what was in the Saurian brandy they were drinking when they cut those orders. Turns out that's all they can spare for now."

"We can't wait until more backup's available?"

"It won't be for forty-eight hours, and the relay can't wait that long to be fixed."

Security chiefs are all alike, Fabian thought as he watched Corsi fold her arms. She had the universal cranky look that all the security chiefs that Fabian had ever met had.

"We'll arrive at Phicus in twelve hours." Gold then gave Salek a nod.

The Vulcan, who had been sitting with his elbows on the table and fingers steepled together in front of his face, leaned back and unclasped his hands, leaving them to rest on the tabletop. "We will continue our examination of the Dominion device until we arrive at Phicus. At that point, Duffy, Blue, and I will commence with repairs on the communications relay. Stevens, 110, and 111 will continue their examination of the device, with the assistance of Okha and Abramowitz."

"Hey, maybe we'll luck out and dope it out before we get there," Duffy said with a smile.

Salek turned to Duffy. "Luck is not something upon which we should depend."

Still smiling, Duffy said, "S'why I said 'maybe.' "

"Let's get to it, people," Gold said, rising from his chair. Everyone else did likewise.

Corsi, Fabian noticed, still looked aggravated. Okha and Tydoan looked bored. The rest of the team, however, seemed eager to get at the problem, as everyone made a beeline for the lab.

I think I'm gonna like it here, Fabian thought.

Twelve hours later, Fabian wasn't liking it here so much.

The Bynar pair had attempted to interface with the golf ball, but had found no way to access the systems. Sensors indicated *some* kind of mechanism, but if there was a computerized intelligence behind it, they couldn't find it.

At least, they couldn't find it via sensors. Ideally, they would just open it up and take a peek, but they found no access ports either.

"Geez, even a real golf ball has *seams,*" Fabian finally said in frustration as the latest attempt to gain ingress met with failure.

"Not this one," Duffy said with a sigh.

Pattie made one of her tinkly noises. "Perhaps we should attempt to use a phaser on the golf ball."

"That is an unacceptable risk," Salek said. "The device was found on the bridge. Logically, that means it might well be a weapon—or, at the very least, be booby-trapped."

"Yeah, the Jem'Hadar wouldn't have it on the bridge," said Duffy, "if it wasn't important."

"Or if it wasn't theirs."

Fabian turned to see that Abramowitz was speaking.

"You're all leaving out one possibility," she continued. "What if the Jem'Hadar found it and they don't know what it is either? Maybe it really *is* a golf ball with a pituitary problem."

"There is an indication—" 110 started.

111 finished. "—of electronics within the golf ball."

"So?" Abramowitz shrugged, her short black hair bouncing slightly. "Maybe it's a gyroscope to keep it on track after it's been hit off the tee."

Laughing, Fabian said, "You play golf?"

Abramowitz nodded.

"Go fig'. I thought my grandfather was the only person left in the Federation who played."

"Nah," Duffy said, "I had an aunt and uncle who played too. My parents used to send me to stay with them whenever I was being too annoying."

Fabian found himself speaking without thinking, his frustration at twelve hours of dead ends lowering his resistance. "Spent a lot of time with them, did you?" He immediately regretted speaking up. True, Duffy had a relaxed manner, but he *was* an officer, and they didn't usually take kindly to the enlisted folk making snide remarks.

To Fabian's relief, however, Duffy just laughed and said, "More than I would've liked to, yeah. Never took to the game, though. I was always about eight million over par."

"As diverting as this discussion of human gaming practices is," Salek said, "we should return to the business at hand. While Abramowitz's suggestion has merit, we must assume, for the nonce, that this belongs to the Dominion or one of its allies."

Blinking, Fabian looked at the golf ball again. *One of its allies.* Once again, he had that familiar feeling, and those words triggered it.

Then, finally, it hit him. "That's it!"

"What is 'it'?" Salek asked.

"I *knew* I'd seen something like this before." He turned to the others. "A few years back, I was serving on the *Defiant.* We went into the Gamma Quadrant to mediate a trade dispute involving the Federation, the Karemma, and the Ferengi. A couple Jem'Hadar ships attacked and we all wound up in the atmosphere of a gas giant."

"All?" Duffy asked, sounding serious for once.

"It was us, two Jem'Hadar, and a Karemma ship. At one point, the Jem'Hadar fired on us, but the torpedo didn't detonate on impact like it was supposed to." He smiled. "Dumb luck, really, but it kept us alive long enough to get out of it in one piece. The funny thing is, the torpedo was designed by the Karemma."

"Aside from the obvious irony," Pattie said, "how does that help us?"

"The surface of this thing is made of the same material as that torpedo. It didn't have any visible seams, either, but Quark managed to get it open."

110 and 111 exchanged glances. "You got it open—"

"—with a subatomic particle?"

"Uh, no," Fabian said, trying to hold back a laugh. "Quark is a Ferengi bartender."

"The *Defiant*'s a warship that's even smaller than this," Pattie said. "How did you have room for a bartender?"

Fabian felt himself losing control of the conversation. "He wasn't the bartender on the ship, he—"

Salek mercifully interrupted. "As fascinating as this discussion is, I'm afraid it will have to wait. We will be arriving at the Phicus system in ten minutes, thirty seconds. Duffy, Blue, you're with me. The rest of you, carry on."

Fabian stared at Okha, Abramowitz, and the two Bynars. "'Carry on,' huh?" He shook his head. "So, should I finish the story?"

"There was a story?" Abramowitz asked.

"*Sorial estarifo,*" Okha said suddenly.

Everyone looked at him.

Okha shrugged. "That's the closest I can come to 'sis-boom-bah' in Old High Andorii."

The Bynars stared at the linguist for a moment, then turned as one toward Fabian. "How was this bartender—"

"—able to get at the mechanism—"

"—of the torpedo?"

Fabian sighed. "He wouldn't tell us. He said he

used a regular tool kit, and made a comment about never revealing a trade secret." He looked up. "Computer, compare sensor readings of the device to that of the Jem'Hadar torpedo confiscated aboard the *U.S.S. Defiant* on stardate 49265. Is there a design correlation?"

"Material used to house specified Jem'Hadar torpedo is a ninety-nine-percent correlation to the material used for the surface of the device."

"Okay, so it's almost definitely Karemma."

"Do they play golf?" Abramowitz asked.

"Not to my knowledge," Fabian said, finding himself unclear as to whether or not the cultural specialist was serious. "What I need is a standard emergency tool kit."

Okha snorted. "Good luck." At Fabian's questioning look, the linguist continued. "This is an S.C.E. ship. There's nothing 'standard' on here. Everything is top-of-the-line and refurbished and toyed with and tinkered with."

Fabian sighed and started putting together a mental list. Quark managed to get the torpedo open with nothing but the equipment found in a standard emergency tool kit, and Fabian was damned if he was going to let that Ferengi troll outdo him. . . .

Salek fit the ODN conduit into the communications relay with a gloved hand. That meant that he was now done with seventy-six percent of the work he had assigned to himself to do, and should have his tasks completed within the hour. He reached into the supply case that he had magnetically attached to the side of the relay in order to retrieve another new ODN conduit. Several dozen of them had been vaporized by the Cardassian attack, and several more damaged, as were many isolinear optical chips. Salek had appointed himself the task of replacing them. Even as he did so to one of the outer sections of the relay—remaining tethered to it via his magnetic boots—Duffy was reattaching the relay's hull plating in another section. Both of them wore EVA suits. Blue, meanwhile, had gone to work on the transmitter array.

As he pulled out the latest conduit, he activated the communicator in his EVA suit.

"Away team, report."

"Aft hull plating's almost welded on," Duffy reported. *"Then I can get to the fore. Pity I don't have the golf ball, then I could play through."*

Blue's voice then came over the comm line. *"Transmitter array should be online in about twenty minutes."*

"Excellent. I have replaced half of the ODN conduits and all of the isolinear chips. Carry on."

Salek, of course, did not bother to rein in Lt. Commander Duffy's humorous excesses, having long since realized that they were part and parcel of his personality, and they never interfered with his ability to perform his duty. Salek, therefore, had no reason to complain.

His sister had cautioned him against signing on with the S.C.E. She had encouraged him to take a post on the *T'Kumbra,* with its all-Vulcan crew, but Salek did not see the logic in that. Besides, there were no positions available for a lieutenant commander on that vessel, and he saw even less logic in taking an inferior position.

"The humans are so—emotional," his sister had said, as if this were some great revelation.

"Of course they are," he had told her. "And Betazoids are telepathic, Tellarites are aggressive, and Andorians are blue. These are well-documented facts. I see no reason for any of them to interfere with my choice of posting. Unless you think so little of me that you expect me to succumb to emotionalism simply by being around them."

"No," his sister had replied. "I simply do not wish you to suffer needlessly."

"I fail to see how I will suffer."

His sister had dropped the subject after that, for which Salek was grateful. He had found his assignment as first officer of the *da Vinci* to be most satisfactory. They performed an important service for the Federation, and the crew under him was exemplary.

Salek was especially pleased with the arrival of the Nasat engineer. P8 Blue could survive without an EVA suit in a vacuum for as long as she could hold her breath—a figure measured in hours—and that, combined with her multiple, more flexible limbs, allowed her access to places a suited humanoid couldn't get at. Her presence cut their repair time by a factor of ten—a not inconsiderable amount, especially given the precariousness of this system. Lt. Commander Corsi's fears regarding the Cardassians were well founded.

Looking out into space, Salek saw the hulls of the *Sloane* and the *Appalachia*—illuminated by running lights—in a defensive position proximate to the relay. At present, he could not see the *da Vinci*, as its orbit had taken it to the other side of the relay relative to Salek's own position.

"Uh oh."

Frowning, Salek activated his comm link to Duffy. "Report." He commenced with replacing the next ODN conduit.

"I just found something that I think is—oh, crap. Duffy to da Vinci*."*

"Go ahead," said Gold's voice.

"There's a beacon of some kind in the comm relay—it looks like Cardassian tech. As far as I can tell, it's relaying sensor data via a subspace comm link."

"Deactivate it immediately," Salek said.

"I'm not sure I can yet, but even if I do, I don't think

it'll make a difference. I'm picking up a Cardassian trans-porter trace on the thing."

Salek's eyebrow raised. "In all likelihood, the Cardassians who attempted to take this system beamed it into the relay."

"Damn," Gold said. *"Duffy, hold off on deactivating it for a minute. What kind of data is it sending?"*

"Not sure yet. Give me a minute."

"Sir, we cannot allow the beacon to remain active," Salek said. He continued his work on the ODN conduit, as he was easily capable of splitting his focus. "It represents a security risk."

"So does deactivating it. It means they know we found it and they may come back to try to take another shot at the comm relay. It might be more useful to us as a decoy. If it's there to eavesdrop on our comm channels, we might be able to turn it to our advantage. Deliberately feed false intel through the relay."

Not for the first time, Salek was reminded as to why Starfleet did not assign engineers to captain the S.C.E. vessels. Sometimes a more galactic perspective was needed on their missions. It was a most logical setup, as Salek had not thought of the possible tactical uses of the beacon.

"It's a nice idea, sir," Duffy said, *"but I don't think it's gonna work. I just tapped into what, exactly, this thing is sending. If my tricorder's reading its Cardassian right, it just sent an SOS out. It knows we found it."*

Salek heard a sigh from Gold. *"That tears it, then. Yellow alert. McAllan, alert the* Sloane *and the* Appalachia *that we may be having company soon, then see if Starfleet can deign to send us some backup. Duffy, kill that thing before it sends over full technical specs of all three ships. Salek, how much time do you have left?"*

"Approximately forty-four minutes, twenty-nine seconds."

Gold snorted a laugh. *"The* proper *definition of the*

*word 'approximately' you should someday learn, Salek.
All right, get a move on. Can you get the work done faster
with more people?"*

Just as he finished replacing the latest ODN conduit,
he replied, "Negative. There are only two areas that
need repair work of the type that can be accomplished
by humanoids in EVA suits. Additional personnel would
simply be in the way. The remaining tasks can only be
performed by Blue."

"Gee," Blue said, *"only on board a few hours and
already indispensable. It's good to be me."* She made a
noise that corresponded in the Nasat lexicon to laughter.

*"So why are you wasting time jabbering at me? Gold
out."*

Salek, of course, had been working while talking to
the captain, but there was little to be gained by reac-
quiring the comm signal and pointing that out.

"Got it!" Duffy said. *"Okay, this puppy won't bark no
more."*

Salek interpreted this comment to mean that he had
successfully deactivated the beacon.

The second officer continued. *"If the Cardassians
want to know what's coming through this relay, they'll
have to come here themselves."* A pause. *"Not that I,
y'know, want that or anything, but—never mind. Duffy to
Feliciano. Diego, lock onto the piece of equipment half a
meter in front of me and beam it to the lab. Tell the new
guy not to touch it."*

"Yes, sir."

As Salek began removing a damaged ODN conduit,
he wondered how Stevens, 110, and 111 were proceed-
ing with the attempt to ascertain the function of the
Dominion device.

A sonic driver. A lousy, rotten, stinking sonic driver.
Fabian had managed to cobble together the actual

components of a standard emergency tool kit from
the assorted tool kits on the *da Vinci*—all of which
were far better equipped than any tool kit he'd
worked with on the *Defiant* or on Deep Space 9.
While he did so, a small device that—to Fabian's
experienced eye after serving on a Cardassian-built
space station for two years—looked to be of Cardassian design was beamed into the lab. Chief Feliciano
said that Duffy had told "the new guy" not to touch it.
Fabian plotted several types of revenge on Duffy for
the crack while he started trying each of the tools on
the golf ball.

For whatever reason, the emissions of the sonic driver had two effects—they made 110 and 111 wince and
they removed a panel of the golf ball. Said panel had no
visible seams until after it came off.

"How'd you do that?" Okha asked.

"Don't know, don't care," Fabian said, taking out his
tricorder. Then his eyes widened at what the display
told him. "Wow." He looked over at the Bynars. "Are you
two reading what I'm reading?"

"If you are reading—"

"—several dozen weapons systems—"

"—a propulsion system—"

"—and a sophisticated computer core—"

"—then yes, we are reading—"

"—what you are reading."

Fabian sighed. "I wish I could say that was a relief."
He was about to tap his combadge when an indicator
light went on over the doorway to the lab.

The *da Vinci* was at yellow alert.

Abramowitz pursed her lips. "That can't be good."

"Never is," Okha muttered.

"Stevens to bridge. This may not be the best time, sir,
but we've pried open the golf ball, and, uh—well, it's
interesting."

"Good job, Stevens. Report," Gold said.

Taking this as a sign that he could go on at greater length despite the alert, Fabian said, "Apparently this is some kind of small, mobile weapon. The outer casing is designed to survive space travel and protect the components, which is why we couldn't read it until we got it open. We're gonna do a more thorough analysis now. Unless there's a more pressing concern?"

"Not for you. We're just playing it safe up here, waiting to see if the Dominion wants to crash the party. Let me know what you find out."

"We will, sir. Stevens out." He turned to look at the diminutive, bald-headed aliens next to him. "Okay, Mutt, Jeff, let's get to work."

"I am 110."

"I am 111."

"There is no Mutt—"

"—or Jeff here."

Again, Fabian sighed. *Stick with Duffy for the jokes,* he admonished himself.

As he ran the tricorder over the golf ball, he decided to brave a question. "If you two don't mind my asking, how did a couple of Bynar civilians wind up on the *da Vinci?*"

"None of our kind—"

"—has ever joined Starfleet—"

"—although we have assisted Starfleet—"

"—in many computer-related endeavors."

"It was decided—"

"—that one pairing—"

"—should serve as observers on a Starfleet Corps of Engineers vessel—"

"—during this time of war—"

"—to render assistance where needed."

Smiling, Fabian said, "That's very considerate. You consider enlisting for real?"

The two Bynars exchanged glances. "We have—"

"—*considered* it."

Fabian wondered if he had hit upon a sore point. Before he could pursue it, however, two security guards entered. At least, Fabian assumed them to be security. True, they were enlisted personnel, based on their lack of rank insignia, and their uniforms had the gold trim of operations, but Fabian knew a grunt when he saw one. For one thing, they were armed; for another, they had that tense, coiled look that every security guard he'd ever known had—and that no engineer he'd ever met could master. When engineers got tense, they became all frazzled; when security guards got tense, they shot things.

"Can I help you guys?" Fabian asked.

"Yellow alert," the shorter, paler one said. "SOP is that we stand guard on any projects. Core-Breach's orders."

Fabian laughed. "'Core-Breach'?"

"That's Lt. Commander Corsi's nickname behind her back," Okha said with a grin. "Nobody's had the guts to say it to her face."

"Well," the darker, taller guard said with a grin, "not twice, anyhow." He stuck out a hand. "I'm Vance Hawkins."

Fabian returned the handshake. "Fabian Stevens. Just came on at the starbase."

"Stephen Drew. Welcome to the loony bin, Stevens."

"We have—"

"—found something."

Turning around, Fabian saw that the Bynars looked excited. At what, he wasn't sure. They didn't carry tricorders, and they had spent the time since Drew and Hawkins entered communicating with each other in a high-pitched whine. Fabian asked them what they found.

"We have found—"

"—access to the computer core—"

"—of the golf ball."

" 'Golf ball'?" Drew said with a smirk.

Okha looked with annoyance at Stevens. "See what you've done? Now even the twins are doing it. This is how we wind up with bad names for things."

Primly, Abramowitz said, "There's nothing wrong with golf balls."

Looking at his tricorder, Fabian said, "Maybe, but there's a lot not to like about this one. Can you guys access the core?"

"Of course," 110 and 111 said in perfect unison.

Then they went back to their high-pitched whine. Looking at Okha, Fabian asked, "What is that they're doing?"

"It's a rapid-fire form of communication in straight binary code, and moving at a somewhat ludicrous speed."

"Have you ever tried to translate it?"

Okha frowned. "No. Why would I?"

"Oh, I don't know," Abramowitz said, "maybe to get some insight into another culture?"

"That's your job," Okha said with a shrug.

"It *should* be our responsibility."

Suspecting that he was opening an old argument between these two, Fabian said, "Never mind." He turned back to look at the Bynars, who had now placed two hands—one the left hand, the other the right hand—into the opening Fabian had created in the golf ball. "Should they be touching it like that?"

The high-pitched whine got a bit louder, and the Bynars' eyes seemed to roll up into their heads. Fabian noticed that whatever they were saying was perfectly matched. They were uttering their rapid-fire binary code in perfect unison—which, he realized, was why it seemed louder. He had been recording everything with his tricorder already, but now he set it to make a separate record of just the Bynars' utterances, and to attempt a translation once they were finished. It was as much for his own curiosity as any-thing, but he thought it might also provide insight into the golf ball.

"That's really outstanding." Fabian looked at Okha and Abramowitz, who seemed less than impressed. "I mean, that level of communication with a computer, it must just be—" He shook his head. "Outstanding."

Abramowitz smiled. "You said that already."

Shrugging, Okha said, "We've all gotten used to it."

A very loud, high-pitched wail cut off any response Fabian might have made. He—and everyone else—turned to see 110 and 111 crying out in what looked like pain.

"Get them out of that!" Okha cried.

Even as Hawkins and Drew rushed over to the golf ball, Fabian said, "Wait! We don't know what separating them will do!"

Ignoring this admonition, Hawkins grabbed for 110.

That was followed by a flash of light, a massive elec-trical discharge, and Hawkins being hurled across the lab and into a bulkhead, which he hit with a rather sick-ening thud.

Drew tapped his combadge even as he backed off from 111. "Drew to sickbay. Medical emergency in the lab."

"On my way," came Tydoan's voice.

Neither 110 nor 111 had budged, though they were still screaming. Fabian listened carefully. "I think they're still screaming out binary code."

"Who cares?" Okha said. "We have to separate them."

"I'm open to suggestions," Drew said.

Fabian ran over to the assorted tools he'd found when he was trying to reassemble his tool kit. He needed one particular tool that he'd seen. He was amazed when he saw it before, as he thought his mother was the last person in the entire galaxy who actually had one.

C'mon, c'mon, it's in here somewhere.

The Bynars' screams continued.

Finally, he found what he thought might work.

As he rummaged, Drew said, "What, you've got some super-scientific gizmo that'll get 'em outta there?"

"Something like that," Fabian said as he stood up, holding a long piece of metal, with two small prongs at the end of it. One of the prongs was movable.

Drew frowned. "What the hell is that?"

"A wrench." Fabian rummaged some more and found a pair of nonconductive gloves. "Everybody stand back," he said as he put them on.

Abramowitz and Okha did so—Drew did not, but stayed about a meter behind Fabian. *Fine, if Mr. Security Guard wants to keep an eye on me, who am I to say no?*

Slowly, Fabian approached the golf ball. 110's (or was it 111's?) left hand was in the left-hand part of the opening, with 111's (or 110's) right hand in the right-hand part. Both their mouths were wide open, letting loose with a maddening barrage of high-pitched ones and zeroes. This close, Fabian could see the arc of electricity linking them to the golf ball—indeed, that was all that linked them. Neither hand was actually touching any part of the inner workings of the golf ball, which made Fabian's life easier.

I hope to hell this works.

He shoved the wrench in under 110's (or 111's) hand.

A flash of light encompassed his eyes, and the next thing Fabian knew, he was lying on the floor, on top of something rather lumpy, and feeling a bit dazed. "What happened?" he asked in a slurred voice.

"You fell on top of me is what happened," came a muffled voice from under him, which he realized was Drew.

Clambering into a standing position, Fabian chuckled. "I *did* tell you to stand back."

Drew also got upright. "Remind me to listen to you next time."

"Fine. Listen to me next time."

Sighing, Drew said, "Yeah, you're gonna fit in just fine here." He looked around.

Fabian did likewise and was at once glad to see that 110 and 111 were now separated from the golf ball and distressed to see them unconscious—possibly dead—on the floor. The little boxes they each wore on their belt—some kind of processing unit, he knew—were broken and smoking, small components falling onto the deck next to them.

Tydoan entered then, along with two other people, one an older human male, the other a young human female, all in blue-trimmed uniforms.

"What is it *this* time?" the Bolian asked. Then he noticed the security guard against the bulkhead. "Not Hawkins again. I'm going to just give him his own damn bunk in sickbay. Copper, Wetzel, look him over. I'm gonna take a look at the twins."

The other two started examining Hawkins while the elderly Bolian knelt down next to 110 and 111. As he ran the scanner over them, he started muttering, "Damn stupid engineers sticking their noses in where they don't belong, and then they wonder why they're hurt all the time. Should just retire and be done with it."

"Will they be okay, Doctor?" Fabian asked.

Tydoan ignored Fabian as he finished his examination. Then he stood upright, groaning. Fabian thought he heard the Bolian's knees actually crack. "They'll be fine," he finally said. "Bynars can take a heaping dose of juice, but this was more than a heaping dose. I'll bring 'em to sickbay and—"

"That won't—"

"—be necessary."

Fabian looked down and saw that the Bynars were both starting to rise.

"Hang on, you two," Tydoan said. "You took a major jolt, and—"

"The 'jolt' we took—"

"—is well within—"

"—standard Bynar tolerances, Doctor."

As they spoke, Fabian's tricorder beeped. He looked down at the display, and his jaw became unhinged. *Oh, this isn't good.* Quickly, he switched his tricorder off and purged the records of the Bynars' utterances, suddenly quite grateful that he'd isolated them.

"We thank you—"

"—for your concern—"

"—but it is unwarranted."

"Besides, we have critical information—"

"—that we must impart to Captain Gold—"

"—right away."

Fabian looked at Tydoan. "I'm afraid they're right, Doctor."

"Fine." The doctor threw up his hands. "Don't take care of yourselves. What do I care?" He walked over to Hawkins.

"Stevens to Gold," Fabian said, tapping his combadge. "We have some more information on the golf ball, sir. And it's not good."

Fifteen minutes later, Fabian sat in the observation lounge, along with Gold, Corsi, and the two Bynars. They had waited that long to have the meeting only because 110 and 111 needed to replicate new data boxes. apparently their ability to function at a slow enough level to interact with other life-forms was aided considerably by those boxes, and without them, they'd never be able to process data slowly enough for anyone else to understand.

"The golf ball appears to be a multipurpose weapon, Captain," Fabian said, calling up the sensor schematics from his tricorder on the lounge's viewscreen. "Its housing, as I said before, is the same as that used by the Jem'Hadar for their torpedoes. It can survive the ravages of space and of atmosphere with little difficulty. It's also equipped with three different miniaturized directed energy weapons of similar design to that of a Jem'Hadar warship."

"How powerful?" Corsi asked.

"The yield is roughly equivalent to that of a *Defiant*-class ship's phasers."

"*Gevalt,*" Gold muttered.

"There's more, I'm afraid." Fabian touched a control, and the image focused in on another component of the inner workings. "What you're looking at there is a propulsion system that allows the golf ball to travel at speeds up to full impulse. In addition, it contains a computer core that is *very* complex, which 110 and 111 were able to commune with briefly."

"We are still—"

"—recovering from the shock—"

"—but we learned that the device—"

"—is capable of independent motion—"

"—and firing, based on a sophisticated—"

"—artificial intelligence."

Corsi shook her head. "A self-sufficient, self-directing, obscenely fast mobile weapon?"

"More than that—"

"—we're afraid, Lieutenant Commander."

Gold shook his head. "Much more, I don't think I could take."

"The golf ball can transmit—"

"—a computer virus."

Fabian smiled wryly. "It almost ate my tricorder. I was recording what 110 and 111 were saying, and they were screaming the code for the virus. Luckily, I purged it before it got too far—though if they'd gone on much longer . . ."

"We have already begun a diagnostic—"

"—of all the computers on the ship—"

"—to make certain that no other systems—"

"—besides Mr. Stevens's tricorder—"

"—were affected."

Gold leaned back in his chair. Fabian thought it interesting that, while Corsi looked a frightening combination of appalled and angry, Gold only looked thoughtful—and not nearly as shocked as Fabian would have expected. *Almost as if he knew what was coming.*

"How pervasive," the captain asked after a moment, "would this virus be?"

"It transmits—"

"—in machine language."

"There is no known computer system—"

"—that would *not* be vulnerable to it—"

"—in theory."

Leaning forward, Gold asked, "In practice?"

"We believe that we were in contact with the program—"

"—long enough to devise a countermeasure."

"Good." Again he leaned back. "In a set of reports from Starfleet Intelligence that I received two weeks ago, they mentioned that the Dominion was working on something like this. The mobility, they mentioned. The weapons, they mentioned. The virus, they didn't mention. They also thought the prototype would be ready to go within a month."

Corsi pursed her lips. "Two weeks is within a month."

"That's what both Admiral Ross and I were afraid of when they found that thing. And now we learn that it's worse than we thought."

"Red alert. Captain Gold to the bridge."

Gold tapped his combadge even as the alert lights bathed the observation lounge in a red glow. "Report, McAllan."

"Two Galor-class Cardassian warships and a Jem'Hadar

strike ship have warped into the system, sir. The Appalachia *and the* Sloane *are moving to intercept."*

"Damn. Get us between them and the relay. Our priority is to protect the away team. Gold to Salek."

"Salek here."

"The Dominion just came to find out what happened to their beacon, Commander. How much more time do you need?"

"For a satisfactory repair, nineteen minutes, ten seconds. For a repair that will suffice until such a time as this star system is more secure, four minutes, thirty seconds."

"Good." Gold rose from his seat and headed toward the exit. "Transporter room, this is Gold. Get a lock on the away team and beam them back here—"

The doors closed on him, leaving Fabian with Corsi, 110, and 111. The security chief rose from her chair and headed toward the other exit.

"Uh, excuse me?"

Corsi stopped, turned, and regarded Fabian with a look that made the engineer want to crawl under the table for the next six months. "What?"

"Ah, I'm new—I don't really know what my duty station *is* during red alert."

In a tight voice, Corsi said, "Unless you've been given a specific duty assignment, which you *obviously* haven't, you're to report to your quarters."

Without another word, Corsi turned on her heel and left.

"Is she always that—direct?" Fabian asked the Bynars.

"No," 110 said.

"Usually she is worse," 111 added.

"Lovely. Well, I guess I should go to my quarters." Fabian hadn't even been in his quarters since he came on board. *And to think, I gave up Utopia Planitia for this. . . .*

*   *   *

"Captain on the bridge!"

David Gold rolled his eyes at the words of his tactical officer. "McAllan, knock that off and give me a report." Since reporting to the *da Vinci* two months ago, McAllan had insisted on that bit of protocol even though the captain himself found it unnecessary at best and embarrassing at worst. Leaving aside any other consideration, the *da Vinci* bridge was tiny enough that Gold's presence there would be patently obvious to anyone on it without the need for it to be blared from the tactical station. . . .

"Enemy vessels closing in at full impulse. They'll be in weapons range of the *Appalachia* and the *Sloane* in two minutes."

Gold looked at the recent Academy graduate at the conn station and struggled to remember his name. Finally, it came to him. "Wong, position report."

Wong turned to face his captain. He didn't look old enough to shave. "Holding position at thirty thousand kilometers from the relay, sir."

Turning to the redheaded Bajoran at ops, Gold asked, "Ina, what would be the effect of extending shields around the relay?"

Ina ran her fingers over her console, then said, "Shields' effectiveness would be reduced to sixty-five percent."

Damn. If these were just the Cardassians, that might be enough, but Jem'Hadar ships were just too damned powerful to go in with that much reduced shield effectiveness. "So much for that idea. Wong, keep your fingers nimble. We have to keep that relay intact, clear?"

"Crystal, sir."

"Good."

"*Appalachia to* da Vinci."

Gold had been expecting to hear from either Don

Walsh or Ahmed al-Rashid before long. *I guess Ahmed won the coin toss.* "Go ahead, *Appalachia.*"

"We shall do our best to keep the enemy at bay, David. How soon will your team be finished?"

In response, McAllan said, "Sir, Commander Salek is signaling for beam-out."

"There's your answer, Ahmed. We'll hold position, try to keep the relay in one piece."

"Excellent. It would be more so with a Sovereign-*class vessel or two at our backs, but we must make do with what we are granted."*

"Sad, but true. Go get 'em, Ahmed. We'll watch your back. *Da Vinci* out. McAllan, lower shields." He opened an intercom channel, then. "Transporter room, get the away team back here."

"Aye, sir," Feliciano said.

"McAllan, get the shields back up as soon as they've materialized, and put the tactical display on the main viewer."

The screen changed from a view of the comm relay to a computer-generated overview of the battle arena. On the left-hand side of the screen, the two *Steamrunner*-class ships. Coming in on the right-hand side, two Cardassians and one Jem'Hadar. And at the bottom, the communications relay and the *da Vinci* itself. Small text next to each vessel indicated the status of each ship—shields, weapons, life support, etc.

Here we go, Gold thought, forcing himself to sit up straight.

As the first exchange of phaser fire among the combatants began, Gold wondered how long this would go on. Over his five decades in Starfleet, he'd seen plenty of combat, but nothing like what he'd had to endure against the Dominion.

One of the Cardassian ships was trying to maneuver around toward the comm relay, but *Appalachia* cut them off, taking quite a few hits into the bargain.

Gold's most fervent desire, of course, was to die in bed, surrounded by as many of his children, grandchildren, and great-grandchildren as were still alive and could fit in the room. However, he knew that such a fate was not terrifically likely—and had become somewhat less likely since the likes of the Borg and the Dominion came along, not to mention those skirmishes with the Klingons during the year and a half that the alliance with the Empire broke down. It was, in fact, during that eighteen-month period that Gold had seriously considered turning in his combadge for good. One of his oldest, dearest friends, Captain Mairin ni Bhroanin of the Starship *Huygens*, had been killed in action against the Klingons, and he told his wife, Rabbi Rachel Gilman, that he was considering retirement.

The *Appalachia* let loose with a phaser barrage on one of the Cardassian ships. "The *Appalachia*'s penetrated their shields," McAllan reported. "Hull breach."

Ina added, "Jem'Hadar moving in on *Appalachia*'s position."

"C'mon, Ahmed, move your *tuchis*," Gold muttered.

Ironically, given that she would be the greatest beneficiary of having her husband home on a permanent basis, it was Rachel who had talked him out of retiring. *Probably*, he thought ruefully, *because she saw how miserable I was when I was assigned to Earth*. After Gold's first command, the *Schiaparelli*, was decommissioned, he requested an administrative post on Earth in order to be near his family. That lasted about six months.

"You belong in space," Rachel had said at Mairin's funeral.

"I belong with my family."

"You'll always belong with your family, but for now you also belong in space. Someday, it'll just be the one. *Then* you come home."

Ina interrupted Gold's reverie. "One of the Cardassian ships is moving in on our position."

"Steady, Wong," Gold said. "Keep us between the Cardassians and the relay."

Luckily, Gold's continued ability to survive to retirement was aided by Starfleet's decision to give the S.C.E. a better class of ship. For a long time, the S.C.E. had only the use of half-refitted decommissioned ships, held together with little more than self-sealing stem-bolts and happy thoughts. Later, they were given more current vessels, but still very much bottom-of-the-line. With Starfleet's recent focus on ships better able to defend themselves, prompted by the *Enterprise*'s encounter with the Borg nine years earlier, Starfleet had set aside four of their newest ships—the *Saber* class, intended mainly as a small, maneuverable combat vessel—for the S.C.E.'s use, knowing that sometimes they would need to do more than just crawl around alien wrecks.

Like right now, Gold thought irritably as Cardassian phasers plowed into the *da Vinci*'s shields. "Return fire, full phasers!"

"Firing," McAllan said.

"Ready quantum torpedoes, fire on my mark."

Ina said, "*Sloane* firing on the Cardassians—they're moving off."

"Phaser fire ineffective," McAllan said.

"Fire torpedoes." Gold clenched his left hand.

"Firing."

"*Sloane* is continuing to fire," Ina added.

McAllan sounded a bit more triumphant as he said, "Cardassian shields are down!"

The *Sloane*'s phaser fire combined with the *da Vinci*'s torpedoes to destroy the Cardassian ship.

Gold took no joy in the destruction of the Cardassian vessel. He wouldn't have done a single thing differently given the chance—the Federation was at war, after all—

but he saw no reason to take any pleasure in death. One of the reasons why he jumped at the assignment to the S.C.E. when Admiral Sitak offered it to him was that the Corps of Engineers' purpose was to *fix* things.

So why do we always wind up in the position of destructor?

He put aside such philosophical musings, as they were pointless in times of war, and focused on the tactical display. Again, he clenched his left fist—the *Appalachia* had suffered considerable damage, though they'd also done likewise to the other Cardassian ship.

Most depressing was the display that indicated a total lack of significant damage to the Jem'Hadar, who were the more worrisome of their foes.

"Hold position, Wong. And let's hope Don and Ahmed can keep this up. . . ."

Fabian sat on his bunk in the incredibly dull quarters that he shared with Chan Okha. The linguist himself sat on his own bunk, reading a padd. Fabian had made three attempts to start a conversation, which were met with one-word answers.

I need to do something.

He went over to the computer terminal on the small desk near his bunk. The quarters were slightly larger than the cabins on the *Defiant*, but only slightly, and at least he hadn't had to live permanently there—his quarters were on Deep Space 9. Living full-time in these cramped confines was going to be more of a challenge.

Calling up the tactical display from the bridge, he saw that the battle was going decently, but not great. The *da Vinci* was still in one piece, as were the Jem'Hadar, but the other four were taking a beating.

Looking over the field, as it were, it was obvious that the two *Steamrunner*s were an even match for the two *Galor*s. *No, make that one* Galor, he thought as a combination of *da Vinci* torpedoes and *Sloane* phasers took out a Cardassian vessel. But still, the *Appalachia* had taken a massive pounding, and wasn't going to be a player in the fight for much longer.

And in an even fight, we don't stand a snowball's chance in hell against a Jem'Hadar ship. Which means we have to even the odds a bit. Do something to modify the weapons or improve the shield frequency, or use something—

Fabian smiled. *Or use a weapon they don't know we have.*

Standard procedure notwithstanding, Fabian headed to the doors to his quarters.

"Where you going?" Okha asked.

"Lab. Want to try something."

Okha shrugged. "Your funeral."

"That's what I'm trying to avoid," Fabian said as he walked through the doors.

He got to the lab door and saw Drew and one other security guard standing outside the door. Fabian started mentally rehearsing how he was going to justify his presence at the lab.

However, upon seeing him, Drew simply said, "Figured I'd see you here before too long. The Bynars and Commander Duffy are already in there."

"Ah."

Drew smiled a knowing smile. "You were expecting me to give you a hard time and say that the lab was off-limits while we were at red alert, right?"

Fabian smiled sheepishly. "Yeah, kinda."

"Only way to enforce that on this ship is to stick all of you in the brig until the red alert's over. Mind you, Core-Breach probably considered that. . . ."

Laughing, Fabian said, "I believe it."

He entered to see, as Drew had indicated, 110, 111, and Duffy standing around the golf ball.

Duffy looked up. "Ah, the new guy joins us. Couldn't keep away from the gizmo, huh, Fabe?"

" 'Fraid not, Commander. Besides, I just checked in with the bridge."

Growing more sober, Duffy said, "Yeah, I know. Salek's up there now, giving the captain a hand. I thought I'd be more use down here."

"If we can get this thing to work for us, we might be able to use it on the Jem'Hadar."

Grinning, Duffy said, "That's what I was hoping too. Great minds think alike."

"And so do ours," Fabian said, without missing a beat.

As one, 110 and 111 looked up at the two humans. "We believe that—"

"—we have come up with a way—"

"—to defend our computers—"

"—against the virus."

"Well, that's good news," Duffy said.

"We will program the virus protection—"

"—into the *da Vinci* computer now."

"This protection will need—"

"—to be programmed into all—"

"—Federation and allied computers."

Duffy nodded. "Good work, guys. Get to it." He turned to Fabian. "Meantime, we'll see what we can do about getting the hang of our golf game."

Fabian smiled. "Let's play through . . ."

"Shields down to forty percent."

Salek stood next to McAllan at the tactical station. "Damage control teams, report to deck six."

Gold pounded a fist on the command chair. The second Cardassian ship and the *Appalachia* had both been destroyed. He muttered a quick *Kaddish* for Captain al-Rashid, and wondered if he'd live to give Fayah and their children the bad news in person.

The *Sloane* was limping along with no shields, weapons, or communications capacity, very little power, and life signs indicating that a quarter of the crew were dead. Gold hoped that Captain Walsh was one of those still living, if for no other reason than that Don still owed Gold a rematch for that chess game Gold lost last year at Starbase 96.

Amazing the things you think of under pressure.

"Captain, we cannot continue to trade blows with the Jem'Hadar."

Gold sighed at Salek's statement of the obvious. "Have we done any damage?"

"Their shields are down to sixty-five percent," McAllan said. "Another hit, sir—our shields are at ten percent."

One more minute and I have to abandon to the comm relay.

"Duffy to bridge. Captain, we've been able to gain control of the golf ball."

Smiling, Gold remembered why Starfleet engineers had reputations as miracle workers. "Can we use it on the Jem'Hadar?"

"Definitely, sir. We can deploy it through the cargo bay. Stevens rigged a tricorder that can feed it instructions. The weapons'll plow through their shields, and then we can hit 'em with the virus."

"I find it difficult to believe," Salek said, "that the Jem'Hadar would not have a defense against their own computer virus."

"Sir, 110 and 111 think they can make it work for us. And even if they can't, we'll only need a few seconds of distraction to keep them from defending themselves."

Another shot from the Jem'Hadar hit. "Shields are gone," McAllan said.

"We're out of options," Gold said. "Get going, Duffy."

"Yes, sir."

Salek said, "McAllan, prepare all remaining torpedoes. Fire them when Duffy and Stevens deploy the weapon."

"Jem'Hadar coming in for another pass," Ina said.

Tapping his combadge, Gold said, "Now would be good, Duffy."

"Give us a sec, sir. We're just getting into the cargo bay now."

Gold then said the words he'd been unable to say until now, but he had no choice. "Wong, evasive, pattern alpha, full impulse." They couldn't protect the comm relay if they were vulnerable. He just had to gamble that the Jem'Hadar would pursue the *da Vinci* and attempt to finish them off before going after the relay.

That gamble, at least, paid off. "Jem'Hadar in pursuit," Ina said.

"We're ready to go," Duffy said.

Salek said, "Fire torpedoes."

McAllan fired the torpedoes, a combination of photon and quantum, which managed to do a certain amount of damage to the Jem'Hadar's shields.

One torpedo did not hit the Jem'Hadar, however—mainly because it wasn't a torpedo, but Duffy's "golf ball." Energy weapons fired from the tiny projectile right at the Jem'Hadar.

"Enemy shields are down," McAllan said, sounding surprised.

"Their power signature is decreasing rapidly," Salek added, "well out of proportion to the damage they have taken. Logic would dictate that the computer virus has infected them—and that same logic would suggest that we finish what it is starting. McAllan, fire phasers."

"Yes, sir."

A moment later, the Jem'Hadar ship exploded, the victim of the *da Vinci* phasers.

The bridge was silent for several seconds.

"Sir," McAllan said, breaking the silence, "we're being hailed by the *Sloane*. I guess they got their comms working."

"Put it through."

"Nice job, David."

"Good to hear your voice, Don."

"Good to be heard. I don't know what kind of magic your S.C.E. people worked, but I'm grateful."

"I just wish we could've pulled it off before we lost Ahmed and his people."

"Yeah, me too. In any case, we're gonna need a tow."

With any other crew, Gold would have thought Walsh was crazy to think that a *Saber*-class ship could tow a much larger *Steamrunner*-class vessel.

With this crew, however, Gold just smiled and said, "We'll get right on it. Gold out." He turned to Salek. "Good work, Salek—and a big *mazel tov* to 110, 111, and the two new folks. Blue's unique abilities got the relay fixed fast, and from the sounds of it, Stevens was a big help with Duffy."

"Thank you, Captain."

"Now, let's see what we can do about the *Sloane.* . . ."

ANDROSSI VESSEL OVERSEEN BY BIRON STARDATE 53679.3

Biron finished reading of the *U.S.S. da Vinci*'s retrieval and usage of the Dominion mobile weapon and was, despite himself, impressed. Once again, the crew of that ship had improvised and managed to defeat a demonstrably superior foe in the Jem'Hadar.

Just as they had twice defeated Biron, also a demonstrably superior foe.

He read the remainder of the log entries, including the account of the deaths of Commander Salek and Dr. Chan Okha. It had, he decided, been worth the expenditure of time to obtain these log entries. He had learned much about the crew of this vessel in his perusals: psychological susceptibility to the ravages of combat; inappropriate grieving over the deaths of lesser beings; relationships between workers and officers; all of these and more were vulnerabilities that Biron could exploit.

He made several notes as to courses of action he could take that would cripple the crew of the *U.S.S. da Vinci* and prevent them from interfering with his proper duties ever again.

The first thing he needed to do was ascertain the location of Dr. Tydoan. The former chief medical officer for the *U.S.S. da Vinci* had resigned from service in Starfleet after the cessation of hostilities with the Dominion. Biron did not possess any record of his activity following his resignation, since such records were beyond the purview of what he had originally requested from the now-deceased Yridian.

"Attention, Overseer. We have received a subspace communication from the sponsor. It requires your immediate attention."

The voice was Sub-Overseer Howwi's. All thoughts of petty revenge against the crew of the *U.S.S. da Vinci* fled Biron's mind temporarily. His primary duty—indeed, his *only* duty—was to his Elite sponsor. A communication from him took precedence over anything else. Biron would locate Dr. Tydoan at a later date.

However, the time would eventually come when the opportunity to take revenge on Captain David Gold, Commander Sonya Gomez, Lt. Commander Kieran Duffy, and the rest of the crew of the *U.S.S. da Vinci* would present itself.

Biron found himself looking forward to that time with somewhat inappropriate, yet rather enjoyable anticipation.

WILDFIRE

David Mack

1

Captain Lian T'su tightened her grip on the armrests of her seat. The *Orion* main viewer showed another huge web of lightning bolts tear through the roiling, red-orange clouds of the gas giant's atmosphere. Electrical discharges rendered the clouds visible for little more than a second and were followed immediately by a bone-rattling boom of thunder that reverberated through the decks of the *Steamrunner*-class starship.

"Do you have a lock on that signal yet?" T'su said to her tactical officer, raising her voice slightly to be heard over the din of the ship's groaning outer bulkheads.

"Negative, Captain," said Lieutenant Ryan. "Atmospheric interference is still too heavy. Switching to a delta-channel isolation frequency."

The hull of the *Orion* had begun shrieking in protest soon after they had descended ten thousand kilometers into the gas giant's turbulent lower atmosphere. Now that the ship had dived below twenty-five thousand kilometers, one-fifth of the way to the planet's core, the eerie sounds of fatiguing metal were becoming almost constant, and the vibrations through the hull were growing more severe by the minute.

Twelve years ago, when T'su had been an ensign, she had been at ops aboard the *Enterprise*-D as it skimmed the upper atmosphere of Minos while under fire by an automated attack drone. At the time, she'd thought that was a rough ride. *Compared to this, that was noth-*

ing, she thought, wiping the sweat from her palms.

T'su turned back toward the main viewer, which now showed only a dim outline of the thermal disturbance they were speeding toward. The test of the Wildfire prototype had been about to commence when Lieutenant Sunkulo, her operations officer, had detected an unknown energy signal that mysteriously vanished the moment sensors had been trained on it. If there was another ship in the atmosphere, following the *Orion*, the mission's security was at risk. T'su had orders to keep the prototype out of the wrong hands at all costs, and she was well aware of the potential for disaster if she failed.

Right now, however, she was more concerned about the threat to her ship posed by the planet itself. "Current hull temperature and pressure?" she asked, trying to keep her voice steady. *Always project confidence*, she reminded herself.

Sunkulo tapped a few keys and answered calmly. "Temperature is eleven thousand four hundred degrees Celsius. Pressure is twenty-two million G.S.C." Anticipating his captain's next request, he added, "Structural integrity field still holding."

T'su nodded. Around her, the rest of the bridge crew was quiet, intensely focused on their work. Lieutenant Fryar was making constant, minor adjustments at the helm to keep the ship steady while Ensign Yarrow relayed his data from the science station to Ryan at tactical. They were using active tachyon scans to map the atmosphere's thermodynamic layers and currents in order to plot the course the Wildfire device would take to the planet's core. The data was being constantly uploaded to Lieutenant ch'Kelavar, the ship's Andorian second officer, who was in the forward torpedo room with the Wildfire development team.

Another lightning flash caused the main viewer to flare white for a split second. Another thunderclap, magnified by the density of the gas giant's atmosphere, drowned out the sounds of the *Orion*'s groaning hull plates and shook the ship violently. The lights on the bridge flickered for a moment, and several display screens became scrambled and failed to recover even after the shaking ceased. T'su winced as the acrid odor of burned-out isolinear chips assaulted her nostrils.

Commander Dakona Raal, the ship's imposing first officer, placed a reassuring hand on T'su's shoulder. She silently smiled her thanks to him, and he nodded almost imperceptibly in return and moved his hand away before anyone else on the bridge noticed it had been there.

A native of Rigel V, Raal had been mistaken for a Vulcan by almost every member of the crew when he first came aboard last year. He had responded by shaving his head bald, growing a goatee, and making a point of leading a Klingon folk music sing-along during the crew's last shore leave. He also had learned to cook a *hasperat* so spicy it could knock the nasal ridges off a Bajoran, and Dr. Cindrich, the ship's chief medical officer, had described Raal's unrestrained laughter as "infectious."

Raal was unorthodox, brash, and sometimes a bit too obviously attracted to T'su for her comfort, but at times like this she was glad to have him close by. This was her first command, and although ferrying a contingent of Starfleet Corps of Engineers specialists wouldn't have been her first choice of assignments, the past month had taught her it was rarely boring. Through it all, Raal had proved himself to be an exemplary first officer, the one T'su could always count on in a crisis.

But this crisis was getting too close for comfort.

"Lieutenant Ryan, stand by to deploy the Wildfire device on my mark. Helm, as soon as it's away, get us out of here, best possible speed."

Ryan and Fryar both acknowledged and continued to

tap keys. "We're ready, Captain," Ryan said. T'su leaned forward in her seat, about to give the order, when the image on the main viewer changed.

The low hum of activity on the bridge ceased as everyone turned toward the viewscreen. A latticework of glowing colors seemed to be growing around the ship like a coral reef; grids of light, in parallel and perpendicular rows, surrounded the *Orion* like a cage of energy. T'su snapped her crew back into action. "Tactical, what is that? Is it Tholian?"

"Negative, Captain. The energy signature doesn't match any known configuration."

T'su swiveled toward her science officer. "Yarrow, tell me something useful."

Yarrow studied his display. T'su could tell something was wrong; when Yarrow was alarmed, his mane puffed out and his whiskers twitched. Right now, his mane was twice its normal size. "It's a photonic energy grid, Captain, source unknown. I can't determine its—"

"It's shrinking!" Sunkulo said. T'su spun back toward the main viewer in time to see the image dissolve into static. Sunkulo's console was rapidly dominated by warning lights. "We're losing power all over the ship!"

T'su clenched her jaw as a powerful shock wave rattled the ship. "All decks! Damage reports!"

"We just lost comms," said Ryan. He pressed futilely at his console, which was stuttering its way into darkness like every other panel on the bridge. T'su found herself barraged with reports from every direction at once. Helm wasn't answering, auxiliary power was failing, tactical was offline. The voices overlapped, frantic and hoarse, struggling to be heard over the din of wrenching metal. One voice cut through the clamor, firm and quiet.

"Captain," Raal said gravely. "We're about to lose the structural integrity field." T'su looked at Raal, saw the hardness of his expression, and realized this was the no-win scenario she'd been warned about at the Academy all those years ago. "Recommend we release the log buoy, sir."

T'su nodded curtly, and felt her thoughts turn inward as Raal bellowed the order to Sunkulo. Seconds later, the buoy was away. T'su shivered from adrenaline overload as the bridge lights faded and the bridge slipped into total darkness. She covered her ears as the shrieking of the hull became deafening and the atmosphere's turbulence hammered her ship.

As a flash of lightning a hundred times larger than anything T'su had ever seen on Earth tore through the bridge, the last thing she felt was a hand on her shoulder.

2

Bart Faulwell strolled into the *da Vinci*'s mess hall and passed Carol Abramowitz on his way to the replicator. He glanced at the short, dark-haired woman, who was so deeply engrossed in whatever she was reading on a Starfleet-issue padd that she had allowed her raisin oatmeal to go cold and congeal into a hardened mass in the bowl in front of her.

"The butler did it," he said. Abramowitz seemed not to notice his comment. Then, with some effort, she pulled her attention away from her reading material.

"Huh?"

"I said, 'The butler did it.'" He noted the complete lack of comprehension in the cultural specialist's expression. "You were so entranced," he said, "I figured you must be reading a mystery of some sort."

"No, no. Actually, I've been fascinated by Keorgan art ever since that mission we went on with Soloman a few months ago. I had no idea their photonic cloud sculptures could be so elaborate. Understanding their aesthetic is like opening a door into their collective psyche."

"Sounds fascinating," he said. "Want to see something completely different?" Abramowitz looked up at the bearded, middle-aged cryptographer and linguist. He was keenly excited about his latest endeavor and was certain that if he didn't show someone soon, he'd simply burst. Carol put down her padd and sighed.

"My answer makes no difference, does it?"

"Not really." Faulwell turned to the replicator. "Computer: Faulwell Test One." With an almost musical hum of activity, a swirling vortex of molecules began to reorganize themselves inside the replicator's service area. A few seconds later, a dog-eared and coffee-stained leather-bound copy of Melville's *Moby-Dick* had formed.

Faulwell picked up the book, flipped it open to its title page, and handed it to Abramowitz. She examined it and saw his signature, the ink seemingly as fresh as if he had just signed it. "Perfect, right?" he said. "Accurate down to the indentation the pen made in the page. It even has the same smell as the original," which, he noted with pleasure, was a comingling of old paper and worn leather.

She looked back up at Faulwell. "So?" He picked up the book and snapped it shut in one hand with a theatrical flourish.

"The point, my unobservant friend, is that for the past year, I've been a fool."

"I could have told you that."

"More specifically," Faulwell said, ignoring her remark, "I've been writing my letters to Anthony on paper and reading them to him in subspace messages. Then, on those rare occasions when I get to see him in person, I've been giving him letters he's already heard me read to him."

"So you've decided to start reading him chapters from *Moby-Dick?* That's romantic," she deadpanned. He sat down across from her and held up the book in both hands.

"What if I told you this book is actually still in my quarters right now? Or, I should say, the *original* is still in my quarters."

Abramowitz caught on. "You made a replicator pattern of your book."

"Exactly. And I can do the same for my letters to Anthony and send them to him, attached to subspace messages."

She took the book from him and began flipping through it. "Very clever. You worked this out yourself?"

Faulwell shrugged. "I had some help from Diego," he said, referring to the *da Vinci's* transporter chief, Diego Feliciano. "He seemed happy to have a project to work on," Faulwell said. "I think he's as bored as the rest of us, going around in circles out here."

"You see, that's your problem: You don't know how to appreciate downtime." She put down the book, stood up, and placed her bowl of now rock-hard oatmeal back into the replicator for matter reclamation. She touched the control pad, and the bowl vanished in a whirlpool of dissociated atoms. She turned back toward Faulwell. "Gomez and her team are having a grand old time building their . . . whatever it is—"

"It's a mobile mining platform and refinery."

"Whatever. There's no one trying to steal it, kill us, or start a war. Do you *want* Gold to send us off to some remote planet? With no backup or hope of rescue when our supposedly simple mission inevitably goes tragically wrong?"

He pretended to think about that for a moment, even though he knew the answer was obvious. "No."

Abramowitz leaned in close and whispered into his ear with an intensity that was only half in jest. "Then *shut up.*"

Captain David Gold lay on his back on the biobed, with his arms folded behind his head, admiring the details of the ceiling of the *da Vinci* sickbay. Dr. Elizabeth Lense, the ship's chief medical officer, stood beside the bed and methodically waved her medical scanner back and forth above her commanding officer's torso. The scanner's high-pitched oscillations rose and fell in a steady cadence.

"Three minutes you've been scanning the same spot," Gold said. "Maybe something I should know?"

"No, sir. Physically, you check out in perfect shape."

"You mean, for a man my age."

"No, I mean you're in perfect shape." She put away her medical scanner and entered some notes on a padd. "Though I am considering putting you down for a psychiatric consult."

Gold sat up slightly, supporting himself on his elbows. His white eyebrows were raised in an expression of displeased surprise. "Excuse me?"

Lense held her poker face for a very long two seconds, then broke into a wide grin. "You might be the first captain in Starfleet history to volunteer for his annual physical." Gold's expression softened, and he swung his legs off the bed and sat up. "Most skippers," Lense added, "have to be hounded like a Ferengi on tax day to show up for their exam."

The captain stood and stretched his lean, thin body. He let out a relieved groan as the crick in his back went *pop* and vanished.

"How do you think I stay in such good shape? Not by ignoring my doctors." Gold picked up his uniform jacket from on top of the console next to the bed. He put it on and studied Lense as she walked to her desk and transferred her notes into the computer. "And how have *you* been, Doctor?"

"You mean physically?" she said, in a tone that let Gold know she understood exactly what he was really asking. A few weeks earlier, he had had to call her to task for letting her work slip because of problems with depression. She had begun relying too much on Emmett, the ship's Emergency Medical Hologram, to handle her everyday patient care. Gold, fortunately, had stepped in and helped Lense get back on track.

"I mean, in general," he said.

Lense sat down in her chair, her posture straight yet relaxed. "Busy, believe it or not," she said. She folded her hands in front of her. "With security and engineering escalating their little practical joke war over the past two weeks, I've had to deal with some interesting cases. Lipinski and Robins came in with the ends of their hair fused together at a molecular level." She chortled softly and shook her head. "The smell was horrendous. Separating them without shaving their heads made for a very entertaining afternoon."

Gold chuckled. "I'm sure it did. Any idea who the culprit was?"

Lense nodded. "My best guess would be Conlon."

"Mine too. And you avoided answering my question."

The doctor tapped her index finger on the desktop for a moment. "You're right. But I think what you need is a second opinion. Computer, activate Emergency Medical Hologram."

A blurry, humanoid-shaped holographic image appeared between Lense and Gold and quickly formed into the trim, dark-skinned, and friendly visage of Emmett. He came into focus, surveyed the serene sickbay, and smiled at Gold. "Good afternoon, Captain," he said, then turned his head to offer a friendly nod to Lense. "Doctor."

"Hi, Emmett," Lense said warmly. "The captain requires an update on my medical status."

Emmett turned to face Gold. "Doctor Lense has shown marked improvement over the past few weeks, sir. Her sleep patterns have returned to normal, and her energy level has increased. Overall, I would evaluate her psychological status as stable. Emotionally, she seems to be in good spirits."

Gold cocked an eyebrow and flashed a crooked grin at Emmett. "Really? Good news. Very good." Gold stroked his chin. He hated to continue this line of inquiry, but he needed to be sure she was really recovering and not simply masking her symptoms. He respected Lense, but he couldn't afford to be too trusting. "What percentage of sickbay's walk-in cases have you treated over the past six weeks, Emmett?"

"Actually, sir, I haven't attended a patient in the past four and a half weeks, since shortly after we arrived in the Tenber system. Dr. Lense has activated me only to assist with her lab work, and only when her scheduled sleep cycles coincide with those of Medical Technician Copper and Nurse Wetzel."

Gold nodded, very pleased with the report. "Thank you, Emmett."

Emmett smiled back. "You're welcome, sir. Is there anything else I can do for you today?"

"No, thank you, Emmett. We'll let you know if we need you."

Emmett nodded, then blurred and dissolved with a barely audible hum of photonic generators shifting into standby mode.

Gold looked at Lense, who couldn't conceal her expression of self-satisfaction. Normally, her cockiness would have irked him, but considering the turnaround she'd made, he couldn't hold it against her. "Well, Doctor. Sounds to me like you've earned a bowl of my wife's matzoh-ball soup. Or, at least, a fairly good replicated facsimile of it. Join me for lunch?"

"It would be my pleasure, sir." Lense rose from her desk and fell into step next to Gold. They reached the door, then halted as the comm chirped. The voice that followed was that of Lieutenant David McAllan, the ship's spit-and-polish tactical officer. *"Bridge to Captain Gold."*

"Gold here."

"Captain, we're picking up an emergency signal from a Starfleet vessel, with a message on an encrypted channel."

Gold frowned. "Put it through to my ready room. I'll be there in a moment. Gold out." He looked at Lense, and sighed heavily. "I'm afraid I'll have to give you a rain check on that free lunch, Doctor."

Lense shrugged. "That's okay, sir. I've always known there's no such thing."

Commander Sonya Gomez, first officer of the *da Vinci* and leader of the ship's S.C.E. contingent, monitored her team's progress as she stood and sipped her Earl Grey tea at the center console on the lower level of the operations center aboard Whiteflower Station. The spacious, two-level, state-of-the-art command area of the traveling mining platform was large enough to accommodate up to thirty people during normal operations. Right now, however, its only occupants were Gomez and Lt. Commander Kieran Duffy, her second-in-command on the S.C.E. team.

Duffy was at the rear of the upper level, half-inside an open bulkhead, his beeping and chirping tricorder in one hand and a sonic screwdriver in the other. The tall, blond engineer was searching methodically, but with expiring patience, for a fault in the command center's wiring that the diagnostic program was unable to track down, for reasons that were equally elusive. Gomez caught the sound of muffled swearing from behind the bulkhead, but couldn't make out the words.

She heard an echoing, metallic banging that she surmised was Duffy's sonic screwdriver being pounded like a hammer against a duranium bulkhead. "Everything all right?" she said teasingly, amused at Duffy's mounting frustration over what initially seemed to be a simple problem.

"Fine," Duffy said, clearly irritated. "Never better."

"You should take a break."

Duffy sighed heavily. He turned off his tricorder, put it back into a holster on his belt, and pulled himself free of the bulkhead. He looked around the nearly finished operations center. Two of the three large monitors that dominated the front wall showed the *da Vinci*'s two new "Work Bugs"—larger, three-seat versions of Starfleet's one-person work pods, designed for heavy-duty industrial operations.

P8 Blue was piloting Work Bug One like a natural. Fabian Stevens was piloting Work Bug Two, but with far less finesse. Blue had spent the past five weeks showing Stevens the ropes, teaching him the finer points of the crafts' controls. Together with two assistant engineers in each pod, Blue and Stevens were making excellent progress securing the station's pristine white exterior hull plates.

For the past five weeks the *da Vinci* had been in orbit around Tenber VII, a strikingly beautiful, ringed gas giant planet. Gomez and her team had been assigned to construct a mobile mining platform and refinery that would roam the planet's rings, seeking out such precious ores as dilithium and ultritium, which a Starfleet advance scout had detected here in abundance a few months ago.

The S.C.E. team had been busy since they arrived. Most of them had volunteered for double shifts on the mining station and refinery, which they soon nicknamed "Whiteflower" because of its gleaming, ivory-hued duranium hull plating and the five, teardrop-shaped sections that extended outward at regular intervals from the equator of its hemispherical, central engineering hub. Not long afterward, the name became official, much to the crew's collective amusement.

Duffy sleeved the sweat from his forehead as he walked to the replicator. He rubbed the back of his aching neck as he ordered. "Computer: quinine water with a twist of lime."

"That item is not currently listed in the replicator data-bank," the computer said.

Duffy stared at the replicator with a glare of equal parts anger and disgust. He closed his eyes and drooped his head in defeat. "You've got to be kidding me." He stood, arms akimbo, waiting for the computer's inevitable, overly literal reply. It didn't come. He opened his eyes, then turned and looked down at Gomez.

"How do you like that, Sonnie? Doesn't it usually make some kind of Vulcanesque remark when we say things like that?"

"I had Soloman reprogram it to ignore rhetorical questions." She reached under her console and picked up a thermos. "I figure I just saved you about an hour per month that you'd have wasted in pointless arguments with the mess hall replicator." She pushed her dark, wavy hair out of her eyes, waved the thermos, and flashed him a come-hither smile. "Care to guess what this is?"

"You know me so well," he said. With a grin he jogged to the short stairway that connected the two levels of the operations center. He hopped up to a sitting position on the rail and slid down it to the lower level, landing on his feet with casual athleticism in front of the petite brunette. She handed him the smooth, metallic, curve-topped thermos. He removed the cap and gulped down two mouthfuls of quinine water, then gasped contentedly. "That hit the spot."

He's like a boy sometimes, she thought as she sipped her Earl Grey and studied him out of the corner of her eye, watching the bobbing of his Adam's apple as he downed another swig of quinine water. They had been attracted to each other almost immediately when they had met aboard the *Enterprise* over a decade ago, and had dated briefly, but it ended amicably when she transferred to the *Oberth*. Then, after nearly eight years apart, they found themselves together again aboard the *da Vinci*.

But the situation had changed: she was now his boss, and that had made their renewed romance more than a little awkward. She constantly had to remind herself that reigniting their affair had been her idea, part of the "live life while you can" philosophy she had embraced after her brush with death on Sarindar. She thought she could live in the moment, the way he did, but lately she was becoming less certain. *I love him, and I know he loves me . . . but he's always leaping from one adventure to another. He never thinks about the future.*

"Sonnie," he said, suddenly unable to look her in the eye, "I've been thinking."

Oh, no.

"About tonight—"

"You mean dinner with Fabe and Domenica?"

"Yeah." He self-consciously combed his fingers through his short hair. "I was wondering, I mean—"

"Tell me you're not canceling."

He inhaled through clenched teeth. "Not exactly. I was thinking we might . . . reschedule?" She tilted her head to one side and glared reproachfully at him.

"Kieran, you were the one who said we should have dinner with them, that you wanted to 'bury the hatchet' with Corsi. You even had real Betazed oysters and Risan white wine brought in on the last supply ship."

"I know, it's just . . . well, I wanted tonight—"

"What is it about her that makes you act like this?"

"What're you—"

"Do you hate her *that* much?"

"I don't hate her, Sonnie, I—"

"Then what is it? Why do you get weird every time her name comes up? What, are you two having an affair or something?"

Duffy's face was flushed red and his voice pitched upward. "Damn it, Sonnie, this has nothing to do with her."

"Then what's it about?" She looked at him, trying to read through his eyes what was going on in that mysterious mind of his. His jaw was moving, but no sound was coming from his mouth. She had seen him go through this kind of struggle only once before, when he had asked her out on their first date aboard the *Enterprise*. He took a deep breath—

Their combadges both chirped. *"Gold to all personnel."* Gomez noted that Gold's voice was unusually grim and terse. *"We have new orders. Secure the Whiteflower station and report back to* da Vinci *immediately. S.C.E. staff, assemble in the observation lounge on the double. Gold out."*

Gomez looked at Duffy, who clearly had detected the same bad omens in Gold's message that she had. She tried to lighten the moment. "You were saying . . . ?"

He frowned. "I guess it'll have to wait." He turned away from her and climbed back up the stairs toward the operations center's only working turbolift. She hesitated, then followed him up the stairs and into the turbolift.

"Level six, transporter room," he said as the turbolift doors slid shut with a pneumatic swish.

"Kieran, are you okay?"

"I'm fine," he said in a clipped, neutral tone that she knew meant something serious was on his mind. "Never better."

3

Domenica Corsi, the chief of security aboard the *da Vinci*, hurried down the corridor toward the briefing room, fumbling to get her hair tied back into its customary, tighter-than-regulation bun. She had switched from alpha shift to gamma shift four weeks ago and had finally become accustomed to her new sleep schedule. Gold's urgent summons had just roused her from a particularly pleasant dreamscape, her first in a long while.

She blinked her eyes hard to dispel the fuzzy border around the edges of her vision, finished securing her blond hair into place, and stepped inside the observation lounge.

The room was unusually quiet. Captain Gold was already there, standing behind his regular seat, his expression somber as he stared at the reflective black surface of the table. Lense, Faulwell, and Abramowitz had taken their seats and were conspicuously not speaking.

Corsi moved to her own seat as Soloman, the ship's Bynar computer specialist, entered behind her, followed moments later by engineers Fabian Stevens and P8 Blue, a Nasat whose compact, insectoid form Corsi sometimes envied for its resilience. P8, whom most of the ship's complement called "Pattie," settled into a seat specially designed for her multilimbed physiology, located at the far end of the table from the captain.

Last to enter the briefing room were Duffy and Gomez. Duffy looked scuffed, while Gomez was the very picture of composure. Corsi sensed an unusual level of tension between the two, but under the circumstances, it was difficult to know how to read their moods. Gold looked up at Gomez as she moved to her chair, immediately to his right. His speech was curt and direct.

"Commander, are all *da Vinci* personnel accounted for?"

"Yessir," Gomez said quickly, a bit surprised by Gold's sudden formality. If he noticed, he gave no sign of it that Corsi could see.

"Gold to bridge."

"Go ahead, sir," McAllan said over the comm.

"Set course for the Galvan system, maximum warp. Engage when ready."

"Aye, sir."

Gold leaned forward slowly, as if he were resisting a terrible weight pressing down upon him, and rested his palms flat on the tabletop. The throbbing hum of the small ship's warp engines kicked in, distant, deep and familiar.

"About an hour ago, we received an automated distress call from the Starship *Orion*," Gold said. "She ejected her log buoy after suffering a massive onboard failure while navigating in the atmosphere of a gas giant. The data from the buoy's flight recorder is not good." Corsi watched Gold's hands close slowly into fists as his jaw clenched. "We have reason to believe the *Orion* went down with all hands, including seventy-one S.C.E. personnel."

"Oh, God," Gomez said, a look of dread draining the color from her face. She composed herself and looked quickly back up at Gold. "The *Orion* was Lian T'su's ship, sir. I—" A look passed quickly between her and Duffy. "She was a friend."

Gold nodded compassionately at Gomez, then looked back at the rest of the group. "There's more, of course. What you're about to hear is classified."

Corsi started. If classified information was being bandied about, she wondered whether or not noncoms should be present. Eyes-only information usually wasn't for the eyes of enlisted personnel like Stevens, Faulwell, Soloman, Blue, and Abramowitz. But she trusted that the captain knew what he was doing.

"We've been informed by Starfleet Command that when the *Orion* went down, her S.C.E. team was testing a new, prototype stellar-ignition warhead, code-named Wildfire."

Gold turned toward the monitor behind him and activated it. It displayed a detailed schematic of a torpedo-shaped device and a seemingly endless scroll of technical data running up the screen along one side. "It's protomatter-fueled, and capable of initiating stellar-core fusion. Its stated purpose is to aid in terra-forming by turning gas giants—such as Galvan VI—into small dwarf stars to provide extra energy sources for remote planets."

Corsi considered the device's other potential uses. Every scenario she could think of gave her a sick feeling in her stomach. She had to ask.

"What if this device were deployed into an existing star?"

Gold fixed her with a stern look. "It would depend on the mass of the target," he said. "Small stars would supernova within a matter of minutes. Midsized ones might take up to an hour to explode. An extremely large star could possibly be turned into a supermassive black hole that would begin swallowing neighboring systems." Gold scanned the faces of his staff; the dismayed glances that were crisscrossing the table confirmed they all grasped the scope of the crisis. "So, as I'm sure you all understand, Starfleet is particularly anxious for us to recover the device."

"Sir," Duffy said, straining to keep his tone of voice diplomatic. "What about the *Orion*?"

Gold cleared his throat—more, Corsi suspected, out of diplomacy than out of genuine need. "She went down in neutral territory, which means salvage rights go to whoever reaches her first. Starfleet has made our chief priority the safe recovery of the device—with the salvage of the ship and the rescue of her crew, if possible, a close second."

Corsi nodded, envisioning numerous potential complications. "Sir, we should also be prepared for the possibility that the *Orion* was the victim of a hostile action," she said. "And even if it wasn't, its distress signal might have attracted unwanted attention."

"I already have McAllan working on tactical options, coordinate with him," Gold said. "We'll reach Galvan VI in about nine hours, and we'll be going into the atmosphere as soon as possible after that. Faulwell, Abramowitz: Work with McAllan and Corsi—give them any insight you can into threat forces we might run into out here. Gomez, you and your team have nine hours to work out a plan for recovering the device." He glanced at Duffy. "And hopefully, the *Orion*."

Gold didn't look Lense in the eye as he spoke to her. "Doctor, I don't expect there to be survivors aboard the *Orion*, but prepare sickbay, just in case."

"We'll be ready, sir."

"That's it, then. Reconvene here at 2100 hours. Dismissed."

Corsi lagged behind as the rest of the group filed out. She understood now why Gold had included the entire S.C.E. team in the briefing despite the high security—in this instance, they did need to know if they were going to do their jobs right.

Duffy, Corsi noted, walked quickly out of the lounge, Gomez half a step behind him, with no eye contact passing between them. *He's pretending not to be hiding something,* Corsi deduced, *and she's pretending not to be bothered by it. Wonder what's going on there?* Before she could think of possible explanations, she realized Fabian Stevens was standing just behind her right shoulder.

"I guess this means no oysters tonight," he said.

Corsi sighed. "Guess so."

She still didn't know what to make of her budding friendship with Stevens, whom she had begun calling "Fabe" whenever they were alone together—a situation that had become more frequent during their extended assignment in the Tenber system. It had been several months since their spontaneous, synthale-fueled one-night stand. She'd asked him to keep the matter to himself and not expect anything to come of it. To her surprise, he had done exactly as she asked.

At first she had been grateful for his discretion, but as time passed she had found herself inventing reasons to be near him on away missions and planning her schedule so she'd be in the mess hall when he was. There had even been a few more occasions when they'd been alone together.

When she accepted Gomez's invitation to join her, Duffy, and Fabe for dinner tonight aboard Whiteflower Station, she had stood in front of the mirror in the quarters she shared with Dr. Lense and asked her reflection, "What are you doing?" As she and Stevens exited the briefing room in pensive silence, she still had absolutely no idea.

4

Gomez blinked, not sure she had heard P8 correctly. She considered the possibility that being sequestered in the science lab for over four hours, weighing their options, had caused her to begin having auditory hallucinations. "Towing cables?"

P8 responded to Gomez's dismissive question by switching the image on the science lab's main viewer to a computer simulation of the atmosphere of Galvan VI. Blue streams represented fast-moving currents of frigid, supercompressed gas that plunged in vortices from the upper, colder regions of the atmosphere toward the planet's superheated core. Reddish patterns indicated upswells of superheated, lower-density gas and fluid. Green and yellow patterns marked areas of intense electromagnetic disturbance.

"The icospectrogram we received from Starfleet only goes down to around ten thousand kilometers," P8 said. "That's less than half the distance to the *Orion*, and the severity of ionic disturbances at that depth will disrupt our shields, phasers, transporters, and tractor beams. Assuming the *Orion* is incapacitated, a series of five-centimeter duranium towing cables is our best hope for pulling it out."

Gomez tapped her finger on the side of her half-full mug of Earl Grey tea, which had long since changed from steaming hot to room temperature. She shook her head. "I don't know, Pattie. It just seems so . . . low-tech."

"Sometimes the best solution is the simplest one," Stevens chimed in. "We have about two hours before we make orbit. We could replicate the cables with time to spare if we start now."

Gomez looked at the other specialists gathered in the lab. Ensign Nancy Conlon, a petite brunette human, and Lieutenant Ina Mar, the ship's athletic, red-haired Bajoran senior ops officer, stood next to one another. Both women nodded slowly as they considered P8's proposal. Gomez glanced at Duffy. He was nodding, as well. "I think she's right," Duffy said. "We don't have time to recalibrate the tractor beams. Crazy as it sounds, this is the way to go."

"With our shields offline, we'll have to reroute all

shield generator output to the structural integrity field," Stevens added. "Otherwise, the pressure in the lower atmosphere will squash us like a bug." A split second later he winced and turned toward P8. "No offense."

"Just wait till I find a good analogy for a bag of meat," the Nasat said.

"All right," Gomez said, cutting them off. "Fabian, start replicating the cables to P8's specs. Pattie, go over the schematics for the *Orion* and plan where you want to anchor the tow lines. You and Fabian will handle the hookup with the new Work Bugs."

"Oh yippee," Stevens said glumly, which prompted a tinkly laugh-equivalent from P8.

Gomez issued a string of orders. "Kieran, you'll try to restore *Orion*'s auxiliary power—maybe we can fly her out instead of towing her. I'll search for survivors while Corsi retrieves the Wildfire device and Soloman recovers the logs. Nancy, since we can't transport to the *Orion,* I'll need you to whip up some null-field generators to help us pilot the Work Bugs in that atmosphere. Mar, you're in charge of rerouting *da Vinci*'s shield generators to the SIF."

She noted with satisfaction that even once she stopped talking, she still held everyone's full attention. "Everyone clear?" She was met by a chorus of acknowledgments. "All right, let's get to work. Dismissed."

As the group broke up and moved toward the door, Gomez reached out and gently took hold of Duffy's sleeve. He stopped and waited until the others had left. Stevens was the last person out, and he tossed a sympathetic glance Duffy's way as the door shut with a soft hydraulic hiss.

"What's going on?" Duffy said with a nonchalant half-grin.

Gomez normally found Duffy's ability to smile his way out of a tense situation charming. Now, suddenly, she found it maddening. "I was going to ask you the same thing. You were about to tell me something when we were back on Whiteflower. What was it?"

Duffy wasn't smiling anymore. "Now probably isn't the time, Sonnie." Gomez felt acid churning in her stomach. Something was wrong, and he was stalling.

"Kieran, I can tell something's on your mind." She moved close to him, reached up and softly pressed her right palm against his cheek. She was always amazed at how warm his skin was. "You know you can talk to me. What do you want to tell me?"

He reached up and took her hand in his, and slowly lowered it away from his face. Gomez steeled herself for the breakup speech she could see coming from light-years away.

With his free hand he reached inside his uniform jacket and, still holding her hand, kneeled in front of her. Gomez watched numbly as his hand emerged from his jacket, an exquisitely crafted gold band, set with a diamond, held firmly between his thumb and forefinger. He handed it to her as he looked up. With great effort, she looked away from the diamond ring in her hand and back at him.

"Sonya, I love you," he said in the most sincere tone of voice she had ever heard him use. "I want us to share the rest of our lives together. And before you start lecturing me about Starfleet and duty, I want you to know I'll resign if I have to, because I'll pick you over Starfleet any day. So, to make a short question long, I'm asking for the honor and privilege of being your husband. Sonnie . . . will you marry me?"

For several long seconds, Gomez was convinced her heart had stopped beating. She forced herself to breathe, but despite her best efforts she couldn't think of a single word to say to Duffy, who was now looking very self-conscious and awkward down on one knee. Five seconds of silence stretched into ten, at which point Duffy stood up, his hopeful expression melting into one of desperation.

"Sonnie, please say something."

Gomez closed her eyes and pressed her free hand to her forehead to stave off the fever she could feel forming.

"Sonnie?"

Gomez felt the strength in her legs ebbing. She sat down next to the center worktable and let out a heavy sigh. *We're on our way to recover a device of unspeakable destructive potential from the wreck of a ship on which one of my first friends at the Academy just died. Under the circumstances, I probably could've handled being dumped. But this—*

She opened her eyes as she heard the *swish* of the lab door opening. Duffy was halfway out the door before she called out to him. "Kieran!" He kept going without looking back, and the door slid shut behind him.

Gomez stared at the closed door, then looked back at the sparkling diamond and noted its latinum setting. The fact that the stone was set in latinum meant the ring couldn't have been replicated. *It must have cost Kieran a fortune,* she thought. *He must be the sweetest man I've ever known. . . . So why don't I know what my answer is?*

As she tucked the ring into her inside jacket pocket and made a mental note to return it to Duffy later, a fresh wave of acid provoked muted growls from her stomach.

5

McAllan stood up from the center seat on the bridge as Gold stepped out of the turbolift. "Captain on the bridge!" he said as he moved to his post at tactical.

Gold nodded politely to McAllan and strode to his chair. He had resisted McAllan's insistence on formality and protocol when the young lieutenant first came aboard a few years ago. After McAllan's first year on the bridge, Gold had learned not to mind it so much. Lately, he'd grown accustomed to it and had started letting McAllan take the conn from time to time.

"Report," Gold said as he sat down.

"We're in standard orbit over Galvan VI, sir," McAllan said. "Ensign Conlon has finished prepping the Work Bugs for deployment into the atmosphere. The away team is standing by."

"Good," Gold said. "Ina, do we have a lock on the *Orion?*"

"Affirmative," she said. "Active tachyon scans show her circling the planet's equatorial region at a depth of approximately twenty-nine thousand kilometers. She appears to be derelict, sir, being pulled by a descending current."

"What's the weather like down there?"

"Atmospheric pressure is over forty-two thousand bars, temperature is approximately eleven hundred degrees Celsius," Ina said. "Velocity of atmospheric currents varies from four thousand to seven thousand KPH. And it looks like *Orion's* heading for some choppy weather—she'll hit a region of severe thermal upswells in less than two hours. After that, her path intersects a vortex that'll pull her down into a layer of liquid-metal hydrogen."

Gold turned his chair to face McAllan, who was studying a readout at his station. "Any sign of company?" Gold said.

"No, sir," McAllan said. "Long-range scans are clear, and we haven't picked up any ships in orbit or in the atmosphere."

"Faulwell, any signal traffic I should know about?"

"None," Faulwell said from the communications station, where he'd been since they warped into the system. "We thought the Gorn might send a patrol to investigate the *Orion*'s mayday, but they don't seem to have detected it—or us."

"Let's keep it that way, if we can." Gold studied the deceptively placid-looking, bluish gray sphere of Galvan VI on the main viewer. "Wong? Think you can handle that?"

Songmin Wong, the *da Vinci*'s boyish-looking helm officer, turned and looked back at Gold. "No problem, sir. It's well within our operating parameters."

"It was within the *Orion*'s parameters," Gold noted grimly. "Plot an intercept course for the *Orion*, best possible speed."

"Aye, sir."

Gold took a slow, deep breath as he watched the shape of the gas giant grow larger on the main viewer and finally fill it completely. The planet's subtle striations of color grew more distinct as the *da Vinci* plunged headlong toward the upper atmosphere. Then the viewer crackled with static, and the ship lurched violently as it penetrated the upper cloud layer and began its descent into the semifluid darkness.

"Time to intercept?"

"Twenty-one minutes, sir," Wong said.

"Gold to Gomez. Prepare to deploy your away team."

"*Aye, sir,*" Gomez replied over the comm. Gold detected the rising howl of swift, powerful atmospheric currents buffeting his ship—and he felt his fingers tighten reflexively on the arms of his chair.

The *da Vinci* shuttle bay buzzed with activity as Conlon and four other engineers scrambled to make final tweaks to the null-field generators they'd just installed on the two yellow Work Bugs. The industrial-grade work vehicles were bulkier, more durable, and more powerful than the average Starfleet-issue Work Bees, but they were slower and would need all the protection possible.

Gomez tried to ignore the muffled shrieks of high-velocity wind that were audible even through the *da Vinci*'s hull. She focused instead on checking the seals and readouts on Corsi's environment suit. Several meters away, Stevens and Duffy were completing their own suit checks, and behind them, Soloman and P8 took turns verifying each other's specially made environmental gear. Soloman's was fitted for his short, slender body and larger-proportioned head. P8's suit permitted full mobility with all of her eight limbs, and she could retract its arms if she needed to assume her curled-in, defensive posture.

The first officer slapped her thickly gloved hand on Corsi's shoulder. "You're good to go," she said. "Everybody ready?"

Stevens gave Gomez a thumbs-up signal, and P8 and Soloman nodded. "All right," Gomez said, "Corsi, you're with me and Pattie. Kieran, Soloman, you'll be flying with Fabian. Let's go." The two trios split up and clambered awkwardly into the Work Bugs.

Inside Bug One, P8 settled comfortably behind the controls, her small size compensating for the added bulk of the pressure suit. She began powering up the Work Bug as Gomez sealed the hatch. Normally, the vehicles could seat three comfortably, but in full environment suits it was a tight fit, a situation that for

Gomez only exacerbated the sense of confinement she felt whenever she put on the clumsy gear. She settled into the vehicle's rear seat as Stevens's voice came over the comm. *"Bug Two is all set, Commander."*

"Acknowledged," Gomez said. "Gomez to bridge. We're ready to launch, Captain." A powerful tremor shook the *da Vinci* and rattled both Work Bugs as a resounding boom of thunder echoed through the ship.

"Stand by," Gold said. *"Three minutes to intercept."*

Gomez felt the first bead of sweat trickle down her spine. *Three minutes,* she told herself. *Three minutes sitting still in this suit, while the ship flies straight into a navigational nightmare that I'm about to face in this souped-up cargo pod.* The claps of thunder and violent shaking became more intense and frequent. She closed her eyes, took a deep breath, and began counting backward from one hundred eighty.

It took every shred of willpower Duffy possessed to sit still. He almost wished he were piloting Bug Two instead of Stevens, but his friend was the one who had spent the past month learning to fly the heavy-duty utility craft.

Despite the acoustic insulation of his environment suit and the Work Bug itself, Duffy could hear the unmistakable groaning of stressed metal as the *da Vinci*'s hull protested its descent into the crushing depths of the gas giant's atmosphere.

"Would you listen to *that,* Fabe? Sounds like we're really putting *da Vinci* through her paces."

"Tell me about it," Stevens said. "I haven't heard anything like this since Captain Sisko took the *Defiant* into a gas giant to save a Karemma ship from the Jem'Hadar."

"Please," Soloman said, "not that story again."

"He's right, Fabe, it's the only one you ever tell."

"This from the man who never seems to tire of the

Tellarite story," Stevens said. "Fine, I'll change the subject. Did you ask her?"

"Ask who what?" Soloman said, confused.

"He was talking to me," Duffy said. "And yes, I did."

"And?"

"And nothing. She didn't say a damn thing."

"Pardon me," Soloman said. "Who and what are we talking about?"

"No one," Duffy said.

"It's nothing," Stevens said.

"You asked a question about nothing to an entity that does not exist and are surprised to have received no answer," Soloman said, shaking his head in dismay. "And humans wonder why they have trouble communicating with one another."

Duffy stared in mute amusement at Soloman, wondering when the Bynar had found time to master the fine art of sarcasm.

The image on the *da Vinci* main viewer was little more than static punctuated at random intervals by flashes of lightning that whited-out the screen and revealed swirling eddies of various liquefied gases raging past the ship at thousands of kilometers per hour. A computer-generated grid of longitudinal and latitudinal markings was superimposed over the image, along with a reference point indicating the position of the *Orion*. That reference point was just above the artificial horizon line and quickly drawing near.

Ina checked her console. "Sixty seconds to intercept."

A powerful impact knocked Gold forward, halfway out of his seat, and pinned Wong and Ina to their consoles. As Gold pulled himself back into the center seat, he noticed, out of the corner of his eye, McAllan scrambling back to his feet, trying to look like he'd never lost his balance. "Report," Gold said.

"Thermal upswell, sir," Ina said. "Small, but enough to overload our inertial dampers."

"A lot of these we should expect?" Gold said.

"Impossible to predict, sir," Ina said. "Convective columns have been drifting, disappearing, and reappearing in a chaotic manner. But the *Orion* will be drifting into a region of intense convection activity within ninety-six minutes."

"Let's get this over with, then," Gold said. "Wong, take us to within two kilometers of the *Orion*, then use thrusters to maintain minimum safe distance. The tide down here is fast and rough, so you need to leave room to compensate."

"Aye, sir," Wong said. Gold watched the young ensign confidently guide the ship through the maelstrom, seemingly oblivious of the ominous roar of the atmosphere, which they'd been unable to mask with acoustic dampening frequencies, despite numerous attempts.

The *Orion* appeared on the *da Vinci* main viewer, hazy behind a bluish silver veil of swirling gases. The sight of it reminded Gold of a story he used to read to his son, Daniel, when he was a boy—*The Flying Dutchman*, a tale about a cursed sailing vessel. Looking now at the lifeless husk of the *Orion* on the viewer, Gold couldn't help but recall the image of the battered, seatorn *Flying Dutchman* emerging from a wall of fog.

"Gold to away team. We've reached the intercept point. Launch when ready."

"*Acknowledged,*" Gomez said.

Gold anxiously folded his arms as he watched the main viewer. Between the *da Vinci* and the *Orion* enormous bolts of green lightning sliced through the darkness, and he felt the *da Vinci* shudder as bolt after bolt struck its hull.

The two Work Bugs appeared on the viewer, looking tiny and fragile as they awkwardly dodged the electrical discharges on their journey to the derelict starship. *We jump from star to star with ease,* Gold mused. *Now, two kilometers looks longer than a light-year.* Oy, gevalt.

Gold sighed. There was nothing for him to do now but wait.

6

Stevens struggled with the sluggish controls to prevent the shearing currents from slamming Bug Two into Bug One. The null-field generators Conlon had installed were helping tremendously—in fact, without them, piloting the Work Bugs in this environment would be impossible—but they consumed enormous amounts of power, and each burst of emerald-colored lightning disrupted the null field just long enough to tumble Bug Two like a rolling die, tossing Duffy and Soloman against one another and the back of Stevens's seat. The inertial dampers were overloading with each lightning strike, and the cabin of Bug Two was thick with smoke and the odor of fried circuits.

The deafening roar of wind had become so omnipresent that Stevens was learning to tune it out, treating it as white noise. Ahead of the Work Bug, the lightning offered him irregular, strobing images of the *Orion* looming closer, but he chose to rely on the outline of the ship, complete with flight readouts and range to target, provided by the computer in the form of a heads-up display superimposed over the cockpit windshield. The two Work Bugs were now within less than a hundred meters of the *Orion*. He keyed the comm to Bug One.

"Commander, we're close enough to start a visual survey."

"Acknowledged," Gomez answered. *"We'll take the dorsal hull, you take ventral."*

The two Work Bugs separated. Bug One maneuvered to survey the *Orion* from above, while Stevens slowly guided Bug Two beneath the *Steamrunner*-class starship, which was nearly twice the size of the *Saber*-class *da Vinci*.

"Activating filters," Stevens said as he keyed a switch. Like a wash of color, a tint swept across Bug Two's windshield, neutralizing much of the haze and distortion that blocked their view. Suddenly, the *Orion* became clearly visible, dominating the view outside the cockpit. Duffy inched forward past Soloman to get a view of the crippled vessel, and craned his neck sharply to look up at its underside.

"Damn," Duffy muttered. He pointed upward. "Fabe, look at that." Stevens glanced where Duffy was pointing. The *Orion*'s secondary hull was blasted away in large sections, the framework beneath it twisted and bent inward. Duffy activated the scanners as Stevens keyed the comm.

"We're seeing some heavy damage on the ventral secondary hull," Stevens said. "Looks like concussive damage from atmospheric shock waves."

"Readings are consistent with antimatter detonations," Duffy said. "Could've been photon or quantum torpedoes."

"Dorsal hull is intact," Gomez replied. *"We're not reading any life signs in the primary hull. Do you have any in the engineering section?"*

"Negative," Duffy said. "And it looks like she's partially flooded. Internal pressure is reading just over two hundred bars."

"That's not too bad," P8 said over the open channel. *"It means* Orion *still has some hull integrity."*

"It's time to go in," Gomez said. *"We'll dock Bug One at the forward ventral hatch. Fabian, dock Bug Two at the starboard dorsal hatch. Once we're in, you and Pattie will continue your survey, figure out where to attach the tow lines."*

"Acknowledged," Stevens said as he swiveled Bug Two around and began moving it toward *Orion's* starboard docking hatch. Duffy and Soloman secured their helmets in place. Duffy grabbed a portable tool kit. Soloman picked up a slender case containing an emergency data-recovery terminal. Stevens fastened his own helmet into place, looked over his shoulder at the pair, and grinned. "Get ready for a little bump," he said.

Bug Two slammed hard against the *Orion*. The impact knocked Duffy and Soloman hard against the bulkhead and sent them toppling to the deck. The clang of the magnetic docking seal finding its mark rang out like a bell inside Bug Two. It was followed by the grinding of docking seals securing themselves. Duffy and Soloman got back on their feet as the airlock on the other side of the hatch depressurized with a muffled hiss.

"Nice flying, Fabe," Duffy deadpanned.

"You know the rule, Duff," Stevens said. "Any landing you can walk away from. . . ."

Duffy shook his head and opened the hatch. "I think we need to raise our standards."

"I concur," Soloman said as he followed Duffy into the airlock and sealed the hatch behind them.

Gomez paused, her magnetic boots yanking her foot back onto the deck. She strained to see through the souplike, semiliquid atmosphere that had flooded the corridors of the *Orion*. Her palm beacon was set to maximum intensity, but it was unable to penetrate more than a few meters into the murk ahead of her.

Considering the carnage that filled the corridors of

the *Orion*, Gomez decided that was probably for the best.

Temperatures inside the ship had been hot enough to sear the flesh off most of the dead, leaving behind skeletons in scorched rags or—in many sections of the ship—pulverized piles of bone and little else. As Gomez pushed forward she felt a rib cage disintegrate, crushed underfoot by her heavy magboots.

The miniaturized null-field generators Conlon had built into the away team's environment suits alleviated much of the pressure they were experiencing inside the ship, but Gomez's muscles were already growing fatigued from pushing through the dense mixture of partially liquefied gases, as well as the added strain of fighting against the planet's intense gravity. The *Orion* was slowly rolling on its Z-axis as it drifted, and rather than walk on the ceilings or walls, the away team had resorted to magnetic boots. Unfortunately, the planet pulling in one direction and the boots pulling in another made for very slow progress in the flooded passageways.

Her tricorder scanned a twenty-meter radius around her position and relayed its data to a display projected on the inside of her helmet visor. The mean temperature inside the ship had climbed to nearly one hundred thirty degrees Celsius—a mere fraction of the temperature outside the vessel, but more than hot enough to have long since killed any humanoid life-forms on board.

Gomez reminded herself that anything was possible—there might be a shielded area deep inside the ship where survivors held out hope of rescue—and continued her search, even as her hopes of finding anyone alive decreased with each scan.

Soloman emerged from the interior pressure lock that led to the *Orion*'s main computer core and breathed a sigh of relief. The multiple redundant fail-safes that were a standard element of Starfleet ship design had proved their value once again: Even though all the compartments surrounding the main core had been flooded with semiliquid gases, the core itself had remained undamaged, its structural integrity uncompromised.

His tricorder indicated the core was offline, without main or auxiliary power. Its last remaining backups—small emergency batteries built into the core assembly itself—had activated and were keeping the core operating at a minimal level. Soloman opened the case containing the data-recovery terminal and patched into the *Orion* main computer core. Within seconds the core powered up with a majestic hum and established a link with the small but robust portable unit. Soloman initiated the recovery of the *Orion*'s logs—all of them, from sensor logs to personal and official logs from every member of the crew—and activated his comm.

"Soloman to Commander Gomez," he said, his delicate, high-pitched voice echoing inside his helmet. "I've reached the main computer core and started the recovery of the ship's logs."

"Good work," Gomez said, the strain in her voice belying her exhaustion. *"Notify me as soon as you're finished."*

"Acknowledged." Soloman closed the channel and stood patiently, staring up at the ceiling of the lower core chamber some fifty feet above his head. He knew, based on the rate of data transfer possible between the portable unit and the main core, that this operation would take at least twenty-eight minutes. He also knew, from his review of the core's design schematics, that the core was structurally stable, that he was standing in one of the safest areas of the ship. But he still wished he were leaving this ship now instead of later.

* * *

Duffy wished he were in the *da Vinci* mess hall wolfing down a triple-decker roast beef sandwich with his usual quinine water. Somewhere between decks eighteen and nineteen his stomach had reminded him that, in the flurry of activity that had followed the *da Vinci*'s new orders, he had forgotten to eat lunch—and dinner.

He had already written off the *Orion*'s impulse engines as a lost cause. The main fusion reactor had been breached and caused a cascade failure of the entire impulse system. Half the compartment had been destroyed by the initial blast, and the rest had been exposed to atmosphere.

Now he was slogging his way through the main engineering compartment, his palm beacon barely cutting through the dark shroud of liquefied gases. He was surrounded by the scorched-black skeletons of the *Orion*'s engineering crew, many of whom appeared to have died while trying to don pressure suits.

Why didn't she answer me? Duffy shook his head. *Stop that. Don't think about Sonnie. Think about the warp reactor. At least warp reactors make sense.*

Duffy felt his way to the railing that circled the warp core, and followed it to the dilithium crystal chamber. He scanned it, and was pleased to find the crystals inside were undamaged. Then he scanned the interior of the core and wondered why it had been purged. It was structurally sound, and its auxiliary systems were intact, but it had been deactivated. *Correction,* he thought. *At least warp reactors usually make sense.*

He opened the access hatch to the lowest level of the ship and descended slowly, the planet's gravity pinning him against the ladder as his magboots struggled to gain purchase on the rungs. After reaching the bottom deck of the *Orion*, he opened the emergency bulkhead to the antimatter pod storage compartment.

Turning slowly, he surveyed the massive room, which was now little more than a series of empty pod frames and twisted duranium hull plating. He looked away as a flash of lightning forked past outside the ripped-open hull, and held on to the door frame as a clap of thunder knocked him backward. Catching his breath, he closed the bulkhead and keyed his comm.

"Duffy to Gomez."

"Go ahead."

"I have a new theory on what tore open the belly of the *Orion*. All her antimatter pods have been ejected."

"They lost containment and tried to eject the pods—"

"—but the ejection system was made for zero-G vacuum and the pods failed to reach safe distance before they exploded. Man, what a mess."

"So, no chance of restoring power?"

"Negative. Once her batteries go, her integrity field'll collapse and this'll become the biggest hunk of duranium origami you ever saw."

"Okay, come back up and start working your way forward to help me finish scanning for survivors. We'll meet back at the starboard hatch on deck three."

"See you there. Duffy out."

Duffy trudged back toward the access ladder. He remembered how arduous the climb down had been, and he looked back up the ladder to his destination, seventeen decks away.

Damn, Sonnie . . . the things I do to keep a date with you. With aching shoulders and a growling stomach, he started climbing.

7

Corsi felt her way through the *Orion*'s forward torpedo room, inching toward the launcher assembly, where her tricorder indicated the Wildfire device rested on a loading rail. She searched the area with her palm beacon, struggling to discern the narrow, conical shape of the device from the wreckage of the collapsed ceilings and flooring. Then the beam of her palm beacon fell upon the tip of the device, which lay half-buried in a tangle of optical fibers.

She tried to pull the fibers off the device. They resisted, caught fast on something underneath—a protrusion from the warhead casing, she surmised—and she tugged harder. Like kelp tearing away from the hull of a sunken ship, the cables came free, and she tossed them aside. As the trailing ends of the cables passed behind her, she saw that they had been tangled up in the corpse of one of the *Orion*'s crew, the skeleton of a male Andorian, whom she guessed was probably Lieutenant ch'Kelavar, the *Orion*'s second officer.

Scanning the Wildfire device, she saw her tricorder was receiving no readings from it whatsoever—and remembered that the device was heavily shielded. She slowly ran her hand along its surface, feeling for its control panel. A few seconds later, she discovered the slight indentation in the device's casing and pressed down. The surface of the device suddenly was wrapped in a shimmering, holographic cocoon, and through her helmet visor she could barely hear the standard feminine Starfleet computer voice, heavily distorted by the dense, semiliquid gases that filled the compartment. The image of a standard interface panel formed on the outside of the device's holographic shell. *"Verify security clearance."*

Gold had been ordered to give the device's top-secret access codes to as few people as possible; for this away mission he had entrusted them only to Corsi. Corsi entered the project's specific code sequence, followed by her personal authorization.

"Verified."

The hologram changed again; now it displayed vast amounts of data, including the device's current depth in the atmosphere, its target depth, its countdown preset and its operational status—which, Corsi grimly noted, clearly indicated it was armed. She keyed her comm.

"Corsi to Gomez. I've located the device."

"Status?"

"Active. If it drops to its target depth, it'll start its countdown automatically."

"How long until—" The comm crackled with static, swallowing Gomez's reply. Corsi tapped the side of her helmet, mostly out of frustration. The static persisted, with a few stray words slipping through intermittently: *"—device . . . return to—"* Then Corsi's comm spat out a long burst of static.

"Commander? Your signal is breaking up. Please repeat. Commander, do you copy? Commander, do you—"

The static turned to silence, and Corsi paused as the room quickly grew darker. Her palm beacon dimmed rapidly, as did the small indicator lights on her pressure suit. She reflexively looked to her tricorder, only to find it had lost power, as well. Within seconds, the compartment was swallowed by darkness, and the only sound she could hear was her own breathing, ragged and loud inside her helmet.

She knew she was respirating too quickly. *Remain calm*, she thought. She concentrated on controlling each breath, keeping her lungs' ebb and flow slow and even. *Probably just an ionic disturbance in the atmosphere. It'll pass in a few seconds, just stay calm.*

Slowly, a violet glow of light returned and suffused the cramped compartment. *There, no problem, just a simple—*

She looked down and saw her palm beacon and tricorder were both still without power. Then she noticed her shadow stretching slowly across the Wildfire device. The light was coming from behind her, and it was getting brighter.

With great caution, she turned toward the light.

Stevens reached the aft end of the *Orion*'s secondary hull, looked up at the underside of the starboard nacelle, and shook his head in disappointment as he keyed the comm. "Starboard nacelle's got multiple fractures where it meets the engineering section," he said. "Any luck on port side?"

"Negative," P8 Blue said. *"Massive damage along the entire port nacelle assembly. I do not think this will work."*

"Want to do one more sweep forward before we—"

"Gomez to Work Bugs. We've lost contact with Corsi. Can you confirm all channels clear?"

Stevens tried not to think of worst-case scenarios while he checked his Work Bug's comm relay circuits. Because the *Orion*'s main computers were offline, the away team's communications were boosted through the Work Bugs' onboard systems.

"Bug Two, all channels clear."

"Work Bug One, all channels clear."

"All right. I need visual confirmation that the forward torpedo compartment is still intact."

"On our way," Stevens said.

"Acknowledged," P8 Blue said. *"Reversing heading now."*

Stevens could just barely see Work Bug One, up

above the *Orion*, as he rotated Work Bug Two for the return trip along the *Orion*'s underside. As he completed his rotation maneuver, he saw an incandescent, narrow double helix of energy that emerged from the deepest layers of the atmosphere and extended upward, disappearing into the underside of the *Orion*'s saucer section.

"Pattie, do you see that?"

"Affirmative."

"Stevens, report," Gomez ordered.

"Some kind of energy beam, Commander. Coming up from the planet and penetrating the ship's saucer."

"I am unable to lock scanners onto the phenomenon," P8 Blue added, *"but it appears to be entering the* Orion's *hull directly beneath the forward torpedo compartment."*

"Gomez to all away team personnel. Corsi might be in trouble. Who's closest to the forward torpedo compartment?"

"This is Duffy. I'm on deck five, section twelve. I can reach her in two minutes."

"I'll meet you there," Gomez said through the increasing static on the comm. *"Everyone else, get to the emergency rendezvous point. Stevens, tell the* da Vinci *we might need to abort."*

"Acknowledged." Stevens stared at the shimmering ribbon of light piercing the *Orion*'s hull, thought of Domenica Corsi being on the receiving end of it, and again tried not to imagine the worst as he activated his Work Bug's emergency channel. "Stevens to *da Vinci*, priority one."

Corsi stared in awe as the lattice of light emerged from the floor, creeping upward like a vine ascending an invisible wall. Each tendril was made of small beams of energy, some only a few centimeters long while others stretched vertically for more than a meter. Every beam was either parallel or perpendicular to another beam, and they built upon each other, new tendrils of light appearing through the floor, pushing the ones above upward, like a twisting ladder. It extended through the bulkheads on either side of the torpedo room, and was several meters deep from Corsi's point of view—which meant it was blocking her only avenue of escape.

The structure stopped moving upward and began growing outward, toward Corsi. She backed away from it, but after a few steps she had no more room to retreat. The wall of light pushed in and enveloped her.

An electrical shock coursed through her nervous system. Her fingers curled into a rictus, and a metallic taste filled her mouth as her teeth clenched with enough force to crack their enamel. She convulsed violently. Her face twisted into an excruciating, death's head grin.

She struggled to keep her grip on consciousness. *I won't go out like this!* The nausea was overwhelming. Her skin felt like it was on fire. *Can't panic, can't panic, can't panic, can't panic. . . .*

Vertigo erased her balance. She thought she might be floating, but since she couldn't feel her feet she couldn't be sure. The edges of her vision began to fade and push inward, and she felt herself sinking into the comfort of oblivion.

No! Fight, damn it! Fight!

The tunnel bordering her vision grew longer with each moment, and her desperate inner voice felt small and impotent against the promise of darkness.

Not like this . . . not like—

Gold strained to see the double helix of light through the constantly shifting wash of static that dominated the *da Vinci*'s main viewer. "Ina, can you clean that up?"

"Filters are at maximum, sir," Ina said.

"McAllan, what are we looking at here? Is that beam coming from a weapon?"

The tactical officer studied his console and frowned at the lack of information it offered him. "Not sure, sir. The beam is absorbing all our scans, and we can't look deep enough into the atmosphere to find its source."

"I'm going to need more than that to—" Gold stopped as the main viewer showed the mysterious tendril of energy dim and fade away beneath the *Orion*, vanishing like a phantom into the swirling hydrogen mists. "That's either very, very good," Gold thought aloud, "or very, very bad."

Duffy slogged down the flooded corridor at the fastest pace he could manage, his muscles burning with fatigue as he forced himself forward through the thick semi-fluid hydrogen. His hot, ragged breaths fogged the transparent aluminum faceplate of his helmet as he stumbled across the walls and ceiling. He broke his constant, sideways falling with his arms while the ship rolled slowly around him. To move more quickly, he had reduced the settings of his magnetic boots to the minimum he needed to keep his footing, and he had decided that whatever the planet's gravity said was "down" was fine by him.

He reached the intersection closest to the forward torpedo compartment at the same time as Gomez, who had adopted the same tactic for moving through the corridors. He fell into step behind her as they approached the open door to the torpedo room. It was still open, and the compartment beyond was completely dark. Gomez and Duffy moved quickly inside, the beams of their palm beacons crisscrossing in the reddish amber murk.

Gomez gestured with her tricorder toward the back of the room. *"Back there,"* she said, her voice echoing inside Duffy's helmet. Corsi was slumped in a sitting position against the far wall. Duffy shone his search beam into Corsi's face. The blond security chief was unconscious. Gomez continued scanning with her tricorder. *"She's alive—barely. Let's get her out of here."*

Duffy and Gomez each grabbed one of Corsi's arms, pulled her to a standing position, and began dragging her toward the corridor. *"Gomez to Stevens, report."*

"I'm docked at the rendezvous point," Stevens said. *"Soloman's aboard and Pattie's standing by to dock Bug One as soon as I'm clear."*

"Tell Soloman to take Bug One with Duffy. You'll be bringing Corsi and me back to da Vinci."

Work Bug Two bobbled and rolled violently as it sped toward the *da Vinci,* now less than a kilometer away. Stevens was making no effort to fly smoothly or gracefully—just as quickly as the Work Bug's engines and the planet's atmospheric turbulence would allow. Forks of neon green lightning sliced past the cockpit windshield, but Stevens's only fear right now was time—or, more precisely, how little of it Domenica might have left unless she reached the *da Vinci* sickbay.

A violent upswell spun the Work Bug nearly two full rotations around its forward axis, its thrusters screeching as Stevens fought to regain control. The utility craft had barely recovered its heading before Stevens once again pushed the thrusters to full-forward.

"Stevens, go easy," Gomez said. She was kneeling over Corsi, doing what little she could with a first aid kit to help the fallen security chief, who was in deep shock—or worse.

No, not worse, Stevens told himself. *She'll be okay. Just keep going. Just get there.* "I'm all right, Commander," he said, not believing it at all.

Through the swirling haze Stevens recognized the familiar shape of the *da Vinci,* less than four hundred meters away.

With a little luck, I can have us in the shuttle bay in ninety seconds. He stole a quick look back at Corsi, whose porcelain-smooth skin had become terrifyingly pale. He hoped that for her the next ninety seconds wouldn't equal a lifetime.

8

"She suffered a severe neuroelectric shock," Lense said, looking away from the diagnostic screen to face Gold and Gomez, who stood on the other side of the biobed, eyes fixed on Corsi, who lay unconscious. "Her central nervous system was badly disrupted, and there was damage in her prefrontal lobe and motor cortex. I've repaired most of the major problems, but she's still comatose."

"For how long?" Gold said.

"Hours. Days. Maybe the rest of her life."

Gold shook his head, unable to find words for his dismay.

"Can you tell if this was caused by a natural phenomenon or a weapon?" Gomez asked. Lense shook her head.

"Hard to say. There was no specific point of impact, so I'd say it wasn't a directed attack. But I really can't rule out any possibility."

Gold glanced at Lense. "Let me know the moment anything changes," he said, gesturing toward Corsi.

Lense nodded. "Of course."

Gomez stayed at Gold's shoulder as he took a few steps away from the biobed, then paused. "Bring the rest of the away team to observation in ten minutes," he said quietly.

"Aye, sir." Gomez exited quickly. Gold lingered in sickbay for a moment, then moved toward the door. He stepped into the corridor, then looked back. He watched silently as Lense stood over her patient and gently stroked a wayward lock of blond hair from Corsi's temple.

The sickbay door slid shut, and Gold found himself alone in the corridor. If Corsi didn't make it, she would not be the first person to die in the line of duty under his command. But bitter experience had taught him that each loss affected him differently—especially when it was someone he considered a friend.

Stevens was the last member of the away team to reach the briefing room. "Sorry I'm late," he said, his voice quavering with what Gold surmised was suppressed worry over Corsi. "I just stopped in sickbay to—"

"Stevens," Gold said in a tone of voice that was deliberately gruff, "what's the *Orion*'s status? When can we pull her out of here?" The verbal slap seemed to have the effect Gold had sought. With effort, Stevens regained his composure and looked his captain in the eye.

"She's got severe structural damage at most of her major stress points, sir," Stevens said. "The engineering section is completely compromised, and the primary hull has enough damage that if we try to attach towing lines, she'll just rip in half."

Gold turned his gaze toward P8. "You would agree?"

P8 uttered a brief series of clicking noises. "Yes, Captain," P8 said. "Stevens is correct. We will not be able to tow the *Orion* using duranium cables."

"What about this light you and Stevens encountered? How did it disrupt power and comms?"

"Unknown. We were unable to scan the phenomenon," P8 said.

"We need to know if it was a natural event," Gold said. "It could just be an atmospheric effect caused by the Wildfire device. But if it's a weapon. . . . Did it show any sign of intelligent control?"

Stevens and P8 looked at each other. Stevens shook his head, and P8 waved two sets of arms in a gesture equivalent to a humanoid shrug. "We really can't be sure, sir," Stevens said.

"Can you tell me anything about it? Anything *definite?*"

"It was bright," P8 said.

Gold frowned, then aimed his furrowed brow at Soloman. "Were you able to recover the *Orion*'s logs?"

"Not all of them," Soloman said. "I downloaded the flight data and most of the primary sensor logs. The mission was aborted before I could copy the crew's official and personal logs, which you indicated were low-priority."

"I understand," Gold said. "Good work. Have McAllan start analyzing them as soon as possible."

"He's already started, sir."

"Since we can't tow the *Orion* back to orbit, our only priority now is to recover the Wildfire device," Gold said to everyone as he activated the monitor on the wall behind his chair. It showed a map of the planet's atmospheric currents. An ominous patch of shifting reds and oranges, indicating violent thermal disturbances, lay ahead of the *da Vinci*'s projected course.

"We don't have much time," Gold said. "We and the *Orion* are being pulled toward some nasty weather that leads down to the deepest layers of the atmosphere. *Orion* probably won't survive the trip. We have about thirty minutes to go over there, get the warhead, and get back. Blue, you'll be flying Duffy back to the *Orion*. Bring him back safely, please."

"Aye, sir."

"Duffy, stay behind a moment. Everyone else, dismissed." Gold and Duffy waited while the rest of the group filed out of the briefing room.

Gold handed a padd to Duffy. "These are the security codes for the Wildfire device. Don't reveal them to anyone."

Duffy stared at the padd and scrutinized the codes. "Fairly standard," Duffy said matter-of-factly. Gold regarded the young officer with a grave expression.

"Duffy, before Corsi's transmission was cut off, she told Gomez she believed the device had been armed. If that's true, you'll need all sixteen of those codes to shut it down."

"No problem."

"I don't want any heroics from you, Duffy. If you don't think you can shut it down before *Orion* hits the vortex, get out of there. Once the device hits detonation depth, we'll have less than three hours to get out of orbit."

"How long will it take the device to reach detonation depth?"

"What, I'm a fortune-teller? Depending on the size of the thermal vortex, it might reach the core in an hour, a day, or never. But if you're aboard the *Orion* when it takes that ride, it'll be a one-way ticket. Understand?"

"Perfectly, sir."

"Good. Get down to the shuttle bay and suit up. You have three minutes." Duffy followed Gold out the door into the corridor, where they turned in opposite directions. Duffy stopped Gold with a question.

"Why me, sir?"

"Excuse me?" Gold said, turning to face him.

"Why did you pick me for this mission?"

"Your experience with protomatter-based systems and your ability to perform well under pressure."

"Oh," Duffy said, a bit embarrassed. "I thought you were going to say 'Why not.'"

Gold nodded and answered over his shoulder as he

walked away. "That was my other answer. Two minutes and thirty seconds, Duffy. Don't be late."

9

The thermal eruptions around Work Bug One were becoming more frequent and more powerful with each passing minute, and P8 Blue was using four of her limbs to hold herself steady as the industrial utility craft shivered from each massive thunderclap. Buffeting currents threatened to shear Bug One away from the *Orion*'s forward starboard docking port, whose interlocking metal rings screeched in protest as their limits were repeatedly tested.

P8 made yet another adjustment to the Work Bug's null-field settings, hoping she could minimize the effects of the turbulence and the volume of the thunder that followed each slashing bolt of lightning. The immense green electrical discharges were also becoming more intense, and now were arcing around the *Orion* in a nearly constant, blinding macabre dance.

The Nasat engineer wished she could simply pull her appendages inward and roll into her defensive posture, but if she did she would be unable to watch the console and monitor Duffy's vital signs, which currently appeared to be normal and steady. P8 noted the timer counting down the minutes and seconds remaining before *Orion* intersected the thermal vortex that lay ahead, and she keyed the comm switch. "Bug One to Duffy. Fourteen minutes, Commander."

Several seconds passed with no reply. P8 checked

Duffy's vital signs, which still appeared normal. She was about to repeat her transmission when his voice crackled weakly over the staticky channel.

"I know," Duffy said. *"Stand by."*

P8 let out a few worried clicks as she listened to the grinding of metal against metal coming from the docking port. She was a structural engineer by training and knew that what she was hearing was a very bad sound. *Stand by,* she thought cynically. *Easy for him to say.*

Every muscle in Duffy's body felt like it was being tied into a knot as he strained to separate the control cone of the Wildfire device from its protomatter payload. Duffy had ascertained the device was in the final stages of prelaunch when disaster struck the *Orion,* which meant the device was fully armed. The only way to disarm it now was to separate its trigger from the protomatter that would fuel the artificial stellar ignition.

The first twelve steps had been easy for Duffy. He simply followed the codes Gold had given him, entering them in sequence into the device's holographic interface. But now, four steps away from finishing the procedure, his progress had come to a halt over a simple lack of leverage.

The device rested on the loading rail into the firing tube, which was at roughly chest height for Duffy. Between the height of the loading rail, the proliferation of debris cluttering the small compartment, and the fact that without main power the device would have to be decoupled and taken off the rail manually, Duffy was in a difficult position.

He adjusted the settings of his magboots and half-walked, half-pulled himself up the wall where the loading rail entered the firing tube. Then he took two careful steps, placing one foot on each side of the metallic rail, and began slowly shuffling toward the device. Within a few seconds, he had managed to seat himself on top of the warhead trigger. With enormous effort, he bent his leg farther than he thought anatomically possible and braced his foot against the front edge of the protomatter payload casing. Gripping the edge of the warhead with both hands, he began to push with his foot.

Duffy held his breath and exerted himself with a migraine-inducing grunt. A wave of pain started in his groin and extended into his temples. He tried to use the pain to his advantage, as a focus for his efforts. *Come on, dammit! Shake loose before I hurt something important.*

His grunt evolved into a shout of agony and frustration as his first attempt failed. A gust of breath burst from his lungs, and he gasped quickly, determined to try again as soon as the red spots swimming in his vision faded a bit. He blinked once and noted the countdown on his helmet's visor display. He had eleven minutes to get this warhead off the *Orion* before it got sucked down a one-way turbolift to hell.

He drew a deep breath and felt the tension coiling in his gut as he braced his foot for a second go. Another grunt welled up from somewhere just below his diaphragm. Suppressing his fatigue and pain, he struggled against what he was quickly coming to think of as "the immovable object."

His left foot slipped off the edge of the device. He lost his balance and tumbled backward off the rail, flailing in a slow-motion descent through the dense hydrogen murk, onto the detritus-strewn deck.

Shaking off the fall, he swept the beam of his palm beacon through the compartment. The narrow band of polarized light revealed a grim tableau of skeletons entangled in ODN cables, ruptured bulkheads, and dormant consoles. Then he saw something, half-buried, that might prove useful. He scrambled on all fours over to the corner of the room, and pulled a narrow piece of broken duranium hull plating from beneath a pile of fiber-optic wires. The metal was roughly a meter and a half long, and just over two centimeters thick—an ideal lever.

Duffy carried his new, makeshift tool over to the Wildfire device, his confidence bolstered. *Time for a rematch*, he thought. He wedged the lever between the warhead and its payload and summoned his irresistible force for another round versus the immovable object.

The mood on the *da Vinci* bridge was tense but subdued. On the main viewer, the *Orion* was barely visible through the swirling currents and increasingly violent lightning storm, and the muted rumble of thunder had swelled into an ominous, near-constant presence, like the hammer of a titan beating the *da Vinci* in an irregular tempo.

Gold walked slowly around the perimeter of the bridge, past several dimmed consoles. Every nonessential system had already been taken offline to add power to the *da Vinci*'s structural integrity field, yet the hull continued to moan from the immense pressure of the gas giant's atmosphere. He noted that some of the bridge officers seemed unfazed by the tumult—Ina and McAllan both maintained a coolly professional demeanor—while others, such as Soloman and Wong, seemed now to be wishing they had never joined Starfleet in the first place.

The captain joined Gomez and McAllan at the tactical console. Gold saw McAllan had divided his display into two equal halves. On the left he was reviewing the *Orion*'s flight data from the moments before its disastrous power loss; on the right he was monitoring the current status of Work Bug One and the structural integrity of the *Orion*, as well as keeping an eye on the countdown to the *Steamrunner*-class ship's impending descent into the planet's core.

"Any theories yet?" Gold said, careful to keep his

voice down. McAllan remained focused on the changing screens of data from the *Orion*'s flight recorder.

"I don't think you'll like it," McAllan said quietly.

"Try me," Gold said.

McAllan tapped a few commands into his console and showed the captain a series of reports generated by probes sent into Galvan VI. "The S.C.E. surveyed this planet sixteen times over three years to prepare for the Wildfire test. None of the probes encountered anything like the energy-dampening field that crippled the *Orion*." McAllan presented a few more screens of information. "They scanned the planet's thermal layers down to nearly forty-five thousand kilometers. The S.C.E. computer-modeled most of the rest."

Gomez studied the thermal-imaging scans, then shook her head. "Looks like they got it wrong. These convection patterns shouldn't be possible in a planet this size."

"That's what the Wildfire project leader said." McAllan called up a written status report. "That's why the S.C.E. retrofitted *Orion* with a specialized active-tachyon scanning system. Their orders were to map the planet core, feed the data to the device, and send it on its merry way."

Gold could already see where McAllan was headed. "You think there's a connection between the scans of the planet's core and the attack on the *Orion?*"

"There was no sign of this phenomenon before *Orion* shot those tachyon pulses down there," McAllan said. "It appears to be localized around the *Orion*, and it seems to be drawn to the Wildfire device—which just happens to be the one thing that might completely obliterate this planet. If you ask me, Captain, I'd say this looks like self-defense."

Gold nodded. "You may be right," he said. "In which case, the sooner we get the device out of the atmosphere the bett—"

The *da Vinci* heaved violently upward, then rolled quickly to port as the ship's inertial dampeners reset themselves. The impact knocked Gomez halfway over the railing that circled the upper deck of the bridge. McAllan landed hard on the floor, along with Gold and most of the rest of the bridge crew. Ina and Wong clung to their consoles as Gold struggled back to his feet.

"Report!" Gold shouted over the howling din.

"Thermal upswell, sir," Wong said. "We took a direct hit."

"Damage report," Gold said as he stumbled across the pitching deck and landed with a grunt against his chair.

Ina scanned the alerts quickly appearing on her console. "Plasma leaks in starboard warp nacelle . . . shield generator three overloaded . . . ventral-side hull damage near the aft impulse reactor."

"Casualties?"

"Minor injuries in engineering—scrapes and burns."

Breathing a cautious sigh of relief, Gold said, "Wong, keep an eye out for those upswells."

"Aye, sir," the young helmsman said.

Gold squinted at the main viewer, as if that would help him pierce the curtain of static flurrying across it. He could feel it in his fingertips and in the soles of his feet—his ship, trembling beneath him, its every shudder an echo of the violence surrounding it in this nightmarish place.

Every instinct Gold possessed told him to abandon the *Orion* and take his ship back to the placid vacuum of space. But he had his orders, and he thought of Duffy and Blue, whom he had sent into that maelstrom. He wasn't leaving until they were safely back on the *da Vinci*.

A nova-bright flash of light flared on the main viewer. Gold lifted a hand to shield his eyes, and the rest of the bridge crew followed suit. A second later, the flare dimmed.

"Magnify," Gold ordered.

Ina adjusted the main viewer, which still showed only overlapping lines of zigzagging interference. Within seconds details returned, and Gold's mouth felt painfully dry as he saw the glowing, smoldering gash that a bolt of lightning had just sliced across the *Orion*'s forward hull.

He glanced over his shoulder at Gomez, who was staring anxiously at the main viewer, then looked at McAllan.

"That's it," Gold said to McAllan. "Get them out of there."

What happened? Where am I?

Duffy reached toward his face, tried to rub his eyes—only to find the faceplate of his Starfleet pressure suit in the way.

Pressure suit. I'm in a . . . I'm on the floor.

Duffy felt the tremendous pressure of the semifluid hydrogen that filled the ship crushing down on him. He lay on his back, legs splayed apart, rumpled like dirty laundry over the wreckage on the deck. He licked his lips, which were dry, cracked, and bleeding. The sharp sting of saliva in the tender wounds helped him edge closer to consciousness.

He keyed the switch for his palm beacon. The beam sliced through the haze as he began to notice a terrible, erratic throbbing that felt like either a headache or his heart pounding its way out of his chest.

The beacon's intense bluish beam fell upon a metal bar fused to what looked like a modified photon torpedo casing. The bar was probably close to two meters long, but it was twisted—melted?—into an S-shape. Above and beyond the misshapen metal bar, large sections of the bulkhead were blasted apart, glowing white-hot and smoldering.

*Not a headache . . . not my heart. That's . . . thunder.
That's thunder.*

Crackling noise filled Duffy's ears, which were ring-ing and felt like they were packed with wax. The sound was just a faraway scratch of electronic spatters at first, then he was able to discern words. *"Duffy, do . . . read . . . —bort . . . Please resp— . . . Blue to Duff—"*

His confusion began to clear, and clarity returned in waves. *The* Orion. *I'm on the . . . I'm retrieving the device. Wildfire device. It's armed . . . I . . . I need to get up.*

He keyed his comm and increased the gain on the transceiver. "Duffy to Blue. I'm okay, I think."

P8 responded through the yowling, high-frequency signal disruptions, which were quickly growing worse. *"Get back to the Bug. Gold's orders are to abort. We have four minutes to get back to the* da Vinci."

Duffy looked up at the metal bar, conjoined to the Wildfire device's outer casing at the molecular level, and was suddenly grateful he hadn't become part of that impromptu sculpture. He grabbed onto a piece of bulkhead jutting out from the wall and pulled himself to his feet. "Get ready to fly," Duffy said. "I'm on my way."

"Be careful, sir," P8 said.

Duffy fought to overcome an attack of vertigo as he lifted his foot over a lightning-cut, half-molten gap in the wall that was now the only exit from the compart-ment. "A bit late for that," Duffy said.

Setting his magboots to minimum grip, he broke into a clumsy walk-jog through the rolling, mangled, smok-ing corridors of the *Orion.* He hoped Pattie and the Work Bug would both still be there when he arrived.

"More power to stabilizers!" Gold shouted. "Keep her steady, Wong!"

At the helm, the young ensign struggled to comply, but the turbulence around the tiny starship had grown more violent. Another blast of superheated, superdense gas erupted beneath the ship, which listed sharply to starboard. The roar of the storm outside the vessel had become overpowering, and the bridge lights flickered erratically.

Gomez looked up from the damage reports that were flooding in from engineering and glanced at the main viewscreen. The small, vulnerable-looking Work Bug was fighting its way through the fiery maelstrom, back to the *da Vinci*, but the constantly shifting currents tumbled the tiny craft end over end, spinning it in all directions, trapping it halfway between the two starships. *Come on*, Gomez thought as she watched the Work Bug struggle forward. *Another half-kilometer, you can make it.*

A massive, spinning pillar of liquid-metal hydrogen—fresh from the planet's core—formed between two enormous cloud layers and grabbed the Work Bug, pulling it in quickly shrinking circles toward what Gomez realized would be almost certain destruction. She thought of Kieran, trapped inside the small craft, and felt a chill wash through her as she watched Bug One accelerate toward its doom.

"Wong," Gold said, "Take us in fast. Angle the shuttle bay doors toward the Bug and try to disrupt that twister."

The conn officer set the *da Vinci* on a course directly into the swirling column of scorching, liquid-metal hydrogen.

"McAllan," Gold said as the spinning wall of semi-fluid fire grew large on the main viewer, "tell them the cavalry's coming."

The view outside the Work Bug's cockpit window was a blurry wash of moving colors, and Duffy—pinned to the port bulkhead by the centrifugal force of their inward spiral—felt extremely dizzy. He gasped for breath after his second round of painful dry heaves, and was suddenly very glad he had missed two meals in a row today. He was barely able to hear P8 over the deafening cacophony of thunder crashing in an unbroken chorus around the craft. He tapped in front of his ear, which P8 understood meant he wanted her to repeat herself. She spoke slowly, with overly perfect diction.

"The *da Vinci* is coming to get us," she said, fighting to regain helm control. Duffy, with great effort, nodded once. He could no longer turn his head far enough to see what she was doing at the controls; all he could do was relax and remain stuck against the inner hull of the Work Bug, waiting either for death or a Starfleet-issued miracle. *There isn't a damn thing I can do now,* he thought. *This could all be over in a few seconds. . . . I might never see Sonnie again.*

Duffy was hurled from the port bulkhead. He slammed hard into the starboard airlock door before rolling ass-over-elbows toward the front of the Work Bug. Before he could ask P8 what was happening, a jarring collision knocked him backward, then upward— which was now downward—onto the Work Bug's ceiling, and he heard a sound that on any other day would have made him cringe, but right now was sweeter than a Trill lullaby: the high-pitched scrape of duranium on duranium. Duffy rolled onto his stomach, blinked, and realized P8 had made a textbook-perfect, upside-down, backward-facing crash-landing in the *da Vinci* shuttle bay.

"Good landing," Duffy said without a hint of irony.

"Thank you," P8 said.

Duffy reached up to help P8 out of her pilot's seat harness. Outside the cockpit windshield, beyond the shuttle bay entrance's crackling, overtaxed protective force field, he could barely see the shape of the *Orion*, ringed by lightning, roughly a kilometer away. He keyed his comm circuit and was about to hail the bridge when the *Orion* suddenly was silhouetted by an incandescent flash from a huge, explosive thermal upswell. Duffy squinted hard and lifted his arm to block the glare.

P8 let out a panicked string of high-frequency clicks.

Duffy lowered his arm to see the *Orion* flying like a *targ* out of *Gre'thor*, directly toward the *da Vinci*.

It all happened in three-point-five seconds.

Everyone on the *da Vinci* bridge saw the flash on the main viewer, the eruption directly behind the *Orion* that sent the *Steamrunner*-class starship speeding toward them.

McAllan reacted first. "Collision alarm!" he shouted, sounding the shipwide alert klaxon as he did so.

"Evasive!" Gold ordered. To Gold, the moment seemed trapped in amber. Wong entered commands at the helm, but he seemed to move in slow motion, as did the *Orion*, rolling toward them through the swirling mists like a blazing wheel.

"Brace for impact!" Gold ordered. The burning husk of the *Orion* filled the main viewer. Gold grabbed the arms of his chair and focused on the rising whine of the *da Vinci's* impulse engines, which strained against the planet's crushing gravity and dense, smothering atmosphere.

The image on the main viewer shifted, but not quickly enough. Gold felt it before it happened. *This is what it feels like when your luck runs out,* he thought.

The *Orion* smashed like a hammer into the *da Vinci*.

10

The moment of impact was the most terrible thing Gold had ever heard; he could swear the *da Vinci* howled in pain as the *Orion*'s primary hull rammed into its underside. The tremor from the collision flung him from his seat, and the echoing boom sent a stabbing pain through his eardrums. The rest of the bridge crew seemed to be tumbling in slow motion through the air, caught in the strobing flicker of the malfunctioning main viewscreen and stuttering overhead lights.

He hit the deck hard, on his back, his breath knocked out of him. Fighting to inhale, he pulled himself back toward his chair. To his right he saw Gomez, clinging to the railing and shouting orders over the sound and fury of explosions and alarm klaxons. "Damage report!" she said, sleeving a broad smear of blood from her forehead to reveal a jagged cut that immediately resumed bleeding.

"Comms are down," Ina said, her voice betraying the first signs of panic. "Sensors are offline, we're losing pow—"

Another explosion rocked the *da Vinci*. Gold felt the deck heave and lurch, and he knew another thermal upswell had pummeled his ship. He fell hard against his seat as the bridge lights flickered out, and the only illumination came from the exploding science console to his left.

Then he saw McAllan moving through the air toward him.

Gold thought an explosion had tossed McAllan forward, but then he realized the tactical officer was intentionally vaulting over his console, directly at him, one arm outstretched. McAllan's hand slammed into Gold's shoulder, knocking the captain off his feet. As Gold fell he saw the bridge ceiling's central support hub—which was located directly above the captain's chair—collapsing down in a heap of twisted duranium. Gold, still unable to breathe, lay paralyzed as the wreckage crushed his tactical officer—and his own left hand.

At first, Gold felt nothing from his hand, which he knew must have been pulverized. Then agonizing pain shot up his arm. He would have screamed, but his lungs continued to resist his attempts at breathing.

The bridge was in chaos, filling with panicked voices and billowing smoke, but to Gold, who was rapidly growing weaker, it all seemed light-years away—unreal, like a bad dream or a holodeck illusion.

He summoned a mental image of his wife, Rachel. She had always said his impatience would be the death of him. *Guess you were right, sweetheart,* he thought, as consciousness slipped from his grasp. *Forgive me.*

The impact of the *Orion*'s collision with the *da Vinci* had knocked Work Bug One onto its starboard side, placing its hatch on the floor. As the shuttle bay began to collapse around it, Duffy decided that having only one exit hatch from the utility craft definitely qualified as a design flaw.

The view beyond the force field was spinning wildly, which he realized meant the *da Vinci* was out of control. They had to get out of the shuttle bay now. "Fire starboard thrusters!" Duffy said as the shuttle bay's force field began to collapse.

"The navigational thrusters aren't designed to—"

"That's an order!"

P8 keyed the thrusters as a second jolt pummeled the *da Vinci*, lifting the Work Bug half a meter off the deck. The combined force of the impact and the thrusters rolled the small craft wildly toward the side wall of the shuttle bay. Duffy tumbled inside the rear of the vehicle like a specimen in a centrifuge, cursing as he banged roughly off every solid surface. The Work Bug struck the wall with a hollow thud and came to a stop resting right side up.

Duffy shouldered open the battered hatch and looked back to make certain P8 was with him. Taking advantage of her specially designed EVA gear, she curled herself into a ball and rolled quickly across the floor to the aft-corridor exit. She forced the sliding door open while Duffy sprinted to the shuttle bay's auxiliary control panel. He tapped at the sparking console for a few seconds, trying to reinforce the collapsing force field or close the outer shuttle bay doors, but the system was in near-total failure. He gave up and followed P8 out of the shuttle bay.

The shuttle bay force field collapsed as Duffy reached for the exit's manual closing lever. The rushing wall of superdense, semiliquid gases propelled a shock wave of compressed air that knocked Duffy backward, away from the lever, and lifted the abandoned Work Bug and tossed it forward like a toy in a tornado. P8 grasped the lever and yanked it with four arms. The door slid closed as the corridor rang with the sound of the Work Bug striking the shuttle bay's aft wall.

Chief Engineer Jil Barnak shielded his face with his arms as he dodged through the flames that were spreading rapidly through main engineering. He checked the antimatter containment field and was relieved to find it intact, which, he mused cynically, made it unique among the ship's systems at the moment.

The warp core had gone offline at the moment of impact. Main power had failed almost instantly. Consoles all throughout main engineering had exploded and were now belching columns of acrid black smoke. But his engineers were still at their posts.

"Orthak!" Barnak shouted over the blaring alarms. "Get your flippers over here and shut down the EPS taps, we're venting plasma! O'Leary, transfer impulse power to the—"

A second explosion rocked the ship, knocking the gray-haired Atrean chief engineer off his feet. The smoke was now too heavy to see through, and Barnak choked and coughed as it burned his lungs. He reached for a breathing mask and drew in a few desperately needed breaths of clean air. He turned to finish his order to O'Leary, only to discover the man was now dead, a jagged piece of shrapnel wedged in the back of his skull.

Then Barnak saw the fracture in the matter-antimatter reaction assembly.

The other engineers—those who were still standing—were shouting overlapping damage reports and asking Barnak for his orders, but he had stopped listening. He had to make a critical decision in the next five seconds. He had two options.

He could attempt an emergency shutdown of the warp core, and hope the contents of the reaction assembly could be expelled before that ten-centimeter-long fracture exploded. Purging the core could take up to eleven seconds, and it might take days to repair the fracture. But if he gambled wrong, if the fracture ruptured before he purged the antimatter from the reaction assembly, the resulting explosion would vaporize the *da Vinci*.

His other choice was to eject the warp core, guaranteeing the short-term safety of the ship, but leaving them without warp power until they could be towed back to a starbase. The actual ejection of the core would take only a fraction of a second—but evacuating main engineering with the turbolifts offline would take more than thirty seconds. Barnak was certain the reaction assembly wouldn't last thirty seconds. It might not last ten.

He keyed the safety override and initiated the emergency core-ejection. He knew it was the right decision; his only regret was that he had no time to tell his engineers what was about to happen.

Barnak wondered if his wife would be waiting for him in the afterlife. When he was a young man, his wife, Sindea, had passed away of a sudden illness a few months after they were married. That was more than forty years ago. He had never remarried, choosing instead a solitary life in the service of Starfleet.

A quickly rising hum was all that preceded the electromagnetically propelled ejection of the *da Vinci*'s warp core, which shot down and out of the main engineering compartment in a blur, exiting the ship in a hundredth of a second. The vacuum created by its departure tore the breathable air from main engineering, and pulled Jil Barnak and seven of his engineers out into the atmosphere of Galvan VI, less than four seconds before the warp core exploded.

"Get that force field up!" Stevens said, pointing the beam from his pressure suit's wrist beacon past Faulwell, toward the door to the forward sensor control room. Faulwell, also suited up for the worst, was straining to pull the manual-release lever for the emergency bulkhead in the middle of the corridor.

"I can't," Faulwell said through teeth gritted with effort. "Internal force fields are offline." Stevens cursed under his breath. Without the force fields, they would have to manually close the emergency bulkheads to seal off compromised areas of the ship. He sprinted across the trembling deck to Faulwell's side, grabbed hold of the release lever, and pulled. The lever came free, and both men briskly stepped clear of the quickly closing twenty-centimeter-thick door.

"C'mon," Stevens said. "We have to get down to deck four." Faulwell followed Stevens, who, although an enlisted man, was in charge of the ship's damage-control teams during this kind of crisis. They rounded the corner and practically ran over Abramowitz, who was assisting security guards Eddy and Lipinski. Stevens was glad to see all three women were wearing lightly armored full EVA gear—which he had months ago made a standard for all *da Vinci* damage-control personnel—even though he knew the garments would offer only limited protection without the null-field generators that had been added to the away team's pressure suits. *Still,* he reasoned, *better a small amount of protection than none.*

"Did you secure the science lab?" Stevens asked Eddy. She shook her head.

"It's already gone. We had to seal corridor two."

"Damn. Let's get down to deck four."

Stevens led the way to the turbolift. As he stepped in front of the doors, he realized they were quaking. A thin spray of blistering, liquefied hydrogen jetted out of the crack between the sliding doors and struck his pressure suit like a red-hot scalpel. He dived to his left, tackling Abramowitz as the turbolift doors bulged outward and a jet of superheated semifluid hydrogen began flooding into the corridor. The wall beyond the turbolift buckled inward.

"Run!" Stevens said. "Get to the ladder!"

The five of them sprinted as quickly as their bulky EVA gear would allow, the churning flood of inferno-hot gases lapping at their heels as they retreated. With the rushing, knee-deep flood rebounding off the bulkheads only seconds behind them, they rounded two corners and logjammed at the emergency access ladder. It was claustrophobically narrow for one person even in a regular uniform, and barely navigable for one wearing a pressure suit. Stevens pushed Abramowitz forward and up the ladder. "Climb, fast."

Abramowitz scrambled up the ladder as quickly as

she was able. As soon as she had climbed high enough for another person to get on the ladder, Stevens pulled Faulwell forward. "Go." Faulwell grabbed the rungs of the ladder. Stevens looked up to see Abramowitz opening the hatch to deck two and climbing through. Faulwell followed as quickly as he could.

Stevens turned toward Eddy and Lipinski. "Don't even think about it," Eddy said. "Move it, Stevens." Stevens grinned and climbed, his hands hitting the rungs the moment Faulwell's foot was clear. Stevens glanced down as he neared the top, and saw Eddy on the ladder just below him. As he pulled himself over the lip of the opening onto deck two, he heard an explosion from the deck below and looked down.

Lipinski was at the bottom of the ladder, looking back into the corridor. Stevens thought she was about to say something, when a wall of searing liquefied hydrogen slammed into her with terrifying speed and force. She went limp without making a sound, and the flood raced up the ladder shaft.

Eddy, still on the ladder, looked up at Stevens, her expression calm as she pulled the manual release for the access ladder's emergency bulkhead. The thick barrier snapped shut between her and Stevens, and the upswell of liquid metal struck it with a gruesome, muffled thud.

Faulwell reached down and offered his hand to Stevens. "Come on," Faulwell said. "We have to move."

Stevens, numb, took his friend's hand. Faulwell helped him to his feet, and gently prodded him forward as they moved to seal the next bulkhead.

Duffy stumbled to a halt as he found the corridor ahead blocked by imploded walls and burning plasma conduits. He turned back and saw P8 Blue was still right behind him; her annoyed clicking noises, rendered hollow-sounding by their suits' short-range transceivers, echoed inside his helmet. *"If the starboard side is blocked, we're trapped,"* P8 said as she followed Duffy toward their only other route off this deck.

"Lucky for us I'm a gambling man," Duffy said. The pair turned the corner, and at the far end of the starboard corridor saw Security Guard Loten closing an emergency bulkhead. Duffy waved frantically at Loten and quickened his pace toward the Bajoran man, who noticed Duffy as the bulkhead began to close. Loten reversed the lever, opening the door, and gestured to Duffy and P8 to hurry. Loten pulled the release lever for the bulkhead as the pair scrambled across the threshold, and P8 squeezed through the narrowing gap barely in time.

Duffy and P8 were just getting their bearings on the other side of the bulkhead as Loten started hurrying off port-side. Duffy keyed his suit's comm. "Loten. What's the fastest route to the bridge?"

Loten stopped, turned back toward Duffy, and forced open a pair of sliding doors leading to an empty horizontal turbolift shaft. *"Only way forward, sir,"* he said, pointing into the shaft. *"Breaches all over this deck. Ladder's still clear in section one."* Loten turned away and resumed his rush toward the port-side corridor. *"Gotta seal the mid-hatch before we lose this deck. Good luck, sir."*

He sprinted clumsily away in his EVA gear and vanished around the corner.

Duffy and P8 stepped into the horizontal turbolift shaft, closed the sliding doors behind them, and activated their wrist beacons. Until now, Duffy had thought of the *da Vinci* as a small ship. Suddenly, it looked much longer than he had remembered.

As he and P8 moved toward the front of the ship, the sounds of the crumpling outer hull seemed to grow louder and more distinct. Then he realized it was because the thunder and roaring currents he had been tuning out for the past several hours had suddenly ceased. For a moment, he wondered if they had escaped the storms and made it out of the atmosphere.

Then the shrieks of collapsing metal from the ship's outer hull grew worse than ever, and Duffy realized that the *da Vinci* hadn't climbed above the storms. The ship wasn't on its way back to space. It had been pulled below the storms, into the thermal vortex.

It was sinking.

Concentrate, Chief Diego Feliciano reminded himself as he worked. *Focus.* His thoughts kept drifting homeward, to his wife, Arlene, and only son, Carlos, and he had to keep tearing himself back to the present. He and Damage Control Team Four were racing to boost the power to the ship's structural integrity field, which was failing under the steadily rising pressure of the atmosphere.

To Feliciano's left, security guards Friesner and Frnats were at the end of the dead-end corridor, following a series of extremely simplified directions being given to them by Lieutenant Keith Kowal, the ship's gamma-shift operations officer, who was standing at the other end of the corridor, working on his own tangle of wires and pile of burned-out circuits. Friesner had no trouble identifying this or that piece of hardware, but Frnats didn't know an ODN cable from an isolinear chip, and Kowal was quickly growing impatient with the Bolian woman.

"Just take the small, red rectangular thing out of the top left slot, and throw it on the floor," Kowal said. Frnats did as he instructed, and for the moment things seemed to be on track.

"Chief," Kowal said, "how're we doing with the holo-generator bypass?"

"Almost done, sir," Feliciano said. If Kowal's numbers were right, they had less than two minutes to increase the SIF's power before the entire ship imploded. As soon as Kowal finished his EPS tap, Feliciano would shunt it and the ship's other auxiliary power sources to the new bypass. As long as they didn't have to explain to Frnats what any of that meant, they might just make it.

Or they might not.

The corridor's outer wall began to warp, and the deck under their feet heaved and contracted. This corridor was seconds away from disintegrating. Feliciano saw his own look of recognition reflected in the faces of Kowal, Frnats, and Friesner.

Kowal turned his attention back to the EPS bypass in front of him. "Feliciano, I need you to stay," he said, then nodded his head sideways toward the open doorway beside him. "Frnats, Friesner, move forward and seal this bulkhead behind you."

Friesner continued rerouting various independent power sources to Kowal and Feliciano's new relay. "Seal it yourself, sir," she said, her hands moving quickly inside the mangled machinery. "I'm still working here."

Frnats turned to face the bank of glowing isolinear chips in front of her. "Ready for your next order, sir."

Kowal nodded. "Connect circuits one and two."

Feliciano saw the pieces of his own engineering puzzle quickly coming together. "Ready for bypass in ten seconds, sir," he said confidently. *Just a few more seconds. We can do this.*

There was a deafening roar as the wall behind the damage control team splintered. Feliciano felt the searing heat on his back even through his radiation-shielded pressure suit. It reminded him of the worst sunburn he ever got, when he was a boy visiting his grandfather's house in Havana, where his wife and son now lived and were home waiting for him. Carlos's seventh birthday was nine days away. Diego had missed his son's last birthday, and he had promised Carlos he would make it home this time. "Cross my heart and hope to die," he had said, drawing an X with his finger across his chest, while his son mimicked him and flashed a smile wider than the Crab Nebula.

Kowal shouted something to Feliciano, then turned and reached for the manual bulkhead release. Feliciano couldn't hear the lieutenant over the wrenching of metal and the howling of liquid-metal hydrogen geysering up through cracks in the deck. He felt his footing slipping.

He made an educated guess that Kowal's EPS tap was ready; with one hand he opened the switch to his own makeshift circuit, and with the other he made the sign of the Cross. *Dios te salve, María, llena eres de gracia* . . . The jury-rigged power relay pulsed to life.

Feliciano saved his last thought for Arlene and Carlos as the deck disintegrated and the outer wall exploded.

Lense's eyes adjusted from the glare of her medical tricorder to the dimly lit sickbay. She was standing over Nancy Conlon, who'd been carried in by security officer Stephen Drew (who was unhurt, as usual) a few moments ago with a sizable chunk of broken duranium protruding from her shoulder blade.

Lense looked from one end of sickbay to the other and counted only six people besides herself: Drew, Conlon, Corsi, medical technician John Copper, Nurse Sandy Wetzel, and Emmett—the Emergency Medical Hologram—who probably didn't even really count as a person. Of the six, only Corsi and Conlon were patients. Lense knew that was a bad sign—in a crisis of this magnitude, few wounded meant many more dead.

She removed the jagged shrapnel from Conlon's shoulder. The petite engineer bit down on her lip and stifled a cry of pain—not that anyone but Lense would have been able to hear her over the melancholy wails of the *da Vinci*'s crumpling outer hull. Wetzel shone a light on Conlon's wound, and Lense was glad to see it was clean of any metal fragments. "Emmett, hand me the sterilizer, please," Lense said.

The holographic physician passed the tool to Lense. "Sterilizer."

Lense used the device to clean the wound, then handed it to Copper and looked back to Emmett. "Dermal regenerator," she said. Emmett reached for the device on the rolling cart next to him. His hand passed through the cart, then a static flicker disrupted his holographic body.

"Emmett?" Lense said. "Are you losing power?"

"A moment, Doctor, I'm running a diagnostic." Emmett's eyes darted from side to side, as if he were reading an invisible book at tremendous speed. He looked up, past Lense, to his program's manual interface on the far wall of sickbay. "Doctor," he said sharply. "Evacuate your staff and patients immediately."

"What's—"

Emmett's voice became distorted and plagued with bursts of harsh static. "The computer that runs— *snnrkkzzzt*—my program is experiencing cascade— *grzzzrrttt*—hardware failures. That wall has been breached from the other side."

Lense grabbed her field surgery kit from the rolling cart. "Wetzel, Copper, grab everything you can!" She slung her surgical kit diagonally from her left shoulder and reached for a first-aid kit. "Surgical supplies, hyposprays, anything!" Wetzel and Copper scrambled to collect every portable piece of sickbay they could find. Lense slung the first-aid kit from her right shoulder and turned toward Conlon. "Can you walk?"

"I think so," Conlon said.

"Go. Drew, you carry Corsi. Everybody move!"

Drew lifted Corsi and moved straight for the door, with Conlon right behind him. Lense sprinted across the room to her office, scooping every loose item within reach into her first-aid kit. She leaned into her office and grabbed from her desk the thank-you plaque she'd been given by the president of Sherman's Planet, and dropped it in with the hypospreys and neural stimulators.

She stepped quickly to the door, and paused in front of Emmett, whose program was rapidly disintegrating. She had told herself hundreds of times he was just a program, a simulation and nothing more. But watching him come apart was like watching a person die, and she couldn't hide her tears, which were undeniably real. "Good-bye, Emmett," she said.

"Good-bye, Doc—*skrrzzk*—tor," he said. As his program collapsed, his garbled, disembodied last words echoed in the empty sickbay. "It's been an honor serving with you."

Lense had forgotten she was still standing in sickbay until Drew shouted her name. "Dr. Lense! Come on!"

She sprinted out of sickbay as the back wall began to collapse. Drew closed the door behind her, then grabbed her arm and pulled her roughly down the pitch-dark corridor. "Sickbay won't hold," he said. "And without pressure suits you folks are sitting ducks. We have to get you up to deck two."

Lense ran behind Drew, trying to follow the thin, quaking beam of light from his pressure suit's wrist-mounted palm beacon. They turned the corner and found Wetzel, Copper, and Conlon waiting for them. Copper and Wetzel were carrying Corsi; each of them had one of the comatose security chief's arms draped across their own shoulders. Conlon had activated her own palm beacon and was widening its beam to better illuminate the corridor ahead. Drew pointed forward.

"Move out," he said. "Double quick-time."

The group hurried down the narrow corridor toward an access ladder. They all had just congregated beneath it, when the corridor behind them reverberated with a thunderous explosion, followed by a shock wave that knocked them to the deck. They heard the rapidly growing roar of something coming toward them.

Drew sprinted away from the group, back the way they had come. Lense had never seen anyone run so quickly, in or out of a pressure suit. "Go!" he yelled back over his shoulder. "Get up the ladder!" Conlon scrambled to get a handhold on the rungs. Wetzel and Copper, holding Corsi between them, froze.

Lense glanced back and saw the flood of superheated liquid-metal hydrogen raging around the corner less than ten meters away. Drew leapt toward one of the emergency bulkhead levers, located just a few meters ahead of the oncoming wall of destruction. He grasped the lever with both hands and let the weight of his falling body pull it down. The emergency bulkhead emerged from the wall and closed quickly as the flood raced toward it.

Drew was on the flood side of the bulkhead. His momentum had carried him past the safe side of the door, and he was unable to get back on his feet in time.

The barrier closed. The corridor vibrated with the low-frequency rumble of the flood striking the bulkhead with enough force to annihilate anything in its path. Lense forced herself to turn away from what she had seen and focused on what she had to do next.

Save the living first, she thought, reminding herself to think like a doctor. She concentrated on remaining calm, detached, professional. *Save lives now. Grieve later.* She'd done it before, when her entire medical staff and half the crew of the *Lexington* were killed at Setlik; she'd do it now.

"Are you all right to climb?" she asked Conlon.

"I'll make it," Conlon said. Lense helped her onto the ladder, and Conlon started her ascent. Lense stood beside Wetzel and Copper and stared back down the corridor at the sealed bulkhead. *Grieve later.*

As soon as Conlon was far enough ahead, Lense stepped onto the ladder and began climbing.

"Hawkins, get those fires out!" Gomez said to the muscular, dark-skinned security guard who'd been assigned to the bridge. She tripped over a chunk of the debris that had killed McAllan and dodged out of Vance Hawkins's way as he hurried past her to extinguish the flames erupting from the science station and licking madly at the ceiling. The bridge was thick with smoke, the stench of burned circuitry, and the smell of blood. The few display screens that hadn't been destroyed now showed only infrequent static.

"Depth nearing fifty-three thousand kilometers," Ina said without looking up from the ops display. She was still at her post, desperately wringing every bit of information she could from her failing console. "Hull pressure is thirty-five million GSC and rising."

"Wong," Gomez said, "increase power, pull us up!"

"We've lost the warp core and impulse power's offline," Wong said. He was trying to pilot the ship with only one hand and half a helm interface. The left side of his console had exploded and shredded his left hand with hundreds of tiny pieces of shattered data crystals and tripolymer membrane.

"Thrusters," Gomez said. "All thrusters to maximum." She knew it was illogical to think navigational thrusters alone could enable a ship the size of the *da Vinci* to reach escape velocity from the gravity well of a gas giant, but she had to try.

Wong complied, but the banshee-like groan of the ship's collapsing hull was punctuated by another deep, muffled explosion—the sound of another section of the ship being compromised and flooded.

"Ina, can we get more power to the structural integrity field?"

"Not from here," Ina said. "It's already at maximum."

"How long will it hold?" Gomez asked, dreading the answer.

"On auxiliary power?" Ina tapped a few keys. "Seventeen hours, forty-one minutes." Her console chirped a warning. "But we're about to—" The bridge's emergency lights flickered erratically, then dimmed rapidly. "—lose auxiliary power," Ina said, finishing her thought as her console went dark.

Wong turned away from his console to face Gomez. "Helm's gone, Commander," he said flatly. "She won't pull up."

Activity on the bridge halted. There was nothing more to say, nothing more to be done. Gomez sagged to the floor next to Captain Gold, who lay unconscious, his left hand pinned under a ton of duranium. Soloman was kneeling next to the captain, providing whatever first aid he could.

Gomez considered recording a final log entry, then realized she couldn't—there was no power for the log recorder. All around her, the bridge crew seemed dazed, paralyzed. She wiped the blood from her brow and smeared it across the front of her uniform jacket. As she did, she felt the bump of something in her jacket's inside pocket. She reached inside and took out the ring Duffy had given her nearly seven hours ago.

The diamond was flawless. It caught even the dimmest glimmer of light from the emergency illumination above Gomez's head and seemed to shine in her hand. She didn't know if Kieran and Pattie had made it back aboard the *da Vinci* before the *Orion* made impact. Caressing the gem's cold facets with her fingertip, she tuned out the cries of distress from the *da Vinci*'s fracturing outer hull.

An ear-splitting, bone-jarring impact rocked the ship. As the last of the emergency lights went out, the last thing Gomez felt was the diamond ring clutched in her hand.

11

Gomez awoke to the snap of Ina Mar cracking a chemical flare to life. Its pale violet glimmer bolstered the dim glow of other flares she had scattered around the smoke-filled bridge. Gomez brushed a lock of her hair from her forehead, then gingerly touched the gash on her forehead with her fingertips. The wound was still sticky with half-dried blood.

Even after several minutes the emergency lights had not come back on, which meant auxiliary power was gone. The only thing keeping the ship's structural integrity field from collapsing under the pressure of the gas giant's atmosphere was a very small number of industrial-grade sarium krellide batteries with what were now certain to be very abbreviated life spans.

The bridge was eerily quiet. There was no throb of engines, no hum of life-support systems, none of the muted vibrations through the deck that became routine elements of the environment when one lived aboard a starship. Now that the ship had sunk below the meteorologically active levels of the planet's atmosphere, the cacophony of thunder and thermal swells that had buffeted the ship for hours before the accident were conspicuously absent.

The groaning of the hull had also diminished significantly; Gomez grimly concluded that most of the outer compartments and lower decks had imploded after the collision with the *Orion,* and the habitable areas of the ship were now likely limited to the central areas and uppermost decks. Fortunately, that included the bridge, which, though damaged, was still mostly intact. Gomez surveyed her surroundings; it stank of charred wiring, chemical flame retardant, and blood. Hawkins was extinguishing the last of the small fires inside the shattered aft console displays; Ina was lighting another chemical glow-stick; Wong exited through the bridge's aft door to the corridor outside, where the crew had set up a makeshift triage area.

Dr. Lense knelt in the center of the bridge, next to the unconscious Captain Gold. The white-haired captain's left hand and wrist were pinned under a heavy mass of fallen ceiling support beams; the small mountain of metal would have killed him had McAllan not leapt forward and sacrificed his own life to push the captain most of the way clear. Lense glanced at the display of her medical tricorder and shook her head as she reached into her shoulder bag for a laser scalpel. With quiet precision she activated the beam, and a faint odor of searing flesh crept into Gomez's nostrils as Lense began amputating the captain's left hand just above the wrist. She cut quickly through muscle and bone, the beam cauterizing the flesh as it went. She clicked off the scalpel and put it back into her shoulder bag.

"Commander?" Lense said to Gomez, nodding toward Gold. Gomez helped her lift the captain from the deck; he seemed surprisingly light. They carried him out to the corridor, where Wetzel and Copper tended to five patients, who sat on the floor. The light from Wetzel's and Copper's palm beacons slashed back and forth in the darkness as the pair moved from one patient to another.

The two women gently placed the captain between the gamma-shift helm officer, Robin Rusconi, who was awake and grimacing as she bore her pain in silence, and gamma-shift tactical officer Joanne Piotrowski, who was unconscious. Lense took a dermal regenerator from her shoulder bag and slowly repaired the jagged wound on Gomez's forehead. Gomez stood still and let

Lense work. She watched Wetzel and Copper position a handful of violet glow-sticks Ina had just brought them, trying to maximize their area of illumination. She looked back at Lense as the doctor finished and put away the regenerator.

"Do we have a head count, Doctor?"

Lense nodded and watched Wetzel and Copper as she answered. "Four confirmed dead: McAllan, Eddy, Lipinski, and Drew. Another eighteen missing and presumed dead—most of them in the engineering section and damage-control teams." She gestured to the five patients in the corridor. "We have five seriously injured: Gold, Corsi, Piotrowski, Rusconi, and Shabalala. The rest of us I'd call 'walking wounded.'"

"How soon can you have them back on their feet?" Gomez said, gesturing toward the wounded. Lense shook her head.

"Without a sickbay? No time soon." Lense held out her medical tricorder and flipped through several screens of data while interpreting it for Gomez.

"Shabalala has third-degree burns over almost half his body," she said, referring to the beta-shift tactical officer. "Rusconi has a shattered femur and fibula, a broken knee, and a fractured pelvis. Piotrowski has a serious skull fracture and concussion, a broken clavicle, and multiple internal injuries. She's lost a lot of blood, and she's still hemorrhaging. Lucky for her she has the same blood type as Wetzel. We'll start transfusing her in a few minutes, then I'll begin surgery."

Gomez frowned. "Gold and Corsi?"

"Gold's in shock. Corsi's still comatose, but stable."

"Keep me posted, Doctor." On the edge of her vision, Gomez caught the flicker of a new beam of light emanating from around the corner at the end of the corridor. The shaft of light bobbed with the walking motion of whoever was carrying it, revealing by degrees the curling ribbons of acrid smoke that snaked lazily through the corridors. A long shadow was cast ahead of the beam, its shape amorphous but growing more distinct as its owner neared the corner.

A moment later, Gomez was relieved to see the familiar, diminutive eight-limbed shape of P8 Blue. P8 was walking upright and appeared unharmed. The palm beacon silhouetting her body was still behind the corner. Then P8 stepped forward, and Duffy entered the corridor behind her. He swung his beam across the row of seated patients, then onto Gomez.

"Everybody hurt?" Duffy asked. "Anyone all right?" Gomez usually appreciated Duffy's sarcastic humor, but this time his instinct to deflect tragedy with a flip remark annoyed her. She said nothing as he and P8 walked over to her.

"Sorry we're late," he said quietly as he settled in next to Gomez. "Traffic was a—"

"Round up everyone who can walk and join me on the bridge immediately," Gomez interrupted. She turned and strode purposefully back to the bridge.

From behind her, she heard Duffy's quiet reply: "Yes, ma'am."

Duffy and Stevens, both free of their bulky environment suits and back in regular uniform, stood together at the aft end of the bridge, leaning against the railing and looking over the pile of broken metal that was now hard not to think of as McAllan's burial mound. Gomez paced over a short open patch of deck in front of the mound, reversing direction after every third or fourth step, being careful always to turn in the direction that kept her from making eye contact with Duffy. Her every motion was watched by eleven of the fourteen remaining, assembled active members of the *da Vinci* crew, besides herself. Only Lense, Wetzel, and Copper were absent, busy preparing for surgery on Piotrowski.

"Where, exactly, are we?" Gomez said to Wong. The once-boyish-looking Asian man cradled his crudely bandaged left hand as he sat in front of his scorched, shattered helm console. Gomez noted that Wong seemed to have aged in the past few hours. The look in his eyes had changed, had become hard and distant.

"We're about fifty-nine thousand kilometers deep in the atmosphere," Wong said, "drifting around the planet's equator, suspended in a layer of superheated liquid-metal hydrogen. The structural integrity field is the only thing keeping our hull from melting. Once the SIF runs out of power, it's anyone's guess whether we'll burn up or be crushed first."

Gomez turned toward Ina, who was seated at what was left of her regular post at ops. "Engineering damage report?"

Ina checked her tricorder. "The warp core's been ejected, leaving us without main power or warp propulsion. The impulse system's ruptured, and all fusion cores went into auto-shutdown as a fail-safe. Auxiliary power failed when the strain of maintaining the structural integrity field overloaded the EPS taps. Right now, we're running on half emergency battery power, and most of that's going to the integrity field, which'll collapse in less than an hour."

"What about escape options?" Gomez said, turning toward Stevens. "Can we abandon ship? Or send a distress signal and hang on until a rescue team arrives?"

"Afraid not, Commander," Stevens said. "Subspace transmitters are gone, and both our shuttles were destroyed by a hull implosion—not that they'd survive long this deep in the atmosphere. Life support's offline, and we're down to four hours of breathable air. Most of the escape pods and a lot of the spare environment suits were lost when the outer compartments imploded. And, even if we could get a signal out, the nearest rescue's at least eighteen hours away. We'll either be out of power or out of air long before then."

Gomez rubbed the stinging sensation from her eyes with the palms of her hands. "What about the main computer?"

Soloman cocked his head slightly. "Tricorder scans indicate the computer core is still intact, but without power we will not be able to bring it back online."

"Could you power it up with one of those portable kits?" Duffy said. "Like the one you brought aboard the *Orion?*"

"Yes," Soloman said. "But I do not think I can reach the access hatch to the core."

"Most of the corridors on that deck are either flooded or have imploded," P8 said.

Gomez nodded, and turned to Conlon. "Conlon, we need to buy ourselves some time," Gomez said to the young woman. "Three more hours, to be precise. Is there any way for you to bring auxiliary power back online for just three more hours?"

Conlon looked petrified by the question. "By myself? Commander, the whole engineering staff is gone, except for me. How am I supposed to—"

Gomez cut her off. "Nancy. We need power to keep the structural integrity field operating for the next three hours while we look for a way out of the atmosphere. I don't care how you do it, but find a way, and do it before the reserve batteries run out in"—Gomez checked her tricorder's chronometer—"about forty-five minutes. Just buy me two more hours after that."

"Why only two hours?" Abramowitz asked.

Hawkins turned to her and answered plainly. "Because that's when we estimate the Wildfire device will detonate, igniting this gas giant into a small star. If we're not gone by then, we're dead no matter what."

Faulwell sighed heavily and shook his head. "I'm so glad you asked that, Carol. Really, I am."

"I know we're down to a skeleton crew," Gomez said, trying to sound reassuring as she looked around the bridge at the desperate faces surrounding her. "But we need to restore power to the SIF in the next forty minutes. Once that's done, we'll focus on escaping the atmosphere." She turned quickly from one person to the next as she fired off orders in a tone that brooked no questions.

"Duffy, Stevens, you're with me. We'll reroute any independent power sources we can find to the emergency batteries.

"Robins, Hawkins, find a safe route to the main computer core for Soloman. Check all emergency bulkheads along the way, make certain they're holding.

"Conlon, Pattie, look for a way to purge main engineering, the impulse core, or any other compartment from which you can reroute primary and auxiliary power.

"Faulwell, Abramowitz, search all secure areas of the ship for extra environment suits, drinkable water, rations, first-aid kits, light sources, tools, tricorders, anything that might be even remotely useful.

"Soloman, Ina, Wong, stay here and try to restore bridge operations.

"Everyone report back here in exactly twenty minutes. And do your best to come bearing good news."

12

Faulwell and Abramowitz struggled for breath as they forced the sliding door half-open and peeked into Lense and Corsi's quarters. The air in the ship was quickly growing hot and stale without the life-support system to counter the heat radiating through the hull from Galvan VI's searing atmosphere.

Faulwell slipped inside the room first, leaving behind in the corridor a makeshift sack he had fashioned by knotting together bedsheets taken from Lipinski and Eddy's shared quarters. The sack was now almost filled with salvaged first-aid kits and small pieces of standard-issue equipment collected from throughout the ship.

Abramowitz followed Faulwell into Lense and Corsi's dark, tiny room, the beam from her palm beacon set wide and casting an enormous, sharp shadow of Faulwell on the far wall.

He quickly riffled through Lense's side of the room, in a routine at which he was quickly becoming too proficient for his own comfort. Looking over his shoulder, he noticed that Abramowitz seemed to be procrastinating, dwelling too long on the small knickknacks that had fallen from a shelf and landed in a random arrangement on Corsi's bunk.

"Carol?" he said. "You okay?" She nodded. "Then we need to hurry," he said. "Check under her bunk—maybe she keeps a spare phaser rifle."

Abramowitz crouched, pulled open the drawers below Corsi's bunk, and started to toss aside articles of civilian clothing. Faulwell finished his own search, which had yielded a spare medical tricorder and a first-aid kit—both of which Lense kept conveniently under her pillow—and turned to see Abramowitz lifting from Corsi's drawer a rectangular wooden case with a clear top. Inside the case was an antique axe. It had a broad, squarish, spike-backed steel head, its red paint heavily scuffed. The head was affixed to a meter-long, gently curved wooden handle whose rough grain and faded flecks of yellow paint betrayed its antiquity. The base of the handle was sheathed in thick, black rubber. The head of the axe rested on a triangle of folded, dark-blue fabric decorated with white stars.

At the bottom of the case, on the glass, there was a small brass plaque bearing an inscription:

> *A firefighter performs*
> *only one act of bravery in his life,*
> *and that's when he takes the oath.*
> *Everything he does after that*
> *is merely in the line of duty.*
> *In Memoriam—September 11, 2001*

"Looks like a family heirloom," Faulwell said.

Abramowitz looked up at Faulwell. "Corsi would want this. We should bring it to her."

"I don't think it's what Gomez had in—"

"Fine, I'll carry it," she said sharply. She stood, cradled the cumbersome box in her arms, and walked toward the door.

"Carol, we're gonna make it out of this," he said, unsure whether he sounded convincing.

She stopped and rested the end of the box gently on the floor, her back to him.

"What if we don't?" she said. The angry tone of her question caught him off guard. She turned back to face him. "If you die out here, what will Anthony do?"

He recoiled for a moment, then cocked his head slightly, chuckled, and took his best guess. "I figure he'll throw a party."

"A party?"

"Mm-hmm. Invite all our friends, serve my favorite lasagna. Play my favorite Chopin nocturnes. Probably try to eulogize me as some kind of Starfleet hero instead of the—" He paused. "Instead of the glorified academic I am." He looked at Abramowitz's face and realized he had been mistaken—she wasn't angry, she was afraid. Her sardonic façade was crumbling as he watched. Her eyes were wet, her voice quaking with emotion too long kept under lock and key.

"There's no one to throw a party for me, Bart."

"Carol? Are you—"

"I've been on the *da Vinci* for almost three years, Bart, and you're the only one I'm really friends with. I just haven't been able to make a . . . a *connection* with any of the others, and I don't know why."

"Maybe it's the *drad* music," he said with a smile, hoping humor could steer her out of her downward spiral.

"Bart, I'm serious. I don't want to be alone anymore."

"What're you talking about? You're not alone, you're—"

"Oh, c'mon, Bart. I *get along* with Pattie and the others, but I don't . . . I don't have any *family* besides you. At least, not anybody who would make the effort to throw a party in my honor. And if we both die here . . ." Abramowitz wiped the tears from one eye with a rough swipe of her palm, then from the other with the back of her hand. "There won't be anyone back home who'll be interested in making up kind lies about me." She took a breath, choked down the beginning breath of a sob. Faulwell felt his own emotions stir in empathy, as if she were radiating her sorrow to him in waves. "I feel alone in the world, Bart. I don't want to die alone. I don't want to die without falling in love, just *once.*"

Her revelation stunned him. He'd always seen her as his not-too-personal confidant, fellow gossipmonger, and sarcastic conversational foil. He'd never considered she might be hiding something like this. She was quick, sharp, a paragon of control; twenty-four hours ago he would have denied she could even form tears. "You've *never* been in love?" he said, trying to sound sympathetic. She glared at him. He guessed she had taken his words the wrong way. She turned away from him.

She picked up the case containing the axe and squeezed through the half-open door, back to the corridor. Still clutching the medical tricorder and first-aid kit, he followed her out, hoping the next bunk he searched might contain the comforting words he suddenly couldn't find.

Elizabeth Lense was reluctant to perform invasive surgery while seated on an unsterile blanket in a smoky corridor, but she knew that Ensign Piotrowski would certainly die if she didn't take the risk. Copper knelt on the other side of the patient, holding a palm beacon above her torso, the beam aimed directly down and focused to provide maximum illumination.

In medical school, Lense had heard a centuries-old Earth saying about surgeons: "Sometimes wrong; never in doubt." She reminded herself that surgery never came with guarantees, no matter how advanced the technology. No physician's knowledge or skill are ever perfect; even with the simplest procedure, it can't be assumed the patient will come through improved—or even alive. The key was to know this and cut anyway.

She activated the laser scalpel, ignored the sickly sweet odor of burning flesh and fatty tissue as she deftly made a long inverted-Y incision below Piotrowski's sternum, and reached down and exposed the interior of the abdominal cavity.

Lense suppressed her response to the adrenaline rush she experienced as she felt Piotrowski's blood warming her hands through the sterile surgical gloves. She marveled at the raw physicality, the carnal beauty of this type of hands-on surgical technique. It had been a long time since she'd had to cut open a living patient by hand—not since her time on the *Lexington* during the Dominion War. Emergency field surgery was a required course at Starfleet Medical School, but almost no one specialized in it. Lense wondered whether that was because Starfleet doctors were too arrogant to think any situation could ever be so dire as to warrant performing surgery anywhere but in a state-of-the-art operating theater, or because someone in Starfleet was afraid surgeons might once again learn to enjoy wielding the calculated violence of a scalpel.

"Cardiac regulator," she said, her voice steady and authoritative. Copper hesitated as he eyed the array of medical instruments laid out on the sterile cover in front of him, then picked up the long, needlelike device and handed it to Lense. She took it quickly and, in a smooth, measured motion, pushed it inside Piotrowski's torso.

Lense concentrated on the subtle tactile cues she sensed as she pushed the device deeper. She felt it travel easily through a pocket of fatty tissue, catch slightly on the denser muscles beneath, then tremble with a subtle change in resistance as it pierced the wall of the thoracic aorta. She keyed the device's main switch, and it threaded itself forward into the heart, stabilizing Piotrowski's pulse and blood pressure.

"Clamp."

Copper handed her the instrument, and she set to work securing the inferior vena cava so she could repair damage to the vein. She cast a brief glance at Wetzel, who was lying still next to Piotrowski. All of Wetzel's vitals were normal, and the transfusion was running smoothly.

Lense visually inspected Piotrowski's intestinal wall for perforations. She was certain it was undamaged but decided it would be best to get a second opinion. "Copper, run a scan and make sure the lower colon is intact."

Copper checked the readout of his medical tricorder, which hummed with an almost musical oscillation as he scanned Piotrowski. "All clear, Doctor." Lense nodded. There was still much work to do repairing the pancreas and the ruptured left kidney, but she had no doubt she would save Piotrowski.

She just hoped she wasn't wrong.

Gomez held the dimming, crooked chemical flare at arm's length in front of her as she navigated the pitch-dark corridor by a combination of memory, instinct, and hearing. Ahead of her she heard the muffled sounds of someone swearing from behind a bulkhead and the clang of a metallic object being struck repeatedly against something hard. Both sounds grew louder as she continued forward.

She stopped as she reached the origin of both noises, which continued unabated. "How's it going, Kieran?" she said.

The swearing and clanging ceased. "Never better," Duffy said, his voice muffled behind the bulkhead. "You?"

"Can't complain," Gomez said. "Nancy and Pattie found a working extractor in cargo bay two. They expect to have main engineering cleared in less than an hour." She paused as Duffy tumbled out of a ragged gap in the wall, his uniform catching on every protruding edge. "Will the *da Vinci* still be here in an hour?" she said, offering him her hand. She helped him to his feet. He stood bathed in the magenta light of her dying flare.

"Good question," Duffy said. "Fabe thinks we can boost the auxiliary system with the backup phaser generators, if we can override their security lockouts."

"How long will that take?"

"A few seconds—once the main computer is back online. The command lines are intact, but right now there's no way to reach the generators directly. The computer's the only way."

Gomez frowned, then sighed. "Any other ideas?"

"None that'll work. Have Hawk and Robins checked in?"

"Not yet," Gomez said. "I'll have them brief Soloman on the best route to the core. Find Fabian and go help get engineering ready."

"You got it," Duffy said as he picked up his tools. Gomez started to move toward the forward ladder to deck two, then stopped as Duffy added, "I am glad for one thing, Sonnie." She stopped, turned, and looked back at him. He continued, "Time like this, I'm glad you're in command."

Gomez nearly laughed. "Yeah?" She shook her head. "I'm not." She walked away, slowly shaking her head in disbelief. It was then she noticed that the hand she'd used to help Duffy was now coated in some kind of grease. She wiped it off across the front of her already filthy uniform jacket, and felt the bump of the diamond ring he had given her only hours earlier still tucked safely in the jacket's inside pocket.

She reached in, took out the ring, and turned back. She wondered what she'd say to Duffy as she gave it back to him, wondered how she would explain that she shouldn't have accepted it at all . . . at least, not yet.

Duffy was already disappearing around the far corner, on his way to find Stevens. Gomez considered calling out to him, then thought better of it. This wasn't the right time.

Less than thirty minutes ago I was clutching this ring like it was my last hope, she thought. *Now I can hardly wait to give it back.* She put the ring back into her jacket's inside pocket and shook her head. *I hate irony.*

13

Soloman stood next to Gomez in the deck one corridor and studied the schematic on the first officer's tricorder display, flipping through it one screen at a time. "You'll have to cut through this bulkhead into the Jefferies tube here," Gomez said.

Robins and Hawkins had detailed a circuitous route, through maintenance crawlspaces and narrow gaps between various systems that were tightly packed together inside the *da Vinci*'s primary hull, to a Jefferies tube that would enable Soloman to reach the main computer core. He eyed the still-smoldering opening that Hawkins and Robins had just cut from the wall with their phasers. "I am not sure I can fit between the comm relay junction and the secondary EPS conduit," the slightly built computer expert said. Gomez gestured to the narrow space depicted on the schematic.

"Hawkins and Robins think the relay shifted when the outer hull buckled on the other side of it," she said. "You should have enough room to get by, even in a pressure suit."

Soloman imagined himself being sucked out a narrow opening in the hull and crushed in the blistering depths of Galvan VI's liquid-metal lower atmosphere. "If the hull has ruptured there, it might present an impassable hazard."

"The atmosphere at this depth is less active than it was where we boarded the *Orion*," Gomez said reassuringly. "With the null-field generator already installed on your suit, you shouldn't have any trouble reaching the main computer core."

Soloman was not reassured. He picked up the portable kit he had carried aboard the *Orion* to reboot its core. "After I restore power to the core, what is my first priority?"

"Reroute backup phaser-generator power to the structural integrity field," Gomez said. "That'll give us enough time to work out a plan for getting back into orbit."

"What is my secondary priority?"

"Sensors and navigational control."

"Understood." Soloman stepped through the phaser-cut portal and squeezed into the narrow crawlspace, pulling in his portable data-recovery terminal behind him. With his other hand, he activated his suit's helmet beacon. The narrow beam revealed an awkward and claustrophobically tight space he would have to traverse to reach Jefferies tube One-Bravo. As he lowered himself down and reached for a handhold, he heard behind him the gentle thud of the hastily cut bulkhead plate being put back into place, followed a few moments later by the high-pitched screech of it being phaser-welded shut.

Lense finished closing the incision in Piotrowski's abdomen and permitted herself a sigh of relief that the young ensign's vital signs all appeared stable. She turned off the dermal regenerator and handed it back to Copper.

"Can you take care of disconnecting the transfusion?" she asked him.

He nodded. "Yes, Doctor," he said.

Lense stood and pulled off the blood-caked surgical gloves. She dropped them into a waste-collection canister she'd set off to one side of the corridor and moved to check on the condition of the beta-shift tactical officer, Anthony Shabalala.

As she passed Corsi, a rectangular shape caught her eye.

She glanced over to see that while she had been busy operating on Piotrowski, someone had retrieved Corsi's family-heirloom firefighter's axe and tucked it under the left arm of the tall, blond woman, who remained comatose. The image of Corsi lying supine with her axe under her arm reminded Lense of a drawing she had once seen of a dead Viking warrior resting on a bier with his weapon at his side.

Kneeling next to Corsi, Lense reached out, and felt with her fingertip for Corsi's jugular. She closed her eyes and concentrated on sensing the weak pulse. It was faint but steady.

Lense opened her eyes and gently touched Corsi's face, then silently moved on to tend to Shabalala.

Ensign Songmin Wong tried again to close his left hand around the sonic driver. His wounded appendage refused to obey. He winced as needlelike stabs of pain jolted up his arm, and he shifted the tool to his right hand.

He was fairly certain his helm console could be repaired. The power supply capacitor had overloaded, causing half of the console's surface to explode outward. He had already replaced the capacitor; now all he needed was a new surface panel.

With his right hand operating the sonic screwdriver, he used his left to hold steady an interface panel he was cautiously removing from the port-side auxiliary engineering station. This console had been spared the fate of several of other key stations on the bridge; if he could attach it to the primary conn circuit, the da Vinci would be ready to fly within the hour.

While he worked, he listened to Gomez and Ina talking Soloman through his long climb-crawl to the ship's main computer. Wong was glad he wasn't the Bynar right now.

"I've reached the comm relay junction," Soloman said, his voice small and hollow-sounding through Gomez's combadge. Until the ship's main computer was back online, the crew was limited to direct combadge-to-combadge transmissions.

"Is it passable?" Gomez said. The first officer stood at the aft end of the bridge, behind the tactical station, her arms folded and her brow wrinkled with concentration.

"*Affirmative,*" Soloman said. "*Hawkins and Robins were correct. The secondary EPS conduit has broken free and shifted point-nine-eight meters to port, away from the relay.*"

"Is the hull behind the relay intact?" Ina said.

There was a long delay before Soloman replied. "*Negative,*" he said. "*I am seeing a break approximately seven meters long fore-to-aft, and three meters wide port-to-starboard. The structural integrity field is preventing atmospheric intrusion, but the field appears to be weakening rapidly at this location.*"

"Move quickly, Soloman," Gomez said, her voice sharp with concern. Wong caught the worried looks that flashed between the first officer and Ina. "Get to the Jefferies tube and start cutting through now."

Wong detached the engineering console and carefully slipped his left forearm underneath it, taking care not to put pressure on his wounded hand.

"*Commander, I have reached the Jefferies tube and—*" Soloman's comm signal was overwhelmed momentarily by static. "*—now. Estimate entry to Jeff—*" Another burst of white noise drowned out the Bynar's transmission, this time for several seconds. Gomez tapped her combadge anxiously.

"Soloman? Soloman, please respond."

Wong paused in his work as the scratching drone of audio interference dragged on. Then, Soloman's voice broke through just long enough for him to utter words that gave Wong a sick feeling in his stomach.

"*Commander, something is happening. . . .*"

*   *   *

Soloman tethered his safety line to one of the Jefferies tube's exterior structural supports.

"Commander, I have reached the Jefferies tube and am preparing to cut through now. Estimate entry to Jefferies tube in approximately ninety-five seconds."

Soloman drew his phaser and steadied his arm to make a circular cut, on an angle, through the curved side of the Jefferies tube. He paused as his helmet beacon dimmed. He started to check its connections, and froze when its beam was suddenly extinguished. He keyed his comm. "Commander, something is happening. I am unsure what—" His suit's heads-up display blinked out, and he became aware of the sudden, terrible silence that enveloped him. Then he felt his weight increase to an excruciating degree, pinning him down against a series of pipes and assorted device casings.

Trapped against the machinery in the *da Vinci's* outer skin, Soloman stared upward at the hull rupture. The integrity field covering the tear in the hull began to flicker erratically. Soloman concluded his odds of surviving a hull implosion and atmospheric breach were negligible.

The integrity field fizzled and blinked out. The atmosphere rushed in, a flood-crush of liquid-metal hydrogen under so much pressure that it was as hot as the surface of a star. Soloman was thankful that his end would, at least, be swift.

He closed his eyes.

Seconds later the end seemed, to Soloman, oddly overdue.

He opened his eyes to see the swirling, churning fluid mass of the atmosphere suspended mere centimeters away from him. *The radiation alone should have been sufficient to terminate my life processes,* he thought. *This is quite unusual.*

His surprise increased as the torrent of liquid-metallic atmospheric gases slowly withdrew from the confined space, retreating finally to hold its ground outside the gash in the hull. Soloman stared in wonder at this blatant refutation of the laws of physics and fluid dynamics.

The gases outside the rupture became suffused with an amber glow. A double-helical latticework of light descended like a ladder from the semifluid darkness into the narrow crawlspace, where it slowly grew and began to rotate on its vertical axis in front of Soloman. He suddenly felt weightless, and he realized that his freedom of movement had been restored.

The perplexed Bynar studied what, to him, resembled a three-dimensional sculpture of photonic energy. It was built in complex layers, each composed of dozens or even hundreds of tiny, moving beams of light. Some beams were nearly half a meter long; others were as short as a few centimeters and radiated from the longer beams, like branches on a tree. Each horizontal layer contained beams perfectly parallel to those in layers above and below; in some places, two or more horizontal layers were bridged by vertical beams of light.

Soloman marveled at the range of hues he perceived in the double-helix of light as it turned slowly counterclockwise in front of him. He realized the layers were undergoing myriad chromatic shifts too subtle for him to detect in their entirety.

He observed the behavior of the individual layers; watched how they rotated at slightly offset rates; noted how the beams that linked them shifted vertically, some rising, others descending; witnessed scores of individual beams—some nearly as fine as a human hair—fade out of existence while others shimmered randomly into being elsewhere in the lattice. . . .

No, he thought, a sudden flash of understanding taking hold. *Not randomly. There is an order to it*. He reached out slowly and let his gloved finger pass through the latticework. He felt an electric tingle not unlike the surge he sometimes experienced when making direct neural contact with a powerful computer. This sensation was far less mechanical, but it still had the flavor of an intense, data-rich energy stream.

He drew back his hand and saw that the beams had changed color around the point where he had made contact. Ripples of indigo radiated away in widening concentric circles. He saw complex patterns taking shape in the movement and arrangement of the beams, the patterns of their colors, the tempo with which they changed, appeared, or vanished. . . .

As quickly as it had appeared, the luminescent phenomenon suddenly withdrew, fading into oblivion even as it retreated. Soloman steeled himself for the sudden, catastrophic return of the atmosphere—then was startled by the hum of his pressure suit returning to normal function. Above him, the structural integrity field crackled back into place—still struggling to keep the high-pressure atmosphere at bay, but undeniably once again functioning.

Soloman turned back to the exterior of the Jefferies tube, braced himself, and prepared to cut through with his phaser. He aimed his phaser, then keyed his comm circuit. "Soloman to Gomez. I am preparing to cut through to the Jefferies tube now."

"Soloman! Are you all right?" Gomez said, her voice pitched with anxiety. *"We lost contact. What happened?"*

Soloman triggered his phaser and started cutting through to the Jefferies tube. "I will make a full report once I have reached the core, Commander." He executed the circular phaser-cut with tremendous geometrical precision. "I suspect you will find my report . . ." He at first resisted the impulse to pun, then gave in to the moment: "Enlightening."

14

"You're sure it wasn't a natural occurrence?" Faulwell said. He and Abramowitz had joined Gomez, Hawkins, Robins, Ina, and Wong on the bridge to hear Soloman's report. "Some primitive crystalline life-forms are known to emit energy in patterns of prime numbers. It fooled more than one deep-space contact team back in the early days."

"I am quite certain that what I saw was neither random nor natural," Soloman said. Everyone had strained to hear his voice from Gomez's combadge until she interplexed the Bynar's signal to everyone else's combadges as well. *"It did not repeat in simple progressions, but I am certain there was a pattern to its organization."*

"Could it have been a probe?" Ina said.

"It is possible," Soloman said. *"However, when I made contact with it, I—"*

"You made *contact* with it?" Hawkins said in an accusatory tone that Faulwell suspected the goateed young man had inherited from Corsi.

"Only for a moment," Soloman said. *"My impression is that the phenomenon is information-rich . . . possibly a photonic life-form."*

Faulwell noted a sudden pattern of raised eyebrows making a circuit of the personnel on the bridge. His own imagination raced at the notion of a light-based intelligence. For a moment, he almost forgot the *da Vinci's* current predicament. Gomez, apparently, had not.

"Soloman, is the main core back online yet?" Gomez said.

"I am completing the patch-in now, Commander," Soloman said. *"Powering up the core in nine seconds."*

Wong drummed his fingers on his now-repaired helm console. "Maybe it's a kind of living computer program," the young conn officer said. "A kind of advanced optical matrix."

"Perhaps," Soloman said, although he clearly did not endorse the idea fully.

"Computer program, photonic life-form, alien super-weapon," Abramowitz said. "What's it doing *here*, inside a gas giant?"

Robins frowned and looked up from her arms, which she held folded across her chest. "And did Starfleet know about it before it scheduled the Wildfire test?"

"Of course not," Ina said. "Starfleet wouldn't—"

"We don't know *what* Starfleet would and wouldn't do," Abramowitz said. "For all we know, this thing was Wildfire's real target all along."

"That's highly unlikely," Gomez said.

"If I might interrupt," Soloman said. *"I have rebooted the core and established manual control. I am disabling the phaser generator security lockouts now."*

"Good work," Gomez said. "Notify Duffy and Conlon when you're done."

"Acknowledged."

"Until now, every encounter with this phenomenon has centered around the Wildfire device, yes?" Faulwell said, thinking aloud. "What if this energy we've encountered is sentient? Could it have been acting in self-defense?"

"I think we're getting a bit ahead of the game, here, Bart," Gomez said.

"Commander, if he's right, then this . . ." Hawkins let the statement hang fire while he searched for the right word. He gave up and continued. "Whatever it is, it might've destroyed the *Orion* on purpose."

"Okay, we have lots of theories and no facts," Gomez said. "But right now our first priority is to stay alive, then to restore power. Further debate on *this* topic can wait."

"Just one more thing, Commander," Faulwell said.

Gomez looked at him with a glare that he interpreted as, *This had better be good.* "If we determine that what we've encountered is an intelligent life-form that lives in this planet's atmosphere, the Wildfire device *must not* be allowed to detonate."

Gomez nodded slowly. "I agree. But right now, we don't have the capability—or the time—to find and defuse the warhead. One thing at a time, Bart."

Faulwell nodded his understanding. Gomez turned back toward the group as a whole. "We'll be rerouting phaser power to the integrity field in a few moments," she said. "Report to your stations and stand by. If there's a burnout I want it contained, pronto."

Everyone snapped to and exited the bridge, with the exception of Ina and Wong, who took their seats at ops and conn. Faulwell followed the group into the corridor, picked up a tool kit, and moved quickly to his duty station. He eyed the items in the kit as he walked. *I don't know what half these things are, never mind how to use them,* he thought. *I hope I don't have to fix anything by myself, or we're all dead for sure.*

Duffy was going crazy trying to ignore the itch between his shoulder blades. He was anxious to secure main engineering so he could remove his pressure suit and scratch the spot raw.

He and Stevens stood next to P8, off to one side of the door to main engineering, while Conlon operated the extractor that was pumping the superheated atmospheric fluids out of the compartment beyond. The extractor was close to breaking down because they had forced it to work past all its rated design specifications in order to clear a path, one sealed-and-flooded section at a time, down to main engineering. Fortunately, the remote station for closing the outer bulkhead of the now-empty warp core shaft had been intact, and its display indicated the core-shaft bulkhead had been successfully closed. Assuming the system wasn't one giant malfunction, that one bit of good luck meant they might have a chance to restore partial operations in main engineering.

Duffy winced as Gomez's voice squawked loudly inside his pressure suit's helmet: *"Gomez to Duffy."*

He lowered the gain on his transceiver and replied. "Duffy here."

"Phaser generators have been rerouted to the integrity field. How're you doing down there?"

"We're almost in," he said. "Stand by."

The extractor whined as its magnetic constrictor overheated for what seemed like the hundredth time in the last twenty minutes. Conlon decreased the extractor's setting and looked pleadingly over her shoulder at Stevens. *"Little help?"* she said through her pressure suit's fritzing comm. Stevens stepped over, affixed his liquid-nitrogen canister to the machine's auxiliary coolant valve, and opened the nozzle.

"I'm running low here," Stevens said, his comm signal fading in and out. *"Make it count."* Conlon monitored the thermal gauge for a few seconds more, then returned the machine to full power. The throbbing hum echoed off the close—and now eerily molten-smooth—corridor walls. Duffy keyed his private comm circuit and subtly gestured to P8 to do the same. The short, insectoid structural engineer leaned forward slightly toward him, her body language equivalent of a nod.

"How badly would you say the interior structure's been compromised in flooded areas?" Duffy said. P8 looked around and studied the walls, ceiling, and deck.

"We'll probably lose most of the outer sections once the integrity field drops below forty percent," P8 said. *"After that, these bulkheads will fold like paper."*

"And main engineering will be cut off," Duffy said.

"No, destroyed," P8 said. *"Unless we reinforce the compartment's outer walls from the inside."*

"Congrats, Pattie. You just volunteered for that."

"I figured as much."

P8 and Duffy reset their comms to the main channel as Conlon switched off the extractor. She detached the nozzle from the emergency pump valve. *"Here's hoping the core-shaft bulkhead holds,"* Conlon said, checking her tricorder readings of the main engineering compartment. *"Ready to proceed."*

Duffy wedged a lever between the two halves of the sliding door, which had been partially fused shut by the molten metallic hydrogen. Stevens readied himself at the door's manual-release lever. Conlon and P8 moved back to the emergency bulkhead lever ten meters down the corridor, in case this all turned out to be a big mistake.

Stevens and Duffy forced open the door. Duffy peeked around the corner as Stevens shone his wrist beacon inside.

Duffy squinted, trying to discern shapes through the wavy lines of heat radiation rising off the deck and walls. Main engineering looked mostly intact, except that any nonduranium surface or component had been completely vaporized. Essentially, the room had been reduced to a shell.

Stevens sprayed a cloud of nitrogen coolant across the deck and nearby surfaces. Duffy monitored the temperature changes with his tricorder, then stepped inside as soon as the deck was safe to walk on with the limited protection of the radiation-shielded pressure suits.

You have got *to be kidding me*, Duffy thought grimly as he surveyed the damage. Stevens, Pattie, and Conlon edged into the room behind him. Duffy keyed his suit's open comm channel.

"Duffy to Gomez."

"Go ahead," Gomez said.

"Main engineering's secure, but I don't think it'll be much use. It's gutted down to spaceframe."

"Are any of the key systems intact?"

Duffy looked around at the smooth, featureless walls. "Hard to tell. Computers're gone, consoles, everything. Core shaft is sealed." He glanced at P8 and pointed toward the deck. "I'll have Pattie go below to check antimatter containment." P8 moved off quickly to find an access hatch to the main engineering sublevels. "Fabe and I'll see if any of the spare-parts bays are intact. Maybe we can jury-rig you an engineering console."

"Sounds like a plan."

"Just one catch."

"Wouldn't be a day in Starfleet without a catch," Gomez said.

"Sonnie, the impulse reactors are ruptured and the warp core's gone—I mean, literally, *gone*. And there's no way we're getting outta this gravity well on battery power."

"So what's the problem?" Gomez deadpanned. *"Don't you have a so-crazy-it-just-might-work plan for just such an occasion?"*

Duffy snorted, happy to volley the gallows humor right back at her. "Don't *you*?"

If only this were a laughing matter, he thought as he stared down the empty warp core shaft to see a featureless bulkhead plate where the ventral magnetic injectors should have been.

Soloman worked quietly and efficiently, despite his growing concern regarding the state of the *da Vinci's* main computer. When he and 111 had first reported to the *da Vinci* as civilian observers, they had begun to make many direct interfaces with this system. When 111 died and Soloman relinquished his designation of 110 rather than rebond with another Bynar, he had enlisted in Starfleet, stayed on the *da Vinci*, and continued that program of general upgrading to the ship's computer. He felt he had formed a bond of mutual understanding with the complex computer. Its heuristic networks, anticipatory subroutines, and state-of-the-art interface persona made it as real an entity to Soloman as any of his organic crewmates.

Now, the entire system was disoriented. Input nodes had been cut off, and power surges had crippled key backup circuits. Compounding the tragedy, Soloman realized that physical damage to the sickbay computers had prevented the main computer from initiating a protective backup of the Emergency Medical Hologram's enormous memory database. Years of interactive learning for the EMH's AI had been irretrievably lost.

For the Bynar, this was like seeing a brilliant friend and colleague reduced to a state of dementia.

He isolated the sensor protocols and ran a fast diagnostic. The software seemed uncorrupted, as did the sensor log database. However, without at least auxiliary power to the ship's sensor network, he would be unable to confirm whether any of the ship's vast array of detection devices were still operable.

Analyzing the sensor logs to verify their last recorded data point, he was encouraged to find the database had recorded a significant amount of data during the moment of impact by the *Orion*, and in the critical minutes that followed. The ventral sensor relays had failed on impact, and other sensor failures had cascaded outward from the point of impact as sections were breached, bulkheads collapsed, and power reserves failed.

Now that Stevens and Duffy had rerouted power from the phaser generators, Soloman had sufficient power to perform basic computer operations. But even with the auxiliary generators back online, Soloman knew it would not be enough. There would be no escape from the atmosphere without main or impulse power.

He replayed the visual sensor log and winced as he

watched the *Orion*'s primary hull smash against the belly of the *da Vinci*. The *Orion*'s primary hull, already stressed to its limits, shattered and crumpled inward even as it ripped open the *da Vinci*'s underside from fore to aft. A cloud of wreckage torn loose from the two ships was swept up by the swift-moving atmospheric currents and swallowed alongside the vessels by a thermal vortex. The visual record distorted and degenerated into static as the two ships were pulled down together toward the lightless, crushing core of Galvan VI.

Soloman replayed the sequence again, from the collision to the end of the file. He checked its final seconds, and confirmed he was seeing the image correctly and not indulging in an irrational human behavior known as "wishful thinking." He paused the image on a blurred silhouette of the *Orion*'s shattered hull and keyed his suit's comm. "Soloman to Commander Gomez. I have information you need to see immediately."

Ina watched P8 toggle the switches on her tricorder, which, using a few old tricks and some spare ODN cable, the Nasat had connected to one of the bridge's science station viewscreens. The Bajoran woman wrinkled her ridged nose at the stench of death that permeated the bridge. There had been no time to remove McAllan's body—or Gold's hand—from beneath the mound of duranium in the center of the bridge. The odor of decay was growing worse with each passing minute and was aggravated by the heat.

P8 pointed out details from several enhanced images Soloman had transmitted to her from the *da Vinci*'s visual sensor logs. The images detailed moments from its collision with the *Orion*. Gomez and Duffy stood together opposite Ina and listened to P8, whose spiel was peppered with clicks, whistles, and other telltale signs of her heightened anxiety. "As you can see here," P8 said, "*Orion*'s primary hull struck our ventral hull at an oblique angle. The force of impact crushed most of the *Orion*'s saucer, which had already been weakened from damage it sustained in the atmosphere. That was our *first* lucky break—"

"You call that lucky?" Ina said, wiping sweat from her forehead. The temperature inside the ship was climbing rapidly, and so far only P8 seemed physically equipped to handle it. Ina silently envied the insectoid engineer.

"If her hull had been intact, she would have cut us in half," P8 said.

Ina raised her hands in concession. "Continue," Ina said, breathing a bit more raggedly than usual.

"That initial impact ruptured several sections on our lower decks and cost us our warp core—which, in turn, caused an overload that destroyed our impulse systems."

P8 flipped to an image from late in the sequence. The broken husk of the *Orion* was barely visible, shrouded in atmospheric vapors and blurred by rapid motion. She touched a key on her tricorder and overlaid a wireframe representing the structure of the *Orion*. "This is how much of the *Orion* survived the impact," she said. "This is only a visual log, so we have no guarantee that its hull was strong enough to hold together after it entered the thermal vortex. But if it did, her engineering hull appears in this image to be mostly intact—and Duffy reported that the *Orion*'s warp core seemed to be undamaged during his inspection a few hours ago."

Ina raised her eyebrows disparagingly. "Pattie, are you suggesting we—"

"Locate the *Orion* and salvage her warp core," P8 said. "Yes."

Ina looked at Gomez and Duffy. "Will that work?"

Duffy shrugged. "It's not impossible," he said. "The *Steamrunner*-class ships were built at the same shipyard as the *Saber*-class. Same warp core design."

"That," P8 said, "was our *other* lucky break."

"Even if *Orion*'s warp core is intact, the odds against finding it down here would be astronomical," Ina said. She fought to keep her eyes open and her voice steady. The heat and the stench were making her light-headed. "It could be anywhere."

"Actually," Duffy said, "she probably isn't far from us at all. Assuming the *Orion* was pulled down with us . . ." Duffy advanced the image sequence on P8's tricorder to show the twisted spaceframe of the *Orion* sinking into the darkness alongside the *da Vinci*. "She probably got caught up in the same equatorial current we did."

Gomez nodded.

Ina continued to play Devil's advocate. "We still don't have sensors," she said.

"I'll talk to Fabe," Duffy said. "This reminds me of one of his war stories."

"Even if you find the *Orion*," Ina said, "do you *really* think you can reach it, salvage its warp core, install it on the *da Vinci*, and restore main power in less than two hours?"

Gomez and Duffy looked at each other and shrugged. "It's so crazy," Duffy said, "it just might work."

I hate when he says that, Ina thought with a scowl.

15

Duffy and Stevens stood on opposite sides of the spread-open innards of a Class Four atmospheric probe.

"This really brings back memories," Stevens said, clicking off his dynospanner as he pulled out the probe's passive-sensor assembly and tossed it aside.

"If you start telling your *Defiant* story again, I'm gonna space you," Duffy said, only partly kidding. He twisted his wrist into a position he wasn't certain it could go, reached under the power core, and decoupled the probe's magneton scanner. He set it on the deck as Stevens began adjusting several small components in quick succession.

"Modifying this thing to circle the equator and send out active tachyon pulses to 'ping' the *Orion* is the easy part," Stevens said as various subsystems inside the probe hummed to life. "Problem is, with our comm systems down we won't have any way of getting the data back from the probe."

"I already thought of that," Duffy said. "You'll need to patch a tricorder into one of the *da Vinci's* small passive sensor arrays. We'll divert just enough power to the array to receive a narrow-band signal from the probe."

"A tricorder won't be able to parse the signal without—"

"—a subspace transceiver, I know," Duffy said. "If you can't find one around, use the one in your combadge."

"Good idea. I mean, why would I need my combadge during a crisis, right?"

Duffy glared at Stevens.

"Combadge. Right. Yes, sir," Stevens said.

Duffy sighed and resumed modifying the probe.

"Sorry, Fabe," he said. "It's been a long day . . . for all of us." Stevens nodded and handed Duffy a magnetic caliper. Duffy was about to say he didn't need it until he looked down at the component he was working on and realized he did need it.

"Thanks," Duffy said.

"Don't mention it." The two men worked in silence for a few moments. Stevens glanced up at Duffy. "Have you had a chance to talk to her yet?"

"To who?" Duffy said.

"Who do you think?" Stevens said.

"Not really. Hasn't exactly been a good time."

"There's never a good time, Duff. Sometimes you—"

"Fabe, we're less than two hours away from a fiery implosion. I'd call this a worse time than most."

Stevens considered that. He shrugged. "Touché."

They worked for several seconds longer. Stevens put down his tool and closed the panel he was working on.

"I just thought of something," Stevens said. "With the launchers offline, we'll have to deploy this thing manually."

"We can probably use a Work Bug for that," Duffy said. "Did you secure Bug Two after you brought Corsi back from the *Orion*?"

"Yeah," Stevens said. "Should be safe and sound in Bay Five."

Duffy nodded, picked up his tools, and moved toward the door. "I'll get Bug Two ready," Duffy said. "Finish refitting the tricorder and get it hooked up to the sensor array."

"Sure thing, Duff," Stevens said. "One last thing?"

Duffy paused in the doorway and looked back at Stevens.

"You should at least get the ring back," Stevens said.

Duffy seriously considered spacing Stevens, then recalled that in addition to being his best friend, the enlisted engineer was the only one on the *da Vinci* qualified to pilot Bug Two and deploy the probe. Bug One, which had been fitted with modified seating customized for P8 Blue's physiology, had been lost in the collision with the *Orion*.

"I'll take that under advisement," Duffy said as he made a mental note to revisit the spacing of Stevens at a later time.

The bridge was silent and sweltering hot. Gomez crawled out from under an aft console, stood up, and felt her shoulders sag from exhaustion. Her hair was drenched in sweat, and her normally immaculate uniform was coated in grime and broad swipes of her own dried blood.

The smoke that had earlier choked the bridge had dissipated and wafted out into the corridor beyond the bridge's aft exit, but a thick haze remained. Gomez felt it catch in her throat as she tried slowly to draw a deep breath. She coughed raggedly, hard enough to bring tears to her eyes.

Ina and Wong had made as thorough repairs to the ops and conn stations as were possible under the circumstances. Small standby lights blinked dimly on both consoles, indicating minimal auxiliary power was still online. Gomez had finally restored basic functions to one of the auxiliary consoles, and routed to it a combination of engineering and science functions she thought would be necessary if the *da Vinci* got a chance to make an attempt to reach orbit.

With one hand against the wall to steady herself, Gomez moved slowly toward the aft exit, being careful to monitor her breathing. The air supply was quickly running low and the temperature inside the ship was soaring. With replicators offline and most of the emergency water supplies lost along with the escape pods, dehydration was now as serious a risk as suffocation.

She leaned in the open doorway and looked out at the dimly lit row of her sleeping shipmates, sprawled head to toe, parallel to the corridor walls. The few emergency air supplies Faulwell and Abramowitz had been able to find were given—on Dr. Lense's orders—to Corsi, Piotrowski, Gold, and Shabalala. *Their lives rest in Fabe's and Kieran's hands now,* Gomez thought. The crew had done all they could without main power, and the best thing any of them could do now was rest and conserve air. Recovering the warp core from the *Orion*—if, in fact, it was still in one piece—was the *da Vinci's* only chance of escaping the atmosphere before its integrity field collapsed.

The worst-case scenarios paraded through Gomez's mind, one after another: If Duffy and Stevens failed to modify the probe correctly . . . if the probe failed to locate the *Orion* . . . if the *Orion's* warp core had been destroyed . . . if the *da Vinci* crew were unable to recover, install, or activate the salvaged core in time . . . Gomez's morbid reverie was cut short by the chirp of her combadge, followed by Conlon's voice. *"Conlon to Gomez."*

Gomez turned away from the aft corridor and stepped away from the open door. "Go ahead."

"Partial life support restored in main engineering." Conlon paused to catch her breath, then continued. *"Maintenance bays are intact. Primary deuterium injector repaired."*

"Good work, Nancy. You should get some rest."

"Not . . ." Gomez heard Conlon cough and fight to draw another good breath. She imagined that as hot as it was on the bridge, it had to be far worse for Conlon, who was working alone in main engineering, trying to effect repairs that usually required a full complement of engineers under even the best of circumstances. *"Not yet,"* Conlon said. *"Still have to replace . . . the antimatter injector."*

"What's after that?"

"Just . . . the easy part. . . . Installing . . . and cold-starting . . . a warp core . . . from a floating wreck."

"Hang on, Nancy," Gomez said. "As soon as the probe's ready, I'll send Duffy down to help you."

"Thanks, Commander. . . . Conlon out."

The channel closed with a barely audible click. Gomez slumped down into a chair in front of one of the gutted aft stations, all too aware that she and the surviving crewmembers of the *da Vinci* had just under two hours to perform a miracle.

The near-silent vibration of the medical tricorder in Elizabeth Lense's hand woke her from a groggy half-sleep. She had set the tricorder to alert her if any of her critical patients' vital signs changed significantly. She glanced at its display and saw a strong series of biometric readings from Captain Gold.

Lense sat up quickly, then stopped as a wave of dizziness robbed her of balance. The air had become dangerously rich with carbon dioxide and left her light-headed. She put her air supply to her mouth, pulled a breath of clean oxygen/nitrogen mix into her lungs, and slowly stood up. She exhaled into the rebreather and took another breath as she walked slowly to Gold, who was sitting up against the corridor wall and cradling his left forearm. He stared down at the surgically neat, bandaged stump of his arm—or, more correctly, he stared past it, to where his left hand used to be. He looked up and took the emergency rebreather from his mouth as Lense crouched beside him.

"Doctor," Gold said, his voice rough and dry. He coughed.

"Welcome back, Captain," Lense said. "What's the last thing you remember before waking up just now?"

"I wasn't hit in the head, Doctor," Gold said, raising his left arm and wincing slightly at the effort. "My hand and my tactical officer both being crushed. I remember all too well."

Lense scanned Gold with her medical tricorder and nodded. "You lost a lot of blood, and you went into shock," she said. "I just want to be sure you—" She paused as he used his right hand to begin pushing himself back to his feet. She stood and put a restraining hand on his shoulder. "Where do you think you're going?" she said sternly. He continued to pull himself back to a standing position. Unwilling to force her commanding officer back onto the deck, she relented and removed her hand.

"Captain, please," she said. "You're in no condition to—"

"Doctor, I just woke up in the corridor behind the bridge. I'm missing a hand, nearly half my crew is sleeping on the deck, and it's so hot I feel like I'm living in my wife's oven. I get the impression we're still in trouble, and I'm going to the bridge to get a report from whoever has the conn. Do you have anything you need me to sign before I go?"

Lense sighed. She reached into her shoulder bag, took out a small hypospray, and prepared it with a small dose of amber medicine. "You lost a lot of blood, and the ship's air is going fast," she said. "Let me give you our last dose of tri-ox. It'll help you keep your strength up."

Gold nodded his consent. "That better not be a sleeper shot," he said. Lense took it partly as a joke, but also as a warning. There was a soft hiss as she injected him.

"Not a chance, sir," she said. "I'm saving those, just in case." Gold wrinkled his brow at her.

"Just in case what?"

She didn't want to tell him she intended to sedate the crew if the implosion of the ship became imminent. She wouldn't impair their faculties while there remained a fighting chance for survival, but if the plan she had overheard Gomez and Duffy hatching on the bridge failed, she intended to make the crew's final moments as painless and peaceful as possible.

"Just . . . in case," she said. She closed her shoulder bag and moved aft to check on Corsi and Piotrowski. She felt Gold's eyes linger on her back for a moment, then she heard his footsteps recede as he moved forward to the bridge.

Stevens guided an antigrav sled into the makeshift hangar the crew had set up for the two industrial-size

Work Bug utility craft they had brought aboard five weeks earlier. On the antigrav sled was the probe he had just finished modifying.

Duffy was at the far side of the hangar, making final adjustments to Work Bug Two's auxiliary harness so that it would be able to carry the probe, which was not a standard part of its equipment inventory.

"Still a few things left to tweak," Duffy said, glancing up from his work. "I thought you were going to comm me as soon as the probe was ready."

Stevens parked the antigrav sled next to the bulky, battered yellow spacecraft. "I was going to, but I had to scavenge my combadge's transceiver to get the tricorder interplexed with the sensor array," he said.

"Good idea," Duffy said. "Wish I'd thought of it."

At least he's got his sense of humor back, Stevens thought. "Anything I need to know about launching this thing?" Stevens said. Duffy shrugged.

"I linked the release mechanism to the welding circuit," Duffy said. "That work for you?"

"Sure, no problem," Stevens said. "As long as the null-field generator holds out." The Work Bug suddenly seemed far more beat-up and fragile than he remembered. He wasn't looking forward to making another flight through the atmosphere. Although it was far less turbulent at this depth than it was above, the environment was still hostile and chaotic enough to make Stevens wary of overestimating his own piloting skills.

"You'll be fine," Duffy said as he turned off his sonic screwdriver. "Either that, or we'll all die hideous deaths."

"Have I ever mentioned that you inspire me?" Stevens said.

"No, but I suspected as much." Before Stevens could craft another verbal riposte, Duffy's combadge chirped.

"Lense to Duffy."

"Duffy here. Go ahead."

"Is Stevens with you?"

Duffy shot a disgusted glance at Stevens. "Hey, Fabe, it's for you." Stevens raised an eyebrow, then leaned toward Duffy's combadge and made an exaggerated show of speaking at the second officer's chest.

"Stevens here. Go ahead, Doc."

"The patient you asked about is regaining consciousness," Lense said. Stevens had asked her to inform him if *da Vinci* security chief Domenica Corsi's condition changed. Lense was one of only a handful of people aboard the *da Vinci* who knew of the one-night stand Stevens and Corsi had shared months ago. She also knew that what had begun as a quickly forgotten tryst had recently started evolving into something entirely different.

Stevens looked at Duffy, who was also among the small number of people who knew of the budding connection between him and Corsi. "You can hook this up by yourself, right?" Stevens said, nodding his head sideways toward the probe. Duffy frowned.

"You have to launch it in less than ten minutes."

"I'll be back in five," Stevens said.

Duffy sighed, then nodded. Stevens tossed the antigrav sled's control padd to Duffy and jogged toward the door. "On my way, Doc," Stevens said. As Stevens bounded out of the hangar bay, he barely heard from behind him Duffy's string of grumbled curses, which were drowned out by the sound of a sonic screwdriver being pounded repeatedly against something metallic.

Not like this . . .

Corsi's last thoughts before losing consciousness aboard the *Orion* echoed in her mind as she shuddered awake. Her skin tingled uncomfortably. She was aware she was lying on the deck, and that her pressure suit had been removed. The heat was stifling and the air hazy. A standard-issue Starfleet emergency rebreather covered her nose and mouth.

She tried to lift her right hand to remove the rebreather, but her right arm was numb. *Not numb,* she realized as her right leg also failed to respond to her efforts to stand. *It's paralyzed. I'm paralyzed.*

Staying calm, she concentrated on moving the fingers of her left hand. With great effort, she felt them slowly curl into a fist and uncurl. Her left arm was wrapped around something. She remembered that paralytics and amputees sometimes believed they could sense phantom limbs. Fearing the worst, she gently rolled her head to the left and lowered her chin.

Looking down the line of her arm, she saw her family's twenty-first-century heirloom firefighter's axe, safe in its transparent aluminum case and tucked securely beneath her arm. She opened her left hand and closed it around the case. *I'm back on the* da Vinci, she thought. *I'm home.*

She heard footsteps approaching quickly. Someone running. Straining to focus, she squinted to see who was rushing toward her in the smoky half-light. As the running figure grew closer, the cadence of his steps, the shifting weight and balance of his body as he moved, even the measure and timbre of his breathing were comfortingly familiar to her. *Fabe.*

Stevens sat beside Corsi and gently grasped her left hand in both of his. He wore a bittersweet smile that conveyed both relief and lingering fear. "Hey," he said in a soft voice. His eyes were bloodshot—likely from exhaustion as much as from smoke and fumes inside the ship, Corsi guessed. She mimicked his crooked smile and grasped his hands as tightly as she could.

"Hey, yourself," she said in a brittle voice.

Several seconds passed as they clasped hands in silence. There were so many things she wanted to say to him, but she couldn't find the right words. He lifted her hand to his lips and kissed her palm with a tenderness she was ashamed to admit frightened her.

"That's what *I* wanted to say," she said. She touched his cheek with her fingertips.

He reached down and stroked her sweat-soaked blond hair along her temple, followed it behind her ear. "I hope you get the chance," he said, looking away. Corsi suddenly became aware she was lying at one end of a short row of *da Vinci* personnel who were sleeping in the corridor behind the bridge. She heard no throb of engines, no muted hum of life-support systems. And Fabe was clearly afraid, more so than she'd ever seen him.

"It's bad?" she said. He nodded. "How many—" She hesitated to ask. She wasn't sure she wanted to hear the answer. "How many of the crew—"

"More than half," he said, his voice breaking. She felt the weight of the tragedy suddenly hitting him. He swallowed hard and continued. "We lost almost all the engineers and a lot of security guards. Four bridge officers, too—McAllan, Kowal, Deo, and Bain." He was shaking. She sensed the tremors of his body radiating through his arm into her hand. "I don't know if we're gonna make it out," he said. Now she was frightened too.

"Fabe?" she said. "Are you—?"

"Captain's all right," Stevens said, pulling himself together. He took a deep breath and steadied himself. "Lost a hand, but he'll make it. He's on the bridge with Gomez."

"Are *you* all right?"

Stevens pondered her question. He shook his head and squeezed her hand. "No, not really," he said. "But I have to get back down to the hangar. As usual, we're down to one of Duffy and Gomez's last-ditch, long-shot plans."

Corsi smiled coyly at him as he let go of her hand and stood up. "I feel better already," she said.

"Yeah?" he said, and let out a soft, bemused chuckle. "I don't." He began to turn away, stopped, and pivoted back toward her. "I'll see you on the other side of a million-to-one shot," he said.

She nodded in small motions. "Count on it."

He nodded to her, the edges of his mouth curling into a hesitant smile, then he strode quickly away, vanishing into the smoky shadows at the end of the corridor. Corsi watched his every step, keenly aware she might never see him again—that in fact, it was likely she wouldn't.

No one had ever accused Corsi of being an optimist. As she lay paralyzed and waiting in the darkness for her fate, she hoped it wasn't too late for her to change.

16

Ina hunched closely over the ops console. Gold and Gomez both hovered close behind her shoulders. The captain and first officer scrutinized the Bajoran woman's every move as she monitored the probe Duffy and Stevens had modified and launched a few minutes earlier. The display on her console had been set to parse the echoes of the probe's tachyon "pings," a crude but effective means of pinpointing the location of the wreckage of the starship *Orion*.

The extremely limited, pale-blue glow from the bridge's few working monitors and consoles now provided its only illumination. The handful of chemical flares Hawkins had lit here had been moved down to main engineering, where lighting was most desperately needed.

A series of indeterminate static splotches on the monitor resolved into the familiar configuration of a Federation starship's engineering hull. "I think I've got it," Ina said. She enhanced the scan resolution and enlarged the image for detail. "Approximately one hundred nine kilometers below our present depth, sixty-eight-point-three kilometers ahead of us in the equatorial jet stream."

P8 Blue poked her head in from beneath Gomez's elbow and looked over the scan results. "Engineering hull looks intact along its center line," the Nasat structural engineer said, then made a few thoughtful-sounding clicking noises. "However, the rate of deformation indicates the remainder of the *Orion*'s hull will buckle in less than an hour."

Gold glanced over to Wong, who sat listening to the conversation. "Wong, can you get us to the *Orion* on thrusters alone?" Gold said, as Duffy and Stevens hurried onto the bridge through the aft corridor entrance.

Wong worked at the helm console for a few seconds, then answered, "Aye, sir. It'll take about thirty minutes."

"Lay in a course and engage," Gold said.

As Wong began entering coordinates into the helm control, a second signal began to appear on Ina's monitor. Gomez and P8 noticed it as well. Duffy and Stevens both pushed in and stared down over the shoulders of the much-shorter Gomez.

"Sir," Ina said, "we have a second signal."

"More wreckage?" Gold said, turning back toward Ina and her standing-room-only crowd of onlookers. Ina studied the data from the probe and answered even as she was still finishing her mental analysis of the raw numbers.

"Negative, sir," she said. "Its depth is approximately nineteen thousand kilometers below our current position, and it's emitting a powerful energy signal."

Duffy edged past Gomez for a closer look at the data on Ina's console. His eyes widened and his nostrils flared slightly as he drew a sharp breath. He straightened his posture and looked toward Gold.

"Sir, that's a protomatter-based energy signature. It's the Wildfire device."

"*Oy, gevalt,*" Gold said. "It's at ignition depth?"

"Aye, sir," Duffy said. He looked at Ina for permission as he pointed to her console. "May I?" Ina nodded. Duffy entered a fast series of commands, then studied the data that flooded across the left margin of the display. Ina recoiled as the towheaded second officer laughed darkly and shook his head. "Yup, it's armed, all right," he said. "Eighty-seven minutes to detonation, and counting."

"Okay," Gold said. "Thirty minutes to reach the *Orion*. Gomez, how long to salvage the *Orion*'s warp core, install it on *da Vinci*, and restore main power?"

"No one's ever done a warp-core replacement in less than six hours," Gomez said. "But since we're going to lose the integrity field in one hundred and four minutes when the phaser generators burn out, I'll say we can do it within an hour of reaching the *Orion*." She looked at the data from the Wildfire device on Ina's monitor. "Assuming we don't get vaporized."

"If you can salvage the core," Duffy said to Gomez, "I can buy you the time you need."

Gomez nodded. "Sounds like a plan," she said.

"All right, then," Gold said. "This is your show, Commander. Take what you need—just leave me two warm bodies to run the bridge, and tell me when we have main power."

"Aye, sir," Gomez said. "I'll need Ina and Wong, so I'll have Faulwell and Abramowitz relieve them after we lock in our course to the *Orion*." Gomez turned toward the young helmsman. "Songmin, plot a course from the *Orion*'s position back to orbit, leave it ready to go on a single command, then report to Work Bug Two."

Wong nodded his acknowledgment, and Gomez moved quickly toward the aft corridor. "Fabian," she said, "round up anyone else who can work and bring them down to main engineering on the double." Gomez strode off the bridge, projecting confidence that Ina sus-

pected was a bit too optimistic to be believed. P8 and
Stevens both followed Gomez out, but Ina noticed that
Duffy remained behind. She saw Duffy step close to the
captain, and overheard him speaking to Gold in a low
voice.

"I need to talk with you, Captain—in private," Duffy
said in a quiet but urgent tone. Gold held his cipherlike
expression as he gestured to Duffy to follow him into
the ready room. Ina watched them as they stepped
quickly off the bridge, leaving her and Wong to
exchange silent looks of bewildered concern.

Gold and Duffy stood facing each other in the ready
room, barely able to see one another. Only a small fraction of the weak lighting from the bridge consoles
spilled in through the open door, but the crew had been
adjusting to the steadily decreasing illumination aboard
the ship. When Gold pondered the extent of the damage
to his ship, he was almost thankful for the darkness.

"What's on your mind, Duffy?" he said. "Don't like
our chances?"

"Honestly, sir, I don't," Duffy said. "But that's not
what concerns me."

"Quickly, Duffy."

"Sir, did Commander Gomez brief you about Soloman's encounter with the energy phenomenon?"

Gold blinked and felt a flush of concern. Gomez had
said nothing of a second direct encounter; she had limited her reports to ship's status and casualty lists. "I
don't recall that she did," Gold said in a careful tone.

"Sir, Soloman reported that it had a logic to it—a
unique intelligence. It might've been a probe, but he
said it felt more organic, like an AI. And sir—it could've
let him die when it breached the hull, but it didn't. I
think . . ." Duffy paused, but Gold anticipated the next
statement formulating in the younger man's mind. "Sir,
I suspect it might have been trying to establish contact.

I can't prove anything yet, but I think it might be—well, a life-form."

Gold groaned. He had suspected something similar before the accidental collision with the *Orion*, while reviewing sensor data with McAllan. "That's a whole new can of worms," Gold said, shaking his head.

"Captain, we have roughly eighty-four minutes until detonation. Regardless of whether we succeed in salvaging the *Orion*'s warp core, we *have* to stop the warhead."

"We can't shut it down from here, Duffy."

"I'm aware of that, sir."

"Are you proposing going after it?"

"Yes, sir, I am. We—"

"Damn it, Duffy, you're a propulsion specialist. I need you here to help Gomez get that warp core online."

"With all due respect, sir, I don't think the *da Vinci*'s going to make it. And frankly, this is more important."

Gold was growing irritated. "Duffy, if you think you're going to throw the Prime Directive at me at a time like this—"

"Sir," Duffy said sharply, "if this 'intelligent light' or whatever it is lives here, we might wipe out a species—hell, a *civilization*—if we ignite this planet into a star. We're supposed to seek out new life, sir, not vaporize it. This is a *Starfleet* mess. It's our responsibility to *fix* it."

Gold struggled to breathe and calm himself. "I share your concern, Duffy, but the device is nineteen thousand kilometers deeper into the atmosphere than we are." Gold shot a quizzical look at Duffy. "How do you propose to reach it without being turned into *borscht*?"

"I'm still working on that, sir," Duffy said a little sheepishly. "I'll need to borrow P8 and Conlon to work out the details." Gold rubbed his chin, which was rough with stubble and slick with sweat. The overpowering heat radiating through the fractured outer hull now dominated every crevice of the tiny ship. He glowered at

Duffy from beneath a furrowed brow silvered with age.

"You have ten minutes, Duffy. Ten minutes to show me a plan—*any* plan—for stopping that warhead."

Duffy was fairly certain the plan he was proposing was one of the worst, most half-baked, ill-considered schemes he had devised in all his years in Starfleet. However, as one of his Academy professors had been fond of saying, "A so-so plan right now is better than a perfect plan an hour too late." And considering that he, Pattie, and Conlon had formed the plan—and pulled together all the essential components to show to Captain Gold—in exactly nine minutes and forty-four seconds, he couldn't help but feel a limited swell of pride at the achievement.

"This is moronic," Gold said without a trace of humor, his voice echoing off the bare walls of the auxiliary shuttle bay.

"It's the best chance we have, sir," Duffy said. "I can disarm the warhead in less than ten minutes once I reach it. The trick, of course, is reaching it."

Gold walked around the other side of the enhanced pressure suit, whose backside now was festooned with so many peripheral attachments that it looked less like a pressure suit and more like a tiny spacecraft. Surrounded by a ring of four chemical flares on the deck at its feet, it was cast in sinister, vertical streaks of purple light and ink-black shadow.

The suit—one of the four used during the boarding of the *Orion*—already had a built-in null-field generator. Now, in addition, it was saddled with a shuttlepod's integrity-field coil that had been twisted to half-encircle the suit's torso; a sarium krellide power cell salvaged from spare shuttle parts; and a narrow-band guidance circuit cobbled together from damaged sensor components. The whole assemblage had been fused to a plasma-thruster harness torn from a spare Work Bug chassis.

"This thing'll run out of power before you get halfway there," Gold said as he massaged the stump of his left forearm.

Conlon stepped forward before Duffy could speak.

"Actually, sir, the suit is programmed to maintain minimal levels of support during his descent, to conserve power," she said. "Once he reaches the probe, the integrity field will shift to full power to keep him safe while he works."

"Who'll be keeping an eye on you, Duffy?" Gold said, his voice betraying his lingering doubts.

P8 jumped in to answer the captain. "Duffy's vitals will be relayed to the science station on the bridge, where Dr. Lense can monitor his bio readings."

Gold lifted a suspicious eyebrow at Conlon and P8.

"This question is for Duffy—and *only* Duffy," Gold said. He jabbed a thumb toward the ungainly conglomeration of parts the trio had assembled. "Can you fly this thing?"

"Not to sound like a Ferengi used-starship salesman," Duffy said, "but it actually flies itself. The plasma thrusters are linked to an autoguidance circuit programmed to home in on the Wildfire device's energy signature. It'll take me right to it. I'm pretty much just along for the ride."

Gold narrowed his eyes at Duffy. "You did all this in ten minutes?"

Duffy shrugged and swapped knowing grins with P8 and Conlon. "We had to cut a few corners," Duffy said.

Gold tapped the device and studied it for a moment. He glanced at P8 and Conlon. "Dismissed."

Conlon and P8 stepped quickly out of the shuttle bay, leaving the captain and second officer alone with what Duffy had dubbed "the mother of all pressure suits." He watched Gold fold his hands behind his back—until the slender, white-haired commanding officer remembered he had only one hand. Gold self-consciously let his arms fall still at his sides as he looked at Duffy.

"The thruster system," Gold said. "Your work?"

"Yes, sir."

"Did Blue or Conlon check your numbers?"

"There wasn't time."

Gold nodded. Duffy watched him carefully.

"How soon can you be ready to launch?" Gold said.

"Ten minutes," Duffy said.

"So, you launch at D-minus sixty-three minutes. How long to reach the warhead?"

"Thirty minutes. Less, if I'm lucky."

"Thirty minutes to reach the warhead," Gold said, fixing Duffy with a penetrating stare. "You know how many minutes this contraption will last as well as I do—don't you, Duffy?"

Duffy swallowed. He should have known better than to think Gold wouldn't notice when the numbers didn't add up. "Yes, sir. I'd say it has roughly forty minutes of power before its integrity field fails. Best we could do."

"A one-way ticket," Gold said.

"Yes, sir."

Gold sighed heavily. "I'd rather send Corsi if I could," he said. Duffy nodded.

"She's still partially paralyzed," Duffy said. "And she has other injuries. She wouldn't live through the dive. Hell, *I* might not live through it."

"I know," Gold said quietly. "I know."

Several leaden moments passed while Duffy waited for Gold to speak his mind.

"Are you ready to do this?" Gold said at last.

Duffy thought of Sonya, then forced himself to forget her just as quickly. "No, sir, I'm not. But I have to go." Duffy looked Gold in the eye. "With your permission, sir."

Gold nodded. Duffy coughed, deliberately, to prevent

himself from getting choked up with paralyzing senti-ment. "If I could ask one thing, sir," he said.

"Of course."

"Don't tell Sonya," Duffy said. "She has enough on her mind right now, without this."

Gold nodded and shook Duffy's hand.

"Good luck, Kieran," Gold said. "Godspeed."

Duffy nodded his farewell and smiled sadly.

"And the same to you, sir."

17

Duffy had never been particularly claustrophobic, but now that he was sealed inside the enormous, jury-rigged pressure suit, he felt severely cramped. The hasty modifi-cations had required the new components be allowed to intrude into the suit's interior. Inertial dampening coils jabbed into his lower back; the guidance circuit pressed against his chest. Furthermore, with the entire suit except for his arms secured to the plasma thruster chassis, he had almost no freedom of movement—just enough to reach the Wildfire device and, hopefully, deactivate it.

Through his helmet's wraparound visor he saw Dr. Lense talking at him, but he couldn't hear what she said. Her features were cast in harsh, unnatural shad-ows from the violet chemical flares on the floor in front of the pressure suit. She was standing on an empty, small cargo case, and her face was practically pressed against the transparent aluminum of his visor. He keyed his suit's exterior audio circuit and her voice crackled through in midsentence.

"*—vitals appear steady, and your brainwave patterns are normal,*" Lense said. Duffy nodded, and she continued. "*Conlon tells me this thing will keep its integrity field at a bare minimum while you descend. You're going to experience some serious pressure effects.*"

"I figured as much," Duffy said. "I'll be fine."

"*I'll be monitoring you from the bridge, just in case,*" Lense said. "*If you begin to experience aphasia, nausea, tremors, hallucinations, or euphoria, increase the power to the integrity field until your symptoms subside.*"

"You got it," Duffy said, though he had no intention of doing so. If he increased the suit's integrity field above minimum before reaching the Wildfire device, the batteries likely wouldn't have enough power left to give him time to complete the disarming protocol. "Anything else, Doc? Clock's ticking."

Lense shook her head once. "*Good luck, Kieran.*"

"Thanks, Doc." Lense climbed down off the cargo case, clearing Duffy's field of vision. He looked past Lense to see Gomez standing at the entrance to the auxiliary shuttle bay, arms folded in front of her as she eyed Duffy's creation. Lense strode quickly past Gomez, leaving Duffy alone with her.

"Hey, Sonnie," Duffy said, trying to sound casual.

"*You call this a plan?*" she said. Duffy noted the teasing lilt in her voice, the tilt of her head, her slightly crooked smile. He had always been smitten with her way of kidding him.

"It's so crazy, it just might work," he said. *And I must be crazy to do it,* he thought.

"*The timing's going to be tight,*" she said, tugging on the connections that held the suit to the thruster chassis.

"I've got it all worked out," he said with rehearsed confidence. He studied the small details of her face; the graceful slope of her nose; the full curve of her lower lip.

I'll never get to kiss you again.

She brushed a long curl of sweat-drenched hair from her face.

I'll never get to enjoy the scent of your hair after you've washed with your favorite herbal shampoo.

"You always have a plan," she said. She stepped up onto the empty cargo case and grasped his thickly gloved right hand with both of hers to steady herself. He looked at her hands wrapped around his. He barely felt the pressure of her grasp.

I'll never get to touch you again.

Never get to hold your hand again.

"Maybe when you get back, we can talk about your plans for us," she said.

Duffy smiled, betraying nothing. "Count on it," he said.

He looked into her dark brown eyes. The effort of hiding his thoughts left him with a grotesque churning in his stomach.

She reached up and touched his suit's faceplate with her fingertips. "Good luck," she said. "And hurry back— I'll leave a light on for you."

"I know you will," he said softly. She let go of his hand and stepped down to the deck. She picked up the fading chemical flares and backed away from him, keeping him in her sight as she moved to the corridor exit.

As she passed over its threshold, the auxiliary shuttle bay was engulfed in darkness, and she was bathed in the pale violet glow of the flares in her hands. To Duffy she seemed to shine, like a lighthouse beacon.

I'm never going to see you again.

She pulled the manual door-close lever. As the door slid shut, Duffy activated his suit's null-field generator. He felt the mechanical rumble of the space doors grinding open. He heard the high-pitched whine of the force field struggling to hold the churning tides of superheated metallic hydrogen at bay. With tremendous effort, he forced himself to turn the suit around to face the force field.

Duffy was surprised to see nothing beyond the force field but darkness. For all the immense thermal and magnetic radiation that raged in the atmosphere of Galvan VI, there was virtually no photonic activity at this depth. This final mission, apparently, was to be dark, silent, hot, and crushing.

He adjusted the frequency of his suit's null field to match the force field. Without daring to hesitate, he activated the guidance circuit, keyed the thruster, and passed effortlessly through the energy barrier to the lightless inferno beyond.

Gold stood between Abramowitz, who sat at the ops console, and Faulwell, who sat at conn. To his left, Dr. Lense occupied the science station Gomez had repaired. Lense monitored every minute fluctuation in Duffy's bio readings, alert for any sign that the second officer might be in more trouble than he could handle.

A moot point now, Gold thought. He caught himself about to second-guess his decision to let Duffy go, then shook it off. *No time now for regrets.*

Gomez had drafted Ina and Wong—along with most of the rest of the crew who were able to walk—to assist in the salvage of the *Orion*'s warp core. Knowing that someone needed to remain at conn and ops on the bridge, Gomez had made a coldly logical assessment of which two crewmembers' skills were least suited to the salvage and recovery mission.

Right now, Gomez's logic is the only *thing cold aboard this ship,* Gold thought. He was unsure which was more suffocating—the heat, or the sharply rising CO_2 content in the ship's few remaining habitable spaces. Faulwell, Abramowitz, and Lense all drooped languidly at their consoles, slowly losing their individual struggles against heat stroke and dehydration.

"Conn," Gold said in a level tone of voice that projected perfect equanimity. "Time to *Orion* intercept."

Faulwell checked his display. "Four minutes, sir."

Gold nodded. "Abramowitz, how are we doing for power?"

Abramowitz worked at her console for a moment, then looked over her shoulder at Gold. "Backup phaser generators are starting to fail. Battery reserves are draining rapidly. The computer estimates ninety-one minutes to integrity field failure."

"Time to Wildfire device detonation?"

"Fifty-eight minutes."

"Steady as she goes," Gold said and moved toward Dr. Lense. He attempted to palm the sweat off his face and neck, then gave up and surrendered to his own perspiration.

He watched the numbers parade across Lense's screen.

"How's he doing?" Gold asked. Lense shrugged and frowned.

"Too soon to tell," she said. "He's only four minutes out. It won't start to get really bad for him for another three or four minutes."

Gold swallowed the urge to tell her that, for Duffy, it was already far worse than she could possibly know.

Gomez's voice crackled over the stuttering comm. *"Captain, we're ready to deploy for salvage on your order."*

"Acknowledged. We'll intercept the *Orion* in just under four minutes. Stand by."

Gold returned to the narrow space between Abramowitz and Faulwell. The possibilities of the coming hour seemed to stretch out before him, like time extended on the event horizon of a black hole. Twenty-five minutes from now, the *Orion*'s warp core would be recovered and aboard the *da Vinci*, or it would be lost into the atmosphere. An hour from now, the Wildfire device would detonate, igniting Galvan VI into a small star and vaporizing the *da Vinci*, or it would be disarmed and left floating derelict and abandoned in a fiery liquid-metal sea . . . with Duffy by its side, sharing its fate.

The twisted shape of the *Orion*'s secondary hull remained concealed by the superdense metallic hydrogen in which it and the *da Vinci* were both immersed, but a computer-generated wireframe indicating its position relative to the slowly approaching *da Vinci* took shape on the main viewer. Gold felt the gentle tremor in the deck as the ship's braking thrusters fired and guided the *da Vinci* in a slow, rolling maneuver beneath the wreckage of the *Orion*.

"Sir," Faulwell said, "we're in position."

Gold keyed the switch for the comm. "Gold to Gomez. Deploy when ready." *And God help us all.*

Duffy felt the pressure around him increasing steadily as the plasma thrusters hurtled him downward, toward the core of the gas giant. Minutes earlier, as he had exited the *da Vinci*, he had looked back and watched the ship's dim outline quickly disappear into the darkness that now had swallowed him.

He faced forward now, the view beyond his faceplate featureless and black; all he had to look at was his own worried reflection, staring back at him with varying expressions of regret, terror, and growing disorientation.

The rising pressure inside the suit had caused his ears to pop within a minute of leaving the ship; now he could barely hear Lense's voice trying to soothe him over the comm.

"Just relax, Kieran," she said. *"Your vitals are all still in the clear. How do you feel?"*

He wanted to say, *Like an ant being stepped on by an elephant,* but he couldn't draw enough breath to force the words from his mouth.

His legs cramped up and began to twitch. *Damn,* he thought. *Only eight minutes out and already I'm losing it. And I've still got more than twenty minutes to go.* He concentrated on suppressing the tremors in his legs, but the effort only made the spasms more frequent and severe. *Great. Just great.*

"*Duffy, can you hear me?*" Lense said. She sounded like she was speaking through a thick blanket. "*I'm reading neurological anomalies in your motor cortex. Your central nervous system is beginning to react to the pressure. Are you all right?*"

Duffy struggled to harness a single breath and force it outward. "Okay," he said. It was more of a grunt than a statement.

"*Try increasing the suit's integrity field,*" she said. "*And be careful. Now that you've got the shakes, you need to be on the lookout for pressure psychosis. It might manifest as paranoia, hallucinations, or euphoria.*"

Duffy's ribs started to ache, and he was getting dizzy as his blood pressure climbed. He was sorely tempted to increase the suit's integrity field strength, perhaps just for a few moments. Then he reminded himself the numbers didn't allow it. There was barely enough power to get him to the Wildfire device and spare him five short minutes to disarm it. He glanced at the power-level gauges on his visor's HUD—and was alarmed to realize he couldn't focus his eyes to read them. *Wonderful. Now I'm going blind too.*

He closed his eyes and let the high-pitched whine of the plasma thrusters lull him a step closer to relaxing and enjoying his headlong plunge into the abyss.

Look, Mom, he thought, fond memories of his youth springing to mind. *I'm flying.*

P8 Blue led the way into the *Orion*'s main engineering compartment, followed closely by Madeleine Robins from security. The room was completely flooded and pitch-dark. A fast scan from the built-in tricorder on P8's suit confirmed that most of the surfaces inside the derelict ship had been scoured bare by the superheated metallic hydrogen.

Lucky for us, a warp core is made to contain matter/antimatter reactions, P8 mused. *It has to be tough inside and out. Otherwise, there'd be nothing here to salvage except slag.*

She scanned the core and was pleased to find it still intact. She keyed her suit's comm. "We're good to go," P8 said. "Plant the charges in pattern alpha, just like we planned."

P8 and Robins split up and moved toward different points around the upper and lower perimeters of the warp core. Each began planting specially shielded, shaped explosive charges that P8 had fashioned in a matter of minutes from old geological survey mines left over from one of the *da Vinci*'s past assignments. P8 had made her best educated guess about the optimal placement for the charges, based on the rapid rate of structural deformation the *Orion* was suffering.

"No extra points for neatness," Gomez had told her before the salvage team left *da Vinci*. "Just bring me a warp core."

P8 planted her first charge and primed the detonator. *One warp core coming up.*

Stevens stared out the cockpit of Work Bug Two, straining to see anything other than an unbroken curtain of darkness.

The *da Vinci* was roughly eighty-one meters away from the Work Bug. Inside its main engineering compartment, Gomez and the rest of the salvage team were waiting for the away team to deliver the *Orion*'s warp core.

The *Orion*, meanwhile, was only a few meters away; the Work Bug was docked to its ventral emergency hatch, yet Stevens couldn't see even a hint of it through the superdense murk surrounding it and the battered-but-sturdy utility craft.

A wireframe image and detailed sensor readings projected holographically onto the windshield gave him highly precise position and relative-motion data regarding the husk of the *Orion*'s engineering hull, but being unable to see the ship with his own eyes gave the entire salvage mission the feeling of a low-resolution holoprogram, like the piloting simulations used in Starfleet basic training.

Stevens was surprised to find he wasn't alarmed by the absence of normal visual contact; if anything, the oddly virtual nature of the experience put him at ease. *Just numbers and a few quick maneuvers I mastered fifteen years ago*, he told himself. *Nothing to it. . . . Just don't screw up, or else everyone dies.*

"Salvage team to Work Bug Two," P8 said over the comm.

Stevens snapped to full attention. "Work Bug here."

"We're set and coming out. Get ready for some fireworks."

"I love fireworks," Stevens said, shocked at his own perverse level of cheerfulness as he fired up the engines.

Two minutes later, P8 and Robins scrambled aboard the Work Bug, squeezing into the narrow space behind Stevens, who was strapped securely into the pilot's seat. P8 moved to the port side cargo-arm controls while Robins sealed the starboard hatch.

"We're tight," Robins said over her suit comm. *"Punch it."*

Stevens disengaged the docking clamps and struggled to hold the Work Bug steady as it separated from the *Orion*. He knew from P8's rushed pre-mission briefing that his next destination was the *Orion*'s severely damaged port side.

The shimmering green holographic wireframe image on his windshield rotated slowly as he reoriented the Work Bug and keyed the navigational thrusters. A second, bright-orange holographic diagram appeared, superimposed over the original wireframe. This diagram was P8's best estimate of the escape trajectories for the various shattered pieces of the *Orion*'s hull that were about to be explosively separated.

"Watch out for that one on the left," P8 said.

Stevens snorted in amusement. "No problem," he said. "I've had enough collisions for one day." He angled the nose of the Work Bug back toward the *Orion* as he cleared its port side ventral edge. "What's minimum safe distance?" he said.

P8 made a few quiet clicking noises, followed by a low whistle. *"Five-point-one-four kilometers,"* she said. *"No time. Hold on to something heavy."*

Stevens didn't like the sound of that. "What do you mean hold—"

The shock waves from the quick succession of blasts made his teeth hurt. Each cacophonous explosion stabbed at his eardrums, and for the first time in his life he became aware of each of his internal organs as he felt them shuddering against one another inside his torso.

He jabbed a finger at the null-field generator control and tried to boost its power, only to discover it was already at maximum. The lights inside the Work Bug hiccuped as the hull was peppered from outside by myriad tiny collisions.

"Forward thrusters!" P8 said over her suit's crackling comm circuit. *"Get in there and match the warp core's rotation so I can grab it."*

Stevens fired the main thruster and studied the wireframe of the warp core, which now floated ahead of him, tumbling loose in a cloud of twisted duranium wreckage.

When P8 had described this phase of the recovery mission to him, she had made it sound as if the core would be in a slow, regular spin. He had assumed retrieving it would be as simple as approaching its center point, matching the rotation, and adjusting his bearing to parallel the core's long axis so P8 could snag the core in the Work Bug's cargo claw.

Ahead of him, the warp core tumbled erratically.

Of course it's not that easy, he thought sourly. *It's never that easy.* The core was rotating on one axis, spinning on another, and generally wobbling to and fro as a result of random interactions with invisible but immensely powerful currents in the planet's superdense atmosphere.

"Pattie," he said, "this thing's all over the place. I can't line it up."

P8 pushed forward to study the schematics and sensor data. *"Well, you could always just give up, let it drift away in the atmosphere, and condemn our only hope of survival to a fiery doom,"* she said. Stevens growled in frustration and accelerated.

"Stand by on the cargo claw," he said, and pitched the Work Bug into a chaotic spinning tumble in an effort to match the unpredictable movements of the *Orion*'s orphaned warp core. "And hang on, this is gonna get messy."

Stevens tried following the core's tumbling motion, hoping to discern a pattern he could anticipate and intercept. But the core's movements refused to be predicted. He tried to sneak under it, and it rose away; he tried to roll alongside it and ended up narrowly dodging a potentially disastrous collision. As he chased the core in circles, he became painfully aware of the precious minutes the rest of the team were losing while waiting for him. *Every second I'm chasing this damn thing is one that Gomez isn't hooking it up,* he chastised himself.

He accelerated again and followed the core through

another chaotic tumble-roll. He waited until he saw its balance shift and was sure it would pitch upward to an intercept point.

Then he forced himself to steer in the opposite direction.

The motion of the wireframe on his windshield was a blur. A jolt shuddered through the craft as the sound of a metallic impact echoed inside the cabin. Stevens was certain he'd rammed the core by accident until he heard a long string of satisfied-sounding warbling noises from P8.

"Got it!" she said. *"Nice job. Let's go home."*

Stevens confirmed the cargo claw had a secure grip on the warp core, right on the edge of a structural support element that could handle the stress. The odds of getting this right had been astronomical. Until now, he hadn't dared to let himself believe they would actually succeed. *Damn it,* he thought. *Why don't I ever have this kinda luck when I'm playing* dom-jot?

He keyed the ship-to-ship comm. "Work Bug to *da Vinci.* Did somebody order a warp core?"

Gomez stood in the *da Vinci*'s main engineering compartment, staring down the cylindrical cavity that once held the ship's primary warp core and matter/antimatter reaction assembly. The other members of the salvage team—Ina, Wong, Copper, Wetzel, Soloman, Hawkins, and Conlon—also were grouped around the edge of the artificial chasm, staring down at the darkness beyond its bottom extremity. Only a weak and invisible force field prevented the planet's blistering, liquid-metallic atmosphere from rushing in and instantly vaporizing them all.

No one moved, and no one spoke. Air had become dangerously scarce aboard the *da Vinci,* and had grown as hot and dry as a Vulcan summer. Several crewmembers' nasal passages had begun to crack from dehydration. Gomez seemed to be suffering the most; she wiped away her latest nosebleed from her upper lip and unabashedly palmed the bright-red blood on her pant leg. She was confident no one would see; despite having brought every remaining chemical flare on the ship to main engineering, the room rapidly was dimming as the flares dwindled.

Gomez would have preferred to install a warp core under controlled conditions at a starbase, or, in an emergency, in deep space. Installing the *Orion*'s salvaged core into the *da Vinci* here, in the lower atmosphere of a gas giant, without flooding main engineering, would require a real-time adjustment of the core shaft's containment field. It would have to expand outward to envelop the core, then retract with it until it was locked into place. Because the hard connections to the main computer were still offline, it would have to be done manually.

Hawkins had said that the procedure was similar to extending defensive shields around an allied vessel, so Gomez tapped him to be in charge of modulating the force field. *At least he's got a job that's familiar to him,* she thought as she looked around at the rest of the team.

Except for Conlon and herself, the rest were not engineers. Ina and Wong at least had some advanced technical training; Soloman's help would be critical to adapting the engineering software to the current crisis. But Wetzel and Copper were medical staff; Hawkins was a security guard. Installing a warp core, even just for a basic power supply, was no simple task. It was not a job to entrust to amateurs.

Unfortunately, Gomez thought, *amateurs are all we have left.* She resolved to keep her instructions short and simple.

"*Work Bug to Gomez,*" Stevens said over the comm. "*We're on approach. Standing by to deliver the core.*"

"Bring it in slow," Gomez said. "Make sure it's lined up."

"Coming in now. Get ready to grab it."

Gomez nodded to Hawkins. "Extend the force field."

Hawkins worked at his control padd. Gomez saw him blinking away exhaustion as he made multiple tiny adjustments.

Gomez and her team stared down into the darkness; several seconds later the warp core emerged, like a phantom rising from an abyss. Unseen generators whined with a rapid oscillation as Hawkins used the force field to pull the warp core up into the shaft. "Stand by," Gomez said. "As soon as it reaches the top, activate the magnetic locks in front of you."

Gomez watched anxiously as the core continued to rise. She kept anticipating a mishap, another catastrophe to compound all they had already suffered in the past twelve hours. But this time she was wrong. The top of the core ascended past her eye level, and climbed steadily upward toward the deuterium injector valves. A few seconds later, there was a dull thud as it reached the top of the shaft. Gomez and her team moved in concert, throwing the switches on the powerful magnetic seals that held the core steady at its central point, just below the dilithium crystal articulation chamber.

The warp core was in place, but there still remained more than a hundred small, finely calibrated steps that needed to be executed, to within vary narrow tolerances, before the core could be cold-started. And, to Gomez's chagrin, the chemical flares were fading faster than she expected, so much of this work would have to be done in the dark. She tapped her combadge.

"Gomez to Work Bug. Good job. Get back here on the double. I need you all in main engineering."

"Acknowledged," Stevens said. *"We'll be with you in less than five minutes. Work Bug out."*

Gomez gasped for breath in between orders.

"Conlon, get to the top and hook up the deuterium

injectors. . . . Hawkins, Copper. Go up one level and secure the next set of magnetic locks. . . . Wetzel, Wong. Go down one level and do the same thing.

"Soloman, restore core control circuits here, at the primary node only. Don't worry about the backups. . . . Ina, reconnect the main EPS tap to the core shunt, over there, behind the dilithium crystal chamber. I'll check the crystals.

"Everyone ask me for more orders when you're done. Go."

Fix the big things first, Gomez reminded herself. *Power-related repairs only.* She watched her team move to carry out their orders. There still was almost no talking; only a silent, intensely focused concentration that seemed to propel all the members of the team.

Gomez was about to permit herself a swell of optimism when the silence was broken by the deep, agonized groan of the *da Vinci*'s hull beginning to implode, one section and bulkhead at a time, starting in the aft sections and progressing forward. *The integrity field is retracting,* she realized. *Instead of an hour, we've got thirty minutes—if we're lucky.*

At the moment, Gomez was no longer feeling lucky.

Falling . . .

Duffy snapped back from a daydream he suddenly couldn't remember. He felt the brutal, crushing hand of the atmosphere relaxing its hold on him. *Must be close to the device,* he reasoned. *Suit's powering up its integrity field.*

He could barely hear his own breathing. The prolonged, intense pressure had left his ears ringing and feeling like they were filled with concrete.

Keying the visor display, he saw the tactical readout from the Wildfire device. He was less than ten meters from it and approaching quickly. He waited until he was nearly on top of it before reaching out. His hands made contact, and he grabbed hold of the twisted duranium rod that was still fused to its outer casing. *The sole achievement of my last attempt to defuse this thing,* Duffy mused as he held on to it.

Firing small maneuvering thrusters on his suit, he steadied himself directly above the device's control pad. *Only one chance at this,* he thought as he noted the suit's power gauges decreasing rapidly. *Gotta get it right the first time.*

He had completed twelve of the sixteen steps needed to disarm the device during his first attempt aboard the *Orion,* before a stray blast of lightning had nearly cooked him alive. Now he had only to pry open the casing and enter the final four code sequences directly on the warhead control interface. On the *Orion,* with no leverage and only his own strength, he'd been unable to force open the device's outer casing. With that in mind, he'd taken the precaution of enhancing the suit's myoelectric components, to amplify his strength far beyond its normal range. Gripping the duranium rod in his left hand, he placed his right against the open edge of the device casing and pushed the two apart.

The device opened easily, giving him access to the warhead control interface. For a moment he saw an outline of the device through his visor, then realized it was probably just a glitch in the visor display, caused either by the immense atmospheric pressure, the extreme heat, or the suit's rapidly depleting power reserves. *Or maybe I'm hallucinating.*

Duffy entered the final codes carefully but quickly. He wasn't concerned about beating the detonator, which still had nearly twenty-four minutes remaining; he was worried about his suit's impending power failure. By even his most optimistic calculations, if he kept the integrity field at full power, the suit would run out of energy in less than four minutes. At the minimum survival level, he might last another twenty.

He submitted the final disarming protocol for approval. Several seconds later, the device acknowledged the codes and verified it was aborting the countdown and shutting down all its systems. Duffy breathed a relieved sigh as the device's power signature vanished from his suit's sensor display. He gradually reduced the power to his suit's integrity field and boosted the power to his comm as he opened a channel.

"Duffy to *da Vinci*," he said, realizing for the first time that his suit was less than ten minutes away from running out of air. He'd have to keep this short.

"*Go ahead, Duffy,*" Gold said, his voice sounding distant to Duffy's compromised eardrums.

"Device . . . disarmed."

Gold was grateful for any small bit of good news right now.

"Good work, Duffy," Gold said.

"*Doc?*" Duffy said, his voice quavering oddly. Gold didn't know if it was Duffy's voice that sounded odd, or if it was the transmission that was distorted. "*Something's happening. . . .*"

Fearful looks passed between Gold and Lense, who had watched helplessly when Duffy's vitals went haywire during his dive toward the planet's core. She stared at her monitor, her eyes focused on a point Gold would have guessed was a kilometer beyond the jumbled scroll of bio readings being relayed sporadically by Duffy's pressure suit.

"What's happening, Kieran?" Lense said.

Gold felt Abramowitz and Faulwell grow tense in response to the troubling silence that followed Lense's query. Then Duffy's voice trembled again over the comm.

"*Light . . . getting . . . brighter.*"

Gold leaned close to Lense and looked over her

shoulder at the bio readings. *As if I understand any of this,* he thought sourly. He muted the comm.

"Doctor?" Gold said. "What's his status?"

"Vitals are becoming unstable. His CO_2 levels are rising."

Abramowitz turned her seat toward Gold and Lense. "He might be encountering the same phenomenon that Soloman saw," she said. "He might be making contact."

"Possibly," Lense said. "But more likely he's suffering from pressure psychosis. Captain, we should get him back aboard as soon as possible."

Gold felt Lense watching him as he stepped away without answering her.

The hull of the *da Vinci* howled as another flooded, outer section buckled inward, folding in on itself as the planet's atmosphere tightened its lethal grip. Gold placed his remaining hand against the unusually warm bulkhead.

I know how you feel, he thought. Part of him wanted to believe his ship could hear him and would take heart. *Fight, old girl. Hold together.*

Gold moved to the ops console and opened a ship-wide channel. "All hands, this is the captain. Lt. Commander Duffy has succeeded in disarming the Wildfire device." Gold checked the console's display. "We have approximately fourteen minutes before we run out of power. Make them count."

Gold's announcement was still echoing off the barren walls of main engineering as Gomez looked up from the dilithium crystal articulation frame.

Fourteen minutes? she thought. *Is he kidding me?*

Stevens, Pattie, and Robins had made it back several minutes ago. Gomez had detailed Stevens to hook up the antimatter injector assembly; Pattie was directing the rest of the nonengineers in reconnecting the electro-plasma system to the reactor. Conlon would be finished with the deuterium injector in a few minutes, then would go below to help Stevens. Soloman was promising core control functions in three minutes.

Even with all that done, there would still remain the delicate and potentially disastrous task of manually calibrating and controlling the matter/antimatter reaction process to restart the core. Gomez was ready to do it herself—she was an expert in warp drive engineering—but she would feel a lot better once Duffy was back aboard to help her fine-tune it. He was a propulsion expert, and this was his specialty.

She wiped the sweat from her palm down the side of her jacket and tapped her combadge. "Gomez to Duffy. What's your return ETA? We could really use a hand up here."

Gomez looked up and noticed Conlon was climbing down from the deuterium injector. *Good. She's ahead of schedule.* A few seconds later she was still waiting for a reply from Duffy. She was about to tap her combadge again when she heard his voice crackle weakly over the comm.

"I'm sorry, Sonnie."

Gomez felt the panic rise in her like a wave.

"Kieran? What're you—"

"I love you, Sonnie. . . . I'm sorry." Duffy's final iteration of *I'm sorry* was drowned out by a rasp of static.

"Kieran?" Gomez's voice rose in pitch and volume with her fear. "Kieran!"

Gomez was numb. Her breath caught in her throat. She thought of Duffy, alone, swallowed by searing darkness, crushed, vaporized. . . . She slumped against the side of the warp core. Her jaw trembled and her knees felt ready to fold and deliver her to gravity's mercy.

No. . . . Oh, God, no. . . . A sick shudder racked her body. Her throat tightened to hold in a cry of rage and grief. Through the blurred lenses of her tear-filled eyes she noticed that all other activity in main engineering had ground to a halt.

Can't fall apart, she told herself. *If you're weak these people die. Get up. Get up!*

She banished her grief with an angry growl and blinked hard to clear her vision. She sealed the dilithium crystal chamber and glared at Conlon, who seemed to recoil from Gomez, as if grief were contagious. "If you're done up top, go help Stevens," Gomez said.

Conlon rushed to the hatch that led to the engineering sublevels.

"Let's go, people," Gomez said, loud enough to be heard a deck away. "We have twelve minutes to restore main power, and I don't plan to be late."

Gomez moved toward the impulse power relay, grabbing up tools along the way. She thought of Duffy, dying alone, and wished she was with him. She paused to look at the other members of the crew, all scrambling to finish repairs they weren't remotely qualified to make, fighting for their lives.

If it were just my life, Kieran. . . . She let that thought drift away uncompleted. She stepped to the relay, opened it, and began making the fastest, simplest, good-for-now repairs she could think of. *But it's not just my life. These people need me.*

She had her orders. She had her duty.

And there would be time to mourn later.

18

Falling . . .

The sky had opened up beneath Duffy. He tumbled downward, spiraling in tight circles beside the now-inert Wildfire device. His weight increased with each passing moment, and his vision had long since blurred.

He was no longer in darkness; all he saw were washes of color racing past him—or perhaps he was racing past them. He sensed he was moving with tremendous speed, even though his pressure suit's plasma thrusters were out of fuel.

Then the sensations changed. The pressure abated. He no longer felt the heat. *Lense warned me about this*, he remembered. *Pressure psychosis. I'm losing it.* He wondered which would come first—crushing implosion or asphyxia. He hoped for asphyxia.

Pulling a breath of thinning air into his lungs, he struggled to focus his eyes. He was hurtling headlong through a vertical tunnel of multicolored light, plunging past its spiraling walls toward a bright surface of shifting colors and swirling semiliquid gases.

The multichromatic wall rushed up to meet him. He braced for the impact. Instead, he broke through the luminescent barrier, penetrating it like a bullet.

Duffy emerged into a vast expanse of vacuum, a region of negative space at the heart of the gas giant. The pocket of vacuum was encased in a shimmering, hollow sphere of liquid metallic hydrogen.

At its center was a sphere of light.

The sphere wasn't like a star, or some monochromatic orb; its surface was made up of what Duffy surmised must have been many trillions of individual beams of light with definitive beginnings and endings, collections of coherently ordered light that seemed to be their own source.

Hundreds of colossal tentacles of energy, which reached from the surface of the sphere to the shimmering wall above the vacuum, undulated and twisted around one another; they resembled tornadoes of light and moved in complex patterns that Duffy couldn't help but think of as a dance.

The beams in the sphere and tentacles spanned more hues than Duffy could discern, in shadings and gradations too subtle for him to comprehend. He continued to descend, slipping through a narrow gap in two tentacles as they closed their double-helix into a single strand. He found it difficult to judge sizes and distances without the benefit of his suit's sensors, but he guessed the sphere he was falling toward was at least eight times the size of the Earth.

The surface of the sphere dominated his field of vision; its horizon grew wider and flatter. Duffy felt like he was falling in slow motion as he neared the moment of impact.

He fell into the sphere and sank through its shifting layers of light and energy. The systems of his enhanced pressure suit flickered, then failed.

Duffy was oblivious of the shutdown of his equipment; he was far away, drowning in the deep, swift currents of memory.

Blades of grass prickled young Kieran's neck as he lay on his back, arms folded behind his head. He stared up at the night sky from his parents' backyard. His father sat beside him, listening proudly and only rarely pointing out minor corrections as Kieran named the constellations.

Only seven years old, Kieran already had memorized most of the stellar configurations visible from Earth with the naked eye, and he was well on his way to learning the stars' names as they were known to those who lived on planets that circled them.

"I'm going to go there one day," Kieran declared. "To all those stars and others you can't even see. I'll see them all."

His father, who admired the stars but had always been satisfied with life planetside, responded by smiling and gently tousling Kieran's mop of light-brown hair.

"Someday, son," he said. "Someday. If you work hard. If you study. If you're both smart *and* lucky, you might even get into Starfleet."

Kieran gazed longingly at the stars. He wanted to be out there now, flying in the pure, empty space between worlds. School and Starfleet were so long and tedious; thinking about them made the stars seem farther away than he could stand.

His father seemed to sense his eagerness and the disappointment that followed on its frustrated heels.

"When you grow up," he told Kieran in a wise and gentle voice, "you'll find that the stars are an excellent school for patience."

Duffy plunged through a wispy scattering of clouds tinted pink by the sunset. The gravity boots the lanky teen's uncle had given him for his sixteenth birthday had propelled him skyward for months afterward. Each time Duffy left the ground he went a little bit faster, a little bit farther, a little bit closer to tempting fate.

His mother frequently wailed it would be only a matter of time before he'd go too far, or slam into something and break his neck. His father had been a bit more subtle, nicknaming him "Icarus" over breakfast one morning a few weeks ago.

Duffy wouldn't let their fears hold him on the ground. It felt too good to be free, to be on his own, to make his own rules in a wide-open stretch of sky. Flying without the aid of a spacecraft or even a simple glider, with the air rushing against his skin and through his hair, was about as close a thing to real freedom as the impetuous teenager could imagine.

I should have been a bird, he thought as he soared upward with the wind and sun at his back.

The German shepherd reared up on its hind legs and was nearly twice Kieran's height. Alone with the beast in his family's backyard, Kieran feared the dog's leash would snap, or that the animal might simply pull up the tree to which it was lashed.

Kieran's father had named the animal Alexander—in honor of Alexander the Great—and it barked and yelped with exuberance born of hunger. Kieran recoiled from Alexander, an exceptionally large and spirited example of its breed. Its eyes gleamed with desperate anticipation for the bowl of foul-smelling dog food that the petrified, nine-year-old Kieran had brought for its dinner but was now too scared to put down within reach of the writhing bundle of fur and fangs.

The dog had made a truly lasting impression from the first moment Kieran's father had ushered the slobbering beast out of the transport pod and into Casa Duffy. The dog had spied Pearl, the family's ornery, old, white longhaired cat. Pearl always wore an indelible expression of utter contempt for the world. She was a tough old cat who had survived all manner of indignities, and she certainly wasn't keen on sharing her home with a big, smelly dog.

Alexander, for his part, wasn't going to allow some cat to besmirch his new master's abode, and immediately sprang into action. He galloped toward Pearl, barking and flinging saliva with wild abandon. Pearl sat, stoic as a golem, watching Alexander's frenzied approach with cold eyes.

When Alexander dared to push his barking snout

into her face, she stood up on her haunches and swatted his wet nose like a Klingon beating a piñata with a *bat'leth*.

The dog yelped like a squeaky hinge and scampered back behind Kieran's father, its head drooped in remorseful failure. To avoid further humiliation for the dog, Kieran's dad agreed to tie it to a tree in the backyard.

Now the dog strained against its tree-tethered leash with such might that Kieran was afraid it would either strangle itself or break free.

Breaking free was what this dog did best. It did it so often and well that Kieran's mother had nicknamed it "the Houdini of dogs." Kieran didn't know who Houdini was, but he guessed he must have been someone who once was good at getting out of things. Within a few weeks of its arrival, the dog had proved repeatedly that there was no chain, no leash, no lock, no fence that could hold it. The only activity Kieran dreaded more than feeding the dog was walking it, because that inevitably led to the slender young boy being dragged through the neighbors' shrubbery just before losing his grip on the leash.

Before long, Kieran's father was forced to admit the dog was too clever and free-minded to be contained in a single backyard. Kieran would always remember the bittersweet look on his father's face the day they delivered the dog to an apple orchard in New England. His father seemed genuinely sorrowful to give up the dog to a new owner, but couldn't hide the joy he felt as he watched the golden canine leap away in long strides, bobbing wildly through fields of tall grass and dodging with lightning grace between stands of Granny Smith and Golden Delicious trees silhouetted against an orange-and-indigo sunset.

As the Houdini dog escaped his last cage, Kieran's father looked down at him with the same wistful expression and tousled his hair. "Come on, son," he said. "Let's go home."

Duffy stretched his legs out in front of him and curled his toes in the cool grass. He glanced over at Gomez, who, like him, was attired in civilian clothes. It had been a long time since he and Gomez had had an opportunity to wear civvies, been able to shed their uniforms and ranks and just be together.

A cool spring breeze moved across the lawn, silent and gentle, bearing the perfume of new blossoms on the trees. The band playing under the shell beside the lake was spinning out a cool, bluesy jazz number, strong on bass and piano and wire-brush percussion. Groups and couples surrounded Duffy and Gomez on the wide, upward-sloping expanse of well-manicured grass.

Duffy had almost forgotten how thrilling real, live entertainment could be. Like many people who spent long stretches of time on starships or starbases, he had become accustomed to taking his recreation in holodecks. But after dealing with the holographic constructs of the Enigma Ship, Duffy had had enough of holograms for a while.

He looked up at the stars. The constellations looked very different from here on Betazed. He thought of how he had longed as a boy to roam free between those distant points of light in the sky, how romantic the adventure and exploration had seemed. His uncle Jim—who had given him the gravity boots—had actually tried to talk him out of joining Starfleet the following year. "If you want to fly, fly free," Uncle Jim had said to him. "Being on a starship is being in jail, with the chance of being sucked out into space."

Duffy had ignored his uncle, and enrolled in Starfleet Academy a year later. He had never regretted his decision. But now he felt it was time to choose a new path.

He reached down and held Sonya's hand. Their fingers meshed together easily. Everything with her felt that way—effortless and natural. She turned her head slightly and shared a smile with him. He admired the perfect slope of her nose in profile, the warmth of her hand in his, the way her dark curls framed the subtle perfections of her face.

In that moment, he imagined a new life, one lived not in the cold empty reaches between the stars, but in a place like this—rich and lush and peaceful, far away from the disasters, battles, and emergencies that came with wearing a Starfleet uniform. A life in which he could spend long summer nights listening to music under the stars, with Sonya by his side.

His future became clear to him.

I'm gonna ask her to marry me.

Second-year cadet Duffy stood at attention, his dress uniform still so new and crisp that it chafed against his skin. The sun pounded down, baking the sweat off his skin and almost blinding him. His mother clung to his left arm, her grip tighter than the jaws of a Kryonian tiger. His sister Amy couldn't stop crying.

Duffy watched his father's coffin descend into the ground. Most of the other mourners had already departed for the post-funeral reception. Duffy had insisted on staying to see the coffin lowered so he could toss a handful of dirt into the grave afterward. The funeral director had tried to discourage him, calling the fistful-of-earth tradition "archaic" and "morbid."

"Try and stop me," Duffy had said to him.

The coffin settled with a muffled thump into the bottom of the grave. The cemetery worker operating the hydraulics under the casket stepped away to give the family a few moments of privacy. Duffy gently lifted his mother's fingers from his arm and stepped around the other side of the grave, into the generous shade of a large, Y-shaped tree.

He lifted the dark-green tarpaulin off the mound of cool, black soil heaped next to the rectangular pit. His mother clung with both hands to Amy. Together they watched as he closed his fist white-knuckle tight around a clump of dirt, turned, and extended his arm over the grave.

Duffy let his fist open.

The shower of dirt rained down and spread, fluidlike, across the dark lacquered wood of the coffin, falling with a finality that Duffy found wholly surreal.

Good-bye, Dad.

Lt. Commander Duffy was trying very hard not to feel like a fraud during his first real turn in the captain's chair of the U.S.S. *da Vinci*, but, considering the beating the ship had just taken from the Tholians, it wasn't easy.

All he'd had to do was sit quietly in the captain's seat while Commander Gomez and Captain Gold led an away team into the interspatial rift to retrieve the *Constitution*-class *U.S.S. Defiant*, which had been trapped there since 2268.

Then, without warning or apparent provocation, the Tholians had attacked the *da Vinci* and transformed this into one of the worst days of Duffy's life.

He'd barely succeeded in disabling the attacking Tholian vessel, which had moments ago escaped to rally reinforcements for a rematch with the badly damaged *da Vinci*. If Domenica Corsi was right—and she usually was—the *da Vinci* could expect to be surrounded by Tholian battle cruisers in just a few hours.

When the Federation Diplomatic Corps hears about this, my career in Starfleet will be over. If I'm still alive, that is . . .

No time for that now. Get it together, Duff.

"Our first priority is to get the *Defiant* out," he said. "Fabian, reestablish the tractor be—"

His voice shrank as he stared in shock at the main viewer.

The interspatial rift had vanished, taking with it the captain, the away team, the *Defiant* . . .

And Sonya.

Duffy's muscles convulsed as he continued to pinwheel toward the center of the sphere of light inside Galvan VI.

His jury-rigged pressure suit hung about him like a dead weight. His body was numb. A bitter taste filled his mouth. Dark spots swam across his vision, interrupted by bursts of intense color unlike any he had ever seen before. A low rumble echoed in his bones as much as in his ears.

More fragments of memory flickered unbidden through his mind.

A stuffed toy, his favorite, fell from his three-year-old hand, dropped deliberately out a window. It receded toward the distant ground in hyper-real slow motion.

The light . . . it's the light . . .

His collarbone had broken with a sickening wet snap when he ricocheted off the tree. "Just because you're sixteen years old doesn't mean you're invulnerable," his mother said with a wagging finger, before she confiscated his gravity boots for a month.

My memories . . . the light . . .

Home on midsemester break from the Academy, Duffy awoke on Saturday morning to the aroma of French toast and bacon cooking in his mother's kitchen. . . .

Young Kieran waited patiently beside the signal beacon, staring at the patch of sky above his parents' backyard. . . .

Running late for an engineering staff meeting aboard the *Enterprise*, Lieutenant Duffy passed a young woman with dark curly hair in the corridor. She wore the gold of engineering or security. *Who's she?* he wondered. . . .

It's playing my memories. Like bioelectric recordings.

An intense surge of energy rippled through Duffy's body. His present became distant and obscured, like a coastline shrouded by a gathering fog, until all he was aware of was the continued sensation of falling.

Lieutenant Duffy strode quickly toward the *Enterprise* arboretum on deck seventeen. Lieutenant Gomez had invited him to join her for a symposium on exobotany at 1900 hours. She met him outside the aft door to the arboretum, and they walked in to find the enormous tree nursery devoid of other personnel.

"I guess we're the first ones here," Duffy said as the door swished shut behind them. Gomez reached up, and, using her thumb and forefinger, gently turned and lowered his chin toward her.

"Kieran," she said with a smile, "there's no symposium."

She pulled him into their first kiss. Her lips were softer than he could have imagined. Her hand pressed gently against his cheek, then slowly migrated behind his neck to pull him closer.

It was several seconds before Duffy remembered that his arms still worked. He wrapped them around her, thanking his lucky stars that she had made the first move.

Lt. Commander Duffy's first thought was: *Where the hell am I?*

His second thought was: *Oh my God, I'm blind.*

He reached toward his eyes. He felt the blindfold and pulled it off, then wished he hadn't. The bright morning glare stabbed tiny needles of pain through his eyes into the back of his skull. Lifting his arm to block the revoltingly golden glow of sunrise, he examined his surroundings.

Unless he was badly mistaken, he was in the worst room of the seediest hotel on Freyar. Tattered curtains sagged in front of a grime-encrusted window, outside which shrieking hovercar traffic blurred past. The floor was littered with empty and broken bottles of Romulan ale, Klingon bloodwine, and foul-tasting cheap Ferengi synthale. The matted, dank-smelling carpeting was stained so badly that Duffy could no longer discern its original pattern.

Duffy coughed and spit something out of his mouth that was either a half-chewed fruit stem or a particularly tough insect leg. He lay alone in the filthy bed, his stomach growling with hunger even as his lower intestine gurgled its displeasure with the gluttonous feast he and his new best friend, engineer Fabian Stevens, had wolfed down last night in the hotel bar.

The pair also had made time last night to get filthy stinking drunk, in between losing round after round of *dom-jot* to a sneaky pair of alien women, neither of whose species the two humans had recognized. Stevens had taken a shine to the redhead, however, leaving Duffy to work his charms on the petite gray-skinned girl. Duffy vaguely recalled something fun happening afterward.

He lifted the bedsheet. He was naked. He sat up and realized just how much his head hurt. Then he noticed that nowhere in the room did he see any sign of his uniform.

Oh, you gotta be kidding me. He grunted as he stood, and groaned as he forced his stiff, aching limbs to shuffle forward. There was only one other part of the hotel room to search.

He opened the door to the bathroom. The stench hit him a split-second after the clamor of a rasping snore. The odor was just bad enough to make him wince, but not enough to make him retch. He glanced at the filthy steel commode, sink, and ancient-style bathtub and hydro-shower. The snoring was coming from behind the closed shower curtain. He pulled it open.

Stevens was sprawled inside the bathtub, also completely *au naturel.* Duffy stared down at him with a mixture of amusement and irritation. Duffy flipped the shower toggle to its "on" position and opened the valve for the hydro-shower's cold-water supply. An icy spray sputtered, then streamed out of the shower nozzle, drenching Stevens.

The engineer shrieked like a soprano bat and leapt to his feet, dancing gingerly on his toes for a few seconds before hopping awkwardly out of the shower. Dripping wet and shivering, he wrapped his arms around his torso and glared at Duffy, who turned off the water. "What the hell'd you do *that* for?" Stevens said through chattering teeth.

"They stole our uniforms," Duffy said angrily.

Duffy continued to glare at Stevens for several seconds. Stevens struggled to suppress a chortle, but his mouth was already contorting from the effort of holding in his laughter. Duffy was trying to play this straight—he was the ship's second officer, for crying out loud, and Stevens was an enlisted man—but Stevens's attempts not to laugh made their predicament even funnier.

Duffy guffawed first, and before long both men had laughed until their stomachs hurt. Exhausted, they sat facing each other—Duffy on the commode, Stevens on the edge of the tub.

"How the hell are we going to explain this to Captain Gold?" Stevens said. He opened their one remaining bottle of Klingon bloodwine and took a swig. Duffy shook his head and took the bottle from Stevens.

"Dunno," Duffy said, then downed a mouthful of the tart, potent libation. "But if I were you, I'd be more worried about explaining it to Commander Salek."

"That's the problem with Vulcans," Stevens said, wiping a dark-purple bloodwine stain from his chin. "No sense of humor."

Lieutenant Duffy stood at the airlock gate, blocking Lieutenant Gomez's path. She had a standard-issue Starfleet duffel bag slung over one shoulder. She was leaving the *Enterprise.*

"This is it, then?" he said.

"Kieran, please," she said, her tone all-business. "I need to go. The *Oberth* is waiting for me."

"I know." This was a great opportunity for her; he knew that. She had received a promotion to full lieutenant, and because the *Oberth* was a smaller ship than the *Enterprise,* she'd be on a much faster track to career advancement.

But it killed him to see her go. He wouldn't admit that to her; it would only make this more difficult, for both of them.

"I didn't mean to hold you up," he said. "I just wanted to say good-bye." He was lying. They had said their farewells more than two hours ago. There was nothing left to say. Except that he had come to the airlock with a half-formed plan to ask her to stay, despite the fact that he knew she'd have to say no.

She kissed him softly on the cheek. "Take care of yourself, Kieran." She gently pushed past him and walked resolutely down the gangway toward the *Oberth.*

Toward her future. Out of my life.

"Sir, are you going aboard?" The voice came from behind Duffy. He turned to see a stoutly built, middle-aged human, a Starfleet chief petty officer, looking at him. "I have to seal the gangway, sir." Duffy nodded and moved away down the main corridor. He kept walking until he reached one of the observation lounges.

Duffy positioned himself in front of the twenty-meter-tall transparent aluminum windows and watched silently as the *Oberth* cleared its moorings and powered up its navigational thrusters. The compact starship pulled away from the spacedock and allowed Starbase Control to guide it through the massive space doors.

She's gone, he thought. *She's really gone.*

The *Enterprise* was scheduled to remain here at Starbase 67 for nearly a month to undergo major systems repairs following a rather brutal encounter with a quantum filament. Without Sonya, however, Duffy was certain it would seem much longer than that.

I'm never going to see you again.

The auxiliary shuttle-bay door slid closed, separating Duffy from Gomez. His departure from the *da Vinci* was only seconds away. Once he passed through the force field, there would be no coming back. He knew that the chances of the *da Vinci* and her crew escaping the atmosphere were dismal. He also knew that beating long odds was what this crew did best.

He turned and faced the force field. To step through it, to leap alone into the darkness, would mean releasing his hold on everything and everyone he cared about. His knowledge of what he was about to lose held him back. This would be no accidental death, no calamity met in the spur of the moment.

This was a calculated sacrifice.

Duffy closed his eyes and thought of Sonya.

If I don't go, we'll both die for certain. If I succeed, at least she'll have a chance.

He opened his eyes and faced the dark *tabula rasa* beyond the force field. He imagined all the people and things he treasured as a tenuous clump of cold dirt clutched in his fist, stretched out over a dark chasm. He pictured his fist opening, his handful of dirt falling away in a slow earthen cascade, vanishing into the abyss of time.

Empty-handed, Duffy stepped forward through the force field and surrendered himself to the darkness.

Good-bye, Sonnie.

Falling . . .

Duffy felt weightless, disembodied. He listened to his own shallow breathing, which grew weaker with each labored ebb and flow from his desperate lungs. *I'm not dead . . . yet.*

He opened his eyes.

Half conscious, he drifted slowly into the center of a hollow space within the sphere of energy. This vast emptiness was spherical, a vacuum beyond which pulsed an unbroken surface of radiant energy.

Logically, Duffy knew he should be alarmed; his air supply was reading empty. His suit was out of power. Suffocation was only moments away. Yet he felt peaceful . . . serene . . . unafraid.

They were reading my memories. Duffy sorted through the episodes of his life that he had vividly relived moments ago, as well as countless others that had flickered by so quickly as to be nearly subliminal in their effect. *Memories of flight . . . memories of loss, of separation . . . of Sonya . . .*

. . . memories of them. Duffy searched his mind for several newly made memories, hidden in the fractured puzzle of his own past: Life formed on an unfamiliar world beneath a reddish star; a saurian species rose through stages of evolution; they mastered symbolic thought, built civilizations, waged wars; they soared away to the stars; they evolved, as many other corporeal species before them had done, into nonphysical beings.

They were giving me their *memories as they read mine.*

The Ovanim. They call themselves the Ovanim. Duffy marveled at how much the Ovanim had been able to impart to him in images and mathematical concepts, without ever resorting to spoken words. The Ovanim had long since abandoned physical bodies, and, disdaining contact with physical beings, chose to make their home here, deep within a gas giant, an environment so hostile to corporeal species that they had expected to enjoy their solitude for at least several more millennia. The subatomic legerdemain they'd had to concoct to make this domain a reality was more complex and subtle than anything Duffy had imagined possible.

Too bad I won't live long enough to study it.

The light around Duffy began to dim. He looked around, confused. An image nearly a hundred kilometers tall took shape on the curved inner surface of the hollow sphere in which he floated. The image that formed was that of Galvan VI, as seen from space. Then a new shape appeared—the *U.S.S. Orion*, silhouetted against the glowing, bluish gray gas giant. The ship disappeared into the planet's atmosphere.

Moments later, the flash of the planet igniting into a nova blinded Duffy. He squeezed his eyes shut, and held them closed until the glare subsided.

He peeked cautiously at the newly forming image. It was a short series of quick images, rendered in what, to Duffy's failing vision, looked like the impressionistic stipple of a Monet painting: The *da Vinci* navigating through the hazardous atmosphere; the Work Bugs inspecting the wreck of the *Orion;* Corsi and the warhead; the collision of the *Orion* and the *da Vinci* . . .

Duffy's vision blurred. He struggled to shake off quickly growing feelings of panic and disorientation.

Have to focus . . . have to fo—

—cus . . . Duffy snapped back with a start. *Passed out. Not much time left.*

The image that now towered over Duffy, larger-than-life, was himself, disarming the Wildfire device. The image melted into the likeness of Sonya, shining in violet light as Duffy had last seen her . . . then it became his air gauge, flashing EMPTY on his visor moments before his suit lost power.

The thoughts that whispered in his mind were not his own.

. . . **disruption** . . . **light** . . . **death** . . . **defend** . . .

I understand, he thought. *You defended yourself.*

Duffy focused on making himself heard and hoped his efforts now were not futile. This was going to be his last first-contact mission. He was determined to make the best of it.

We didn't know you were here. It was an accident.

. . . **understand** . . . **accident** . . . **forgiveness** . . . **peace** . . .

Yes. We, too, wish to live in peace. We're sorry.

. . . **duffy** . . . **rescue** . . . **death** . . . **sacrifice** . . .

It was my duty. My life for yours.

. . . **understand** . . . **grateful.**

The images on the inner sphere shifted again. Duffy found himself surrounded by images of Sonya: as he had first seen her that day when he walked past her on the *Enterprise;* smiling at him as she pulled him into their first kiss; running toward him on Sarindar, sun-browned and scarred but also defiant and fearless and beautiful; laughing hysterically at one of his stories of drunken misadventure; graceful in repose under starlight on the night that he knew he wanted to marry her.

Sonnie . . .

Duffy drew a pained, shallow breath, then exhaled and felt his life slip away, like a fist opening into a hand.

19

Ina was grateful not to be on the bridge right now. *I never know what's happening when I'm up there*, she thought. *All I can do up there is sit and wait. At least down here I'm* doing *something.*

Gomez moved from one person to the next, giving so many orders so quickly that Ina couldn't keep track of them all. Minutes ago Ina's task had sounded simple, but the heat and exhaustion had taken their toll. *Can't breathe*, Ina thought, battling back an irrational urge to scream. *Can't get my hands to follow simple commands.* It didn't help that main engineering was growing darker by the minute as the chemical flares expired.

"Mar!" Gomez shouted up at her. "How's that phase adjustment coil coming?"

Ina nodded in reply. "Almost finished," she said over the deafening groans of the ship's buckling spaceframe.

"Step it up, we still have to initialize the power transfer conduit," Gomez said before turning her focus toward Stevens.

Ina finished calibrating the coil and forced herself to climb the ladder to the PTC. *Still so much to do*, she realized. *But at the rate the hull is collapsing . . .* She banished that thought from her mind and moved on to the next task.

Faulwell sat quietly at the helm. A legion of sweat rivulets meandered through his beard.

He looked to his right, toward Abramowitz, who sat hunched over the ops display, her features dimly lit by the feeble blue-green glow of the console in front of her. To his left, Captain Gold was little more than a dark phantom in the shadows, leaning against the railing, his head drooped and his body sagging from injury and exhaustion.

Faulwell stared blankly at the engine function display, which remained resolutely at OFFLINE. His orders were simple enough: If that readout changed from OFFLINE to ONLINE, he was to press the blinking green pad on the helm. He was expressly forbidden from touching anything else.

Nothing like a vote of confidence.

He considered mentally composing a letter to Anthony, but the notion of crafting a death note he couldn't send—and wouldn't want to, if he survived—seemed morbid and futile.

Not to mention melodramatic. Anthony always hated when I—

Hates, Faulwell corrected himself. *It's not a past-tense situation just yet.*

Faulwell fixed his attention on the engine function display and poised his hand above the blinking green pad.

And he waited.

Gomez forced herself to keep moving from one end of main engineering to the other; her legs felt ready to fold with each step. Her every breath was a gasp, hot and toxic with carbon dioxide. All she saw now were indistinct shadows, some of them sprawled unconscious across the deck.

She rotated her attention among the crewmembers who were still conscious as she issued orders, offered suggestions, and lent a hand wherever she thought it would help. Above her, Ina seemed confused and disoriented.

"Mar!" Gomez shouted to the red-haired Bajoran woman. "How's that phase adjustment coil coming?"

"Almost finished," Ina said. Gomez could barely hear her over the shrieks and wails of the *da Vinci* hull being crushed by the atmosphere. *Only a few minutes before it's all over,* Gomez told herself. *Can't let them lose momentum.*

"Step it up, we still have to initialize the power transfer conduit," Gomez said. Ina nodded her acknowledgment.

If it were just me . . . The thought dangled incomplete as Gomez pictured Duffy alone, dying imprisoned in his failing pressure suit; the grieving part of her wanted to surrender now and follow him into the darkness. *But it's not just me.*

She picked up the gravitic calipers and moved to help Stevens finish priming the master EPS control.

Gold hated the waiting more than anything. More than the heat, more than the stench of death on his bridge, more than the threat of sudden destruction. Starfleet Academy never told aspiring young officers about the impotence of command. *In a crisis, a captain belongs on the bridge, they told us—especially when he's missing a hand and can barely breathe.*

There was nothing more Gold could do to help Gomez and her team. The light from the bridge consoles was fading rapidly, and Gold found it almost impossible to distinguish the shapes of Faulwell at conn and Abramowitz at ops.

The minutes and seconds stretched on, bringing with them for Gold a floodtide of nostalgic reminiscences.

He thought of his family as he had last seen them, weeks ago. Rachel, his wife, waved good-bye to him from the visitors' lounge window of the starbase; behind her was their son, Daniel, flanked on one side by his adult sons, Matthew and Michael, and on the other by his wife, Jessica. Running amok behind the two young men were their children—Matthew's son Adam had become fast friends with Michael's boy Tujiro. Matthew's little girl, Jacqueline, was busy being fussed over by her mother, Ilana, and Michael's wife, Hiroko.

Daniel's daughter Esther stood with her Klingon boyfriend Khor. Daniel's other daughter, Leah, had not been there that day. Leah had severed her ties with the family nearly fifteen years ago, after her marriage to Suvak of Vulcan. Gold had heard from a former shipmate now stationed on Vulcan that Leah and Suvak had two daughters.

It pained Gold that he had never seen either of Leah's girls with his own eyes; it hurt him worse to see the lingering sadness Leah's estrangement caused Daniel. Daniel was Gold's eldest and had always held a special place in his heart. In many ways Daniel was the spitting image of his father, tempered by the better qualities of his mother. Gold had to wonder now if he had shown too much favoritism to Daniel during his youth. *Five other children I sired, how many still talk to me?*

It was just bad luck that Gold's first command of a deep-space exploration mission came shortly after his second son, Joseph, had been born. He wished he had spent more time with Joey; he wished he'd had more time with all his kids. He'd tried to atone for his mistakes when Nathan, his youngest son, was born. The attention he'd showered on Nate had only alienated Joey further.

By the time Sarah and Rebeccah had come along, Gold spent so much time away on starships that the two young girls once mistook him for a stranger when he came home on leave. His eldest daughter, Eden, had always seemed distant to him, despite the fact she was his "princess," and that he was as close as humanly possible to Eden's oldest daughter, Ruth, currently expecting the latest in a series of great-grandchildren. As for Eden, Gold hadn't seen or spoken to her in over a year—not since near the end of the Dominion War, after the liberation of Betazed, when most of the extended family had gathered for the funeral of Nathan and his wife, Elaine.

The memory of the funeral was like an open wound for Gold; the merest thought of it stung his eyes with tears. *Can't believe I had to bury my baby boy.* . . . Gold reminded himself that his family had been fortunate—many of his friends' families had buried several children each; some had lost entire generations to the war. Gold took comfort in the fact that Nate and Elaine were survived by two wonderful daughters, Danielle and Simone—two strong young women who clearly had been cast from the same mold as their grandmother, Rachel.

Gold didn't remember now how he and Rachel had ever found time to make six children. Those six children had in turn raised nineteen grandchildren, whom Gold and Rachel—*Well, more Rachel than I,* he admitted to himself—doted on. And now the grandchildren were having children—fifteen so far. Gold had long since lost count of the nieces and nephews his five brothers and sisters had sired, not to mention the grandnieces and grandnephews, and their scions after them.

Like a small army, this family, he thought, with amusement that quickly turned bittersweet. *And when do we see each other now? Weddings and funerals. We need to find some other reason to get togeth—*

Gold winced at a distorted boom of implosion that was both thunderous and delicate, like a giant's foot crushing a glass sculpture underwater. *There goes one of the warp nacelles,* Gold realized. As a similar sound rumbled ominously, signaling the destruction of the other warp engine, Gold feared his family's next gathering would be yet another funeral.

Lense had been unable to stay on the bridge once she'd realized that Duffy wasn't coming back. *I tend to the living,* she had told herself when she bolted away from the science station.

After she had retreated to the solitude of her corridor

full of unconscious patients, she'd realized the real reason she had fled was so that no one on the bridge would see her cry.

She blinked the tears from her eyes and struggled to pierce the darkness. She checked the ampoules' markings by the light of her medical tricorder, and loaded up three full hyposprays of concentrated melorazine.

That should be enough for everyone still on board, she thought. *I just hope I can reach everyone in time. . . . No— wrong.* She closed her hands around the hyposprays and amended her wish: *I just hope I don't need to use these.*

Faulwell stared at the flashing green pad on the helm console. He fixated on it, clung to it as a symbol of his last hope.

The light stopped flashing. It dimmed, flickered weakly for a moment, then went dark—along with all the rest of the bridge stations. No light came from the corridor aft of the bridge. The command center of the ship was dark as a grave.

"Sir?" Faulwell said, unsure how to continue. He swallowed nervously even though his mouth was dry and pasty.

"I know," Gold said quietly from somewhere unseen.

Isolated in blackness, Faulwell heard Abramowitz's shallow, agonized attempts to breathe the stiflingly hot, putrid-smelling air that grew thicker and more rank with every exhaled breath.

He felt a prickly heat spread across his back, dogged by wandering beads of sweat that made him think of insects crawling on his skin.

The ship's outer hull howled like a pack of drowning wolves. Faulwell's knuckles tightened reflexively on the edges of his console. He braced himself for the searing impact of the liquid-metal atmosphere that threatened to surge through the ship in the next few seconds.

The sudden flaring brightness and deafening *whoosh* still caught him by surprise, and he let out a cry of terror—

—which caught halfway in his throat when he realized the sudden brightness was coming from the bridge's main overhead lights, and the *whoosh* was the sound of the resurrected life-support system pumping fresh, cool air into the bridge.

"Engineering to bridge," Gomez said over the comm in a weary monotone. *"Partial main power restored. Starboard impulse engine online."*

Faulwell and Abramowitz turned in unison to look at Gold, who stood cradling his handless left forearm. His eyes were closed; his mouth was pursed tight. He nodded slowly. After a few seconds he opened his eyes, swallowed, and spoke slowly and distinctly in a brittle near-whisper: "Good work, Gomez." Gold looked at Faulwell with a dark and melancholy expression. "Let's get the hell out of here."

20

CAPTAIN'S LOG, STARDATE 53781.3.

At 0441 hours, the da Vinci *escaped the atmosphere of gas giant Galvan VI and assumed a wide orbit around the planet. At 0503 hours we launched an emergency distress beacon. At 0549 hours we received a reply from the Federation starship U.S.S.* Mjolnir *indicating it was en route at maximum warp, with an ETA of approximately seventeen hours, nine minutes.*

Gold sat alone amid the jumbled wreckage of his quarters. On the deck at his feet lay the twisted remains of his antique silver traveling clock, a twenty-fifth-anniversary gift from his wife.

He paused in the dictating of his log and reread what he had so far. He dreaded finishing it.

No point putting it off. He resolved to push ahead, and resumed his log entry.

> *The final total of casualties is . . . appalling. Twenty-three of my crew have been killed, and five seriously wounded, including myself. I'll be assuming responsibility for contacting the families of the following personnel and offering my personal condolences, above and beyond the official Starfleet protocol:*

> - *Bain, Lieutenant (j.g.) Kara—Ops (beta shift)*
> - *Barnak, Lieutenant Jil—Chief Engineer*
> - *Chhung, Alex—Engineer*
> - *Deo, Lieutenant (j.g.) Elleth—Conn (beta shift)*
> - *Drew, Stephen—Security*
> - *Duffy, Lieutenant Commander Kieran—Second Officer*
> - *Eddy, Claire—Security*
> - *Feliciano, Chief Petty Officer Diego—Transporter Chief*
> - *Foley, Manfred—Security*
> - *Friesner, Esther—Security*
> - *Frnats—Security*
> - *Kazzarus, Chief Petty Officer Sa'il—Cargo Chief*
> - *Keegan, Lieutenant (j.g.) Peter—Engineer*
> - *Kowal, Lieutenant (j.g.) Keith—Ops (gamma shift)*
> - *Lankford, Ensign Denise—Shuttle Control Officer*

- *Lipinski, Andrea—Security*
- *Loton Yovre—Security*
- *McAllan, Lieutenant David—Tactical Officer (alpha shift)*
- *O'Leary, Lieutenant (j.g.) Brian—Engineer*
- *Orthak—Engineer*
- *Skernak, Jovun—Engineer*
- *tai'Mio, Ensign Talia—Engineer*
- *Weiland, Lieutenant (j.g.) Norma J.—Engineer*

I am also submitting the following posthumous commendations:

Kragite Order of Heroism: Lieutenant Jil Barnak, Chief Engineer, in recognition of his quick action, which, although it cost the lives of nearly his entire engineering staff, saved the ship.

Starfleet Citation for Conspicuous Gallantry: Lieutenant David McAllan, Senior Tactical Officer, who gave up his life to defend his captain; Stephen Drew, who died to protect injured personnel and the da Vinci medical staff; and Claire Eddy, who sacrificed herself to protect the ship from a massive hull breach.

The Federation Medal of Honor: Lt. Commander Kieran Duffy, whose noble sacrifice exemplified—

"*Gomez to Gold.*" The first officer's voice snapped over the comm, interrupting Gold's log entry.

"Go ahead."

"*Something's happening,*" she said urgently.

"On my way," Gold said, tossing aside the tricorder and darting out his jammed-open door.

The planet pulsed with light, and it was getting brighter.

Gomez was filled with a growing sense of unease as the bridge was bathed in the planet's ominous glow. In front of her, Wong and Ina, back at their regular duty stations, had the luxury of focusing on their displays instead. Behind her, Hawkins kept his attention squarely directed at the tactical console he'd been assigned, in light of the ship's three tactical officers being injured or dead. Gomez and the rest of the crew were still attired in their torn, scorched, and stained uniforms, many of which reeked of stale perspiration and dried blood.

Gold stepped quickly but stiffly onto the bridge. He stopped in midstride when he saw the image on the viewscreen.

"Report," he said to Gomez.

"It began increasing in brightness about two minutes ago," she said. Gold stepped down into the center of the bridge next to her. The pile of debris that had collapsed onto Gold's chair and claimed McAllan's life had been cleared away, leaving only dents and gouges in the deck—and the absence of the captain's chair—as evidence of the calamity.

"The Wildfire device?" Gold said.

Gomez shook her head. "No, that would've been a sudden flash, followed by a shock wave and a shift in the planet's energy signature. This is . . ." She looked at the monitor. "Well, we're really not sure *what* this is."

Ina looked up from her display. "Captain, I'm detecting an energy signature moving up through the planet's atmosphere. It'll clear the topmost layer in five seconds."

Gomez stared at the planet, which was now painfully bright to look at. Its surface flared and whited-out the viewscreen.

"Compensating," Ina said as she adjusted the viewer's settings. A filter cut the glare and made the image tolerable to look at. "Sorry about that," Ina said. "Most of the automated functions are still offline."

"That's all right," Gold said reassuringly. "Magnify that just a bit, would you?"

"Yes, sir," Ina said as she enlarged the image. The increase in magnification revealed a latticework of overlapping beams of light composed of hues from across the entire spectrum. Individual beams within the lattice drifted, or randomly appeared or vanished. The overall effect, Gomez thought, was rather like observing a living sculpture with an intricate, almost indescribably beautiful logic to its geometry.

A soft, synthetic chirp sounded on Hawkins's console. "Captain," he said, "the *planet* appears to be directing a signal toward us."

"What kind of signal?" Gold said. Hawkins worked for a few moments, then looked surprised.

"It's an unencrypted text message, sir, on a Starfleet frequency. . . . It appears to be in English."

Gomez turned toward Hawkins with an expression like an animal caught in a spotlight. She felt a wave of irrational hope surge through her. *Starfleet frequency,* she thought. *English. Kieran.*

"Onscreen," Gold said.

Everyone waited as Hawkins transferred the signal from his console to the main viewscreen. Gomez pressed her palms flat together and held the edges of her hands against her mouth, her thumbs hooked beneath her chin.

"we are . . . Ovanim . . . gas planet . . . our home," the message read.

Gomez felt her hopes sink. *Maybe he's with them,* she told herself. *They've got his frequency, they know English. . . .*

"your ships . . . accident . . . warhead . . . duffy . . ."

Yes, they know his name, good. Gomez knew she was clinging to a fragile hope, but she didn't dare let go. *They know his name, he must have made contact.*

"sacrifice . . . warhead cold . . . sorry . . . grateful . . . peace"

The word "sacrifice" twisted inside Gomez like a knife.

"Hawkins, send a reply on the same frequency, same format," Gold said. His voice pitched upward slightly as he recited the message. "We are the United Federation of Planets. . . . Warhead. . . . Accident. . . . Sorry. . . . Peace." Gold nodded to Hawkins, who transmitted the brief reply.

Ina responded to an audible prompt from her console. "Sir, sensors have detected something emerging from the planet's atmosphere, being rapidly propelled into orbit." Everyone waited quietly while Ina gathered more data. "It's the Wildfire device, sir. And I'm reading something else alongside—" She looked up, alarmed. "It's Duffy."

She magnified the image on the main viewer to reveal Duffy in his modified pressure suit. He drifted through space, floating beside the inert warhead on a slow journey toward the *da Vinci*. There was no sign of activity from his suit's thrusters, no independent movement.

Even before Ina spoke, Gomez felt the bad news coming, like an ill wind preceding a storm.

"No life signs, Captain," Ina said in a soft voice.

Gold stood near the back of the auxiliary shuttle bay, surrounded by nearly all the surviving crewmembers of the *da Vinci*. To his right he saw Corsi, back on her feet, leaning on Robins's shoulder. Faulwell, P8, Soloman, and Abramowitz huddled together off to his left. Directly in front of Gold were Lense, Wetzel, and Copper, awaiting the call to service, medical supplies slung at their sides. Gomez stood alone in front of the others, her arms clutched anxiously to her chest.

Gold had left Ina in command as he followed Gomez off the bridge. Hawkins and Wong had remained at their stations, as had Conlon, who was alone in main engineering. Now, as Gold watched Work Bug Two slowly approaching the *da Vinci* shuttle bay on a return trajectory, towing the Wildfire device behind it in a tractor beam, he envied them for their absence.

Clutched in the Work Bug's cargo claw was Duffy, motionless inside his now-depleted pressure suit.

Stevens adjusted the Work Bug's energy signature so it would pass directly through the shuttle bay's force field. Lense, Wetzel, and Copper waited on the other side of the invisible energy barrier, standing by to do everything they could for Duffy, who was held securely in the cargo claw.

As the Work Bug cleared the shuttle bay force field, its sensors still showed no life signs from inside Duffy's suit. Stevens completed the landing sequence, and the Work Bug touched down on the deck with a gentle bump, followed by a dull thud as the Wildfire warhead came to rest on the deck behind it.

Through the cockpit windshield he saw Lense rush toward Duffy, Wetzel and Copper right behind her, each of them clutching an armful of medical supplies and equipment.

He carefully lowered Duffy's pressure suit to the deck, then released it from the cargo claw. Wiping the tears from his face, he opened the starboard pressure hatch.

Lense and Copper released the safety seals on Duffy's pressure suit and began pulling it away in pieces—helmet first, then the breastplate, followed by the arms. As soon as his helmet was off, Lense was dismayed by the prominent, dark-purple petechial hemorrhages that marred the sandy-haired second officer's face and neck—classic forensic evidence of suffocation.

Wetzel put the cortical stimulator in place on Duffy's temples and began administering pulses of energy directly into Duffy's brain and central nervous system.

Copper scanned Duffy with his medical tricorder, then shook his head at Lense. He showed her the medical tricorder's display. Not only was Duffy not responding, his body was close to entering the early stages of rigor-mortis.

She looked over her shoulder at Gomez, who stood only a few meters away. The first officer was hugging herself and rocking slightly, her eyes rimmed red with exhaustion and tears. She looked more fragile than Lense had ever seen her.

Lense turned back to Wetzel and Copper. "Seventy cc's tricordrazine, prepare for CPR," she said. Wetzel handed her the hypospray. She injected it into Duffy's jugular, then placed her hands at the base of his sternum and began compressions. Wetzel tilted Duffy's head back and checked his airway. After every eighth compression by Lense, Wetzel drew a deep breath and forced it into Duffy's lungs, mouth-to-mouth.

Though she knew it was hopeless, Lense continued compressions until Wetzel gasped for breath. Copper discreetly showed her the medical tricorder's readings, which indicated no positive change. She steeled herself, then turned and looked back at Gomez.

Gomez met her stare and read the awful truth in Lense's eyes. Gomez began to tremble violently.

"I'm sorry," Lense said.

Gomez backed away, tears welling in her eyes.

No, he can't be . . . not like this . . .

Fabian Stevens didn't want to look any longer; he couldn't stand the sight of his best friend's body lying on the deck. He slumped forward against Work Bug Two and cried into his hands. The hard, choking sobs left him unable to breathe.

He felt a hand on his shoulder.

He turned to see Corsi, her hair falling in unkempt tangles over her shoulders. Her face mirrored his own, and he saw in her eyes an empathy and tenderness even deeper than the one she had shared with him one lonely night months ago.

She ushered him into her arms. He surrendered himself to her embrace and wept into her shoulder.

Gomez shook her head, sinking deeper into denial with every backward step she took away from Duffy's corpse.

One tear rolled down her cheek, then another. She felt a scream of rage and anguish build inside her throat. She pressed a hand to her lips—as if that meek gesture would be enough to dam up her ocean of grief. Her pulse throbbed in her ears.

She was beyond words. Her entire body quaked with a terrible, inchoate fury and sorrow. She was hollow, aimless, adrift. Faulwell's hand gently touched her arm in a futile effort to offer comfort. She shook it away with an anger that made the older man recoil and take two steps back.

The small cluster of people behind her parted as she passed through them toward the exit. Her eyes stung, but remained fixed on Duffy's body, which grew smaller in her field of vision as she retreated, the image searing itself into her memory. She backed into the corridor and saw his body framed in the outline of the doorway.

She forced herself to close her eyes and turn away. She opened them to see Captain Gold standing in the corridor in front of her. *Your fault*, she fumed, and glared accusingly at him. *This is your fault*. Pushing roughly past him, she stormed away, deserting the captain in her bitter wake.

Gomez sealed the maintenance lab door behind her. All she wanted was to hide in the sanctity of her own quarters, safe behind closed doors, but that was impossible now. Her private quarters had been destroyed during the final series of implosions that had rocked the *da Vinci*.

All her personal possessions aboard ship had been lost to the atmosphere of Galvan VI: her civilian clothes; a leather-bound twenty-first-century edition of *The Complete Works of Richard Brautigan* that her father had given to her when she was fifteen; the sonic rifle she had wielded in her battle against a crystalline killing machine on the planet Sarindar.

And the pens, she realized with a pang of regret. Duffy had given her a set of Vulcan calligraphy pens for her birthday three months ago, because six months earlier she had happened to mention she was interested in taking a class in written Vulcan. He had often surprised her with small, unexpected gifts: a small pendant adorned with an emerald, her birthstone; a music crystal that played Trill lullabies; a bottle of rare Deltan perfume. . . .

Now they're all gone . . . everything he ever gave me. . . .

She palmed the tears from her cheek and wiped her hand across the front of her uniform. Her fingertips paused on the raised edges of the ring that was still tucked safely within her jacket's inside pocket.

She took out the ring. Flickers of light danced across its stone's facets as she turned it in her hand. She let the ring fall into her palm and closed her fist around it.

Her first sob caught in her chest. Her second burst out of her like a hacking cough. Then her grief escaped in full force, a throaty dirge that echoed off the metallic walls of the cramped maintenance lab. She pressed her back to the wall and slid downward as her knees buckled. Her wails of despair became angry screams.

She tightened her fist around the ring until the stone bit into her flesh. No sound she made, no pain she inflicted on her body, could ease the torment seething inside her. She slumped to the deck, then curled into a fetal position. She opened her fist and looked at the ring, which was daubed with her own blood. Although she had no idea why she was doing it, she slipped the ring onto the third finger of her left hand.

She stared through her prism of tears into the cold fire of the diamond, as if it held the secrets of life and death.

Her funereal cries grew steadily more despondent as the truth took root in her mind:

Kieran's gone.

ABOUT THE AUTHORS

KEITH R.A. DeCANDIDO is the co-developer of the *Star Trek: S.C.E.* series, with John J. Ordover, and, in addition to *War Stories*, he has written or cowritten the stories *Fatal Error*, *Cold Fusion*, *Invincible*, *Here There Be Monsters*, and *Breakdowns*. His other *Star Trek* work includes the novels *Diplomatic Implausibility*, *Demons of Air and Darkness*, *The Art of the Impossible*, and *A Time for War, a Time for Peace*; the cross-series duology *The Brave and the Bold*; short fiction in *What Lay Beyond*, *Prophecy and Change*, *No Limits*, and *Tales of the Dominion War* (which he also edited); the comic book miniseries *Perchance to Dream*; and the first two *I.K.S. Gorkon* books, an ongoing series of novels taking place on board a Klingon ship. Forthcoming *Treks* include *Worlds of Star Trek: Deep Space Nine* Volume 3 (the Ferenginar portion), *Articles of the Federation* (a look at the Federation's government), *Tales from the Captain's Table* (an anthology of stories featuring various *Trek* captains), and *Enemy Territory* (the third book in the *Gorkon* series), with others in development beyond that. Keith has also written novels, short stories, and nonfiction books in the media universes of *Farscape*, *Gene Roddenberry's Andromeda*, Marvel Comics, *Resident Evil*, *Xena*, *Buffy the Vampire Slayer*, and more. His original novel *Dragon Precinct* was published in 2004 and his award-nominated original SF anthology *Imaginings* was published in 2003. Find out more silly things about him at DeCandido.net.

DAVID MACK is a writer whose work spans multiple media. With writing partner John J. Ordover, he co-wrote the *Star Trek: Deep Space Nine* episode "Starship Down" and the story treatment for the *Star Trek: Deep Space Nine* episode "It's Only a Paper Moon." Mack and Ordover also penned the four-issue *Star Trek: Deep Space Nine / Star Trek: The Next Generation* crossover comic-book miniseries *Divided We Fall* for WildStorm Comics. With Keith R.A. DeCandido, Mack co-wrote the *Star Trek: S.C.E.* eBook novella *Invincible*, currently available in paperback as part of the collection *Star Trek: S.C.E. Book 2: Miracle Workers*. Mack also has made behind-the-scenes contributions to several *Star Trek* CD-ROM products. His solo writing for *Star Trek* beyond *Wildfire* includes the *Star Trek: The Next Generation* duology *A Time to Kill* and *A Time to Heal*, the *Star Trek: New Frontier Minipedia*, the trade paperback *The Starfleet Survival Guide*, and the *Star Trek: S.C.E.* eBooks *Failsafe* and *Small World*. His other credits include the short story "Twilight's Wrath," for the *Star Trek* anthology *Tales of the Dominion War*, edited by Keith R.A. DeCandido; and "Waiting for G'Doh, or, How I Learned to Stop Moving and Hate People," a short story for the *Star Trek: New Frontier* anthology *No Limits*, edited by Peter David. He currently is working on an original novel. A graduate of NYU's renowned film school, Mack currently resides in New York City with his wife, Kara.

J. STEVEN YORK & CHRISTINA F. YORK had nearly two decades of married life together before they dared to collaborate. When they—and the marriage—survived the experience, they decided it might be fun to do it again. Besides *Enigma Ship*, they have appeared together in *Mage Knight Collector's Guide* #1 and the upcoming *S.C.E.* eBook *Spin*.

On his own, Steve has published multiple novels (most recently, *MechWarrior: Fortress of Lies*, Roc, 2004), novellas, short stories, and eBooks. He's written fiction for computer games, and scripts for radio. He considers his one nonfiction book an aberration, as he considers himself first and foremost a storyteller, regardless of what form those stories take. He'd be happy scripting amusement park rides, as long as they had character and plot. He's also done collaborations with his friend Dean Wesley Smith.

Chris has published stories in three *Trek* anthologies (*Strange New Worlds*, *Strange New Worlds II*, and *New Frontier: No Limits*), and assorted other venues. Her second solo novel, *Dream House*, will be a hardback release from Five Star in late 2004.

Chris has always lived on the West Coast, and Steve has lived most everywhere. The two met in Seattle, and eventually settled in a remote Federation outpost known as coastal Oregon. There they maintain their home and offices, under the supervision of two feline captains.

KNOW NO BOUNDARIES

Explore the Star Trek™
Universe with Star Trek™
Communicator, The Magazine of
the Official Star Trek Fan Club.

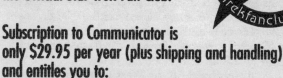

Subscription to Communicator is
only $29.95 per year (plus shipping and handling)
and entitles you to:

- 6 issues of STAR TREK Communicator

- Membership in the official STAR TREK™ Fan Club

- An exclusive full-color lithograph

- 10% discount on all merchandise purchased at
  www.startrekfanclub.com

- Advance purchase preference on select items
  exclusive to the fan club

- ...and more benefits to come!

So don't get left behind! Subscribe to STAR TREK™
Communicator now at www.startrekfanclub.com

www.decipher.com

DECIPHER®
The Art of Great Games®

A VIACOM COMPANY
www.startrek.com
STFC

STAR TREK®

STCR.01

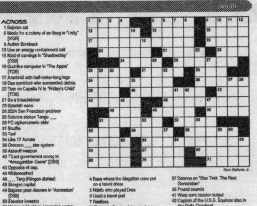

ACROSS

1 Bajoran oat
5 Medic for a colony of ex-Borg in "Unity" [VGR]
9 Author Bombeck
13 Use on energy reinforcement cell
14 Kind of carvings in "Shadowplay" [DS9]
16 God-like computer in "The Apple" [TOS]
17 Arachnid with half-meter-long legs
19 Dax symbiont who succeeded Jadzia
20 Tsar on Capella IV in "Friday's Child" [TOS]
21 Be a breadwinner
23 Spanish wave
24 2024 San Francisco problem
26 Science station Tango ___
28 PC alphanumeric abbr.
31 Studio
33 Feel
34 Like 17 Across
36 Orreros ___ star system
39 Assault weapon
40 T'Lord government envoy in "Armageddon Game" [DS9]
43 Opposite of gap.
44 Whitewashed
48 ___ Targ (Klingon dishes)
48 Shagon rapist
49 Bajoran poet Akorem in "Accession" [DS9]
50 Elevator inventor
51 Homeworld of two assassins sent to DS9 in "Bsash"
53 Leocks before Loron
55 Axtorian beverage served in Ten-Forward
56 Mass- matter word
59 ___ song-slug
61 ___ canna of Po'Mat
63 Lifeform indigenous to the Oxllan homeworld
65 Lt. Paris spent time here
67 Radlals
68 Ferarius commander who offered Kirk tranya
69 Klaang escaped from one in "Broken Bow" [ENT]
70 Caps for Scotty
71 Billiards: Prefix

DOWN

1 Royal letters
2 Samoan friend of Jadzia Dax
3 Chess oaste
4 Base where the Magellan crew put on a talent show
5 Ndefo who played Drex
6 Used a travel god
7 Restless
8 "Enterprise" supervising producer Howard
9 Bouncer in "Violations" [TNG]
10 Tarkassian imaginary friend of Guinan as a child
11 McGivers who befriends Khan in "Space Seed" [TOS]
12 Saturn sector
15 ___ and Loos" [DS9]
22 Alpha-current ___
25 Salver
27 Supralzone shout
29 Member of Klingon intelligence in "Visionary" [DS9]
29 Regime on Ekos in "Patterns of Force" [TOS]
30 Denecan creature Korax compared to Kirk
32 Parent of P'Chan in "Survival Instinct" [VGR]
35 Modernized
37 Degrees on "Star Trek: The Next Generation"
38 Pound sounds
41 Warp-core reactor output
42 Captain of the U.S.S. Equinox also in the Delta Quadrant
45 Author LeShan
47 Tactical officer on night shift in "Rightful Heir" [TNG]
48 Bajoran grain-processing center
51 Kes is kidnapped to this planet in "Warlord" [VGR]
52 Tanandra Bay, for one
54 Show horse
55 Priestly robes
57 "Inter Arma, ___ Silent Leges" [DS9]
59 Seat of the Kazon Collective
60 Miles O'Brien's coffee-cutoff hour
62 Of old
64 Gigabres: Abbr.
65 Fight finisher

Ben Babaad Jr.

STAR TREK CROSSWORD SERIES